the bRoken RoAd

Shannon Guymon

Other Books by Shannon Guymon

Never Letting Go of Hope

A Trusting Heart

Justifiable Means

Forever Friends

Soul Searching

Makeover

Taking Chances

Child of Many Colors: LDS Stories of Transracial Adoption

the BROKEN ROAD

Shannon Guymon

Bonneville
Springville, Utah

The views expressed within this work are the sole responsibility of the author and do not necessarily reflect the position of Cedar Fort, Inc., or any other entity.

This is a work of fiction. The characters, names, incidents, places, and dialogue are products of the author's imagination, and are not to be construed as real.

ISBN 13: 978-1-59955-419-8

Published by Bonneville Books, an imprint of Cedar Fort, Inc., 2373 W. 700 S., Springville, UT 84663
Distributed by Cedar Fort, Inc., www.cedarfort.com

LIBRARY OF CONGRESS CATALOGING-IN-PUBLICATION DATA

Guymon, Shannon, 1972-
  The broken road / Shannon Guymon.
    p. cm.
  ISBN 978-1-59955-419-8 (acid-free paper)
  1. Brothers and sisters--Fiction. 2. Children of criminals--Fiction. 3. Mormons--Fiction. 4. Utah--Fiction. I. Title.

  PS3607.U96B76 2010
  813'.6--dc22

      2010013380

Cover design by Angela D. Olsen
Cover design © 2010 by Lyle Mortimer
Edited and typeset by Kimiko Christensen Hammari and Heidi Doxey

Printed in the United States of America

10 9 8 7 6 5 4 3 2 1

Printed on acid-free paper

To my brothers, Zach and Josh Hill.
You're amazing.

♥

ACKNOWLEDGMENTS

Identity theft is such a prevalent crime these days that it's almost boring now. Stories come on the news, and people shrug and flip the channel. But for people who it has happened to, it's painful. It rips out your heart and shatters your trust in people, especially if the one who stole your identity is a loved one. I remember one lady who read my manuscript, shook her head, and told me, "This is too implausible. This could never happen." Sadly enough, it happens every day. But I hope that this book fills people with hope. Hope in life. Hope in the goodness of people. And hope that God will help all of us find our way.

I'd like to thank all of the people who have helped me and inspired me to write this book. And I'd like to thank all of my readers for their kind comments and emails. You guys are the best!

Love to all,
Shannon

ONe

The bishop sat at his desk and listened to the attractive young lady sitting in front of him. Her eyes looked like shattered glass.

"I feel so, so . . . *angry* sometimes. And today was the worst. I usually love watching the Primary children sing in sacrament meeting, but I just don't think I can take hearing that song 'I Am a Child of God' ever again. You know the lyrics: 'I am a child of God, and he has sent me here, has given me an earthly home *with parents kind and dear.*' What a joke! And that's pretty much our church's anthem. Every time I hear it, I want to run screaming from the room." A tear ran down her cheek.

The bishop nodded in understanding and pushed the tissue box toward her.

"I know. That's a hard one. But don't think you're the only one. Even in this ward, there are many people whose parents are charter members of the great and spacious building. I'll give you the key to loving that song again. As a matter of fact, that song will be instrumental in healing your heart."

The girl looked at him with stunned exasperation. He held up his hands for patience and then started to sing in a rather nice baritone, "I am a child of God, and he has sent me here, has given me an earthly home, with parents *kind of weird.*"

The young woman looked at him for a moment in shock and then burst out laughing. "Are you serious?"

The bishop nodded his head with a smile. "Trust me. You can sing

1

that verse along with everyone else, and no one will know the difference. There's no reason for that song to ever bring you to tears again. Now let's look at the rest of that song.

" 'Lead me, guide me, walk beside me, help me find the way. Teach me all that I must do to live with him someday.

" 'I am a child of God, and so my needs are great; Help me to understand his words before it grows too late.

" 'I am a child of God. Rich blessings are in store; if I but learn to do his will I'll live with him once more.

" 'I am a child of God. His promises are sure; Celestial glory shall be mine if I can but endure.' "

The bishop finished and watched as the young lady in front of him wiped the tears off her cheeks. She raised her gaze to meet his, and he was glad to see her eyes looked a little less shattered.

"I guess that is a pretty amazing song," she said quietly.

"Yes, it is. Your homework is to sing that song to yourself every night for the next week before you go to bed. Can you do that for me?"

She sniffed and nodded. "Yeah, I can do that."

The bishop studied her for another moment and then felt prompted to ask another question. "Something else is bothering you. Can you tell me what it is?"

She looked at him in surprise and then sighed, closing her eyes for a moment.

"It's just hard sometimes. Some people have this perception of my father. That he's a good guy, that he's just had some bad luck or something. They think that I'm being cruel and unforgiving, when all I'm trying to do is protect my brother and sister. And the strangest part of all is that *he* thinks he's a good person. He really believes it. He thinks everyone's out to get him. He has no clue that the things he's done are wrong. I don't even think he's sorry," she said in a bemused voice. "Remember the snake analogy you told me about? The one where you can get bit by a snake and not hate the snake, and you can forgive the snake, but you can make sure you never get bit again? He doesn't even know he's the snake!"

The bishop frowned and looked down at his hands for a moment. He knew exactly what she was talking about. He saw it every week in his office.

"Think of it this way. There are two mirrors," the bishop explained. "One mirror is held up by Satan. The other mirror is held up by Heavenly Father. Let me explain how your father can look in the mirror every day and truly believe that he's a great guy. When your father looks in the mirror, he's hearing Satan whisper in his ear, 'Wow, what an amazing man. You've done so much good in this world. You stop missionaries in the street to give them money for lunch; you take them out to dinner. You have a good heart. Okay, maybe you've had to bend the rules a little here and there, but it's the end result that matters. Your intentions were always pure. What a good guy.' "

The young woman rolled her eyes. "That's him perfectly."

The bishop nodded and continued. "But if he turns and looks in the mirror that Heavenly Father is holding up for him, it's a different story. He's not going to hear what he wants to hear. Heavenly Father will stand there and look at your dad, and he's going to say, 'I love you with all my heart, but it's time we do something about those fangs. I have a Son who's a great dentist. His pliers will hurt, but those fangs of yours have damaged too many people. They're getting too sharp. And all that poison you have inside isn't doing you any good. We're going to have to do a little open-heart surgery before it takes over your whole body. My Son is a good physician, though; you can trust him. It will hurt a lot, but he's the best. And those scales you have all over your body? We've got to do something about them. The only way to get rid of those is with the refiner's fire. It hurts a lot, but in the end, you'll be the man you were supposed to be.' "

The bishop smiled slightly as the young woman nodded. "Do you see why your dad likes looking in Satan's mirror more? It's painless. It's pleasant. It makes him feel good. And it's easy."

The girl sighed heavily. "Yeah, I get it. But how do you honor a snake?

two

Allison watched from her front porch as her brother and sister climbed down the steps of the yellow bus and walked toward her. Nervously, she balled up her hands at her sides. She studied their faces and could tell from their tense expressions that their day hadn't gone well.

"Hey, guys! How was the first day of school?" she called out as they walked up the sidewalk.

Aspen, her younger sister, tried to smile back at her, but her face was unusually stiff. "Oh, you know how first days are. Kind of not so fun."

Allison threw her arms around her sister and gave her a big hug. Aspen's thin arms wrapped around her immediately, and the two of them stood together. "It'll get better, honey. I promise."

Aspen sniffed and pulled away, walking into the house quickly so no one would see her tears. Allison felt like crying with her but held it in as she smiled at her brother, Talon.

"What about you, Tal? Make any new friends?" Allison asked hopefully.

Talon's eyes were so dark with misery, she felt like crumbling right there on the spot.

"Well, let's see if you can figure it out. I had to ride a big stupid yellow bus to and from school. I have to wear clothes from DI. And, oh yeah, as soon as they heard my last name, everyone either looked at me like I was diseased, or they looked at me like I was a diseased piece of snot. So yeah, everyone was flocking to be my new best buddy."

Allison moved out of Talon's way as he pushed into the house and

4

threw his backpack on the floor. She could hear his feet stomping up the stairs to his bedroom and the almost instantaneous sound of loud music. Instead of following her brother and sister into the house, she sat down heavily on the front steps and laid her head in her hands. Her siblings' misery felt so heavy on her heart that she didn't know if she could take it. The weight was almost unbearable. It had been her decision to move back to Alpine. It had been her decision to move them away from their home. But it was also her responsibility to keep what was left of her family safe. And the only safe place left on earth was Alpine, Utah. For some reason, she had thought—*hoped*—that her brother and sister would go to Lone Peak High School and make many wonderful friends and have such a great time that they would forget to resent her and blame her for making them move. No such luck.

Allison lifted her head and looked at their new little neighborhood. They'd been in town for a month now, but she still felt like a fish out of water. When she'd lived here as a teenager, she had felt like she was the princess of Alpine and everyone there was just a little part of her very own magical kingdom. Ten years ago when she had sailed into town with her parents, they had been the first of the ultra-wealthy families to discover Alpine. Her father had built a ten-thousand-square-foot mansion with a ballroom and indoor basketball court and pool. She had walked the halls of Lone Peak with her head high, and anyone who had been lucky enough to be a part of her exclusive circle was allowed into her world of pool parties, shopping sprees, and trips to Hawaii and New York. She hadn't necessarily bought her friends, but they knew who paid the bills.

It was almost tragic how opposite her life was now. Where once she'd lived in a mansion, now she rented one of the oldest homes in Alpine. Before, she'd had the clothes of a runway model. Now, Deseret Industries, a thrift store, was her boutique of choice. Before, she'd had so many friends that her cell phone never stopped ringing. Now? She hadn't had a call from anyone in weeks.

Allison sighed. She knew she needed to get up, finish the laundry, and start dinner, but just sitting there, staring down her street was the only thing she had the energy for.

She watched curiously as her neighbor stepped out onto her front porch and lumbered down her front steps. She was a tall woman with wavy brown hair and an enormous belly. Allison winced as the woman stumbled on her way to the mailbox. Pregnancy did not look fun. Or attractive.

The woman turned, and her mottled red puffy face convinced Allison that adoption would be a nice alternative when it came time to have children. Not that she'd be having any anytime soon. The memory of Jason dumping her made her wince automatically. She could still see his face as he held his hand out for the engagement ring he had given her.

"Hey, there! You must be my new neighbor," the pregnant woman called out.

Allison looked up in surprise and stood nervously, wiping her hands on her worn-out jeans.

"Um, yeah. Look, why don't you stay there, and I'll walk to you," Allison said, walking quickly toward the woman.

The lady laughed and patted her stomach. "Oh, you're sweet. Why don't you come sit on the porch swing with me and tell me all about yourself?"

Allison felt like taking the woman's arm as they walked up the steps, but controlled herself. She watched as the woman sort of leaned back, holding onto the iron chain of the swing for all her life as she slowly lowered herself down.

"You got it there?" Allison asked, hoping to high heaven the swing would hold them both.

"Oh yeah. Sit, sit! Sorry I haven't been over, but this pregnancy has just wiped me out. Just making it out to the mailbox is a huge achievement. I'm Maggie Peterson. What's your name?"

Allison sat down, *very carefully*. "My name is Allison Vaughn, and we just moved here from Dallas. We're renting for now while my brother and sister finish high school. They're both juniors this year," she said, watching the chain swing back and forth and wondering which link would give first.

Maggie looked back at her carefully. "Allison Vaughn. *Hmm*. And you're in charge of your younger brother and sister. You can't be much older than they are. Where are your mom and dad? Why aren't you off at college, having fun?" she asked kindly.

Allison laughed with absolutely no amusement in her voice. "I did go to college for a few years, but life got in the way of my finishing. It's kind of a long story. My dad still, um . . . *lives* in Dallas. And my mom died last year in a car accident. And before you ask, the answer is *yes*, my brother and sister *are* better off with me," she said grimly.

Maggie's eyebrows rose slightly, but she didn't pry. "Sorry about your mom. My mother has worked as a grief counselor, so if you ever need anyone to talk to, just let me know and I can give you her phone number."

Allison stared at her, blinking in surprise. A *grief* counselor? What she needed was a *life* counselor.

"Thanks. I'll let you know. So what about you?" Allison asked, changing the subject as quickly as possible. "How long have you lived in Alpine?"

Maggie smiled and pushed her long, wavy brown hair out of her eyes. "Just a few years now. I've been married for a year and a half, and our first baby is due in a couple months."

Allison's mouth fell open in shock. "You have two more months? Oh my heck, you poor thing," she whispered.

Maggie laughed and rubbed her large stomach. "I know I already look like I'm ten months pregnant. But my doctor says pregnancy hits every woman differently, and it just happened to hit me with a semi-truck. My husband, Luke, says it's to make up for the last twenty-six years. I was always super skinny."

Allison nodded her head but didn't believe her for a second. This woman looked like she was pushing two hundred pounds, easy.

"Did you say your husband's name was Luke? As in Luke Peterson?" Allison asked, sitting up straighter and forgetting for a second about the chain holding up the porch swing.

Maggie nodded her head, smiling. "Yes, do you know him?"

Allison smiled slightly. "Well, not very well. He was older than me. I used to live here five years ago. We moved away right before my graduation. I think he was on his mission then, or he was just barely home from his mission. I'm sure he wouldn't remember me," she said hopefully.

Maggie stared at the woman sitting beside her and laughed. Allison was the original pin-up girl—blonde, tall, and curvy. "Oh, he'd remember you. If you looked anything like you do now, he'd remember. My husband is a reformed lady's man. Now he's a banker. Go figure."

Allison blushed and shook her head quickly. "No, I'm sure he wouldn't remember me. I just remember him because he was popular. Everyone liked Luke."

Maggie nodded in agreement. "He's still like that. I can't wait to tell him about you. We were just talking the other day about coming over and introducing ourselves, but I haven't been feeling well lately."

Allison smiled. "Please don't worry about it. I hear you're supposed to start feeling better when you hit the eight-month mark."

Maggie rolled her eyes. "Yeah, right. I'll believe it when it happens. Now enough about me. Tell me all about you. You're taking care of you brother and sister. You moved here from Dallas. You're gorgeous. Tell me something wonderful and interesting about yourself," Maggie insisted, smiling encouragingly.

Allison winced and sat back in the swing, looking up at the mountains surrounding the little town of Alpine. Something interesting and wonderful? About *her*? She had plenty of horrifying things she could tell Maggie. Interesting, yes. Wonderful, *no*. Should she tell Maggie that her father was in prison, scheduled to be released soon, according to his lawyer, because of overcrowding, but still very much in prison at the moment? She could tell Maggie her mother died in a car accident with her boyfriend, and that was how they found out Felicia Vaughn was leaving her husband of twenty-five years for a much younger man. She could tell Maggie that she had been given custody of her brother and sister and had just enough money from her mother's life insurance policy to survive on, if they didn't mind starving slightly. Or she could just do what she'd been doing for the last year and pretend everything was fine. She was fine, life was fine. Fine. *Fine.*

Allison glanced at Maggie and sighed. Maggie looked back at her with compassionate eyes, as if she could read her soul.

"It's been tough, huh?" Maggie asked sympathetically.

Allison blew a strand of hair out of her eyes and tried not to cry. "Yeah. It's been tough. Someday I'll tell you about it," she said honestly. For some reason, she didn't feel like lying to Maggie.

Maggie nodded and patted her hand kindly. "Anytime you need someone to talk to, I'm here."

Allison nodded and stood up. "I'd better go get started on the laundry and dinner. Aspen and Talon have celiac disease, so I have to make everything from scratch. No calling in for pizza."

Maggie looked surprised. "Isn't that where they can't eat wheat or something?"

Allison nodded tiredly. "Yeah. And practically everything has wheat in it."

Maggie stood up with a lot of grunting and pulling. "Whew! Well, good luck with dinner. Come over tomorrow if you have some free time," she offered.

Allison walked down the steps and smiled over her shoulder. "Thanks. It was really nice meeting you, Maggie."

Maggie waved at her, but Allison's smile disappeared as soon as she turned away. She wouldn't be over tomorrow. As soon as Luke got home from work and learned who his new neighbor was, Allison would be lucky if Maggie even waved at her. Luke would know the whole story of Max Vaughn and how his family had left Alpine in disgrace five years ago. Being a banker, Luke would know of all the money Max had "invested" for his friends and neighbors. And how all that money had disappeared.

Allison walked up the front steps to her house and paused to look back at Alpine before going inside. She had known before she'd put one foot back onto Alpine's soil that she would have no friends here. But none of that mattered. It was the one place her dad wouldn't have the guts to show his face. He wouldn't be able to touch her brother or sister. He had burned too many bridges here. For that reason alone, Talon and Aspen might just get to have a normal life. Allison walked in the house and turned to lock the front door. Forget friends. Aspen and Talon were her first priority. And no way was Maxwell Vaughn going to get his hands on them.

thRee

Allison kicked Talon's backpack out of the way and glared at the large picture of a bulldog that graced her foyer. The previous owner had been a huge dog lover. There were pictures of dogs all over the place. Allison didn't care for the artwork but figured that when you rent a furnished house for super cheap, you can't complain—at least not too much. Allison walked back to the kitchen and ran her hand over the pale green formica countertop that was made to look like marble. She wouldn't trade it for the jet-black granite countertops in her dad's house. Not even for a second. She actually liked her little house. For the first time in her life, she felt . . . What was this strangely peaceful feeling? She smiled and shook her head. She felt *safe*. That was it. No sarcasm. No yelling. No belittling. No manipulating. No one to put her or her brother and sister down. They were finally safe.

Allison smiled and got busy with the laundry and the other chores that full-time homemakers have to do every day. It was a little after five when she finally started making dinner. She hoped Aspen and Talon would join her soon. She figured they'd get sick of their own company and come down when they started to smell something good.

Allison pulled a rubber band out of the front pocket of her jeans and pulled her hair up into a ponytail. Time to get cooking. She grabbed the ingredients out of the pantry to make a gluten-free pizza crust. She called it pizza, but its similarities to real pizza were very slim. She missed the chewy, yeasty taste of real pizza, but she would never eat it in front of Talon and Aspen. It would torture them. She still wasn't even sure Talon really stuck to his diet when she wasn't there to watch him. He was going through a rebellious, "I hate the world, the world hates me, I don't have to do anything anyone tells me to" stage. She'd never gone through that stage as a teenager. The world had loved her, and she'd loved the world right back. She felt for Talon, but at the same time the attitude was getting a little old.

Aspen walked into the kitchen, her face looking blotchy and her eyes red and puffy from crying. Allison winced as she added a teaspoon of xanthan gum to her recipe.

"Whatcha making, Allie?" Aspen asked quietly as she sat down on the bar stool opposite her.

Allison smiled at her sister. Aspen was the exact opposite of Talon. Where he was loud and demanded his rights and made sure the world knew he was there, Aspen was quiet and shy and sensitive. They didn't look like twins either. Talon was tall, lean, and naturally handsome, with the darker coloring of their dad and the fine features of their mother. Aspen had the pale coloring of their mother and the bolder features of their dad. Her mouth was wide, her eyes were large, and her cheekbones were sharp. When she got a little older and grew into her face more, Allison knew Aspen would be beautiful. It was her goal this year to get Aspen to look people in the eyes. Confidence was the first step to real beauty.

"I'm making my specialty—pizza," Allison said, watching Aspen carefully for any wincing or eye rolling. She was still new at the gluten-free cooking thing, so she was still working on making things taste normal.

"That's good. I'm just glad it's not that noodle casserole you made last week," Aspen said gratefully. "That was the worst."

Allison grimaced and shook her head. "Yeah, that was pretty bad. Talon wouldn't even touch it. The smell alone had him running for the cereal."

Aspen gripped her hands together and laid her chin on them sadly. "I hate it when Talon is so sad. I can't stand it. At lunch today some guy came up to Tal and told him he knew who he really was and that he was going to make him pay."

Allison's mouth fell open in surprise. It was only the first day of school and already there was a confrontation?

"So what did Talon do?" she asked, her hands suspended over the bowl and her eyes wide.

"What do you think I did?" Talon said, walking into the kitchen. "I shoved the jerk away and walked off. I didn't want to get kicked out of school on the first day. Tomorrow's another story, though," Talon said as he sat down next to his sister and grabbed a slice of pepperoni out of the bag sitting beside her bowl.

Allison grabbed the cookie sheet and dumped the dough onto it. Then she slid it in the oven and dusted her hands off.

"Sorry, Tal. I guess we should have expected something like that. I was hoping it'd be later not sooner, but since it's already happened, let's talk about how you could get out of those kinds of situations without making anyone even madder," she said, trying to think quickly.

Talon sneered at her before rubbing his forehead. "You just don't get it, do you? These people *hate* us. And the ones who don't hate us yet will hate us tomorrow or the next day or the next. Why couldn't we have gone to California or Florida?" he demanded for what seemed like the millionth time. "Somewhere by the ocean. Somewhere no one's ever even heard of Dad."

Allison felt a headache coming on as she leaned her elbows on the counter to face her brother.

"You know why, Talon. This is the one place you're safe from Dad."

"He's my *dad!* He wouldn't hurt *me*. Maybe *you*, but not me or Aspen. And yeah, maybe he'd steal from everyone else in the world, but he'd never steal from his own son," Talon said desperately, trying to convince himself.

Aspen looked at Allison, expecting her to have all the answers.

Allison sighed deeply and then squared her shoulders. She looked her brother straight in the eye and finally told him the truth.

"Talon, if you and dad were on a plane getting ready to crash and there was only one parachute, what do you think would happen? Would Dad choose to save himself or you? Who do you think he'd save? *Hmm?*" she asked quietly but with a firm voice.

Talon blinked and looked away. "I don't know."

"Your dad. *My* dad. Our dad happens to be your basic bad person. He's polluted his spirit so much with selfishness and greed that he doesn't even know who he is anymore. *I'm* the one looking out for you now, and in my opinion you're safer here, *away* from him. When you get back from your mission, then you can decide if you want Dad in your life. Until then, I'm the one making the rules."

Aspen cleared her throat quietly. "Allie, do you think *we'll* turn out like Dad? I mean, we have his genes, you know? You have his sense of humor and green eyes, and Talon looks kind of like him, and I'm good at math. Do you think someday we'll wake up and try to ruin people's lives like he did? Do you think we'll want money more than love? More than our family?" she asked as she started chewing on a fingernail.

Allison took a second to massage her forehead before answering. She noticed Talon's gaze sharpened as he stared at her, waiting for the answer.

"No. And isn't that the best news you've had all day? As a matter of fact, I know that you and Talon aren't going to turn out *anything* like Dad. It says it all over the scriptures, but I like how the second article of faith says that men will be punished for their own sins and not for Adam's transgression. Yeah, I know that's talking about original sin and all that stuff, but it means more than that. It means I'm my own person. I have my agency. It doesn't matter who my parents are or what my talents are or what role genetics play in my life. I will be who I *choose* to be. I'm going to make my own mistakes. And yes, I'll pay for them, but I will not pay for Dad's mistakes. *He* will," she said, watching her siblings' faces carefully.

Aspen sighed in relief, and even Talon's face looked a little lighter.

"Well, it sure seemed like I was paying for Dad's mistakes today in the cafeteria when that guy wanted to tear my head off," Talon said, not sounding tough anymore.

Allison nodded her head and then turned to take the pizza crust out of the oven. She poured the pizza sauce on to the hot crust and then added the toppings and cheese.

"You've gotta understand, Talon, that you're not the only one who's had a major change in lifestyle because of Dad. Some of the people here lost everything. Maybe that kid had to move from a mansion to a tiny house like ours. Maybe, because of our dad, he doesn't have a cool car to ride to school in either. Maybe he's had to watch his parents suffer. It's a hard thing for *everybody*. So my best advice would be to just avoid anyone who really wants to get in a fight with you. If you can't, try to explain that you had nothing to do with it. And if that doesn't work—" Allison stopped in mid-sentence, stumped.

She had absolutely no experience with fighting or even getting out of fights. Who was she to give her brother advice? Unfortunately, she was the only one standing there.

"I know," Talon suggested, "I can finally use my karate skills. All those after-school classes Mom always made us go to with the nanny. They might actually come in handy," Talon said, flexing his muscles.

"Never throw the first punch," Aspen said earnestly.

Allison and Talon looked at her in surprise. "And you would know because you've been in so many fights, right?" Talon asked sarcastically.

Aspen blushed and flipped her blonde hair over her shoulder. "Don't be an idiot. I'm just thinking of what would happen if the cops were called. So don't throw the first punch, but definitely stand up for yourself. And I will too if I'm there. I promise, Tal. I won't ever let anyone hurt you," she said quietly.

Talon looked down and cleared his own throat. And for the first time that day, he said something without being sarcastic or angry. "I know, Aspen. I know you wouldn't."

Allison turned around to hide the tears in her eyes and to put the pizza back in the oven. Aspen was the closest thing to an angel she knew. Allison just hoped that someday, when she really grew up, she could be like her little sister. She carefully wiped her eyes and sniffed a little before putting a smile on her face and turning back around.

Talon sneered at her. "You're such a baby."

Aspen grinned. "It's okay, Allie. You just have a tender heart. You try to hide it and be strong for us, but you're soft underneath it all."

Allison smiled and shrugged. Aspen had no clue. She wasn't soft. Not anymore. She was reminded of the scripture in the Book of Mormon that said, "He commandeth you that ye not suffer any ravenous wolf to enter in among you." She knew who the wolf was, and she would protect her lambs at all costs. Aspen thought she was soft. What a joke. By no means was she a wolf, but she was definitely a guard dog, and her teeth were getting sharper every day. She was strong enough and tough enough to stop anyone who would hurt her family.

At least she hoped she was.

fOUR

After dinner, Aspen and Talon started their homework, so Allison decided to walk down by the park. The air had cooled off, and she needed a little break. For just half an hour she could pretend that she didn't have any responsibilities, that no one knew who she was, and that she was just a simple girl from Alpine taking a walk.

After telling her brother and sister where she would be, she walked down the porch steps and shoved her hands in her front pockets. She took a deep breath of air and took off, trying to really see Alpine. It didn't look any different than it did five years ago. No street lights. No big commercial buildings. Just same old Alpine. She smiled. For some reason, that was very comforting to her.

Walking quickly past the Petersons' house, Allison could see the lights on inside and Luke's car parked in front. After her talk with Talon about confronting people, she had to admit that she just wasn't ready to be told off by Luke Peterson. He knew everyone in Alpine. That meant he'd know everyone who had been hurt by her dad. And he'd hate her. Who wouldn't?

She walked past the house next to the Petersons' and wondered why no one lived there. She paused as she noticed the very small sign in the window. *The Tierney Gallery.* The sign said it was closed until further notice. Too bad. She loved art. When it reopened, she'd be first in line to see what was inside.

She hurried farther down the street and only slowed down when she couldn't see her house anymore. Sighing, she tried to get her relaxed, happy, safe-Alpine feeling back. She caught view of the park and smiled again. She and her friends had spent many hours there perfecting their cheerleading routines. Those were some of the happiest times of her life. In high school she had been captain of the cheerleading squad, and Daphne had been her second in command. They had spent a lot of time together. Too much, really. Of course, they had grown apart after Allison had moved away, but Allison looked forward to reconnecting with someone in Alpine who didn't hate her. Maybe Daphne had grown up. Allison hoped she had. Maybe a more mature, kinder Daphne would be the friend she needed right now.

Allison paused and then decided to sit on a bench and watch the little kids play for a few minutes. She noticed someone had taken out the old hard bark and replaced it with multi-colored rubber pieces to make the play equipment safer.

Some of the parents looked at her strangely but went back to their Frisbees and their kids when they decided she was harmless. She felt some of the tension ease slowly out of her shoulders. This was good. She noticed a new hair salon across from the park. Five years ago, there used to be a little beauty salon there, but it hadn't been nearly as nice as this one. She would absolutely love to have her highlights touched up. But with her budget, there was no telling when she could afford that.

What she needed was a job. Just something part-time so she could be there for Talon and Aspen after school. Maybe the bishop knew of a local job opening that would work with her schedule. She'd been talking to him almost every week since they'd moved in. It wouldn't hurt to ask.

Allison got up from the bench and continued her walk, going past the city building and the ancient little Alpine museum. When she reached the stop sign, she paused, realizing she should probably head back in case the kids needed any help with their homework. She had turned around and started walking back toward the park when the screech of tires made her gasp and whip her head around. A bright red sports car with black tinted windows had stopped in the street, causing a road block to all the cars behind him. The driver was either having car trouble or had stopped the car to stare at her. She started walking faster and heard the car drive away.

For some reason, her heart was pounding, and she felt nervous. It had been five years. Nobody would recognize her. *Would they?* She started walking faster as she convinced herself that she didn't even look like that cool, rich, confident girl she used to be. Now, she was a woman. She had filled out and grown up. Wearing old faded jeans and a T-shirt with flip flops, she wasn't exactly the fashion plate she used to be. Her hair was much longer now since she couldn't afford a trip to the salon every month to keep her style looking razor sharp.

Allison noticed with dread that the red car had found somewhere to turn around and was now slowly coming back her way. She bit her lip nervously and looked around. The beauty salon—she'd step in there and ask how much highlights would cost. No one would dare accost her inside a place of business. She hoped. Allison sprinted across the street and practically ran the rest of the way to the beauty salon as the car came to a stop across the street and the driver watched her every move.

Allison whipped the door open and flung herself inside, breathing heavily and wishing she had her cell phone with her. She walked into the stylish entryway and peeked out the window. The red car was parked across the street by the park. Was the driver waiting for her to come out? A cold chill ran down her spine, and she shivered. What if it was one of her father's ex-business partners out for blood? Maybe Alpine wasn't the safest place for her after all.

She turned away from the car and looked over the salon. It was charming, decorated in a European style with warm, dark colors and soothing yellows. It had the same feel as the spa in Dallas where she used to go for massages. If only she had the money for one now.

"I'll be right with you!" called a woman from the back of the salon.

Allison smiled and waved. "No problem. I'm just checking out your services," she called back and turned to look up at the hand-painted list on the wall.

Allison looked back out the window and noticed the red car had finally driven away. She felt a wave of relief wash over her and realized her hands were shaking. She glared at a perfectly innocent potted plant and felt like kicking it. She hated being scared of anything or anybody. After grabbing a brochure off the desk, she was about to make her exit when the woman who had called out to her walked forward. Why did she look so familiar, almost exactly like Sophie Reid? Allison frowned, knowing she would have been better off facing whoever was in the red car.

"I must be cursed," she whispered.

Sophie stopped a few feet in front of her, all trace of her friendly professional smile gone.

"Well, if you aren't, you should be," she said with a snap in her eyes and her hands going to her hips.

"What in the world are you doing here in Alpine, Allison Vaughn?" Sophie demanded with a scowl.

Allison felt her back straighten and her hands tighten into fists. "I live here now."

Sophie nodded her head once, looking her up and down, as if she were cataloging all the changes.

Allison rolled her eyes and waited impatiently for the inspection to end. Sophie had changed too. She had always been cute and sparkly. She was still those things, but now she also had a quiet confidence and a strength that hadn't been there before. Allison was impressed.

"Was Texas not good enough for you? Not enough people there to tell you how amazing and perfect you are? You had to come back here so you could rub in to all of us how gorgeous you are now? I bet it would be hard to find an entourage anywhere that could compare with the one you had here in Alpine."

Allison's eyes widened in surprise. Gorgeous? Maybe back in high school, but she was far from gorgeous now.

"Are you crazy? I didn't come back to Alpine to rub anybody's face in anything. I came back for my brother and sister. It was the only choice I had," Allison said, still shocked by Sophie's comment.

Sophie's chin came up as she stared at Allison, trying to discern the truth. What she saw must have satisfied her because she sighed and crossed her arms over her chest.

"You know, Allison, you and Daphne tried so hard to ruin my life. What happened to karma? If life were fair, you'd be four hundred pounds and have flesh-eating bacteria. But look at you. *Still* the most beautiful girl in Alpine, and if I'm not mistaken, almost human now. What in the world happened to you?" she asked in all earnestness.

Allison let out all the breath in her lungs as her shoulders sagged. She looked down at the floor and then back up to meet Sophie's eyes. "I was never the bad guy you liked to think I was, Sophie. But to answer your question, life happened. A whole truckload of life dumped itself right on top of me. Look, I'll get out of your way. I didn't mean to take you away from your client. See ya around," she said and started walking to the door.

"Not so fast. *You owe me.* You owe me so dang much, it's not even funny. All those times you laughed at me behind my back. All those times you sneered at Blake just because he was my boyfriend. All those times you made me feel like I was dirt, a *nobody.* You owe me. I want your story. Your *whole* story."

Allison's jaw dropped as she stared at Sophie, now almost vibrating with holy rage. *She* had made Sophie feel like that? Perspective was everything. Allison shook her head and laughed grimly.

"You want my story, Sophie? Really? Well, it's a simple story, actually. It's about a girl who had everything—money, friends, and the perfect lifestyle. And then she found out that it was all a lie. A big, fake lie. Now all I want is peace. I don't care about money. I don't care about friends. And I couldn't care less about lifestyle. All I care about is my brother and sister. That's it. End of story," she said. Then she headed for the door with quick, determined steps. This was getting too deep and too painful.

"Hold it," Sophie stopped her. "You care about hair, or else you wouldn't be here. Let me guess. A trim and highlights?"

Allison paused with her hand on the door and looked back at Sophie. "Sorry, Sophie. I think your price is higher than I can afford right now. My extra money goes to milk and school clothes."

Sophie smiled slightly and leaned on the counter, looking at her calmly. "Everybody can afford free. How about I schedule you in for nine tomorrow morning? Just you and me and a pair of scissors."

Allison stared at her in confusion. "Why would you do that? You hate my guts. Why would you do anything for me?" she demanded and then paused. "Oh. I get it. You want a chance to chop all my hair off and dye it purple or something, huh? Well, forget it, Sophie. High school ended a long time ago. I'm too smart to fall for that."

Sophie laughed. "You know it's a good thing you moved back now. A few years ago, you might have been right about my intentions. I've grown up a little too. I promise. No revenge. Just some light ash blonde highlights around the face and a little trim. And a lot of questions," she added in a serious tone.

Allison looked into Sophie's eyes and tried to read her mind. But it was just Sophie. The same old Sophie from high school. Sweet, sincere, and kind.

"I'll think about it," Allison finally said and walked out.

She walked quickly home with her head down as she went over and over her conversation with Sophie. She would love some highlights, but at what price? Would Sophie demand answers and then use them against her? Would she spread gossip about the Vaughn family all over Alpine? If she did, it wouldn't bother just her. It would trickle down to the high school and Talon and Aspen. She had a lot to think about.

Allison rushed up the steps to her house and through her door without noticing a pair of icy blue eyes following her every move.

five

Luke shut the blinds and turned to his wife. "I don't want you talking to her. You stay as far away from Allison Vaughn as you can get. I can't believe she's renting Gwen's old house. Doesn't the new owner screen? Haven't they heard of background checks? I can't believe I'm living on the same street as a Vaughn. Start packing, Maggie. We're moving in with my mom and dad. Allison will probably steal our baby and try to sell her on e-bay," he said as he paced around their small living room.

Maggie groaned and rubbed her stomach. "Don't you think you're overreacting just a little, Luke? I talked to her today. I have a huge evil radar, and I'm telling you, Allison is a good girl. She's sweet. I think she's been through a really hard time lately. Maybe we—and by *we*, I mean *you*—should give her a break," Maggie said as she tried to get comfortable.

Luke walked over and picked up her feet and laid them on a cushion. "Maggie, you are so naïve. She's already scammed you. Her dad was the same way. He was even a member of the high council. Everybody, and I mean, *everybody*, loved Max Vaughn. He was probably the most respected and liked man in Alpine. He fooled everybody and then left town with all our money. Maggie, if you even had a clue how many lives were ruined because of that family's greed. I know people, good friends, who lost everything. I know four families who had to move. Some families declared bankruptcy and then ended up renting just to keep their heads above water. I mean, it's been five years, and some people are just now getting back on their feet. And I know one family who never did," Luke said darkly, his eyes almost freezing her with their disdain.

Maggie sighed and rubbed her stomach again. "Okay, I believe you about the father, but what does that have to do with *her*? Five years ago, she was in high school. You can't really be standing there telling me that a young girl had anything to do with all that," she said in a soothing voice.

"Trust me," Luke said quietly and firmly. "That woman is a viper. I bet you a million dollars she's just like her dad. Apples don't fall that far from the tree. Stay away, Maggie. Don't turn the Vaughns into one of your projects. That family can't be fixed," he stated firmly before walking out of the room.

Maggie leaned her head back on the cushion and stared at the ceiling. Luke was so angry, but she knew what she knew. When she'd looked in Allison Vaughn's eyes, she had seen desperation, heartbreak, and pain. The one thing she hadn't seen was evil.

Luke came back a few minutes later with a large chocolate milk shake in his hand. "Here, sweetie, sit up and eat this. Maybe it will settle your stomach."

Maggie grabbed Luke's hand and tried to move her large, aching body into a sitting position. Just breathing was getting to be difficult these days.

"Thanks, hon. And by the way, if I haven't mentioned it, this is the only child you're getting out of me. I will never do this *ever* again," she swore as she took her first sip of luscious liquid chocolate. "Mmm. This is good, Luke."

Luke smiled grimly. "Of course it is. It's kind of hard to mess up ice cream and milk."

Maggie took another sip and then groaned as the baby kicked.

Luke winced and rubbed her stomach soothingly. "I just can't get over this feeling that there's something else wrong with you."

Maggie rolled her eyes. "I'm so sick of being poked and prodded. If I never see another doctor again, it will be too soon, and I haven't even delivered yet."

Luke began to massage her feet as he studied her. "Well, don't get mad, but I made an appointment for you tomorrow with a good friend of my dad's. Dr. Hastings is a great doctor. He's just going to run a bunch of tests on you. No biggie. They'll just take a little blood at the lab. No internal exam, I promise." Luke crossed his heart.

Maggie glared at him but sighed and gave up. "I think you're right. I think something is wrong. Most pregnant women don't feel like I do, or *look* like I do. This has been the worst experience of my life. And I hate that. I wanted to love being pregnant. I wanted to treasure this time while our baby was inside me. And instead, I'm just gritting my teeth until it's over."

Luke frowned. "So does that mean you'll go?"

Maggie took a sip of her shake and gave Luke her other foot. "Yeah. I'll be there."

Luke's eyes turned dark green with love. "Don't worry. I'll be right there with you."

Maggie sighed as her feet started to feel better. "You and what army?"

Luke laughed. "Hey, I've been working out every night this last week. If you fall, I promise I'll catch you."

Maggie sniffed and took another sip of her shake. "Okay, but remember, you signed up for this."

Luke smiled gently at his wife and kissed her. "And I'd sign up all over again too."

Maggie gave in and smiled. Luke was pretty okay. She really should keep him.

Six

Allison waved at Talon and Aspen as they walked to the bus stop down the road. Aspen waved half-heartedly back at her, but all she got from Talon was a flip of his shaggy hair and a sneer. She couldn't even remember the last time she had seen Talon smile.

Allison leaned against the door jamb and frowned. It must have been before their mom had died and they'd found out their father was being investigated by the FBI. Had it been that long? Talon had always been an in-your-face kind of guy, but he'd always been smiling and laughing too. She bit her lip and wondered if Maggie's mom had any experience talking to depressed teenage boys. She might just have to brave the wrath of Luke and ask Maggie.

She closed the door and walked back into the kitchen. She glanced at the clock and felt her stomach jump nervously. It was only 7:30. She still had an hour and a half to decide whether or not she felt like trading her life story for a few blonde highlights.

Allison blew out her breath and started the dishes. She hadn't known that Sophie had such bitter feelings toward her. Sophie had barely registered on her radar in high school. And when she did, Allison had gone out of her way to be nice to her—in her own way, of course, but her intentions had always been good. Maybe she *should* go see Sophie, just to set her straight on a few matters. Allison ran up the stairs and hopped in the shower.

An hour and a half later, she walked nonchalantly through the salon doors. She was wearing another pair of faded blue jeans and an old vintage T-shirt she had picked up for a dollar at the Good Will in Dallas. Her flip flops had been purchased at the dollar store just last week. If Sophie complimented her on her looks again, she would know she was insane. It was that easy.

Allison stood by the front desk and looked around the empty salon. "Hello? Anyone here?" she called out, wondering too late if she had been set up. What if Sophie and that witchy blonde friend of hers were planning on beating her up or something even more hideous? Allison started to walk slowly back toward the entrance when Sophie appeared through the back door of the salon.

"I knew it! No one can turn down free highlights. No one. Well, come on. Have a seat. We don't have all day. Jacie and my mom are coming in at eleven for their appointments."

Allison sighed in relief. This wasn't a set-up. At least not that she could tell. She walked toward the chair Sophie was gesturing to and sat down gingerly.

"So what do you want to know?" Allison asked as Sophie started combing out her hair.

Sophie looked her in the eyes through the mirror and frowned. "I really want to know why you hated me so much. It tortured me to know that you hated me. Sometimes when I tried to talk to you, you'd cut me off, or even worse, ignore me. It made me feel worthless. But then other times you'd stick up for me. I was so confused. Sometimes I thought you were schizophrenic. I really . . . I really wanted to be your friend. *So much.* You were so smart and funny and pretty. Everyone liked you. *Everyone* was your friend. Everyone but me. And I want to know why."

Allison sighed and closed her eyes. As she thought back to high school, she winced. "Well, that's a valid question," she murmured. "Would it make you feel any better to know I was actually trying to protect you? That the best way I could be your friend was to ignore you or walk away?"

Sophie snorted and tugged on Allison's hair a little harder than she should have. Allison sucked in her breath and massaged her scalp.

"If that's all you've got, I'm going to rethink my ban on purple and green hair dye," Sophie said acidly.

"Who was my best friend all through high school?" Allison asked almost casually.

Sophie rolled her eyes. "Daphne, of course. Everyone knew that.

Bad taste in friends by the way," she added under her breath.

Allison gave a half-smile. "Yeah, well, guess who Daphne hated more than anyone else?"

Sophie ground her teeth. "Me, of course. Duh."

Allison nodded. "So then think back. All those times you tried to talk to me, who was walking up to me? Who would have seen you trying to talk to me, and then tortured *you* for it? I do remember one time when we were talking in the library. It was about some research paper for English. I remember wondering why Daphne hated you so much. Because if she hadn't, then I would have loved to have had you as a friend. You always seemed so sincere and open. Fake friends are hard after awhile. They're exhausting. They can be fun and exciting, but after awhile, just having someone to confide in and be real with would have been really nice. Especially someone who wouldn't tell everyone in school the next day everything you had said," Allison said, looking up at Sophie's reflection to see if her words had caused any reaction.

Sophie's eye's had that snappy look again and Allison sighed. She was starting to dread that look.

"You're telling me," Sophie said, "that you ignored my pathetic attempts at friendship with you because Daphne wouldn't have allowed it? Are you kidding me? *What?* Daphne told *you* what to do? I don't buy it. No one told you what to do. You were the queen. Everyone bowed to you. Even Daphne," she spit out.

Allison bit her lip and massaged her cuticles, looking down and away from Sophie's fury. Free highlights weren't exactly all they were cracked up to be.

"No, you're right," Allison said. "Nobody at school ever told me what to do. Only one person did. My father. When I was a sophomore in high school, my dad pressured me into befriending Daphne Martin because he wanted her dad to invest in one of his real estate deals. It was all about making a profit. I was told who to invite to my parties. I was told who to be nice to. And I was told which girls could be my friends. Remember that trip to Hawaii our junior year? I was told to invite six girls. One of them was Daphne. The other five? I didn't even know them. It was horrible. You can believe what you want. It's your choice. But the truth of the matter is, I was just leverage to my father. A *thing* to be used to get him what he wanted. What father wouldn't be grateful that his shy, reclusive daughter had been invited to spend a week in Hawaii with the most popular girl at school? He'd be so grateful, in fact, that when that father was asked to invest in a small growing company, he'd jump at the chance."

Sophie laid her comb down and stared at Allison. Allison looked back, not blinking. Sophie lowered her eyes first.

"Are you kidding me?" Sophie finally asked, reaching for the first foil.

Allison breathed in deeply and then let it out. "Do I sound like I'm kidding you? Of course I'm not. Oh, and my dad's very strict instructions concerning Daphne were to *always* make her happy. If Daphne was happy, then her dad was happy. Daphne is her dad's weakness. Her dad would do anything for her, and my dad is an expert at taking advantage of weaknesses. If Daphne's dad was happy, then my dad made money. Bottom line, keeping Daphne happy meant not being your friend."

Sophie brushed the pale purple bleach across a section of Allison's hair and frowned. "This is all really hard to take in, Allison. I'm not saying you're making it up. I'm just saying it's hard to change your perception of someone on a dime. I mean, what dad would manipulate his daughter's social life? It's just too weird."

Allison shrugged slightly and sighed. "Take your time. Take all the time in the world."

Sophie stared at her and then grabbed another foil. "Some of that makes sense, but then some of it doesn't. Like when I started dating Blake. Oh my heck, I was so in love with him. He was the most gorgeous guy in the world. He was from a normal family and everything. And he really liked me. I was in heaven. For the first time in my life, I felt accepted. And then later that week, Jacie overhears you telling Kerri, Danita, and Jenny that only someone with no taste would date Blake. And we found out it was you who started the rumor that Blake was gay," Sophie said, her eyes looking dangerous yet again.

Allison sat up straighter and stared Sophie down. "Okay, this is it. This is the truth about your cousin Daphne. You started dating Blake on Friday. By Saturday night, Daphne had a plan to steal Blake away from you. She was obsessed with the idea. I couldn't convince her not to do it. I told her that Jake Hartford had a crush on her, and she didn't even care. She wanted Blake as soon as she found out you did. I felt bad for you. I felt bad that Daphne was always trying to put you down. And like I said, if I'd had a choice in friends back then, it would have been you. Not her. So I did the only thing I could to keep Daphne from stealing your boyfriend. And you have to know that if she had gone for him, she would have gotten him. No offense. So I spread it around school that Blake was a loser. The interesting thing is, all of Blake's friends ignored the gossip. But all the popular kids treated Blake like he was a leper. Especially Daphne. She never knew who started those rumors, but she sure listened. You got to keep Blake, Sophie. So what if you hated me. You were happy," Allison added tiredly.

Sophie's mouth fell open as she forgot about the foil and the bleach in her hand.

In the mirror Allison watched a glob of bleach fall toward her head. "Hey!" she yelled, pulling Sophie out of her trance. Sophie brushed the mixture on the foil quickly and then shook her head.

"I can't get over this. I just can't take it in. The wicked witch of the west is actually human. Possibly a nice human. I'm having a really hard time with this. I kind of thought you'd show up and tell me some lame story about how you were actually addicted to meth and you've turned your life around or something," she admitted.

Allison laughed softly. "That's why I showed up today. I don't really like getting the third degree, although free highlights are the best thing that's happened to me in a long, *long* time. But I really just wanted you to know that I actually liked you back then. I would have loved to have been friends with you in high school."

Sophie grabbed a new section of hair, expertly weaving her comb through the strands.

"Yeah, high school is long gone. Thank heavens. But what about now? You got anyone standing over your shoulder telling you what to do now?" Sophie asked in a soft voice.

Allison's eyes went wide in surprise. Sophie *still* wanted to be her friend?

"Sophie, I appreciate the offer, but you don't know what you're asking. Working in a hair salon, you've gotta hear the local gossip. Don't you know what my dad did to people here in Alpine? Why would you want to be friends with me?" she demanded suspiciously.

Sophie frowned and grabbed another foil. "I don't know, to be honest. I just remember seeing you at school and thinking you were kind of an enigma. On one hand you were rich, beautiful, and popular, but then I'd see you always stop to talk to the special needs kids. You never went past Travis Warford without giving him a high-five or saying hi. And when everyone in the school found out Heather Johnson was pregnant, you made such a point of talking to her and being seen with her. I know she was going through the worst time of her life, and you were so supportive. That's the Allison I always wanted to be friends with. Your dad's not here. Daphne can't touch me anymore. Why not?"

Allison let all the air out of her lungs. "Daphne always did say you were crazy."

Sophie laughed. "You have no idea. Now, that's half your head in highlights. I'd like the other half of the story, if you please."

Allison winced and closed her eyes. "Just between you and me?"

Sophie paused and looked at Allison thoughtfully. "I don't gossip about my friends. And it's a possibility that you could be one."

Allison's green eyes warmed, and a smile slowly spread to her mouth. "Well, it's like I said last night. I'm here to protect my little brother and sister. My dad wouldn't dare show his face in this town after everything he did. As you probably know, my dad ran real estate scams here in Alpine five years ago, selling bogus properties down in St. George to people up here. All the people here wanted to do was earn extra money to pay for their kids' missions or weddings or college or to go on missions themselves when they retired. And my dad took it all with a smile and a promise to double their money. And then he got caught. Daphne's dad was the one who brought in a private accountant because he started to suspect what was going on. My dad found out and took off—with us—a week after prom. I didn't even get to graduate with my class. It was horrible and traumatic. My mom was hysterical for weeks. My little brother and sister were so confused. He took us to Dallas, where he had some old friends from his mission days. And then he started scamming all over again."

Sophie put her brush down and took off her gloves. "Let me grab you a drink and a donut. You look like you could use some sugar," she said kindly and walked through the doorway into the back room for a moment, returning almost immediately with a beautiful jelly donut and water.

"Bless you! See, I knew you were nice," Allison said as she bit into the most delicious piece of fried flour known to mankind. "I can't eat these at home. It would kill Aspen and Talon. They can't have wheat," she explained as she devoured the donut in what could only be described as pure joy.

Sophie laughed. "You poor, *poor* thing. You know I'm glad to see you eat a donut. I was afraid you'd turn it down. From what I remember in high school, you never ate. You'd sit in the cafeteria at lunch with a diet Coke and just talk. It was like you were borderline anorexic or something."

Allison smiled sadly and finished the last bite of her donut. "Yeah, well I learned early on in the Vaughn house that if you didn't want to be made fun of or laughed at, or criticized or demeaned, you stayed a size five. I was immediately called out if I put on any extra weight. It was easier to stay thin than to be chastised about being fat. My parents saw being overweight as a sign of weakness. And when I gained even a little weight, it was open season on Allison. I never knew if they hated it when I gained weight or loved it because then they could have so much fun ganging up on me. All I knew was when I was thin, I was safe from all the verbal assaults. When I gained five pounds, I felt less than worthless."

Sophie frowned sadly at her. "Well, you look perfectly normal now. You're like a Swedish Sophia Loren. Who knew? For all it's worth, you look a thousand times better now that you look like a real woman."

Allison smiled at the compliment and took a drink of water. "Thanks, although it's hard for me to get their opinions out of my head sometimes. Every so often I'll look in the mirror and I'll automatically see all my faults and none of the good. But when I took over caring for my sister, I was determined that she would be brought up with a healthy body image. I want her to see me eat and enjoy food. I want her to see me feel good about myself. I would hate for her to feel bad about herself for the way Heavenly Father made her. I just want her to know that her worth as a human being doesn't have anything to do with what the scale says or what the mirror shows her."

Sophie grimaced and went back to work. "Yeah, well, that's a hard one for all of us. After I had my baby, I couldn't get rid of the last twenty pounds. I've had to learn it's important to be fit and healthy but that starving yourself to fit a certain image is just dumb. But back to your parents. You said your dad started scamming people *again*?"

Allison nodded and twisted the lid to her water bottle back and forth. She felt the same old shame and embarrassment wash over her every time someone found out about her dad. "Yeah, he got away from real estate, though. He went in for a nice little Ponzi scheme this time. And it worked great for about three and a half years. Then it all fell apart on him. He was so surprised too. Almost like the people turning him in to the cops were the ones in the wrong. It was so strange, Sophie. He really thought that what he was doing was okay on some level. He thinks the people who pressed charges against him are the bad guys. It's almost like he doesn't even have a conscience anymore."

Sophie shivered and closed her eyes. "Wow, and I thought *my* dad had problems. What exactly is a Ponzi scheme? I mean, I've heard of it and everything. Everyone knows who Bernie Madoff is. But how does it work?"

Allison crinkled up her nose as she thought about it. She only knew what the FBI agent had told her.

"Well, it's not that complicated from what I can tell. He started off with people he knew in Dallas and sold them on high-yield investments. After thirty days, they'd get back their original investment, plus twenty percent. After that, his victims gave them everything they could. But the initial money he'd pay back his investors with was from the money of his newest victims. There was never any real profit, because there was never any real investment. To keep it going, he of course had to have more and more victims to keep the cash coming in. He started advertising in the local paper, and that's when the local FBI got involved. They did a little investigating, and the whole thing fell apart. You know what my dad said in court? He said he didn't deserve to go to jail because he wasn't hurting anyone. Can you believe that? The next day they confiscated his new boat and his Bentley. It just makes me sick," Allison said as she massaged her temples.

Sophie shut her mouth and blinked a few times. "Whoa. That's just so . . . so *evil*. Sorry, but I don't even know what to say to that. Huh." Sophie shook her head and went back to Allison's hair. "So tell me something good. How's your mom doing? Is that why you're here with the kids? Is she in Dallas waiting for your dad to get out of jail?"

Allison looked away and stared off into space for a moment. "Nah.

My mom died a little while after my dad went to jail. She was in a car with her new boyfriend on their way to go on a cruise when they were hit by a drunk driver. She did leave a note for us, though. It said, 'Tell the kids I'll bring them back a souvenir.' She and her new boyfriend, Bob, had planned a cruise to Mexico. That was almost as mind blowing as the Ponzi scheme."

Sophie frowned as she put in another foil. "Wait. Did she divorce your dad when she found out about all of the illegal stuff?"

Allison smiled sadly. "Now that would have made sense, huh? No. According to my father, she knew all about his illegal business dealings from the very beginning. She couldn't care less whether or not something was legal or illegal. She couldn't care less whether or not innocent people were hurt as long as she had her social life, her clothes, her expensive restaurants, her jewelry, and the entire lifestyle she thought she deserved. The reason she was going on the cruise with her boyfriend was that she was bored and feeling neglected."

Sophie stared in horror. "Dang, Allison. You got the short stick, didn't you?"

Allison frowned and looked away. "I guess. I like to think they weren't always amoral. Maybe when they were young like me, they had goals and dreams. I like to think that they knew right from wrong at one point. I don't know what happened along the way to change that. I'd really like to know, though."

Sophie pulled her gloves off and threw them in the trash. "Come over here and get some heat. We don't want you going orange on us."

Allison practically ran for the dryer. Orange would not be a good color for her. Sophie laughed at her and pulled a stool over so they could finish their conversation.

"So your mom died, your dad's in jail, and now you're the guardian of your little brother and sister. Does that about sum it up?" Sophie asked with a compassionate smile.

Allison shrugged. "That's pretty much it in a nutshell. Right now, all I want is for Talon and Aspen to be happy. If that could happen, I think I could relax. Their constant misery is hard to bear sometimes," she admitted with a small catch in her throat.

Sophie nodded in understanding. "I have a little boy myself, and when he's sad, I cry. That's just how it works. Give it some time. They'll find their way."

Allison blinked quickly as she looked at her hands. "As long as their way leads to missions, college, and happy temple marriages."

Sophie laughed, her eyes sparkling. "Now you sound just like every other mother in Alpine. *Hilarious.* So what's your situation? Do you have a job? Are you going to school? Are you dating anyone?" Sophie pushed, leaning her chin on her knees.

Allison laughed. "You are flat-out nosy, Sophie. Um, no job yet, although I need one. I went to three years of college before I came home one summer and realized that my brother and sister were being raised by their Russian nanny who didn't even know English just so my mom could have a life. So no school for me until the kids are on their way. And dating? Oh my heck, no. Not now, not ever again," she said vehemently.

Sophie's eyebrows raised up an inch. "Oh, you've got to be kidding. Someone had the nerve to break Allison Vaughn's heart? Now I am truly shocked."

Allison grimaced. "I don't know about broken, but definitely dented. When my fiancé realized what kind of family I came from, he politely asked for his engagement ring back. He said he wanted his children to be proud of their roots. He wanted his children to have a righteous, honorable heritage. And my background was as far away from good as you could get. So I'm on my own. And that's a good thing right now. Talon and Aspen have been through so much upheaval lately, I don't think me having an active social life would be the best thing for them."

Sophie snorted. "They're not toddlers. Heck, they'll have their own social lives any second."

Allison's eyes went wide. Sophie was right. Aspen and Talon were almost seventeen. They could be dating right now. *Frightening.*

"Okay, let's go rinse you. Follow me, please," Sophie said. She led Allison to the back of the salon where a row of glossy white sinks stood with plush chairs in front of them.

Sophie rinsed Allison's hair gently and then gave her a warm towel to wrap her hair in.

"Now just a trim and a blow dry and you're out of here," Sophie said as Allison sat back down in front of the mirror. "But first I just have one more question," Sophie continued. "Why did you move back? Yeah, I get it, your dad won't show his face here, but why hide Talon and Aspen from their father? He's a crook, but he's still their dad. Maybe he's learned his lesson. Maybe having Talon and Aspen in his life would be good for him. What could he really do to them?" she asked curiously.

Allison frowned, her light green eyes going cold. "You know, that's a hard one to answer. These last few years I've really gotten closer to the Spirit. I listened to the Spirit when it told me that my little brother and sister needed me to come home and be with them. And after my dad was arrested, that same spirit shouted at me to leave and keep my family safe. I've learned to trust that little voice. I don't honestly know what my father is capable of doing. All I know is that the Spirit knows what he's capable of doing, and the Spirit doesn't want us anywhere near him."

Sophie nodded her head firmly. "Well, then you're brilliant. Anyone who listens to the Spirit is doing the right thing."

Allison watched Sophie frown in concentration as she trimmed a couple inches from Allison's hair and added a few layers.

"Thanks, Sophie. I appreciate your support. There are some people who think I'm worse than my dad because I've cut him off. They say I'm not being Christlike or forgiving," she said quietly.

Sophie put her scissors down and ran some product through the ends of Allison's hair.

"What's not Christlike about protecting two innocent teenagers from the influence of an evil man? Forgiveness has nothing to do with being stupid," Sophie said with a sharp nod of her head, making her red waves bounce around her face.

Allison felt tears in her eyes and was grateful Sophie had turned on the blow dryer. She didn't think she could talk right then if she had to.

Five minutes later, after a lot of round brushing, Sophie put down the blow dryer and grinned at Allison. "You know, when I saw you standing in my salon last night, I thought, *finally, here's my chance to give you a piece of my mind.* Closure, you know? But instead, I find out you're not so rotten after all. What a shocker," she said, undoing the strap around Allison's neck.

Allison stood up and pulled the drape off, laying it on her chair. "Life can surprise you. Here I was so desperate for free highlights I was willing to put myself in the hands of the one girl who hated me more than anybody," she said with a laugh.

"Uh, no. That would be *me*," came a cold voice from behind them.

Allison and Sophie turned around to see Jacie staring angrily at them from the doorway at the back room.

"*Please* tell me you did not just make her look even better, Sophie. There's no one in Alpine that deserves split ends and boring hair more than Allison Vaughn. *Are you crazy?* I mean, yeah, you're nice, that's why you're my best friend, but there is no reason on this earth why you should ever go out of your way to do *anything* for her after the way she treated you. This is too much. Its official, Sophie. I am not happy with you," Jacie said. Her eyes crackled with outrage.

Sophie held up her hands and walked toward her best friend. Allison grabbed her purse and edged backward. She'd always been nervous around Jacie. After what Allison had spread around school about Blake, Jacie would actually snarl at her when Allison walked past her in the hallways. And then, of course, Jacie had always had the bad habit of *accidentally* bumping into her in the hallways, making her books go everywhere. Allison had always had a few people right there to pick them up for her, but still—Jacie was a wild woman. The type who would jump her in the parking lot and buzz all her hair off.

"Jacie, just hold on," Sophie started.

"Um, Sophie, I gotta get going. I'd love to stay and catch up, but I'm late as it is," she said, walking quickly backward and keeping her eyes on Jacie in case she was planning a surprise attack.

Jacie's eyes shot to Allison's retreating figure. "She's leaving without paying, Sophie. Call the cops," she demanded, trying to push past Sophie.

Sophie gave up and laughed, shaking her head at her friend. "Jacie, I did it for free. Now just chill."

Allison had almost reached the reception area when Sophie turned and called out to her. "Allison, do you mind if I tell Jacie a little of our conversation?"

Allison paused, swallowing hard at the molten lava now pouring out of Jacie's eyes. "No problem. You have my permission. And thanks, Sophie. It looks great," she said as she grabbed one of Sophie's business cards on her way to the door.

Sophie smiled and waved before turning back to Jacie.

Allison fled the salon and knew she would *never* trust Jacie near her hair. Jacie was probably devising a plan right now to shave Allison's head for old time's sake.

Seven

Allison walked the short distance home and went right upstairs to look in the mirror. Her medium-golden hair now had some streaks of bright blonde running through. It looked like she had just returned from a summer down at Lake Powell. It was perfect. She smiled at her reflection and sighed. Somehow, having her hair look good just made life better.

She ran back downstairs and grabbed the keys to her old Ford truck. It had gotten them here all the way from Texas with their meager belongings. She just hoped it would hold out for a couple more years until she could afford something better. She hopped up into the cab and drove down to Kohler's grocery store. She was suddenly in the mood for almond M&M's. *Forget the budget*, she told herself. She needed to celebrate. Not only did her hair look good, but miracles of miracles, she had mended one very broken fence. Of course she had about a thousand more to go, but one fence was still one fence.

She parked her truck away from all the BMWs and Escalades and walked into the store. She headed right for the candy aisle and noticed a man standing right where she wanted to be. She stared for a minute at the bags of Snickers and Twix and tried to wait patiently. Then she scooted closer to the man, since he obviously didn't even really know what he wanted. There was only one bag of the almond M&M's left. Tons of the peanut kind, tons of the plain, but only one of her kind. No way would he want it. She could just sneak her arm over and grab it, and he probably wouldn't even notice.

She scooted even closer, sensing that she was probably invading his personal space, but she was almost desperate now with the uncontrollable desire for chocolate and almonds. She paused as she sensed him stiffen and inched away quickly, pretending she wasn't even looking at the almond M&M's. The man leaned over and grabbed her bag of M&M's and then turned and smiled at her.

She glared crossly up at him, since he was kind of tall, and then paused in surprise. *Will Carson.* He was taller and more solid now and a lot better dressed too. He had always worn faded blue jeans and old work shirts to school. Not because it was cool, but because his family was one of the last farming families in Alpine, and that was all he had. She stared up into his deep brown eyes and felt something click into place. She'd always liked Will. She used to be madly in love with him, if she was being honest.

"Will! Wow, it's been a long time. How have you been doing?" she asked, shaking her head in wonder. "You look amazing. Really, *really* amazing," she said truthfully. He was dressed in an expensive dress shirt with a fancy wrist watch and dark blue pinstripe dress pants. He certainly didn't look like he was ready for a day at the apple orchard.

Will looked down at her, still holding her bag of candy with a big smile on his face. "Allison Vaughn. I must be dreaming. What are you doing here?"

Allison shrugged and looked away. "I just moved back to town. I'm taking care of my younger brother and sister now. They just started at Lone Peak."

Will looked at her quietly for a few moments and then glanced casually at her left hand. "That's good. Really good. Well, I guess I'll see you around, Allison." He smiled politely at her before moving to walk away.

Allison frowned. He still had her M&M's in his hand. "Um, Will? Hold up there. I hope you don't mind, but I was actually getting ready to grab that bag of M&M's. You wouldn't mind letting me have them, would you? For old time's sake?" she asked as sweetly as she could, even going so far as to look up at him through her eyelashes.

Will walked the few steps back toward her and grinned. "Yeah, actually, I would. Now you'll know what's it like to want something and end up incredibly, horribly, utterly disappointed," he said with raised eyebrows as he turned away again.

Allison frowned and stomped toward him, grabbing his shirt to make him stop. "Hey, wait just one second. What exactly does that mean? Are you mad at me? I've never done anything to you," she said in outrage.

Will turned around and stared at her hand, still on his arm. "I'm not mad, Allison. What I am is even," he said, holding the bag of M&M's just out of her reach. "Don't you remember a few days before prom, when I asked you if you'd go to the dance with me? And what did you say, Allison? Hmm? *Forgot?* Let me refresh. You told me that you were dating a college guy but that he wouldn't mind if you went to the dance by yourself, since he was at Harvard and couldn't make it. You told me that you'd save me a few dances, though. Well, guess who rented a tux and showed up for his three dances? *Me.* I did. Every time I walked up to you to ask for a dance, your coven blocked me. You danced the whole night with Gage Dulaney and your friends while I stood in the corner, waiting for you to notice me and keep your word."

Will no longer looked relaxed and cool. He looked a little ruffled around the edges now, like he was seriously ticked. *Five years later and still ticked*, Allison thought. *Intriguing.*

Allison bit her lip before answering. "I'm sorry, Will. I don't really have an excuse. I honestly don't remember even seeing you at the dance. If my friends were blocking you, it wasn't because I told them to. I do remember dancing a couple times with Gage that night. But I don't remember enjoying it very much. I would much rather have danced with you," she said in quiet sincerity.

Will's eyes softened, and his shoulders relaxed a bit. "And yet, you still don't get your M&M's, Allie. Life is just so unfair sometimes," he said before walking away without a backward glance.

Allison was left to stare at his back in surprise. She had just been told off by Will Carson. Ticked, *gorgeous* Will Carson. Maybe, just maybe, her moratorium on dating should come to an end. She walked back out of the store without buying anything and didn't even notice the shocked and slightly horrified gaze of a cute blonde standing by the balloon counter.

eight

Allison returned home and went back to real life. She pushed good-looking men and the high from highlights to the back of her brain so she could concentrate on more important things. Like budgeting so they had enough money for groceries at the end of the month. Half an hour later, she admitted it was a good thing she hadn't bought those M&M's after all. Their budget was really tight. What with buying new school clothes and backpacks and paying school fees, she was short a few hundred dollars. She really did need a job. The money they received from their mother's life insurance policy came in monthly installments, and it was just enough to survive on. She hated to think where they would be without it.

Allison dropped the rag she'd been washing her front window with as she saw Luke walk slowly with Maggie up the steps to their house. She winced at how excruciatingly slow they went and shook her head at the misery Maggie must be feeling. Adoption just looked better and better every day.

Allison turned around and headed for the kitchen. She needed to sweep and dust and unload the dishes and do everything she had never had to do before. Her family had always had maids when she was growing up. She'd learned how to do the basics when she went away to college, but not before she had been yelled at by her roommates and almost kicked out of her apartment. She'd had to learn pretty quickly to do things herself and not expect other people to do them for her. The real world had nothing to do with the way she had grown up.

Her phone rang, causing her to jump. She couldn't afford caller ID—not yet, anyway. And not very many people knew her home phone number. The only people who knew it were the bishop, the kids, and the school. *The school!* Allison ran to the phone and picked it up, hoping it wasn't the principal calling about Talon. *Please, don't let it be a fight,* she prayed as she picked it up.

"Hello?" she asked nervously.

"Hi, Allison. It's Maggie. I hope you don't mind, but I asked the bishop for your number. If you have some free time, could you come over?" Maggie asked in a quiet voice.

Allison blinked in surprise. "What? I mean . . . *why?* I mean, not to be rude, but um, *why?*" Allison asked, biting her lip. She walked with the cordless phone back into the front room as she talked and peeked through the window. Luke's car was still there. She did not want to go over to Maggie's if Luke was there. No thank you.

"Well, we just got back from the doctor and found out I have celiac disease. The doctor said that pregnancy can trigger symptoms even though I've gone my whole life not showing any signs of the disease. I remember you mentioning how your brother and sister have it, and I could really use some advice."

Allison frowned and stared at Luke's car, wishing he would just leave and make this easier on her.

"Okay. Can I maybe come by later this afternoon?" Allison asked hopefully. Luke would have to go back to work sometime soon.

"Well, actually, I usually take a nap in about an hour. My body just gives out halfway through the day, and I don't have any control over it. It's kind of weird. So if you wouldn't mind, now would be best. Luke wants to be here to listen too," she added.

Allison groaned as silently as she could and closed her eyes in defeat. "Okay, Maggie, I'll be right over."

Allison hung up and stared resentfully at Luke's car. Of course he wanted to be there when she came over. He probably didn't want his wife having unsupervised visits with her. She was a Vaughn, after all. He probably thought she was going to steal all of their valuables when Maggie was looking the other way.

Allison stomped out of the house and walked quickly over to the Petersons', figuring it was better to just get the visit over with as soon as possible.

Luke opened the door before she even had a chance to ring the bell. Allison stared up at Luke and swallowed. He was a lot taller than she remembered. He still had those freaky bluish-green eyes that could change on you. And he wasn't smiling.

"Allison Vaughn," he said, just standing there in the doorway and staring at her coldly.

"Yep. It's me. Um, your wife just called and asked me to come over. Can I come in?" she asked in a surprisingly normal tone of voice.

Luke crossed his long arms across his chest and looked even more intimidating. "Maggie's back in the family room lying down. I just wanted to make a few things clear before you enter my house. Number one, no business propositions. No hitting Maggie up for money or sob stories about how broke you are. She has a tender heart, especially now that she's pregnant, and I don't want you taking advantage of her. Number two, don't think just because my wife has a trusting nature that I do, because believe me, I know all the tricks, and you're not getting anything past me. Number three, just because my wife is asking you for advice, doesn't mean this is an invitation to be Maggie's best friend. Maggie has a lot of good friends. She doesn't have room for *you*," he said, blazing a hole in her with his bizarre eyes.

Allison stood straighter as her heart started to beat faster and the blood ran out of her face. She had known it would be bad with Luke, but this was vicious.

"You always were a cocky know-it-all, Luke. You know what? Now that I've thought about it, I really don't want to desecrate your hallowed home after all. Tell Maggie there's plenty of info on the Internet and I hope she feels better." She turned on her heels and walked quickly down the steps. Forget it. Maggie was a nice woman, but no way was Allison slaying this dragon.

"Hey, *wait*. Look, Maggie really wants to talk to you," Luke called out, seeming to realize that he had overplayed it.

Allison glanced back over her shoulder and felt like giving him a hand gesture but settled with a classic that Talon had taught her and rolled her eyes without saying anything. She kept going, only faster now.

"Hey! Just stop right there. You don't get to act all offended and innocent. I have the right to protect my wife from people like you. On the other hand, Maggie really wants to talk to you. As soon as we got in the car, she was calling everyone, trying to get your phone number. It would mean a lot to her if you would just come in the house and tell her all this diet stuff is no big deal. Calm her down and then take off. Easy."

Allison stopped walking and turned around to stare at Luke. She had a few choices. She could resort to violence. Just the idea of punching that smug, holier-than-thou look off his face had her hands balling into fists. Or she could do something even worse. Maybe she would go out of her way to be friends with Maggie, just to tick him off. It would torture him. She looked at him for a few moments until he had the grace to look away.

"*People like me*? Really? You really just said that. Okay, I'll do it. I'll go talk to Maggie if you explain in detail what you meant by that. I'm really curious," Allison said in a serious voice, hating Luke and every perfect thing about him, from his ultra-righteous perfect parents to his gobs of ultra-righteous perfect siblings. He made her want to spit on him.

Luke cleared his throat. "You know what I mean. It's no secret what your dad did to people here in Alpine. He practically destroyed a few families. And in one case, he did. Remember the Reynolds? Bart attempted suicide when he found out your dad had taken everything. He's okay now, but they're still renting an apartment over one of their old neighbors' garages. Their kids are too ashamed to even come visit them. That's just *one* story. I could spend the rest of the day telling you about all the tragedies your father was the author of. Did you think people would forget what your family did?"

Allison gritted her teeth and felt like crying. She could feel the backs of her eyes prickling as she clenched her hands. She had too much pride to cry in front of Luke. But he had shamed her. For all her talk to Talon and Aspen about paying for their own mistakes and not their father's, she knew it was a lie. What was true for Heavenly Father wasn't even close to true for the rest of the world. They would all pay for their father.

"I was a kid, Luke. I had no idea what my dad was doing. No one did until it was too late. If you want to stand there and tell me I'm a criminal because of who my father is, you go right ahead, but that just makes you a jerk. A mean, judgmental, *cruel* jerk," she said, with her head held high.

Luke didn't even blink in acknowledgment as her words washed right off him. "Just go talk to Maggie," he said tiredly and gestured to his front door.

Allison glared at him and walked with as much dignity as she could muster back up the stairs and into the Petersons' house. She didn't wait for Luke but walked back, calling Maggie's name.

"I'm back here!" Maggie yelled, drawing Allison into a small room off the kitchen.

Allison walked into the family room and immediately noticed the amazing paintings on the wall. The room reminded her of an art museum. She would have taken more time to look, except she noticed Maggie shoving a store-bought Rice Krispie treat right into her mouth.

Allison yelped in horror and rushed over to yank the rest of the snack out of Maggie's hands.

"Hey! I'm starving here," Maggie protested. "What did you do that for? Luke read the ingredients. There's no wheat in that!" Maggie looked heartbroken as she stared at the now mangled square of marshmallow Rice Krispie.

Luke rushed in behind Allison and immediately glared at her, his eyes shooting sparks. "Abusing a pregnant woman. I'm not even surprised. I told you this was a bad idea, Maggie. Allison, I'll show you to the door," he said angrily.

Allison shook her head in disgust. "Luke, could you just back off? For just one second, back off. Just because it doesn't say wheat, it doesn't mean it's not there. There's a lot of little hidden ways of saying wheat. One of them is malt. Look for yourself," she said, gesturing to the empty wrapper on the coffee table.

Maggie grabbed the wrapper and read the ingredients closely. "Oh my heck, Luke. She's right. You just fed me wheat," she said accusingly.

Luke frowned and grabbed the wrapper. "Okay, so there's malt. You're completely overreacting. It's a little teeny, tiny piece of wheat, not a chemical weapon," he said defensively.

Allison sighed as she felt her head start to pound. "Do you think celiac disease is something to ignore or dismiss? Did you know celiac disease can cause miscarriages and intrauterine growth retardation? We found out my brother and sister had the disease when they were around fourteen years old. If they're not vigilant, they pay the price. This is pretty serious, Luke. Sorry if I offended you by grabbing your treat out of your hand, Maggie, but I know how sick and miserable you've been. I was just trying to help you. You know what? I can't do this. Not with Luke, the guardian of all Alpine here. My best advice is to get on amazon.com and order a few books on the subject. Call me if you have a question, but there's no way I'm staying in the same room with him," she said.

Allison ran back to her house and shut the door firmly, leaning her head on the door frame as she felt the tears course down her face. Luke despised her. He thought she was just like her dad. The thought made her ill. She turned and was walking quietly toward the kitchen when the pounding started on her front door. She could see Luke through the glass in the door. She sniffed and very slowly walked back to the front door. She opened it wide, not caring that he could see her crying. What was pride? Whatever it was, she wasn't sure she had any left.

Luke stood quietly for a moment, taking in her tears, and then cleared his throat. "I've been ordered to apologize by my wife. She's pretty furious with me right now. I guess it was pretty rude to ask you to come over to help Maggie and then treat you like garbage for doing it. I'm sorry. I didn't mean to make you cry," he said guiltily.

Allison shut the door firmly in his face and locked it. She walked back to the family room and collapsed on the old plaid couch. The phone rang a few moments later and she knew it was Maggie, upset and wanting to talk to her. *Nope.* She was done with the Petersons for the day. She closed her eyes and wished the day was over. It had started out so good too. Getting her hair done for free had been a gift, and setting the record straight with Sophie had been even better. Then seeing Will at the store had made her think for just a second that maybe she could have a normal life in Alpine. A life that included dating and fun and maybe even friends if she worked really hard at it. But Luke had shoved reality in her face. Alpine hated her and always would. She wasn't Allison. She was Max Vaughn's daughter. And she could never change that. She grabbed an old quilt off the back of the couch and brought her knees up, drawing into herself for warmth. Talon and Aspen would graduate in two years. Could she spend the next two years surrounded by hate? The other choice was living somewhere else, knowing that her father would show up one day.

Allison felt the tears seep through her eyelashes again. She would take the hate.

NINE

Three hours later, Allison had her tears and her emotions under complete control. She stood on the front porch and smiled as she watched Aspen and Talon walk toward her from the bus stop. She studied their faces for any signs of misery—or even better, but less likely—happiness. Aspen looked normal. She wasn't exactly jumping for joy, but she wasn't depressed either. Talon looked expressionless, almost stoic. Maybe that wasn't so great.

"Hey, guys. How'd it go this time? Any better? Any worse?" Allison asked as she held the front door open for them.

Aspen leaned in for a quick hug. "It was okay," she said as she walked in.

Talon walked up to her and shook his head in exasperation. "Look, you're not our mother. You don't have to stand on the front porch every day waiting for us like some weirdo. Come on, we're practically adults here." He brushed past her, throwing his backpack on the entryway floor and walking toward the kitchen.

Okay. So she was a weirdo. True, she wasn't their mother, but she loved them just as much as if she were. More than the one they'd had, anyway. She sighed. *Keep moving,* she told herself.

Allison walked into the kitchen to see both Aspen and Talon digging into the leftover pizza.

"You know, leftover gluten-free pizza just isn't the same as leftover real pizza," Aspen said with a slight frown. "It's that beany flavor from the fava beans in the GF flour. It's kind of strong the next day."

Allison noted that it didn't keep either one of them from putting down their pizza and grabbing an apple.

"Yeah, this is such crap, Al. I wish you were more like Mom. She didn't care if we ate real food," Talon said with his mouth full.

Allison looked at them both in shock. *"What?* Are you kidding me?"

Aspen shrugged and took another piece. "Yeah, you know how Mom was. She wasn't one for details."

Allison shook her head. "Your health isn't exactly a detail. I don't get it. I was *there.* I remember when you guys were covered in rashes. Aspen, remember how you could barely walk because you had those horrible rashes on your legs? And your face was just a mess. And Talon, those stomachaches that kept you up at night? Mom knew. Why would she let you eat something that would hurt you?"

Talon laughed mirthlessly. "Because she didn't *care,* Al. It was easier to just ignore it and call for carry out. If it didn't affect *her,* then it was no big deal."

Aspen sighed unhappily. "Can we not talk about Mom, please?"

Talon shrugged, threw his pizza down, and headed for his room. "Of course not. If anyone says something even remotely like the truth, then that's going over the line, huh, Aspen? Just live in fantasyland." He threw his backpack over his shoulder before disappearing.

Allison and Aspen stared at each other in misery for a few moments before Aspen lowered her eyes. "I don't live in a fantasyland. I just wish Talon wouldn't hate her so much. It's not good for him."

Allison nodded and picked a piece of pepperoni off Talon's discarded pizza. "You have to deal with your relationship with Mom in your own way. Talon's just dealing with it in his way. He's angry that she wasn't that involved, PTA-loving, cookie-making, unselfish, perfect mom. But I think he's angrier that she died."

Aspen shook her head. "Nah, that's not it, Allie. She left us a long time before she died. You know we were raised by *au pairs* and nannies. It's not like we were ever that important to her. He's mad that he has to look at perfect kids every day at school who have moms who don't cheat on their dads and who have dads who don't steal everyone's money. He's just mad about everything. He's even mad at me," she said in a small voice.

Allison leaned her hip on the counter and studied her sister. "Why's that, honey?"

Aspen put her pizza down and looked away. "Remember that boy yesterday that tried to start something with Talon? His name's Rowan Dalton, and he's in my art class. He sat right next to me today. I told him after class that he'd better leave my brother alone. Well, he kind of laughed at me, but then he shook his head and smiled at me. He sat next to me at lunch too, and we talked about everything we had both been through. He's a lot like us, Allie. He's lost everything. He told me he was sorry for what he did to Talon. I really think he means it too. Anyway, when Talon walked into the cafeteria and saw us sitting next to each other and talking, he kind of lost it. I mean, he didn't yell or anything, but you should have seen his eyes. He looked at me like I'd betrayed him. And then he threw his lunch in the trash and walked out. I guess he didn't have anyone else to sit by except me. I was the last person he trusted, and then I let him down too. I feel horrible," she whispered before a tear slipped down her cheek.

Allison sighed and reached a hand out to pat her sister's shoulder. "It's not your fault, Aspen. Turning an enemy into a friend is a good thing. Talon just has to learn to deal with it. He'll get over it. Hey, maybe your new friend and Talon might become friends too." she said hopefully.

Aspen snorted and shook her head sadly as she wiped the rest of the tears off her cheeks. "Yeah right, Allie. You know Talon."

Allison sighed sadly. Yeah, she knew Talon. And she also knew he was hurting. What he really needed was a hug. But she knew that wouldn't fly with him. That only meant one thing. Wrestling. She cracked her knuckles and moved her shoulders up and down to loosen up. She walked out of the kitchen and toward the stairs.

"Hey, Tal! Your chore is yard work today! Get your rear down-stairs. I want this lawn mowed before dinner," she called up the stairs.

Talon's head appeared over the stair railing. "You've gotta be kid-ding me, Al. No way am I doing any stupid chores."

Allison frowned. "Look, Tal, I'm not your servant. We're in this together. We're a family. I do my part to keep our home working and our life in order, and you do your part by getting good grades and helping out around the house. Now get your rear down here or you're going to pay, buddy. I could pin you last year, and I can still do it. You seriously don't want to push me after the day I've had," she warned.

Tal grinned and walked slowly down the stairs, loosening up his shoulders as he went. "You and what army, wimp? You take me down, I'll mow the yard. But if I pin you, you gotta make dessert tonight. Brownies. *With icing*," he said.

Allison rolled her eyes and gestured to the front door. "Ladies first," she said with a theatrical sneer.

Talon laughed and opened the door. He went out and ran down the front steps to stand on the front lawn. "Come and get it, *sista*. And no crying like a girl either when I kick your trash," he warned.

Aspen walked out, smiling brightly in anticipation. "Don't hurt him too much, Allie. He's kind of fragile."

Talon laughed and crouched down. Allison grinned and ran down the porch steps, circling her brother like a wild animal. They had been wrestling forever. Even though Talon weighed more than she did now, she fought dirty. And she had the sneaking suspicion that he kind of went easy on her most of the time.

Talon went for her knees, but she jumped over him and landed on his back, making him grunt. She flipped over, grabbed his neck, and pulled him down. He threw her off and pounced, grabbing her arm and pulling it behind her back. She grabbed a wad of his leg hair, laughing when he yelped in pain. He immediately released her neck. She jumped up, only noticing too late that they had an audience watching. Luke Peterson was watching with his mouth open and a look of total shock on his face.

Talon hadn't noticed their audience and gave out a loud war whoop as he grabbed her around the middle and fell with her onto on the grass, knocking the air out of her lungs and making her gasp. She tried to push Talon off but was surprised when he disappeared a second later. She opened her eyes and saw Luke holding Talon with one arm.

Talon flailed, jerking back and forth as he tried to get away. "Hey! Get off me, you freak!" He yelled in surprise.

Allison couldn't talk yet as she flipped to her stomach and tried to get up. She gasped a few more times and finally got her breath back.

"Get your hands . . ." Gasp. ". . . off my brother . . . you *jack* . . ."

"It looked like you could use a hand there, Allison. It just didn't seem like a fair fight with this big guy going up against a wimpy girl like you," Luke said, letting Talon go.

Talon jerked away and then turned to look Luke up and down. "She's no wimpy girl, dude. She can usually take me. Why don't you mind your own business?"

Aspen ran down the stairs, stopping to pat Allison on the back.

"Don't worry about my brother and sister," Aspen said in a calm, soothing tone. "This is just how they show affection for one another. Talon's at that awkward stage where he thinks he's too cool for hugs and kisses, so Allie wrestles him. They laugh, they joke, they get a little bruised, but it's all out of love. I promise," she said, looking sweetly earnest.

Allison, who'd been leaning over her knees, stood up and went to stand in front of Talon in case Luke wanted to grab him again.

Talon pushed her away and stepped in front of her. Luke grinned.

"Look, I'm not calling the cops or anything. I've got enough brothers and sisters of my own to know wrestling when I see it. I just came over to see if there were a couple teenagers here who could use some work. I've got tons of yard work and odd jobs around the house that need to be done. I've been so busy with work and Maggie that everything's starting to look neglected. I couldn't believe my luck when you guys moved in. I could really use the help," he said, looking guardedly at Allison.

Allison frowned at Luke. *What was he up to?*

Luke turned to Aspen. "My wife, Maggie, has been so ill that I don't think the house has been vacuumed in months. If you're looking for a job, I've got enough work to keep the both of you busy all year, especially with the baby coming soon. Of course you'd have to get your sister's permission, but just so you know, I pay very well," he said smiling his famous smile that Allison remembered from years ago. Luke could be charming when he wasn't being a complete jerk.

Allison crossed her arms over her chest. "Over my dead—"

"I'll do it," Talon called out, silencing his sister.

Aspen walked in front of Allison as well. "How much do you pay per hour?" she asked curiously.

Luke smiled and shoved his hands in his pockets. "Oh, how does seven or eight dollars an hour sound? With a possibility of bonuses if I'm really impressed," he said grinning at the look on Allison's face.

Talon walked forward. "Yeah? *Really?* Just yard work and odd jobs? Man, I could really use a job. We are *so* broke. Allie's got nothing, and I need transportation like you wouldn't believe. When do I start?" he asked excitedly.

Aspen grinned too. "Oh, Allie, this is perfect. I could help you with all of our bills. You won't have to be stressed out anymore."

Allison smiled at her sister and squeezed her arm affectionately. "Just hold on a second, you two. I think I should talk to Luke in private before we agree to anything here."

Talon rolled his eyes. "Yeah, whatever. Just let me run up and grab my sunglasses and my i-Pod. I'll be right back," he yelled as he ran up the stairs.

Aspen ran up the stairs too, leaving Allison and Luke Peterson staring at each other—one triumphant, one extremely suspicious.

"You can really take that brother of yours? I was standing right here, and it looked to me like you were getting your butt kicked," Luke said, looking her up and down disbelievingly.

"If you hadn't interrupted us, I would be watching *my* brother mowing *my* lawn right now. I don't know what you're trying to do here, but whatever it is, it's not going to work. I actually *really* hate you now. I want you to go away. No, forget that, I want you to move to Nebraska and raise sheep for a living. Go find your yard help somewhere else," she said coldly and turned around.

Luke maneuvered himself quickly around her and stood between her and the steps.

"Fine, you hate me. I deserve that. But maybe I've had a change of heart. Maybe, I've realized that I haven't treated you fairly. Maybe I'd like to make it up to you by giving your brother and sister after-school jobs," he said sincerely.

Allison glared at him and crossed her arms over her chest. Talon and Aspen really did need after school jobs. Desperately. But from *Luke*?

"Yeah, well, news flash. Aspen and Talon are Max Vaughn's kids too. They're innocent, good hearted . . . well, Aspen's good hearted at least. Anyway, they're sweet kids. I don't want you treating them like dirt or making them feel like crap just because of their last name," she said.

Luke looked offended. "I would *never* . . . I mean . . ." Luke sighed and rubbed his hands over his face. "Look, I messed up. I overreacted. *I am sorry.* You have my promise that I will never even bring up their father's name to them. I will treat them with respect and kindness and fairness. And by the way, that goes for you too. You have my word on it," he said solemnly.

Allison studied him frankly. Maggie must have really worked him over for him to be so humble and . . . *nice.* Before she could say anything, Talon and Aspen ran out the front door, ready to work.

Luke grinned and slung an arm over each of their shoulders, leading them away from Allison and toward his own yard. Allison watched in silence and then gave up and smiled. Talon and Aspen were both happy. And that was a very good thing.

teN

Three hours later, Aspen and Talon came home to barbecued chicken legs, canned corn, and homemade brownies. *With icing.* Allison sat and listened to them talk for over an hour about everything they'd done for Luke, who was now their best friend. It sounded like Aspen had done more talking to Maggie than actual cleaning, but from the glow on her face, a small detail like that didn't matter. Allison was sure it had been good for Maggie too. Maggie could learn just as much about a gluten-free diet from Aspen as she could from her. But the change in Talon was the most pronounced. Gone was the sullen, angry boy. In his place was the old Talon—happy, funny, and full of life. Who'd have thought that a job could do so much? Well, that and a handful of cash and a game of basketball.

Allison frowned to herself as she loaded the dishwasher. Luke had taken the time to play ball with Talon and really talk to him. Talon couldn't stop talking about Luke's advice on this and that. It looked like Talon had a new case of hero-worship. But *Luke Peterson?* Allison gagged silently to herself. Of all the people in the world. She shrugged. At least Luke was an honest, good person. Any role model was better for Talon than his father.

After the last of the brownies were gone, Allison cracked the whip on the homework. While Talon and Aspen were busy with English assignments and pre-calculus, Allison grabbed the phone and Sophie's card and went to sit in her backyard. She would have preferred the front porch with the old rocking chair, but she'd had enough of neighbors for one day. The backyard wasn't very pretty, to be honest. From what she had been told by the landlord, its previous owner had raised a lot of dogs. The grass attested to that fact. That and the total lack of flowers. There were a few shade trees and a couple scraggly old bushes, but that was it. Allison found an old worn wooden bench under one of the trees and sat down. She dialed Sophie's number and then glanced at her watch, hoping she wasn't interrupting anything important. Sophie had mentioned having a young son. Allison wondered if she should call tomorrow instead.

"Hello?" a low male voice answered.

Allison glanced at the card quickly. She had dialed the right number. It must be Sophie's husband. "Hi there. This is, uh . . ." What exactly should she say? She felt uncomfortable calling herself Sophie's friend. That might be too presumptuous. "Um, this is an acquaintance of Sophie's. Is she around?" Allison asked nervously.

"Oh yeah. We can't get rid of her. Here she is," he said.

Allison blinked, hoping he was kidding. She heard the sound of Sophie's bubbly laughter and relaxed. Okay, he was joking. If that had been *her* parents, she would have known they were completely serious. Allison sighed in envy. It was so nice to hear couples laughing and joking with each other.

"Hello?" Sophie's voice came on.

"Hey, Sophie. This is Allison. Sorry to bother you, but you're the only one I really know in Alpine now," Allison said, laughing shyly.

Sophie made a tsking sound. "Oh my heck, relax. I'm glad you called. What's up? It's not the highlights, is it? Please tell me your hair didn't fall out."

Allison relaxed and smiled. "Of course not. No, the hair is amazing. The reason I'm calling is because I was wondering if you know of any part-time jobs around Alpine. I need a job desperately, but I still need to be home after school and on the weekends," she said with a wince, knowing she was asking the impossible.

Sophie was silent for a moment. "Well, I'll start asking around. But if worse comes to worse, we could always use a shampoo girl at the salon. It wouldn't pay much, though," she said nervously, no doubt thinking about Jacie's reaction to the job offer.

Allison sighed, knowing Sophie had probably just come up with the job on the fly. The look she'd seen on Jacie's face that morning stopped her from jumping at the opportunity. "Thanks, Sophie, but I think I'll keep looking."

"Hey, you know what? I'm having a girls-only night at my house this Friday. Tons of people will be there. Why don't you come? We could ask around then."

Allison picked at the beginnings of a hole in the knee of her jeans. "Um, is Jacie going to be there?" she had to ask.

"Of course she'll be there. But don't worry about her. She talks big, but she's a softy. I'll tell her to leave her shears at home," she said with a laugh before giving Allison her address and the directions to her house. Allison hung up a few moments later and then stared at the phone, feeling suddenly uneasy.

eLeveN

Over the next few days, Allison watched her brother and sister start to smile more and laugh more easily. She still stood on the front porch and watched them come home from the bus after school, but it wasn't so heartbreaking anymore. She loved the way they didn't look so hopeless. It was pretty irritating listening to Talon talk about how cool Luke was, but other than that, their new after-school jobs were working out well for both families.

Watching Aspen and Talon come home with handfuls of cash every night was kind of exciting for everybody. Talon was saving every penny for a motorcycle, even though Allison was trying to change his mind and put it toward his mission fund. She'd had to convince Aspen to spend the money on herself instead of using it for groceries. That was Allison's job—if only she really had a job. It was a little embarrassing to know that she probably wouldn't be able to find a job that paid her as well as her little brother and sister were being paid. She didn't feel so guilty about how much money they were making after Aspen told her that Maggie was actually a famous artist and they had plenty of money, although you couldn't tell by the Petersons' house, clothes, or their cars. Luke and Maggie acted like completely normal people. If it had been Allison's parents, they would have had the Mercedes, the McMansion, and all the accessories that went with that lifestyle. The Petersons were oddballs for sure.

Allison had talked to Maggie a couple times outside, but just for a few minutes here and there. Allison always cut the conversations off fast. It was fine for Talon and Aspen to be with the Petersons, but she just couldn't go there. She'd never forget the scorn and disdain in Luke's eyes. He could soothe his guilty conscious by being nice to her little brother and sister all he wanted to, but he'd lost his chance at friendship with her. He and his wife could live just fine without Allison Vaughn in their lives. Perfectly fine, in fact. She blew off all of Maggie's suggestions to have lunch together. And when Aspen suggested that they all go to the mall together so she could buy some new clothes, Allison nixed that plan immediately. She'd put it down to Maggie's health, but the real reason was that she was determined to have nothing to do with Maggie or Luke. Not in this lifetime, *not ever.*

The kids were at school on Friday, and the only thing on Allison's schedule for the day was the girls night out at Sophie's house later. She still felt a little strange about being friends with Sophie. She was waiting for the moment when Sophie would stop everything and say, "Ha ha, just kidding! I still hate you. You ruined my life in high school, now watch me ruin yours!" But if Sophie was being real, and this was actually an invitation to hang out with her and her friends, then this was the kindest, most Christlike example of forgiveness that Allison had ever seen. And she wasn't going to mess it up.

Allison couldn't even remember the last time she'd hung out with friends. She'd made quite a few in Texas, but when her dad's name had been splashed all over the papers, her friends had all disappeared. No one took her calls anymore. She'd even been blocked on facebook. Not one friend had stuck by her.

She was used to it by now, but the thought of having a night out was still kind of exciting. And scary. She didn't know everybody Sophie had invited. She'd been too embarrassed to grill Sophie about her guest list. What if there were women there who would hate her on sight—like Jacie? Allison wavered back and forth between going and staying home. After an hour of debating, she had a headache and went out in the front yard to do some weeding. Weeding was the best headache reliever in the world.

After grabbing an old shovel out of the garage, she went to work on the front flower bed. She had half of it done when she saw a shadow by her side. Turning around, she saw that Maggie had waddled up behind her, carrying what looked like a canvas.

"Hey, neighbor. How are you doing?" Maggie asked with her usual friendly smile.

Allison shielded her eyes from the sun and sighed. Why couldn't Maggie just get the hint?

"I'm doing well. Looks like you're starting to feel better. You're out and about."

Maggie grinned down at her stomach proudly. "I feel great today. Yesterday I felt good, but today I feel great. I really do. I even walked all the way over here to talk to you, and I didn't feel like stopping half-way and taking a nap. It's a miracle," she said happily.

Allison leaned on her shovel and searched for something to say. *Jeez, you have bad taste in men.* Or she could say, *Wow, how could you marry such a jerk?* Nah. Neither of those seemed appropriate.

"So how's the diet coming? Are you getting the hang of it?" she finally asked.

Maggie nodded and rested her hand on her hip. "Oh yeah. It's coming along. Hey, do you mind if I sit on your porch steps while we chat? You can keep weeding and I can get out of the sun," she said, not waiting for an answer as she gingerly sat down on the second step.

Allison shrugged and went back to work.

"So Sophie told me you're coming tonight. Do you mind giving me a ride?" Maggie asked as she leaned her canvas against the porch railing.

Allison stood up and stared at Maggie in surprise. "You're friends with Sophie? You're kidding."

Maggie laughed and leaned back on her elbows, making her muumuu dress dip between her knees. "Isn't everyone? She was one of my first friends when I moved here. She's a very special person. Very open and very loving."

Allison ground her teeth. *Unlike me is what Maggie probably meant.*

"So how about that ride? Is that okay? Luke doesn't want me driv-ing at night," Maggie persisted.

Allison sighed. "I'm really not sure if I'm going, to be honest. You might want to get a ride with someone else."

Maggie's eyebrows slammed together as she frowned at her. "Okay, that's it. You *were* going and now you aren't just because you know *I am*? What is it about me, Allison? I've tried my hardest to be your friend. I've tried talking to you every chance I get, and you give me the cold shoulder *every* time. Lay it on the line, Allison, because I'm not leaving until we have this out."

Allison forgot about the weeding and let the shovel fall to the ground. "You want to have it out? *Fine.* We'll have it out. You seem like a really nice person, Maggie, but I'm just not interested in being friends with you. So just stop trying, okay?"

Maggie glared at her and stood up. "Not until I know why. I don't give up that easy. From where I'm standing, you look like someone I could really like. You've taken on the responsibility of two teenagers. You obviously love them to death. You've been through some hard times, but you just seem stronger for it. I respect you, Allison, and I would really like to get to know you better. Now, unless you give me a good reason, I'm not going to stop trying. Not now, not ever," Maggie said, her pale blue eyes looking frighteningly serious.

Allison crossed her arms over her chest and stared Maggie down. Fine. If she wanted the truth, she could have it. "I've had enough fake friends to last a lifetime. Friends who love you when you have everything going for you, but dump you the second things get messy. I don't do lunches. I can't afford them. I don't go out and get manicures, or pedicures or massages. *I can't afford them.* I don't go shopping for shoes. *I can't afford them.* I don't do any of the fun girl things that friends do anymore. So you're not missing out on anything. But that's all beside the point. Your husband told me specifically that you have enough friends. You don't need the daughter of Max Vaughn as your new friend. Your husband is trying to protect you from me, Maggie. Just let him," she said and picked up her shovel again, hacking at the weeds with the fury of too many ruined friendships.

Maggie stared at her in surprise. "Luke said that?" she asked softly.

Allison glanced at her and hacked at another weed without saying anything.

"That's why things blew up so fast that first day you came over," Maggie said, putting together the pieces. "It wasn't over the stupid Rice Krispie treats. It was about what Luke said to you outside. What else did he say?" she demanded.

Allison shrugged. "Not much. Just that he had some ground rules. Something like, don't try and steal money from you. Don't try and take advantage of you. Don't be evil. Just your basics. Oh, and that since my dad has ruined so many people's lives, that obviously means I will too," she said, feeling fresh anger rush through her.

Maggie's mouth fell open. "*Okay.* Now it all makes sense. It's not *me.* It's him. I get it. After you took off and he went after you, he came back completely deflated. I've never seen him look so guilty. An hour later he told me his plan to give your little brother and sister after-school jobs. He was trying to make it up to you."

Allison nodded and wiped the sweat off her forehead. "Yeah, I figured. Which I do appreciate, by the way. Aspen and Talon love making the extra money, and they actually seem to really enjoy Luke too," she said in confusion.

Maggie laughed and sat back down. "Well, I know this will come as a complete surprise to you, but most people really like Luke. Of course, he's usually nice and polite. You might be the one exception," she said curiously.

Allison grimaced. "I usually am. So like I said, no offense, but let's just leave things as they are. I'll stay on my side of the fence, and you stay on yours. I think Luke would be happier that way."

Maggie shook her head slowly. "I'm not so sure of that, Allison. After hearing for the last week what an amazing sister you are, I think he's changed his mind. The way Talon talks about you, you're the new Joan of Arc."

Allison snorted and then looked up. "*Talon?* Talon did?"

Maggie nodded and smiled brightly at her. "Yep. And Luke keeps asking them all these questions about you too. It's like he's the district attorney and he's trying to get to the bottom of the case. Last night after the kids went home, we were sitting on the couch and he looked at me and he said, 'You know what, I think Allison Vaughn is one of the most decent people we know.'"

Allison's shovel fell out of her hands as her mouth fell open. "You just made that up."

Maggie laughed and shook her head. "Hey, you're not as surprised as he is. He knows he messed up with you. He knew it that first day, I think, but now he knows he's in big trouble. Teenagers are pretty transparent. They love to tell you what they think if you just ask them. And it looks like your brother and sister are the two best character witnesses you could ask for. Luke has the biggest foot in his mouth known to mankind. I wonder how he'll get it out."

Allison smiled and then gave up and laughed. "That is just hilarious. The one thing I remember about Luke, besides the fact that he was so popular, was that he was such a know-it-all. It used to bug me to death. Luke just got schooled," she said delightedly.

Maggie tilted her head and studied the happy woman in front of her. "Just so you know, Luke told me all about your dad. And what he didn't tell me, Aspen told me. I know what happened in Texas too."

Allison's smile faded quickly as she picked up her shovel and went after the weeds like a robot.

"It doesn't matter to me, Allison. You might have had a lot of friends who were just your friends for the fun times. Friends who left you when you needed them the most. But I'll promise you right now that I will never do that. I'm a friend who sticks."

Allison sighed and looked toward the mountains. After a moment, she looked back at Maggie's patient eyes and nodded her head. "Okay then. But you'll be breaking your husband's heart."

Maggie laughed. "Not likely. So, are you going to pick me up tonight?"

Allison grinned and shook her head in awe. "You are something else, Maggie. I'll give you that. Yes. I will pick you up at six fifteen."

Maggie stood up and picked up her canvas. "Oh, and by the way, this is for you. I like to sit by the window and paint when I'm feeling good. I love how you always stand at the porch and wait for your brother and sister to come home. I'd like you to have it," she said, holding the canvas out to Allison.

Allison put the shovel down and wiped her hands on her pants before taking the small canvas. She turned it around and stared at the picture. It was her, leaning against the porch railing with her arms crossed over her chest, staring out. She looked tired. She looked determined. But there was a look of devoted love on her face. She hadn't known she looked like that. She looked up at Maggie and wiped the tear off her cheek that had appeared out of nowhere.

"Do I really look like that?" she had to ask.

Maggie nodded her head without smiling. "You know how it talks in the scriptures about spiritual gifts? Well, mine is my painting. My gift isn't so much the painting, though. It's the *seeing*. I can see people sometimes more clearly than they can see themselves. You are a beautiful piece of art, Allison. Especially to Talon and Aspen."

Allison laughed shakily as she wiped a few more tears from her face, making dirty streaks where her hands touched.

"Wow. Aspen told me you were a painter. I had no idea. I should have known by the gallery next to your house that you were the real thing."

Maggie grinned and walked the few steps that separated the two women and did something shocking to Allison. She hugged her. It wasn't a quick hug and a couple pats. It was a heartfelt, comforting, loving hug. Allison stiffened at first, but then gave in to the comfort.

Allison pulled away a moment later and smiled. "Okay. Now you've done it. We're definitely friends now."

Maggie let out a whoop and pumped her fist. "Yes! I knew we were destined to be best friends. I just knew it. Well, I gotta go to the bathroom. But I'll see you tonight," she said and then hurriedly waddled home.

Allison grinned as she watched Maggie leave and then walked into the house with her new painting. She knew just where to put it too. The bulldog in her foyer was toast.

tWeLve

Allison automatically walked out to the front porch that afternoon and then looked almost shyly over at Maggie's window. She didn't see anyone sitting there staring at her, so she relaxed. It was kind of weird to think someone had been staring at her and painting her without her even knowing it. Weird, but still cool. She glanced over her shoulder back into the entryway, where the picture now hung. It looked good there.

She pushed the hair out of her eyes and smiled as the bus pulled up to the side of the road. She watched Talon get off the bus with the few other kids who lived on this block and then waited for Aspen to appear. Allison stood up straighter and frowned when Aspen didn't get off. The bus pulled away moments later as Talon walked toward her, grim-faced and alone. Allison walked down the steps, worried.

"Where's Aspen, Tal?" she asked as he reached her.

Talon glared at his feet and then at her. "She got a ride home with her new *boyfriend*. The biggest punk at Lone Peak."

Allison blinked in surprise. *"What?"*

Talon kicked a rock in his way and looked back down the road. "That kid who tried to get in my face the first day. Rowan. I don't know his last name. She's been sitting with him at lunch almost every day. I don't know how she could be friends with that jerk after the way he acted with me. I just don't get it. If some chick came up to Aspen and pushed her around and threatened her, I wouldn't be *dating* her," he said as he stalked up the steps.

Allison shook her head. She could see why Aspen would be drawn to Rowan but could also see why Talon was so upset. She'd have to have a talk with Aspen. If she was going to be friends with him, Rowan would need to make things right with Talon.

Allison turned around and sat on the front porch as she waited for her sister. Aspen hadn't called, so she knew she wasn't going anywhere with Rowan. He'd have to bring her straight home—that and Aspen knew the Petersons were expecting her shortly.

A rusty, old red Subaru station wagon turned the corner of their street and headed right for her. *Ah ha. Rowan and Aspen.* She watched as the car stopped right in front of her house. Aspen opened the door, while a tall, good-looking young man hopped out and practically ran around to hold the door open for her. Allison had to smile at the looks on both of their faces. She'd seen it many times. Even occasionally in her own mirror. High school love. Rowan and Aspen walked toward her, almost touching hands. Rowan was dressed in old jeans and a faded red T-shirt. Basically what everyone wore to school, even the rich kids. It wasn't the clothes that told the story these days. It was the cars.

He was a good-looking guy, though. She could see why Aspen couldn't resist him. Tall and trim, but athletic looking. Square jaw, blond hair, and brilliant blue eyes. He was a Disney-movie leading man just waiting to be animated.

"Hi, Allie. Rowan offered to give me a ride home since he lives only a few blocks away. I hope that's okay," she said, looking nervous all of a sudden.

Allison smiled and stood up. "Of course it's okay. Hi. I'm Allison Vaughn," she said to Rowan, holding her hand out.

Rowan looked at her and then cleared his throat nervously. "Yeah, hi," he said, and shook her hand firmly.

Aspen beamed up at Rowan as if he had just said something amazing. Allison grinned in delight. Aspen's first boyfriend. Maybe she should grab her camera.

"So, Rowan, are you a junior this year or a senior?" Allison asked, trying to think of questions that a parent would normally ask.

Rowan shoved his hands in his pockets and looked down at his feet. "Um, I'm a senior this year. I would have graduated last year, but I had to get a job to help my parents out. The school held me back. But it's no big deal. This way, I'll just go on my mission right after I graduate," he said, looking at his feet.

Allison's smile faded slightly as she exchanged guilty looks with Aspen. He'd had to do that because of *their* father. No wonder he'd gone after Talon.

"That's a lot of responsibility for a guy your age. Your parents must really appreciate you," Allison said softly.

Rowan looked up and shrugged with a small smile. "Yeah, I guess. Now I work part-time at the rec center in American Fork. That way I can get all my homework done. It's a lot better this year."

Aspen reached up and patted his back approvingly. "Rowan is a really hard worker. He's going to be really successful someday. I just know it."

Rowan looked down at Aspen and grinned at her. "Whatever. Um, I was wondering if Talon's home. I kind of wanted to stop by and talk to him."

Allison's eyebrows shot up, and her opinion of Rowan went up too. "Sure. I'll just go get him," she said. Looking at Aspen's glowing face, she hoped this went well.

Allison ran up the porch steps and walked quickly into the house, bumping into Talon, who had been in the shadows, listening to every word. He grabbed her arm and pulled her back into the kitchen.

"No way am I going out there and talking to that jerk. She shouldn't be with a guy like that. I'm not going to be fake and pretend everything's okay. It's n*ot*," he said in fast, angry words.

Allison put both her hands on Talon's shoulders, trying to calm him down.

"Sweetie, just listen to me for a second here. Can you do that? Can you forget how angry you are and how hurt you are and just listen?" she pleaded.

Talon rolled his eyes but nodded for her to say what she needed to say.

"Remember what I said the other day? About how he's been through some tough times too? Well, he has. And all because of *our* dad. Yes, he shouldn't have taken his anger out on you. But he knows that now. He knows he made a mistake, and now he wants to make up for it. He's here to apologize to you. Now you need to be man enough to accept it. Did you know he was supposed to graduate last year, but he had to work to support his family and they held him back? He could be at college right now if it weren't for our dad. He's been frustrated and hurt and probably bitter. *Just like you, Tal.* Can't we just give this guy a break? If not for his sake, then let's do it for Aspen. I just saw her face when she looked up at him, Talon, and I have to tell you that this could be serious. Now, do you love your sister enough to let this go?" she implored.

Talon's shoulders loosened, and his eyes closed as he leaned his head back. "He had to work to support his mom and dad? *Dang*," he said quietly.

Allison didn't say anything. She waited for Talon to make up his mind. He finally opened his eyes and sighed heavily. "Out of all the guys at Lone Peak, Aspen had to pick this one," he said in exasperation.

Allison laughed and let her hands fall from his shoulders. "People's hearts are kind of funny. Love just doesn't make sense sometimes."

Talon smirked. "Yeah, like that loser you were engaged to. That was worse than Rowan."

Allison frowned but followed Talon back down the hallway and out onto the front porch, where Aspen was now holding both of Rowan's hands in hers as they laughed and looked into each other's eyes. Allison could hear another one of Talon's disgusted sighs.

"Hey," Talon said in a voice dripping boredom.

Rowan dropped Aspen's hands and turned to face Talon.

"Hey, Talon. I just wanted to stop by and see if you wanted to hang out with me and my dad this weekend. We're going to take some four-wheelers up the canyon. What do you say?"

Allison bit her lip nervously. This was Rowan's big gesture. It wasn't the most eloquent apology, but maybe it said more than a little *I'm sorry* would have. It said, *Hey, I plan on being around, so get used to me.*

Talon turned his head and looked back at Allison silently, pleading for help. She shook her head slightly and widened her eyes as she tried to let him know that he'd better play nice.

Talon looked back at Rowan and then at Aspen. She stared up at him with bright, hopeful eyes. Allison stopped breathing, knowing that Talon hated letting Aspen down. But this was asking a lot of him. Maybe too much.

"I've never been four-wheeling before," Talon finally said.

Rowan grinned and stepped closer, leaning on one of the porch railings. "Ah, there's nothing to it. It's easy. My cousin's coming too. He's bringing all his fishing gear. It'll be great. My uncle's bringing steaks. We'll be eating like kings. You'll have the best time of your life, Talon. I promise. You have my word on it." He stuck his hand out to Talon to shake on it.

Talon looked at the extended hand and knew what it meant. It was the hand of friendship. After only a slightly awkward moment, he reached out and grabbed Rowan's hand, shaking hard.

"I'll be there," he said.

Rowan grinned and then turned and picked Aspen up, twirling her around while she laughed happily. "See, Aspen, it's all good. Now we're one big happy family," he said, grinning cheekily back at Allison and Talon.

Talon actually laughed and then turned and walked back inside. Allison smiled in relief. She walked back inside too, leaving Aspen and Rowan to say their good-byes. She had to admit, though, that she was a little worried. She was glad Rowan was willing to be friends with Talon, but what about his dad? What about his uncle? Would they be so nice when Rowan introduced his new friend as Talon Vaughn, Max's son? She'd have to talk to Aspen and maybe meet Rowan's dad before this outing had her final approval. *Yuck.* Parenting was kind of complicated.

Allison walked back into the kitchen as Talon grabbed a box of cereal out of the pantry for a snack. She laughed softly at his expression of tragic martyrdom. "You are one good brother, Talon. I'll give you that," she said in all seriousness.

Talon nodded his head in complete agreement. "*I know.* The very best. I just hope they don't roast me over the campfire for dessert," he said worriedly.

Allison frowned. He'd obviously picked up on that one small detail too. "I'll check it out with the dad and uncle, Tal. I won't let you go unless I feel completely comfortable with it, okay?"

Talon nodded and dug into his cereal. "That would be wise."

Aspen joined them a moment later, blushing and smiling as if she were the poster girl for teeth whitening. Allison's mouth fell open in shock.

"Oh. My. Heck. You just got your first kiss, didn't you?" Allison demanded, standing up and grabbing Aspen's hands as she started giggling uncontrollably.

Talon groaned and let his head fall onto his arms. Allison pulled her sister into a hug and laughed with joy. "Your first kiss! Aspen, you will remember this day for the rest of your life. Yay!"

Aspen pulled out of Allison's arms and fanned her face. "I didn't know he was going to kiss me. I think he was just so happy Talon said yes."

Talon groaned. "Great. The guy's going to be my brother-in-law. I can just see Thanksgiving now," he said in despair.

Aspen giggled and went to the fridge for an apple. "He said his mom wants to meet me. Can you imagine? And he says that next week he wants to take me on a date. A picnic somewhere pretty. I wonder if he'll ask me to homecoming," she said hopefully.

Allison laughed and jumped up again, waving her arms in the air and doing a happy dance. She'd been to three homecoming dances, and she still had her dresses. Aspen was going to look gorgeous.

Talon coughed loudly. "Um, excuse me. I'm trying to eat here. This is getting nauseating. And I just want to point out that Aspen would have never met Prince *not even close to Charming* if it hadn't been for me and my butt he wanted to kick."

Aspen flew to her brother's side and kissed him noisily on the cheek. "You are the best brother in the whole world. I just knew you two would be great friends. You're so much alike. Gorgeous, smart, wonderful, and perfect," she said, giving him an extra kiss before he could roll his eyes.

Aspen skipped out of the kitchen with her apple. Allison listened to her sister run up the stairs and laughed happily. "Talon, at least half of that happiness is because of you. You did that. You just made your sister the happiest girl in Alpine. How does it feel?"

Talon shrugged and then grinned, shaking his head as he poured more cereal into his bowl. "It's all right, I guess."

Allison leaned on the counter to talk more to Talon when she heard the doorbell ring. She walked toward the front door and knew immediately it was Luke Peterson. What a way to put a damper on her happy afternoon.

Allison pulled open the door. "Yes?" she said as if she'd never met

Luke before and he was selling magazine subscriptions.

Luke smiled at her knowingly and shook his head. "So you had to tattle on me, huh? You couldn't have kept my dirty little secret just a few days longer?" he said without mincing words.

Allison snorted and walked out, shutting the door in case Talon could hear. She didn't want him to know that his idol had said rotten things to her about their dad.

"Protecting you isn't exactly on my list of things to do, Luke. You're a big boy. I'm sure your self-righteousness can pull you through," she said, looking him straight in the eyes.

Luke grimaced and shoved his hands in his pockets, glancing back at his house. "Yeah, well, you'd be surprised. Self-righteousness only lasts as long as it takes for truth to show up. I honestly thought I'd already apologized. I remember standing right over there and saying, 'I'm sorry.' Didn't I?" he asked, sounding sincerely perplexed.

Allison frowned in fake confusion and leaned back against the door. "I must have missed it."

Luke smiled and shook his head. "Okay, here it is, so pay attention, Miss Vaughn. I was wrong about you. I've never been so wrong in my life. If it takes me a thousand years, I will make it up to you somehow. I am honored to be your neighbor, and I would very much appreciate it if you would accept my humble apology," he said as sincerely as he could.

Allison grinned and noticed Maggie watching her husband from the shadows of their porch. If not for Luke's sake, then Allison should accept Luke's apology for Maggie. Plus, if Talon could forgive, then maybe his big sister had better walk the walk too.

"Okay. It's official. I forgive you for being the biggest, most obnoxious jerk in the world," Allison said with a smile.

Luke sighed happily and glanced over his shoulder toward his wife, looking very proud of himself. "Good. Now that that's taken care of, do you happen to have two of the coolest teenagers in Alpine around? I've got some work for them today."

Allison grinned and opened the door to yell inside. "Talon! Aspen! Luke's here for you."

Talon and Aspen appeared seconds later, looking pleased. "Dude, we know where you live. You don't have to walk us to your house," Talon said sarcastically.

Luke laughed and fake-punched Talon in the arm. "Well, I figured I'd better come over and ask your sister if it's okay if I take you guys to the movies tonight. Maggie's going to some lame girls-only thing, and there's this new movie I've been wanting to catch. You guys have been working so hard this week, I figured you could use a little bonus," he said, grinning at their expressions.

Talon let out a war whoop and loped over to talk to Maggie, who had appeared on the Petersons' porch. Aspen was much more dignified but just as excited as she laughed and ran to join her brother.

"Well, I guess that's your answer," Allison said with a laugh.

Luke grinned after the kids. "Yeah, I figured. I'll have them home before midnight. We might have to stop and grab some milk shakes afterward."

Allison smiled in gratitude as Luke started walking away. "Hey, wait a second, Luke," she called out, walking toward him. Luke paused and turned around.

"Thank you. Thanks for being so good to them. I guess you were giving them a chance out of a guilty conscious at first, but whatever reason you have for doing what you're doing, I'm grateful. It's made a big difference in their lives."

Luke walked closer to her and looked down into her eyes. "You know, when I first saw Talon and Aspen, the Spirit whispered to me, 'Feed my sheep.' I tried to ignore it at first, because of your dad. But the Spirit just got louder and louder. They're really growing on me. I love those kids like they're my own little brother and sister. I'm not doing this out of a guilty conscious anymore, Allison. I'm doing it because Heavenly Father loves your brother and sister. And I do too," he said. Then he walked away.

Allison stared after Luke in surprise. *Huh.* Well, it was definitely a day for revelations.

thiRteen

Allison picked up Maggie in her old truck at exactly 6:15. Maggie told her how to get to Sophie's house up on Traverse Mountain. The ride there was a lot more comfortable than she had expected it to be. Maggie talked half the time about which brand of gluten-free noodle was the best and the rest of the time about Aspen's new boyfriend. By the time they got to Sophie's, they had both agreed that Rowan and Aspen would have really good-looking kids someday.

Allison hopped out and then ran around to help Maggie step down from the truck. Maggie ended up halfway falling on her, but she made it down in one piece. Maggie laughed in embarrassment as she noticed two people staring at them.

"Oh hi, Daphne. I didn't know you were coming tonight," Maggie said in an underwhelmed voice.

Allison whipped around to see her old friend leaning up against a bright red sports car.

"Daphne! Hey!" Allison said excitedly, running over. "I just moved back in town. I'm so glad you're here."

Daphne smiled coldly at her and gave her an ultra obvious once over. Allison felt immediately uncomfortable and looked down at herself, picking her appearance apart the way she'd been taught by her mom and dad. It wasn't a good feeling. She was wearing her best pair of old jeans and one of Aspen's new T-shirts. Okay, so it had a bedazzled butterfly on it. It was the biggest shirt Aspen had that would fit her. Well, at least her hair looked good, thanks to Sophie. But her makeup?

She'd gone with the "less is more" look. Unlike Daphne. Daphne looked like she had in high school. Just as thin. Just as stylish and just as pretty. The oversized shiny, gleaming purse held proudly from her shoulders probably cost more than Allison's truck. Daphne moved it forward on her shoulder so Allison wouldn't miss it. Allison's shoulders drooped slightly as she finally got it. Daphne was the same old Daphne. The only problem was, she wasn't the same old Allison. That meant Daphne would be putting her in her place. It had always come down to places with Daphne, who had always craved being number one in looks, style, and popularity. The look of relish on Daphne's face said it all. She had finally won.

"What in the world has happened to you, Allison? I swear I almost didn't recognize you," she said with a cold laugh.

Allison's face hardened as her smile disappeared. She opened her mouth to say something but was interrupted by Maggie.

"Daphne, grow up. Come on, Allison, I can't wait to introduce you to some of the most *amazing* women. You'll love them," Maggie said in a rock hard voice. She grabbed Allison's arm, pulling her toward the house.

"Wait a second there. You can't just walk off and not say hi to me, Allison," a deep voice called after her.

Allison turned her head around and looked at the man who had been standing in Daphne's shadow.

Daphne flipped her hair and leaned on the red sports car as the man pulled himself up and walked toward her. *Of course.* It was Gage Dulaney, one of the boys she had put off in high school with her imaginary boyfriend from Harvard. He'd grown up. Five years ago he'd been thin and tall and kind of colorless—pale hair, pale eyes, pale complexion. Now, he was harder, bulkier, and even kind of attractive if you squinted your eyes. She noticed the red car he was walking away from and frowned. It was the same red car that had been tracking her when she'd run into Sophie's salon. He was the one who had caught sight of her and had rushed for a second look. She tensed up, wondering what kind of welcome Gage would give her.

He walked slowly toward her, smiling warmly. He got close to her and then enfolded her into his surprisingly strong arms, hugging the breath out of her. She laughed in surprise but immediately pulled away.

"Gage, it's so good to see you again," she said, stepping back toward Maggie.

Gage grinned down at her, studying her face. "I wouldn't have thought it was possible for you to become even more beautiful, but you did it. Please tell me you got rid of that boyfriend from Harvard," he begged, clasping his hands together.

Allison blushed and glanced at Maggie. Maggie rolled her eyes and sighed impatiently. "No boyfriend. You always were such a flirt, Gage. So what are you doing here tonight? I thought it was a girls-only thing."

Gage slipped his hands in the back pockets of his expensive jeans, which pushed out his pumped-up muscles. Allison could tell he was trying to impress her, but she hadn't made up her mind whether to be flattered or amused.

"Daphne called me for a ride. She's my little buddy. I help her out when I can," he said with a roll of his eyes that Daphne wouldn't see.

Allison raised an eyebrow as Maggie tugged on her arm. "Come on, Allison. Sophie's waiting."

She walked backward toward the house as she waved at Gage. "It was good seeing you again, Gage."

Gage smiled at her and saluted. "I'll be in touch," he promised.

Maggie sighed and banged on Sophie's door. "Do not fall for that guy, Allison. *Nothing* but show," she muttered.

Allison frowned and stared at Maggie in surprise. "You know Gage?"

Maggie shook her head. "Not at all."

Sophie pulled the door open and grinned at the two women. "Maggie, the most beautiful pregnant woman in the world. I'm so glad you felt good enough to come. Thanks for bringing her, Allison," she said and then noticed Daphne standing behind them. "Oh, and Daphne," she said with much less excitement.

Maggie laughed and walked in, giving Sophie a big hug.

"Go put your feet up and grab some of the chips and dip. I made your favorite guacamole," Sophie ordered, pointing her finger.

Allison smiled and couldn't help calling out, "Make sure the chips are gluten-free!"

Maggie waved her hand in acknowledgement and zoomed in on the food.

"I'm really glad you came, Allison. I thought for sure you were going to cancel on me. My first party with the coolest girl in town," Sophie said affectionately, giving Allison a hug too.

A loud snort from behind them had both women turning to face Daphne, who was pulling her jacket off.

"Coolest girl in town? Don't you mean most *notorious*? Or how about, poorest girl in town? Yeah, I'd feel real proud if I were you, Sophie. You finally got Allison Vaughn to come to your house, and she's only coming because she doesn't have any friends anymore," Daphne said with a bright toothy smile as she drifted past them and into the crowd of women.

Allison felt her hands start to shake as her face froze in distress. How could Daphne automatically hate her because of a situation she had no control over?

Sophie's arm tightened around Allison's waist. "Just ignore her, Allison. I wasn't even going to invite her tonight. I *never* do. But my mom accidently let it slip to Daphne's mom, and when she found out you might be here, she insisted on coming. She's only here to rub your face in everything. Don't let her get to you. I hope she doesn't ruin your evening," Sophie said, looking worried.

Allison looked forlornly at the front door, knowing all she had to do was walk through it, get in her truck, and leave. Then she wouldn't have to face Daphne. For the most part, she'd let Daphne get away with her cruel sarcastic remarks and her put-downs because of her dad's orders. But her dad wasn't here anymore. It was just Allison and Daphne, and Daphne thought she could walk all over her. She wasn't the same girl she had been five years ago. Allison smiled at Sophie and shrugged.

"For what it's worth, she's right," Allison said. "I *was* friendless. But now I have Maggie. And you if you're up to it?" she asked raising her eyebrows.

Sophie tilted her head, studying her for a moment. Allison winced inwardly, knowing she had pushed the friendship too fast. There was just too much water under the bridge for them to be friends. Friendly acquaintances? Yes. Friends? Who was she kidding? She had told everyone Sophie's boyfriend was gay. It would take someone really amazing to get over that.

"Allison, do you really think I'd invite you to my home if I wasn't interested in getting to know you better and be friends with you? Besides, anyone Daphne hates is automatically my friend. Come on in and grab a plate of food before Maggie eats it all. Last time we had her over, we had to have a few extra pizzas delivered to feed everyone else."

Allison grinned at Sophie and then took a cue from Maggie and reached over and hugged Sophie.

"Thanks for taking a chance on me. Now I have two friends. That's two more than I had in high school. I'd rather have two real friends any day over a stadium of fake friends."

Sophie grinned delightedly as she put her arm through Allison's, drawing her into her home. "Well, since we're friends now, I've gotta warn you. Stay away from Jacie. She's not as nice as me. She hasn't taken an oath against purple dye or attacking people with buzzers. Just keep your eyes open whenever you two are in the same room."

Allison turned pale as she automatically scanned the room. Sophie cracked up. "You're too easy."

Allison felt her heart relax and was able to smile back into Sophie's open, sparkly eyes. Sophie spent the next fifteen minutes going through the room and introducing Allison to all of her friends.

Allison started to forget names after about ten minutes but did the best she could, smiling and shaking hands for Sophie's sake. Sophie really was acting like Allison was still the coolest girl in town. She didn't act like she was embarrassed at all that she was introducing Max Vaughn's daughter to all of her closest friends. Or maybe, Sophie was just a genuinely nice person. Allison smiled at Sophie and started to enjoy herself. If she was going to have real friends for the first time in her life, she was going to enjoy every second of it. She finally took a break from the introductions and got a plate of food, squishing in beside Maggie and a girl she didn't know.

"*Oh my heck*. Are you starving to death?" came a laugh from across the room.

Allison recognized the voice but ignored it as she turned to ask Maggie how she was feeling.

"Of course it's been five years, but you've gained at *least* fifteen pounds. That's three pounds per year. Just think what you're going to look like in twenty more years," Daphne said, holding a glass of water in her hands, proudly not eating one bite.

Allison glanced at Maggie and noticed how red her face was. "You little brat," Maggie said loudly.

Allison patted her arm, halting the tirade. She could fight her own battles. She glanced around the room of women and noticed everyone had heard Daphne's pronouncement. In Daphne's goal to wound her, she had inadvertently wounded *all* of the women.

Allison faced her ex-best friend and raised an eyebrow. "You're right, Daphne. I have gained fifteen pounds since I was a senior in high school. I'm a woman now. If I wanted to weigh a hundred and fifteen pounds still, I'd have to starve myself and exercise for at least two hours a day. But I enjoy eating. I enjoy being a woman with curves, and I enjoy life. Why would anyone want to imprison themselves into thinking that you can only be beautiful if you're as thin and bony as a teenage girl? I think a woman who accepts herself and her body is the most beautiful thing in the world. On the other hand, a woman who tries to pretend she's still sixteen by starving herself, is just, well, kind of sad," she said and then picked up a taco and bit into it as if her life depended on it.

Maggie started clapping, and then Jacie, of all people, joined her. Pretty soon, the whole room was whooping and clapping. Allison laughed in embarrassment and took the napkin Maggie gave her to wipe the salsa off her chin.

"That's so deep, Allison," Daphne said sarcastically. "Really, I'm touched. I remember your mom teaching us how to throw up. Remember that, Allison? She actually gave us lessons on how to be bulimic. I'm still grateful to her for being able to wear size-two jeans my senior year. She was always full of good tips, wasn't she? My favorite tip from your mom was to go smell really awful garbage right before a meal. I wonder what your mom would say now if she could see you," Daphne said with a pitying glance.

Allison felt her heart break as the memories of her mom's lessons came back to her. There had been so many lessons—and all on subjects a mother should never teach her daughter.

Maggie glanced at Allison's stricken face and put her plate down, dabbing her face and staring at Daphne as if she was insane.

"I find it so interesting that a person raised under the worst circumstances and by the shallowest people can still turn out to be an amazing, strong, and beautiful person on the inside. I guess it comes down to character and choices. Allison obviously had some bad examples throughout her life, but instead of embracing them, she rose above them. And then there are people who through no fault of their parents turn out to be shallow, empty, and truly *annoying* people. Isn't that tragic, Daphne?" Maggie said, as everybody stopped talking to see what Daphne would say.

Daphne stood up and glared at Maggie and Allison, jutting out her hipbones in case anyone had missed them.

"I've always had to deal with jealousy growing up. Being the best always brings out the worst in other people. Don't forget to save room for dessert, Maggie. I'm sure Luke won't mind if you gain *another* hundred pounds," she said and flounced out of the room.

Maggie stared after Daphne and then threw her head back and laughed. Allison giggled a little, and Sophie took Daphne's vacated seat and grinned.

"Well, now that's what I call a good start to a party. I say this calls for seconds, everybody."

All the women grinned at each other and then stood up as one to hit the table laden with food. Maybe it was out of rebellion against Daphne's outdated ideas on beauty or a celebration of their womanhood. But for whatever reason, all the women went home that night very full and very satisfied with being who they were.

Allison jumped in surprise when an hour later Jacie sat down next to her. Allison looked at her warily, raising an eyebrow.

"I'm willing to consider that you're not completely evil," Jacie finally said, her ultra-blonde hair framing a face that would always be cute.

Allison licked her lips and sat back, studying Jacie. "I'm willing to consider that you're not a crazed Doberman pinscher."

Jacie grinned with delight. "Really? *A Doberman.* That's how you saw me?"

Allison laughed and nodded. "Yeah, you're kind of scary. I used to have nightmares of being caught in dark alleyways with you."

Jacie smiled and shrugged. "Nah, that was always the thing about you, Allison. You might not have wanted to go up against me, but I always knew you could. You've got steel in that spine of yours."

Allison laughed softly and shook her head. "I don't know about that. I didn't have much backbone in high school, but now I do. I've had to be strong for my brother and sister. I won't let anyone hurt them," she said seriously.

Jacie nodded in agreement. "I get ya. I was like that with Sophie in high school. She's always been so nice and sweet. She needed me to look out for her, or else she would have been eaten alive. Especially by Daphne. I think that's why I was so angry at you. You were always so good at reigning Daphne in when she got out of hand. When she'd go after Sophie in school in front of everyone, you'd always nip it in the bud somehow. But then you turned on Blake, and I was ticked. I felt kind of betrayed. I looked up to you so much, and then you blew it. I understand now why you did what you did, though," she said.

Allison blinked in surprise. "Wow. You looked up to *me*? That's just crazy, Jacie. I was just as bad as Daphne most of the time."

Jacie shook her head in disagreement. "You wore the crown, but for the most part you were a benevolent ruler. And for what it's worth, Blake turned out to be the biggest flake in Alpine."

Allison laughed as she started to relax. "I would love to hear that story."

Jacie shook her head. "That's Sophie's story to tell. And it's a good one," she said with a sparkle in her eyes.

Allison smiled and glanced over at Sophie, who was in the middle of a conversation with three other women over the merits of walking versus yoga.

"You know, Sophie really has grown up to be a beautiful woman," Allison said. "I always thought she would. She always had such a good spirit around her. She has a good husband, a beautiful home, a beautiful child, and a career she loves. And she deserves it all. I'm really happy for her."

Jacie studied her thoughtfully for a moment. "I'm glad you can be happy for her. That's what's killing Daphne. Daphne figured by now *she'd* have the rich husband and the house on the hill with the beautiful children and the perfect life. She dies of jealousy every time she gets around Sophie. It's beautiful payback, but the envy gets kind of old after awhile."

Allison blew out her breath. "Even if Daphne did get it all, she still wouldn't be happy. Somebody out there would always have a richer husband or a bigger house or a cuter kid. Daphne lives by competition. It's almost impossible to be happy when you do that."

Jacie nodded her head slowly. "I think you got it, Allison. You're right. *You're* not like that. How did you figure all that out? Psychology major?"

Allison frowned and looked at her knees. "Nah. My mom was like that. I grew up watching it every day of my life."

Jacie winced and patted her arm. "But look at you now. You're not even competing with anyone anymore and you're still winning. You've gained fifteen pounds, and now you're a tall, blonde Salma Hayek. Its killing Daphne that you're even more gorgeous now. You look better with longer hair too."

Allison rolled her eyes. "Now you're freaking me out. What happened to the blood-thirsty Doberman pinscher I was so used to?"

Jacie laughed and ran her hands through her hair. "She's still here. Just wait, you'll see her again when Daphne comes back into the room."

Allison groaned. "I thought Daphne left."

Jacie shook her head. "Nah, she's hiding in the kitchen, nibbling on the extras so no one will see her eat and find out she's human after all."

"Okay, everyone. I need your attention. It's time for truth or dare!" Sophie yelled. All the women in the room practically ran for the couches and chairs. Some even sat on the floor. All of them were grinning and looking excited. Maggie came and squeezed in between Allison and Jacie.

"Oh, this is so fun. Last time was hilarious. I still can't believe you drove down the mountain just to doorbell ditch Daphne." Maggie whispered loudly.

Jacie laughed and slapped her knee. "Oh, that was the best. Dang, we can't do that tonight. She's here. Now what will we do for fun?"

Sophie held up her hands. "Okay, since this is Allison's first time, she gets to go first. It's only fair. Kind of like an initiation."

Allison winced as every eye turned to her. "Greeeaaat. Now the hazing starts," she said sarcastically.

Sophie and everyone laughed, shaking their heads. "So what will it be? Truth or dare?"

Allison stared up at the ceiling and then looked to Maggie for help. Maggie was no help at all. She was rubbing her hands gleefully, waiting on her answer.

"Okay, truth." Everyone here knew all her deep dark sordid secrets. Nothing they could want to know would embarrass her more than what was already out in the open.

Sophie stared at her and looked at Jacie. Jacie nodded her head in encouragement.

"Okay, we've been dying to know this forever. Who did you have a crush on in high school? You flirted with all the guys, but never dated anyone. You always went stag to all the dances. What's the deal?"

Allison bit her lip and stared at the group of women looking at her unblinkingly. Half of them had known her in high school, but even the half that hadn't still looked at her breathlessly.

"I *never* had a crush on anyone in high school," she said as snottily as she could.

Sophie looked at her in disappointment, and Jacie sighed rudely in exasperation.

"*However.* I was *madly* in love with a certain boy in high school. *Crush* is a word too tame to describe my passionate feelings," she said, grinning at everyone's looks of eager anticipation.

Sophie clapped her hands and jumped up and down in her seat. "I knew it! I knew it, Jacie! Didn't I say so?" she demanded of her friend.

Jacie held up her hand. "Hold it, Sophie. Wait for the name."

Allison sighed and glanced at Daphne, who looked just as curious as everyone else. So she had kept her secret well. Even Daphne hadn't known.

"Will Carson," she said quietly and gasped as Sophie started screaming.

"I was right! *I was right!*" Sophie screamed, grabbing Jacie's hand and pulling her up to dance around the family room. Jacie laughed and danced with her friend before sitting down.

"We had you figured out, Allison. You were so sly, but we watched you like a hawk. You flirted like crazy with all the popular guys, but you never showed any preference. But when Will walked into the room, you always made a point of saying something to him. You'd walk by and drop a pencil, or he'd be helping his sister and you'd help him fix her hair. *We knew it,*" Jacie said in satisfaction.

"That's such crap. Allison, you were *not* in love with Will Carson. You would have told *me* if you had been. Besides, it's just ridiculous. Sure he's hot now, but back then he was so dang poor he had to get free lunch. He wore the same pair of jeans *every* day. His shoes had holes in them. You're lying," Daphne said in a low, disgusted voice.

Allison shrugged. "Believe what you want to, Daphne, but they asked me for the truth and I'm telling them the truth. You might not have been able see past his empty wallet or his clothes, but I did. Will Carson looked like a young Hugh Jackman. He was so gorgeous sometimes I couldn't even breathe when he walked in the room. And he was so nice. He treated his sister like a princess. He would walk her to her classes and make sure she was happy. He was gorgeous. And I loved him," she said honestly.

Daphne rolled her eyes. "You're only saying that because you're broke and he's rich and single. You're just like your dad, looking for the fast buck. Forget it, Allison. Will's out of your league now," Daphne said with a proud tilt of her head.

Allison gasped at being compared so unfairly to her father. She glared at Daphne but could think of nothing to say to defend herself. Now that Daphne had pointed it out, she realized that if she did go after Will, that's exactly what people would think. That she was just in it for the money.

"Daphne, stop judging everybody by your standards. Just because he won't date *you* doesn't mean he won't jump at the chance to date Allison," came a voice from across the room.

Allison peered around Maggie to see who had spoken. It was an older lady sitting next to Sophie's mom, Candy. She had chin-length light graying brown hair and brown eyes in a face just now showing her age around the eyes and neck. She winked at Allison and glared at Daphne.

Allison looked back at Daphne and was surprised to see that Daphne was sitting demurely in her seat, studying her manicure. *Huh.* Someone had finally shut Daphne up. It was a miracle.

Sophie cleared her throat and went on to the next person. The game went around the room, with nearly everybody choosing truth, except for Jacie, who was forced to drive down the mountain, back into Alpine so she could tell her husband that she was pregnant with their second child. The party wound down as soon as Jacie returned, looking red in the face and very happy. They had so much fun talking they never even got around to putting a movie on. Women started lining up at the door, kissing and hugging Sophie and asking when the next girls night night would be.

Maggie was still eating, so Allison made herself useful by grabbing empty cups and plates and carrying them to the kitchen. She had most of the kitchen cleaned up by the time Maggie, Jacie, and Sophie found her.

"Ah, here she is. Our very own little Cinderella," Jacie said, almost affectionately.

Allison felt the shock all over again at having Jacie be nice to her. Life was crazy surprising.

"Yeah, you should see her little brother and sister. We work them hard every day. I guess it runs in the family," Maggie said, smiling kindly at her.

Allison smiled and wiped her hands on a dish towel. "Well, it's not perfect, but I put a dent in it for you. Thanks again for inviting me, Sophie. I haven't had this much fun in a *very* long time," she said.

Sophie smiled before taking a sip of her Fresca. "I know. But this is just the first of many fun nights to be had. You're young, healthy, and beautiful, Allison. This should be the happiest time of your life. And I think we're going to make sure that happens," she said, nodding her head resolutely.

Allison laughed and shook her head. "Yeah, well, ask anyone who cares for two teenagers how fun life is, and you'll know that that might just be impossible."

Maggie leaned up against the counter and shook her head. "Unlikely, but not impossible. Not if you have a few friends on your side."

Jacie nodded and joined Maggie, leaning on the counter. "It's impossible if you don't have a good plan. All it takes is a five-step plan written down on a piece of paper and you're halfway there. You need to be happy. So here's the plan. Number one, job. We're going to get you a job, because honey, those jeans are just sad. Number two, we're going to get you Will Carson. And number three . . ." She paused and looked at Sophie uncertainly. "Did we ever get to number three?"

Sophie patted her chin with her finger and squinched her eyes up. "I don't think we did. We kind of just make it up as we go, anyway. You should have seen the list Jacie did for me. It was crazy, and I think I only got through one or two, but it all worked out anyway."

Allison laughed and crossed her arms over her chest. "I'm completely on board with number one. Did you have a chance to ask anyone

82

about a job, Sophie? Because I could *really* use one."

"Sophie didn't, but I did."

All four women turned to see the woman who had been sitting next to Sophie's mom. She was standing in the doorway with Candy, listening in on their conversation.

"Sorry for eavesdropping, but I couldn't help it. I hear my nephew's name mentioned, and I'm all ears," she said.

Sophie laughed. "Martha! Thanks for putting Daphne in her place. I've never seen her so quiet in my entire life."

Martha smiled and shrugged as she and Candy walked further into the room. "I say it like I see it. So, Allison, remember our family apple orchard? Well, we still do the fruit stand on Main Street. We have all the help we want after school's out, but we need someone in the morning from about nine to two in the afternoon Monday through Friday. You'd have Saturday's off, and we don't sell on Sundays. Of course it is seasonal, but you never know; we might be able to find something permanent. What do you say?"

Allison felt stunned. It was perfect.

Maggie grinned and grabbed her arm. "This way you can be home for Tal and Aspen when they get home from school. Say yes, Allison," she urged.

Allison smiled and nodded her head. "When do you want me to start?"

Martha laughed happily. "Monday will do. Come to the fruit stand fifteen minutes early so Betsy can walk you through everything."

The women talked for a few more minutes, but Allison could tell Maggie was wearing out fast, so they said their good-byes and left.

Driving down the mountain, Maggie couldn't stop smiling. "You know, I just like you, Allison. Daphne threw everything she had at you, and it didn't even faze you. You are one strong chick."

Allison frowned slightly, looking out over the night sky. "I've found nothing good comes from being weak or being quiet. I've seen what human beings can do to each other. And they just keep doing whatever they can get away with until someone stands up and puts a stop to it."

Maggie nodded her head in agreement and told her a little of her own story—how she had come to Alpine and how she'd had to come to grips with her grandmother's part in her mother's abuse as a child.

Allison pulled her truck into Maggie's driveway and just sat there for a moment. "I would love to meet your mom, Maggie."

Maggie grinned and opened the door. "The feeling's mutual. She lives in town now, and I've told her all about you. You're invited over to my mom's house for dinner after church on Sunday. You and the kids. It'll be great. My grandma Tierney is cooking."

Allison grinned and nodded her head. "Just make sure it's gluten-free."

Maggie laughed. "As if it would be anything else. Thanks for the ride, Allie," she said, using her nickname as if she'd always called her that.

Allison walked into her house a few moments later to find Talon and Aspen asleep on the couch with their heads on opposite arm rests. She went to the closet, grabbed two blankets, and gently laid one over each of them. She stood there, silently studying her brother and sister for a moment. They looked so young when they were asleep. So beautiful and so carefree, as if their lives were perfect. No one looking at them would ever be able to tell that their lives had been torn apart less than a year ago. But they were slowly resurrecting their lives. And she was determined that the lives they had now would be lives filled with trust, honesty, and love. Something she'd never had growing up.

fOURteeN

Allison woke the next day to Talon nudging her shoulder.

"*What?*" Allison asked grouchily, glancing at the clock. She knew it was Saturday, so why was Talon even up at seven-thirty?

"Did you call Rowan's dad? Aspen says they'll be here in an hour to get me, and I swear I'm not going if you don't make sure their idea of recreation doesn't include torture and cannibalism."

Allison sat up in bed and laughed a little. Talon was so over-the-top. But in this case, he was right to be nervous.

"No worries, Tal. I called Rowan's dad last night before I left for the party, and we had a long talk. I told him my concerns and how you met Rowan that first day of school and everything. I gotta tell ya, Tal, he sounds like a very nice man. He told me that after Dad stole all his money, it was a big wake-up call. Financially, they've suffered a lot these past five years, and they've all had to make sacrifices, but it's brought them closer together as a family. He says his priorities are right where they should be now, with his family being number one and his bank account way down the list. It doesn't mean he wants to hang out with Dad anytime soon, but he's smart enough to know that *we* didn't have anything to do with what happened to him. And he said that he really wants things to work out with Rowan and you and Aspen. It's all good, Talon. Seriously. You guys are going to ride some ATVs, cook a few steaks, and do a little fishing. You're going to have a good time. And I promise you, if I didn't feel good about it, you wouldn't be going. Okay?" she asked, studying his face.

Talon sat on the edge of her bed, staring off into space. "Okay, I guess. I trust you. And it *would* be nice to have a friend. Even if he is dating my sister."

Allison sighed and smoothed her old comforter with her hands. "I wish I could give you thirty of the best friends in the world, Tal. I wish I could give you the nicest car in town and all the cool clothes to wear. I wish I could make you happy. But all I can do is love you and do the best I can. I'm sorry you've been so miserable."

Talon turned and stared at his sister. "I know, Al. That's what Luke was telling me last night. He told me that most sisters your age would have taken off and left us a long time ago and that we should be more grateful. *I am.* I just get depressed sometimes is all," he said in a soft, serious voice.

Allison reached over, hugged her brother, and thought once more that Luke possibly wasn't the worst person in Alpine. "You're allowed. Now you'd better go get ready for your big day. I bet Aspen is jealous you get to spend all day with Rowan."

Talon stood up and stretched. "Yeah. She wants me to take a camera and get tons of pictures of Rowan doing everything. *As if,*" he said, walking out the door with a grimace.

Allison smiled and flipped her legs over the edge of the bed. Hopefully Talon would have a good day doing manly stuff and hanging out with Rowan. And if not, then at least he'd made Aspen happy.

After a quick breakfast, Rowan arrived with his dad, uncle, and cousin to take Talon away for the day. Allison walked down the steps first, holding her hand out to Ben Dalton. Ben was a big, tall blond man, and Allison knew Rowan would grow up to look very similar to him. He was dressed simply in jeans and a T-shirt and had a carefree smile on his face.

"Well, have mercy, you've grown up," Ben told Allison. "I remember coming over to your house every now and then to see Max, and I remember thinking you were such a cute little thing."

Allison blushed as she shook Ben's hand. "Wow, I wish I could remember you. People were always coming and going back then. So do you remember Talon and Aspen?" she asked, turning and motioning her suddenly shy siblings to join her.

Ben looked around her as Talon and Aspen took their places at her side. Ben smiled at the two teenagers and stroked his chin. "Hmm,

Aspen, you look a lot like this cute little girl I used to see every now and then, but the girl I knew was always on her roller skates in the ballroom. Used to drive your dad nuts. And Talon. Yeah, I remember this kid. I used to have the most beautiful Harley Davidson in the world, and I drove it over one time to show your dad. He took me in the house to talk business and when we came out, you were sitting right on top, pretending to ride it. Your eyes were closed and you had the biggest grin I've ever seen. Of course I know these kids," he said with a laughing smile.

Talon grinned as he remembered that day. "I remember that! Dad was so ticked at me, but you gave me a ride around the neighborhood. That was the best," he said, relaxing.

"Did you ever bring me over to hang out with Talon and Aspen?" Rowan asked, stepping out from the shadow of his father.

Ben automatically put his arm around his son's shoulders and grinned. "There were a few times, and as I recall, you would spend the entire time chasing Aspen around, pulling her hair and teasing her."

Rowan grinned at Aspen and then reached over and gently tugged a strand of soft blonde hair. "Five years later, and I'm still chasing you."

Aspen blushed a bright red color and laughed shyly. Allison took pity on her sister and walked over to the trailer that held the five ATVs.

"Will Talon have a helmet to wear?" Allison asked, looking over the ancient scratched and dented four-wheelers.

Ben nodded. "Don't you worry, big sis. We'll bring your boy home safe and sound. We'll have a lesson on riding before we set him loose. He's going to come home dirty, tired, and happy, I promise you. Next time we go, we'll invite you girls to come."

Allison grinned and walked back to her brother and sister. "I'll wait and get the report from Talon before I agree to anything. But thanks for inviting him. We've never done anything like this before."

Ben smiled as he herded the boys toward his old blue Chevy truck. "Like I said, he's going to have the time of his life. We'll have him home sometime after dark," he promised. Then he hopped in his truck.

Allison knew Talon would never forgive her if she ran up and gave him a good-bye hug and kiss, so she settled for giving him the thumbs-up signal. Aspen waved as they drove off, and Rowan leaned out the window and sent her the sign language sign for love.

Allison watched her sister beam with happiness and laughed as she slung her arm across Aspen's shoulders and walked back into the house.

"Wow, he's had it bad for you since you were little. It's almost fate that we came back here," Allison said, teasing her little sister.

Aspen sighed happily and walked to the fridge to get a glass of milk. "Isn't he the most gorgeous guy in the whole world? And his dad seems so nice."

Allison nodded in agreement, although she disagreed about Rowan's supreme good looks. "Just promise me you won't get married until after his mission. He leaves right after school, so that will give you a year to finish high school and one year at college. None of this running away and getting married in Vegas stuff," she said with a frown.

Aspen giggled and shook her head, wiping milk off her chin. "Of course we wouldn't do that. But wouldn't that be wonderful if we did get married someday? Oh, I would love that," she said dreamily.

Allison smiled happily at her sister. Her first love. It was so cute.

"You'll probably get married before I do. At least promise me I get to be your maid of honor," Allison said as she started to unload the dishes from the dishwasher.

Aspen shook her head. "Nah, you'll be married way before me."

Allison snorted and grabbed a handful of forks and spoons to put away. "Yeah right. Who would date me?" she asked. Then she thought of Gage. She frowned and reached for the plates. Gage would date her in a heartbeat. But for some reason, she'd rather stay single than date him. And she wasn't sure why.

"Allie, you're so pretty, I don't know why you don't have a date every night," Aspen said loyally.

Allison's mouth lifted at one corner. "I could give you a page full of reasons," she said, her smile slipping as she thought of her ex-fiancé.

Aspen walked over and gave her a quick hug. "Just forget Jason. Talon and I *never* liked him. *At all.* We're both glad he dumped you."

Allison shook her head and wrinkled her forehead. "I don't get it. He was the perfect man. He was smart, good-looking, and a hard worker. He was well off. He had everything. Why didn't you guys ever like him?" she asked curiously.

Aspen sat on the bar stool and looked down at the counter, tracing the fake marble pattern with her little finger. "I don't know. He just seemed so cocky. And every time you left the room, he'd go and talk to some other pretty girl. I don't think he ever really loved you. Sorry."

Allison stood up in surprise, holding the dish to her stomach. "You're right. He never did. If he had loved me, he would have stuck by me. But he didn't. I heard he got married last month," she said casually, turning back to the dishwasher.

Aspen gasped. "To who?"

Allison sighed and wished it still didn't hurt so much. "Remember my friend Kenleigh? They started dating the second he took his ring back. Kenleigh and Jason blocked me on facebook, but everyone else was talking about it."

Aspen shook her head in disgust. "Like I said, I'm so glad you didn't marry him. He would have cheated on you," she said matter-of-factly.

Allison had to laugh at that. "Sweetie, you're not even seventeen yet. How do you know so much about men?"

Aspen grinned. "It's my gift."

The sisters puttered around the house most of the morning, cleaning and organizing and mostly being bored. Aspen wanted to use some of the money she'd earned working for the Petersons to buy a new outfit for her upcoming date with Rowan. Allison gave in easily, and they spent a few fun hours browsing the clearance racks at the mall before Aspen decided on a pair of jeans, a T-shirt, and a new pair of shoes. As they drove back into town, Allison slowed down as she came in view of the fruit stand by the side of the road.

"That's where I'll be working from now on," Allison said, pointing it out to Aspen.

Aspen glanced at the fruit stand in surprise. "Really? I thought you might get a job at a store or something."

Allison drove by and smiled. "Well, this way I can be home when you and Talon are home from school, and I won't have to work the weekends. It's the perfect job for me, really.

Aspen frowned. "Are you sure? It just doesn't seem like something you'd do," she said carefully.

Allison gave her sister a wry smile. "The old me wouldn't have. The new me doesn't have a choice. This will help us pay our bills. Things won't be so tight now. It'll be good. You'll see," she said reassuringly.

Aspen frowned but nodded her head. "You really should be at college, dating and having fun and getting your degree so you can have a career. Instead, you're here babysitting me and Talon. It's not very fair, is it? Maybe I *should* run off with Rowan. That way you could be free," she said sadly.

Allison's fingers gripped the steering wheel tightly as she stared at Aspen in shock. "Don't ever say that again, Aspen. It's *not* babysitting. It's my choice, and I choose to be with you because I love you. I'm happy being here with you. Besides, the real reason I took the fruit stand job was so that I could check out Will Carson. He's only the best-looking guy in the whole world," she said with a smile, hoping to get Aspen's mind on something besides the sacrifices she was making for them.

Aspen gasped and sat up straighter in her seat, turning to grin at her sister.

"You *like* someone? You're seriously interested in a guy?" she asked, her eyes shining brightly.

Allison laughed at the immediate change in her sister. "Oh yeah. You wouldn't believe this guy, Aspen. He's the most gorgeous guy in the world. Think Hugh Jackman but *better*."

Aspen sighed happily. "I love Wolverine. Well, so has he asked you out or anything?" she prodded.

Allison shook her head. "Nah, but that's where this job comes in. I figure if I can just hang around him enough, he'll notice me and fall hopelessly in love with me. I used to know him in high school. He was so adorable, and no one ever even noticed. And his little sister, Bella, is an angel, Aspen. You'll love her. She has Down's syndrome, and she's the sweetest person in the world, besides you, of course. I can't wait to introduce you to them."

Aspen jumped up and down in her seat, squealing happily. "Yes! Allison, this is perfect. I can't wait to meet them."

Allison grinned to herself as Aspen talked the rest of the way home about how to attract a man. Allison sighed deep inside, knowing that nothing would ever come of her very real attraction to Will. From little pieces of conversation here and there, she knew Will was now very wealthy. He lived in a different world than she did. And she knew from experience that people from different worlds seldom, if ever, jumped from one to the other. But her goal had been to divert her sister from the unglamorous aspects of working at a fruit stand. And she had. Almost too well.

Later that night, a little after nine o'clock, Talon walked through the door with a big, but tired, grin on his face. Allison saw it and immediately relaxed. She jumped up and ran to the door so she could thank Ben again. He surprised her and gave her a quick hug.

"That's a good boy you got there, Allison. He's a little wild on a four-wheeler, but give him time and he'll be a pro. Next month we're kidnapping all of you," he promised before he turned and walked back to his truck.

Allison left Aspen on the front porch to say good-bye to Rowan and found Talon leaning on the kitchen counter, drinking a glass of water.

"Well . . . ? How was it?" Allison asked, smiling encouragingly at him.

Talon smiled and lifted his shirt. "Check this out. I totally wiped out and ran into a tree. Isn't that sick?"

Allison's smiled quickly disappeared as she ran to get the first aid kit. How could a kid think a goopy, bleeding abrasion was something to be proud of? She cleaned and bandaged his scrape while he told her all about his day. His whole face was alight as he described the food and the terrain and the deer they saw.

Allison sat in happy silence as she listened to him go on and on. It was ten o'clock before Talon finally yawned and stood up. "I'm exhausted. Good night."

Aspen and Allison watched as he walked out of the room and then turned and grinned at each other.

"Well, you lucky little thing," Allison said. "I didn't think it could be done, but it looks like everything will be fine now between Talon and Rowan."

Aspen nodded her head and smiled. "I knew it would work out. Rowan said it would. He really was sorry about getting in Talon's face that first day. I told him he had to fix things if he wanted to be more than friends with me. So he did."

Allison shook her head at her little sister. Aspen was a power to be reckoned with. Rowan never stood a chance.

"By the way, we're invited to dinner at Maggie's mom's house tomorrow after church."

Aspen nodded and stood up. "Yeah, I know. Luke told us yesterday. He said we're in for the best food in the world. I don't know how the best food in the world could be gluten-free, but I'm willing to hope," she said and walked out of the kitchen with a tired good night.

Allison turned the lights off and went up to bed, smiling with relief. It had been a good day. She knew now that every good day had to be treasured. There were just too many bad ones to let the good ones go by unappreciated.

fifteen

The next day looked to be just as good as the last. After church, they followed Maggie and Luke over to her parents' house in their old truck. Allison thought it was kind of strange that Maggie's mom and grandma lived right next to each other, but she didn't say anything. She couldn't imagine wanting to live next to her parents.

The house was large and old-fashioned, with wide porches and tall windows. It sat back in the trees as if it were hiding from the world. Allison thought it was magical.

They all hopped out of the truck and followed Maggie into the backyard, where a huge picnic table was set with plates and a cute red-and-white checkered tablecloth. The trees were tall and shady, and the flower beds were bright and colorful. Allison couldn't help wishing her backyard was half this beautiful.

Maggie jumped right into the introductions, grabbing Allison's hand and pulling her first to her mother and stepfather.

"Allie, this is my mom, Lisa, and my stepdad, Terry. They used to live in St. George, but they're Alpiners now."

Allison smiled at the two people in front of her and felt a little nervous. Lisa was a beautiful woman with long, wavy dark hair. And Terry was the ultimate cowboy with his super short dark blond hair and his Wrangler jeans and humongous belt buckle. Lisa grabbed Allison's hand in a warm shake and smiled into her eyes.

"I hope you don't mind, but Maggie told me a little bit of your history. I'm really glad to meet you. You're an extraordinary young woman from everything I've heard," she said simply and sincerely.

Allison blushed and looked away for a second. She was never good at receiving compliments, so she settled with a quick thank you. She shook Terry's hand before Maggie pulled her over to her Grandma Tierney.

"Now this is my grandma, Bonnie Tierney. You'll love her. She's the best cook in the world," Maggie said proudly.

Allison smiled at the older woman, immediately liking her style. She obviously took good care of herself. She was fashionably dressed in denim capris and a bright lime green button-down shirt. Her hair was spiky and white-blonde, but it was her watchful eyes that stopped Allison from reaching her hand out. Allison's smile slipped as the older woman stood still for a moment, just watching her as if she were looking for something wrong or out of place.

Maggie looked puzzled by her grandmother's reaction. "Grandma?" she asked questioningly.

Bonnie blinked and then smiled, stepping forward as if she had been in a daze. "Don't mind me. I was just having myself a good look at you. I'm Bonnie, this wild woman's grandma," she said, holding her hand out.

Allison shrugged off the cold stare and shook the proffered hand, smiling back. She soon met Maggie's Grandpa Frank, a big teddy bear of a man, and then everyone sat down to eat. She was glad when she was seated next to Lisa and Maggie, and even more grateful that Bonnie was down at the other end of the table with Luke, Talon, and Aspen.

Allison had second helpings of the mashed potatoes and gravy and the fried chicken and corn on the cob. But when she saw the peach pie Bonnie brought out for dessert, she knew she was in heaven. She couldn't help herself from asking, just because everything had tasted so good.

"Um, Bonnie? Are you sure all of this is gluten-free? I've been cooking gluten-free for over a year now, and I haven't made anything that has tasted half this good," she said with a smile.

Bonnie raised an eyebrow. "Of course it's all gluten-free. Would I poison my only granddaughter? I'll admit I've been on the Internet ever since I found out, trying to find all the best recipes. Now the gravy is easy. I can give you my recipe. No flour, just cornstarch. And the pie crust is no big deal. You just have to know which of the gluten-free flours to use for what. I'll write it all down for you before you go. I'm going to send the extra chicken home with you as well. You've got two teenagers to feed. I remember how much Robbie would eat. It can put a crimp in anyone's budget," she said with a sad smile.

Allison relaxed and smiled as she took a large piece of pie that Lisa held out to her.

"Bonnie is the best. She loves to take care of everyone. She still takes care of me," Lisa said happily.

Allison smiled at the love between the two women. Bonnie was Maggie's dad's mother, but she acted as if Lisa were her own daughter. A painful yearning filled Allison's heart as she wished someone would adopt her and be her mother. What she wouldn't give for someone she could turn to, feel safe with, and be loved by unconditionally. She looked down at her plate, but Lisa had seen her sad smile.

"You okay?" she asked softly.

Allison looked up in embarrassment. "Oh yeah. I'm fine. It's just nice to see the love between a mother and daughter. That's all."

Lisa reached over and patted Allison's knee. "Honey, I know exactly how you feel. Bonnie has been a blessing to me, but it wasn't always like this. I didn't have a loving relationship with my own mother, either. It's hard, I know."

Allison sniffed and nodded. "I feel like an orphan, to be honest. Maybe someday I'll find a new mom, like you did," she said with sad eyes.

Lisa patted her and nodded. "Heavenly Father will bring people into our lives when we need them. He'll give us mothers and fathers who aren't bound to us by blood, but by the Savior's love."

Allison smiled genuinely this time and picked up her fork again. "I hope so. I think moving back to Alpine was the right decision. Maggie and Luke have been wonderful neighbors. They've been so good to Talon and Aspen. And Maggie has been so determined to be my friend. I'm not sure I deserve a friend as good as Maggie."

Lisa grinned and looked across the table at her daughter. "Having Maggie in your life is always a good thing."

The peach pie was gone in minutes, and then Frank Tierney roped Talon, Aspen, and Luke into playing horseshoes. Allison stood and watched them happily while they laughed and enjoyed themselves. As Talon and Aspen joked and interacted with the kind older man she felt her heart relax. True, they weren't growing up with the influence of a father who held the priesthood to love, encourage, and watch out for them, but like Lisa had said, Heavenly Father was very generous with substitutes. Luke gave Talon a high-five and then threw his horseshoe. Life had a way of working out.

"Allison, why don't you come help me with the dishes while Maggie puts her feet up? Lisa, Maggie looks like she could use a foot massage there, Mama," Bonnie said with a steel-laced smile.

Lisa pulled Maggie toward a rocker swing happily, glad to have her daughter to herself. Allison swallowed nervously. That meant she was on her own with Bonnie. For some reason, she had the feeling Bonnie didn't like her very much. She felt her heart turn cold as she wondered if Bonnie and Frank had been victims of her father. She grabbed an armful of dishes and followed Bonnie into the cool, clean kitchen, decorated in yellows and warm earth tones.

"What a beautiful home Lisa has," she said nervously

Bonnie smiled. "We picked out all the colors together. They lived with us next door while they built. What a year that was. I think I loved every second of it."

She turned on the water and motioned for Allison to join her at the sink. They scraped and rinsed plates before putting them into the dishwasher.

"So . . . you're Felicia's daughter," Bonnie said with a small shake of her head.

Allison felt her stomach twist nervously. "You knew my mom?"

Bonnie nodded her head and rinsed a cup. "Oh yes. I knew your mom as well as I wanted to. I was her visiting teacher," she said as she handed the cup to Allison.

Allison had a feeling that Bonnie hadn't enjoyed visiting teaching her mom very much. She didn't feel like dancing around the real issue, so she decided to confront Bonnie head on.

"You obviously didn't like my mom very much. Does that mean you're automatically going to dislike me too?" she asked, turning and looking Bonnie in the eyes.

Bonnie sighed and looked up to meet Allison's eyes. The two women stood there staring at each other before Bonnie grabbed a dish-rag and wiped her hands on it before handing it to Allison.

"Wipe your hands and let's go sit down for a chat. Everyone else is fine without us for a while. And you and I need to have a talk."

Allison took the rag obediently and followed Bonnie after wiping her wet hands. She walked into the family room just off the kitchen and sat down nervously on the leather couch, uncertain of what she was about to hear. She wished with all her heart that she was outside with her younger brother and sister, throwing horseshoes.

Bonnie sat down opposite her in a chair, rather than beside her. "I didn't like your mother, Allison. And I like most people. But I couldn't take more than ten minutes with Felicia. I am curious to know if you take after her," Bonnie said with a surprisingly hard voice.

Allison sat up straighter and stared at Bonnie with narrowed eyes. *Who is she to make judgments about me?* "And why should I care what you think?" Allison said just as coldly.

Bonnie raised her eyebrows at the response and sat back in her chair, studying the young woman in front of her. "You don't have to care what I think, but I'll tell you why I'm worried. Maggie means the world to me. I love her more than my own life. And I don't want to see her spirit diminished by competition and false friendship. I watched your mom turn every church event into a fashion show. She had to make sure that she looked better than everyone, had the best clothes and nicest shoes and most stylish purse, and of course the most exciting life. She brought competition into our Relief Society and turned a group of loving, caring women into juvenile miserable idiots. And that was just the women. A few marriages were strained by your mother's incessant flirting as well. I celebrated the day your mother moved away," Bonnie said as she crossed her legs.

Allison sighed tiredly and rubbed her temples for a moment before answering. At least she wasn't being judged by her father this time. But would she ever be judged for herself?

"Look, I apologize on behalf of my mother for the problems and heartache she caused you and your friends. The only excuse I can make for her is that she was just a very insecure person. She grew up very poor and very shy. She had two sisters and a mother who were extremely competitive with her. They taught her from an early age that if you weren't the prettiest, then you just didn't matter. And then, to make matters worse, she met my dad on a blind date, and he pretty much turned her into the fashion plate you knew. She was just another token of his success. My mom soon realized that the only worth she had to my dad, and therefore as a human being, was that of a beautiful, desirable object. She had no clue that her greatest worth was what she had inside," she said with a shrug as she glanced at her watch. *Maybe she could grab Talon and Aspen and slip away with the excuse of homework.*

Bonnie studied her with her head tilted and her arms crossed over her chest. "And how did *you* grow up, Allison? You were raised by her."

Allison smoothed her faded jean skirt over her knees and wished she was anywhere but sitting across from Bonnie Tierney. But she looked up and met Bonnie's eyes straight on, because she knew if she didn't stand up for herself, no one else would.

"I grew up the same way. Measured and categorized and held up against an invisible standard of beauty and thinness *every day*. If you want me to sign a contract stating that I promise to never weigh less than Maggie or have a better purse or car than Maggie, I'll do it. I plan on being Maggie's friend. Mostly because Maggie won't have it any other way. So I would like to put your mind at ease, but even if I can't, facts are facts. We're friends. I don't hurt my friends, and I don't compete with them either."

Bonnie smiled slightly and relaxed her shoulders as she continued to study the girl in front of her. "Well, you're quite different than I imagined you'd be, Allison. I remember going to your home a couple times when you were younger, and you were always rushing out the door to be with your friends. You always seemed so controlled, so perfect, and *so cold*," she said in a softer voice.

Allison bit her lip and nodded as old memories rushed over her. "Well, when you're raised by Max and Felicia Vaughn, you learn at an early age to put up as many barriers as you possibly can, because then hopefully, if you're lucky, it won't hurt so much that your parents don't love you, don't like you, and couldn't care less about you. So, are we done here? Talon and Aspen have homework to do," she said, getting up and shoving her hands in her front pockets.

Bonnie nodded her head, looking slightly stunned, and stood up too. "Yes, yes, we're done," she said as Allison whirled around and walked quickly to the sliding glass doors leading to the backyard.

Allison stepped outside and breathed in a grateful breath of warm September air. *Freedom.* She walked quickly to where Aspen and Talon were still playing horseshoes and put on a false smile.

"Hey, guys, sorry to interrupt, but it's time to go. You both have homework due tomorrow."

Maggie struggled up from her seat. Luke looked at her quizzically and then turned to study Bonnie's somewhat guilty face.

"Please don't go yet," Maggie said, reaching out and taking Allison's hand. "We were going to light a fire in my grandpa's outdoor fire pit and roast marshmallows. You'll love it," she promised.

Aspen and Talon were both watching Allison with worried expressions on their faces. It was Talon who came to her rescue. "That's okay, Maggie. We're stuffed from the pie, and we really do need to get our homework done," he said, surprising Allison.

Allison stiffly thanked Bonnie and Frank for their hospitality and then fled to her truck. The ride home was silent as Aspen and Talon watched their sister wipe stray tears off her cheeks every few seconds. When they got in the house, Aspen took her hand and led her to the family room couch, sitting her down like a child and grabbing her other hand.

"So what happened in the kitchen?" Aspen asked, not caring at all about her homework due the next day.

Allison shrugged and tried to smile. "I'm sure Bonnie Tierney is a very nice woman. She just has a hard time with me being friends with Maggie. She used to know Mom, and she thinks I'm going to be just like her. She thinks I'm going to flirt with Maggie's husband and demean her and ruin her self-esteem."

Talon glared at the floor and shook his head angrily. "That's such crap! Why would she think that? You're *nothing* like Mom. You're nice and you love us and take care of us, and you don't even care what you look like," he said in her defense.

Allison laughed at the backhanded compliment. "Thanks, Tal. You're sweet. I told Bonnie I'd sign a contract if she wanted me to, promising to not be mean to Maggie, but I don't think that would matter. Once a Vaughn, always a Vaughn," she said, giving in to the bitterness that crept up on her every now and then.

Aspen's face collapsed in distress. "You told us we could cleanse the name. You said we can be great people, that it doesn't matter what happened in the past or who our parents are." Allison swallowed and nodded, rubbing a hand down Aspen's silky blonde hair. *Okay, time to back track.* She had to be strong for Aspen and Talon. Self-pity wasn't something she could indulge in.

"That's true, Aspen. It is our responsibility to cleanse the Vaughn name so all of our gorgeous little future Vaughns will grow up being proud of us. But in the meantime, we still have to put up with people who think we're guilty until proven innocent. It's not fun. And it's not fair. And it can make us sad. But you're right. We have to look at the bigger picture and not let other people pull us off track. The only way we can prove everyone wrong is by our actions. We have to be happy, good, nice people. And then, we'll start being judged for ourselves," she said, nodding her head to stress her words.

Talon leaned back on the couch and kicked his feet up on the old scarred coffee table.

"Man, I really liked Bonnie too *and* her cooking. I was dreaming of her inviting us over for Thanksgiving dinner. But now, *I just hate her guts.*" He said it with such venom, both she and Aspen blinked in shock.

"*Talon!*" Aspen whispered.

"Honey, please don't feel that way. I guess I shouldn't have said anything. But here's the deal. Even good, wonderful, nice people will make wrong judgments about us," she said, trying to soften her brother's heart.

Talon shook his head angrily. "No they don't. Good people don't judge. Jeez, it even says it in the Bible. *Thou shalt not judge.* If they think we're rotten, then they're even worse," he said, scowling at his sisters' concerned faces.

Allison sighed and felt bad for Luke for just a second before she threw him under the bus. But she had to make her point, or Talon would go through life being overly harsh.

"Okay, let me ask you a question then. Do you like Luke?"

Talon and Aspen looked at her like she was an idiot. "Of course we do. Luke is the best. The man can burp the alphabet," Talon said.

Aspen nodded in agreement. "We *love* Luke. He's the coolest guy in the world, and he always pays us more than he should. I love that."

Allison smiled warmly and nodded. "Well, okay then. You just proved my point. Guess what? Luke knew every bad thing about Dad when we moved in, and he told me to stay away from Maggie. He told me that she had plenty of friends and she didn't need the daughter of

Max Vaughn anywhere near her." Allison paused and studied Talon's and Aspen's shocked faces. They looked heartbroken. Their idol was now human.

"But guess what. We all proved him wrong. He realized he made a mistake in judging me before he knew me. And he got in *huge* trouble with Maggie when she found out what he'd said to me," she said with relish.

Talon's eyes looked cold and mean. "He really said that to you? And you let us go work for him?"

Allison nodded. "You two are the best Vaughns in the world. I couldn't think of a better way than to shove the fact that you guys rock in his face," she said, only slightly altering the truth.

Aspen smiled. "I bet Maggie was royally ticked at Luke."

Allison laughed. "Oh yeah. He came over *twice* to apologize. And thanks to you two, he now thinks *I'm* one of the most amazing people he knows. So it's a waste of time to hate people who hate us. All we have to do is let them get to know us and they'll come to their senses. If they don't? Well, then we don't need their friendship, do we?" she said almost cheerfully.

Aspen nodded with a smile, but Talon still frowned. "Sorry, but I still feel like punching Luke in the face."

Allison frowned and grabbed her brother in a tight hug, until he squirmed. "Sweetie, sometimes, we just gotta let it go. Like me. Bonnie hurt my feelings today. And now, I'm going to let it go. You just found out Luke made a mistake. But here's the deal. You and Luke are great friends. What's the point in ruining a great friendship over a little mistake? I'm *fine*, Tal. We're good. So you need to be good too," she said, running her hand through his wavy brown hair.

Talon sighed and shrugged. "Fine, I guess. But I need to think about it. And next time we play basketball—man, I am going to kick his trash," he said lethally.

Aspen laughed and stood up. "As if you could."

Allison smiled as they both went up the stairs to start their homework. Crisis resolved. *Hallelujah.*

She was straightening up the family room and wishing she had a good book to read when she heard a soft knock on the front door. She walked quickly down the hall to see Maggie and Luke standing on the other side of the glass-fronted door. *Uh oh. Now what?*

She opened the door with a curious smile. "Hey, guys."

Luke stepped forward, studying her face carefully. Allison frowned and hoped she didn't look like she had just cried all the way home. But she must have because Luke now looked even angrier and turned to look at Maggie with a pointed look on his face.

Maggie winced and stepped forward, enveloping Allison in a hug before she even said a word.

"Allison, *please* forgive my grandma. She just loves me more than she should. She felt kind of bad about the things she said to you in the kitchen and told us about your conversation," Maggie said as she pulled away.

Allison felt embarrassed and uncomfortable. "It's okay. I've already forgotten about it. Really," she said, blowing the whole thing off.

Luke shook his head, looking stubborn. "No, it's not okay. I saw the way you looked when you walked out of the house. Like someone had just punched you in the stomach. I love Bonnie, but if she doesn't come over here personally and apologize to you tomorrow, I'm going to get bent," he said, sounding truly ticked off.

Maggie laughed nervously. "If it makes you feel any better, Luke read my grandma the riot act. She got an earful, and she feels absolutely horrible. I don't know if she told us everything, but she said she sat you down and told you how she felt about your mom and wanted to know if you were like her. She said she was worried about the two of us being friends." Maggie frowned. "And then she said she was worried about you trying to steal Luke from me," Maggie said with a snort and a grin. "She has no idea how much you can't stand him."

Luke grinned and shook his head. "I know! And I told her that, but she doesn't believe me. She thinks I have this strange power of attraction over all women."

Allison had to laugh at that one. Maggie giggled too. "It's because of Jennie Benchley. Before we got married, he had so many women after him that he's a legend now. I guess my grandma just figured you'd worm your way into our hearts and then steal my husband from me and leave me alone with a baby to raise all by myself. Or something along those lines."

Luke looked uncomfortable and turned red in the face. Allison frowned and shook her head. "If it will put your mind to rest, I honestly won't. I mean, Luke's okay *now*. I don't want to run him over with my truck anymore, but seriously, I'd *never* . . ."

Maggie held up her hand. "Please. *Please.* We know. We explained everything to my grandma, and I think even my mom's mad at her. She knows she's in the wrong here. And we just wanted to check and see if you were okay. I'm just sorry she brought back bad memories and hurt your feelings. You're my friend, and I hate to see you hurt. Especially by someone I love," Maggie said, looking miserable.

Luke nodded. "Me too. I can't stand it either. I guess that makes you my friend."

Allison laughed and closed her eyes. "What a crazy, crazy life. *Me.* Friends with Luke Peterson, my ultra nemesis. *Wow.*"

Luke grinned. "I'm your ultra nemesis? Sweet."

Maggie sighed and rolled her eyes. "So will you give my grandma another chance, Allie? She has a good heart, I promise."

Allison chewed on her bottom lip. Regardless of the pep talk she had just given her brother and sister, she had planned on staying far, *far* away from Bonnie Tierney. But Maggie was her friend.

"Of course I'll give her another chance. Heck, I gave Luke one."

Maggie and Luke smiled and then looked worried as they stared at something behind Allison. Turning around, Allison saw Talon and Aspen, looking very cold and unfriendly.

"Hey, guys," Luke said with a worried smile.

Talon walked around his sister to stand in front of Luke. "Dude, if you ever say anything mean to my sister *ever* again, we're done," he said, sounding way too grown up and very serious.

Luke looked surprised and then frowned. "Allison, have you been telling on me *again*?" he asked, looking at her with his strange eyes turning a stormy green.

Allison blushed and grabbed her elbows, feeling guilty now. "I kind of had to. They were determined to hate your grandma, and so I told them that even good, nice people can make mistakes and that we have to just let things go sometimes. I might have used you as an example to show that even a pretty decent person can misjudge someone, *but* nevertheless deserves a second chance."

Luke sighed and then stared up at the sky for a second before looking Talon in the eyes, man to man. "If it will make you feel better to punch me, then you'd better just get it over with."

Talon's mouth fell open. He hadn't been expecting that. Luke stood there staring at him for a moment, but Talon was at a loss, so Luke turned to Aspen. "Okay, sweetie, get over here and kick me in the knees. Then we can move past all this mess. Okay?"

Aspen giggled nervously and looked to Allison for help. "I don't want to kick him."

Luke looked at everyone and then turned and walked down the porch steps to stand on their front lawn.

"Well, if it works for Allison, it should work for me. Talon, you and Aspen can wrestle me for the honor of your sister. No punching, kicking, biting, or hair pulling. If you win, then Allison's honor is safe. If I win, then I never have to apologize to your sister *ever* again," he said with his hands in a prayerful position.

Maggie laughed and went to sit on the front porch to watch the show. "This is why I love Luke. He's always surprising me."

Allison tried to smile as she sat next to Maggie and watched as Talon and Aspen walked slowly down the steps, looking at each other in silent communication.

"Man, I hope they don't hurt him too bad," Allison murmured as she began to chew on her nails.

Maggie looked at her in surprise. "Um, excuse me, but my husband is awesome. I don't mean to point out his gorgeous body—my grandma would have a heart attack if I did—but he's built. No one can take Luke," she said confidently.

Allison gagged slightly to herself and then watched as Talon circled one way and Aspen went the other. She remembered that Luke, although a talented basketball player, had never been a wrestler. He'd never been much of a fighter either. Luke was at a supreme disadvantage.

Allison grinned as she watched Talon dive at Luke's knees, bringing him down like a cougar taking down a deer. Luke lost his breath as Aspen jumped on his back, twisting his face into the grass, while Talon wrenched his arm behind his back.

"Hey!" Luke sputtered.

Aspen quickly shoved handfuls of itchy grass down his shirt and some into his gaping, shocked mouth. Talon twisted Luke onto his back while Aspen made sure his legs were intractable.

"So do we understand each other? My sister is off-limits. People should be judged for their own actions. Not their parents' crappy decisions," Talon said, panting now as Luke twisted this way and that, trying to knock him off.

"Fine," Luke said as he spit more grass out. "I will now officially adopt Allison into my own family. She will now be known by the name of Allison Peterson. Anyone who maligns her honor will be dishonoring me and therefore will have to pay dearly. Are we square?" he asked, as he stopped wiggling.

Talon sat back and thought about it. "Can me and Aspen change our names to Peterson too?"

Luke grinned and then threw both of the teenagers off and spent the next twenty minutes throwing them around the yard as if they were rag dolls. Allison would have been alarmed if it weren't for the grins and laughter. She knew instinctively that Luke would never hurt them. She and Maggie laughed and giggled as the three of them played in the front yard like puppies.

"Do you think they'll ever stop?" Maggie asked, looking on jealously.

"They'll wear out soon. You almost look like you want to join in."

Maggie laughed and rubbed her stomach. "You bet I do. I never had little brothers or sisters. As soon as I have this baby, we should have a wrestle mania. Girls against guys. You too, Allie. It'll be a blast."

Allison shook her head. "I don't know. Someone's got to hold the baby."

Maggie smiled and stood up. "Responsible as always. That's you, Allie, always thinking about everyone. Okay, guys! I'm exhausted just watching you. Luke, will you pry yourself away and walk this tired old pregnant woman home?"

Luke immediately hopped up and went to his wife, taking her hand and carefully guiding her down the steps. He was breathing hard, but his grin said it all.

"Good night, sis," he said in parting and took off with a wave.

"Did he just call you 'sis'?" Aspen asked, waving at Luke and Maggie.

Allison nodded her head and stood up. "Yeah. How weird is that? Luke's my new older brother. You'd better not mess with me or he'll beat you up," she said with a happy laugh.

Talon smiled at her as he walked up the steps. "You mean no one better mess with you, because your *younger* brother will beat him up."

Allison threw her arms around her little brother and couldn't help tearing up. "That's exactly what I meant, you stinker. You are the *best* brother in the whole world," she said, kissing him loudly on the cheek, whether he liked it or not.

Talon blushed and pulled away but smiled too. "Yep, and you'd better not forget it," he said, walking into the house.

Aspen smiled happily at the empty doorway. "Now we're all good again. I love wrestling. There's just no better way to clear the air, is there?"

Allison put her arm around her little sister as they walked back into the house. "You were kind of scary there too, Aspen. I didn't know you were that mad at Luke."

Aspen shrugged. "I didn't know I was either until I saw him there on our doorstep. And then I felt like punching him too. But not any-more. He totally let us win that first time. Can you believe that? He's going to have to take a shower. I swear he has a pound of grass down his back," she said proudly.

Allison laughed at the memory of her little sister gleefully shoving grass down Luke's shirt. If only she'd had a camera.

The rest of the night was strangely quiet and peaceful. Allison went to bed with a light heart and a new confidence. The day had proved that although some people were going to misjudge her, others wouldn't. And it was the people who would look past her circumstances to the real Allison that she wanted in her life.

Sixteen

Allison waved to Talon and Aspen as they walked to the bus stop, and then walked back inside the house to finish getting ready for her first day on the job. She changed out of her pajamas into a pair of jeans and a faded BYU T-shirt. She really didn't have too much to choose from. She pulled her hair back in a ponytail and then put on sunscreen. Because she would be sitting or standing in the sun for long periods of time, she had to be careful with her fair complexion. After putting on just the barest hint of makeup, she studied herself in the mirror. She didn't look like she was trying to impress anyone. However, she did look like she was ready to work. *Perfect.*

Allison smiled at herself in the mirror, knowing she was going against all of Aspen's careful advice about how to get a man's attention. And how Aspen knew this, she wasn't sure she wanted to know.

She grabbed her truck keys and headed out the door. It was a beautiful early September morning—still warm but with just a hint of coolness. She loved it. It only took her two minutes to get to work. Another plus for her. She parked her truck off to the side of the fruit stand and walked into the large shed. She waited until her eyes adjusted and then looked around. *Wow.* They had tons of fruit and vegetables—watermelons, strawberries, corn, peppers, cantaloupes, squash, and zucchini.

"It's bigger than it used to be, isn't it?" someone asked from behind her.

Betsy Carson looked almost the same. She had worked at the fruit stand five years ago when Will couldn't, and she'd always had on a worn-out sweat suit, and her bleached, permed, frizzy hair was always up in a high ponytail. She loved her makeup too. She was usually partial to blue and purple eye shadows but would sometimes, if the mood struck her, indulge in green. Allison grinned and walked forward. She'd always liked Betsy Carson. She was still wearing a sweat suit, but now it was a beautiful, expensive, silver-gray velour sweat suit. Her hair, once frizzy and damaged from all of the home processing, was now almost luxuriant and fell to her shoulders in a classic blonde A-line bob.

"Wow, you look amazing, Betsy," Allison said, grinning.

"I clean up pretty good, don't I?" Betsy said, turning around in a circle with her hand on her hip.

"Yes, you do. I love your hair. It's perfect for your face shape," she said, noticing the extra confidence and sparkle that Betsy had also acquired in the last five years.

"Will made me go see Candy at the salon, and I've been looking good ever since. I had a date last Saturday night too. I have to tell you, when a woman starts paying attention, the men start paying attention."

Allison laughed delightedly. "Well, good for you. I'm glad you're having fun. You deserve it," she said honestly.

Betsy sighed but her smile stayed in place. "Well, I don't know if I deserve it, but I'm still going to enjoy it either way. Now look at you—all grown up and beautiful too. I remember you'd always come by at least once a week and buy boxes of fruit. I always wondered if you were a health nut or if it was something else that brought you by our humble fruit stand," Betsy said with a twinkle in her eye.

Allison blushed and looked at a box of blackberries as if she were entranced by the fruit. "Well, you guys had the best fruit around. Who could resist?" she said nervously, remembering all those times she'd stop and buy peaches or whatever they were selling just so she could see Will for a few minutes.

Betsy made a snorting sound and walked toward the front of the shed. "Well, for whatever reason you stopped by, you were always good to my Bella. She always thought of you as one of her best friends. It just about broke my heart when she died two years ago of pneumonia. You were so sweet to her. She'd be happy the entire day and talk on and on about how you had given her a pack of gum, or a bracelet you didn't want anymore, or a cookie. From what Will told me, you went out of your way at school to make sure she was treated like a queen. And for that alone, I'd give you a job. Anything you need, you come to me," Betsy said with a firm nod.

Allison's face fell at the news of Bella's death. She'd barely heard anything else Betsy had said. "*She died?*" Allison whispered.

Betsy glanced back at her over her shoulder and then turned around and gave her a quick hug. "Sorry, sweetie, I thought someone would have told you. Didn't mean to tell you that way. It was time, dear. She's in heaven now, and there's no Down's syndrome in heaven. I know she looks down on me from time to time and watches out for me. I can feel her with me most days. It's okay, sweetie," Betsy said, patting Allison on the back soothingly as Allison wiped a few tears from her eyes.

"I'm sorry. It's just that I loved Bella. She was so pure and innocent and good and sweet. If I brightened her day, it was nothing compared to what she did for me. I looked forward to going to school, just so I could see Bella and—" Allison stopped before she could embarrass herself further. She'd almost said Will.

Betsy grinned and nodded. "Now, *that* I believe."

"Making your new employee cry on her first day of work? What kind of boss are you?"

Betsy and Allison turned so see Will standing in the side entrance.

"The best boss ever, as you well know. She didn't know Bella passed. I just mentioned it and she got a little teary. Nothing to worry about," Betsy said.

Will walked closer, studying Allison's face as she quickly wiped the rest of the tears away.

"Bella talked about you during her last week with us. She was always making presents for you, even after you moved away. She didn't understand that you weren't coming back. She made this super long colored macaroni necklace and she made me promise to give it to you. She said you were her best friend and you needed to have it. I still have it boxed away for you. I just didn't know where to send it," he said with a sad smile.

Allison turned around as new tears came. Bella had always been giving her pictures she'd colored for her. And she still had every one. She felt a warm hand on her shoulder.

"Hey, it's okay," he said and then surprised her by turning her around and pulling her into a strong, warm hug.

"She sure did love you," he murmured into her hair.

Allison nodded silently as she leaned her head on Will's chest and felt the comforting beat of his heart. She sighed deeply, not wanting to move, but pulled away quickly in case Betsy saw more in the hug than the friendly gesture it was.

"Thanks, Will. I'm okay. It was just a shock. I was actually thinking I'd see her today, and then to find out she died . . . I don't know . . . I just can't believe it."

Will rubbed her arms and then stepped back, glancing at his mom, who had taken a phone call in the meantime. Betsy had her back to them as she talked quietly, so Will turned to Allison.

"I never thought I'd see Allison Vaughn working at my fruit stand. I might have dreamed it a few times, but I never thought I'd see it," he said with a wry smile.

Allison sniffed her last tear away and smiled back. "Hey, I'm grateful to have this job. It's perfect for me. This way I can be with Talon and Aspen when they get home from school, and I can have my weekends off. I'm lucky your aunt Martha offered me the job."

Will leaned up against an old wooden fruit display and studied her. "Martha does the books for us and takes care of the hiring. Mom and I were kind of surprised when she called us Saturday and told us about our new employee. I am curious, though. Your little brother and sister are teenagers. You could have gotten a better job than this. You might have had to get home around five or six, but they're old enough to watch themselves."

Allison picked up a peach and rubbed a speck of dirt off of it. "Studies have shown that most teenagers get into trouble between three and five in the afternoon. Plus with the year they've had, they need me there. They need stability and the assurance that I'll be there for them. I'm all they've got left," she said simply.

Will looked down at his feet as if he were thinking hard about something, but then looked back up at her with a smile. "Well, you're just how I remember then, aren't you?" he said, smiling bigger now.

Allison shrugged and walked closer to Betsy. She had no idea what he was talking about.

"Yep, it's the same old me," she said airily.

Will followed her closely as she pretended to study the different fruits and vegetables as if she were at a museum, instead of fruit stand.

"So, Allison, I've been wanting to ask you, are you busy—"

"*Will!* Martha wants to talk to you," Betsy said, interrupting whatever Will was about to say by sticking her cell phone in his face.

Allison laughed at his put-out expression and watched as he walked away to take the call.

Betsy grinned at her boy before turning back to Allison. "Okay, here's the deal, kiddo. My son has held a torch for you for at least eight years that I know of. And yes, I'm serious. He's dated every girl from Alpine, to Cedar Hills, to Highland, and even girls from Salt Lake. But no one can ever compare to his memories of you. I'd really like to see some grandkids before I kick the bucket, so I'm going to give you a little advice. He's gotten a little spoiled and lazy these last few years. He needs a little challenge. If you want my son, and honey, *who doesn't*, don't throw yourself at him. You're a good girl, and I've always liked you. You never sneered at us, and you were good to my little girl. So I'm behind you and so is Martha. So don't screw this up," she said, ending in a whisper as Will came back into the shed.

Will looked from Allison's shocked face to his mother's too innocent expression and looked suspicious. "And what were you ladies talking about just now?"

Betsy smiled brightly. "Well, I just suggested that all we have to do to sell more fruit now is to put a big sign out by the side of the road, saying, 'Allison Vaughn is home! Come buy a peach from a real peach,'" she said, using her hands to emphasize each word.

Allison shook her head immediately. "Um, I don't think so."

Will laughed. "You know, I bet we'd double our profits. We need to have someone come by and take her picture. We'll blow it up and put it on a billboard by Kohler's. Great idea, Mom," he said, winking at Allison before kissing Betsy on the cheek and waving good-bye.

Allison frowned, not knowing if he was serious or not. Betsy laughed at her expression and took her by the elbow, leading her outside. Betsy showed her the till and the scale and how to make change. She stayed with Allison through the first three customers but then left her on her own.

Someone had added a large umbrella to the fruit stand so Allison didn't have to bake in the sun all day, which she was very grateful for. A couple hours later, Betsy brought her out a plate of sliced fruit and fresh tomatoes sprinkled with salt and pepper. Betsy then surprised her when she brought out a chair and her own plate of fruit and veggies and joined Allison.

"So what do you think so far? Will thinks you'll last a week and then be gone. He sees you more as the dental-assistant type or a secretary. He doesn't want to see you get your fingers dirty," she said with a raised eyebrow.

Allison sighed and took a sip of water. "Well, I don't have that much dirt under my fingernails, and I'm sticking. Like I said, this is the perfect job for me. I'll be here as long as you need me," she said, looking Betsy in the eye.

Betsy nodded. "You've got grit, girl. Good for you." She looked out over Alpine as if she were seeing it five years ago. "Life is so good now, almost too easy, to be honest. I remember how hard it used to be for him. It was hard to be his mom and know how wonderful he was and all he sacrificed to help our family survive and then to know that he was being laughed at and picked on and looked down on. I wish I had been smarter about business and money. When Will came back from his mission, I turned everything over to him, and he immediately sold off half our land. I'd had offers before, but I didn't trust anyone. It's a good thing too. When he sold, dirt was gold here in Alpine."

Allison munched on her fruit as she watched Betsy. She'd had a hard life, but the love she had for her son showed brightly through her eyes.

"Will's a good businessman. He develops land, builds houses, and does investments. He's got so many things going on, I've lost count. And no one laughs at him anymore. I always prayed for the day when Will could hold his head up high and be proud to be a Carson. Yep, things have changed. But me, I just want to stay here with the fruit. It's what I know, and it's what I love. He keeps telling me to go home and relax. Heck, he already pays a lady to clean my house for me now. What am I going to do at home? At least this way, I can see my friends and chat with everyone. I wouldn't trade this job for soaps or talk shows," she said, leaning back in her chair and lifting her already bronzed face to the sun. Betsy was a true sun-worshipper.

Allison smiled. "Betsy, Will might have been laughed at and picked on, but he was never ashamed to be a Carson. He's always been proud of who he is. That's one of the reasons I always looked up to him."

Betsy turned toward her, opening her eyes in surprise. "Well, I'll be danged. Martha's right. You are in love with him."

Allison choked on a tomato and had Betsy jumping up to pound her on the back.

"Now don't get hysterical. Facts are facts. No need to be embarrassed for loving someone. I'm flat-out happy you do. But don't you go working at his fancy office down the street. That would ruin everything. You just stay here with me, and things will work out just fine."

Allison wiped her mouth with her napkin and wished Betsy wasn't quite so outspoken.

"Betsy, it's been five years. I don't know what my feelings for Will are. Right now, I'm just impressed with the man he's turning out to be. I think we should leave it at that. And you can rest your mind. I won't quit on you."

Betsy sniffed. "It's Will I'm worried about. Not you. He's already called me once this morning, asking me if I wouldn't mind loaning you to him for the week to answer his phones. He just wants you all to himself. 'Uh-uh,' I told him. She's mine. I got her first," Betsy said with a cackle.

Allison laughed and looked at her knees. "I'm sure that's not what he meant."

Betsy shook her head and grabbed a slice of cantaloupe off her plate. "Honey, my Will has been beside himself since he found out you were back in town. It's only a matter of time before he makes his move. He thinks he can steal you away and make you some secretary. What a man. His daddy would have liked that one, though." She stood up. Lunch break was over.

Allison smiled to herself as she watched Betsy disappear and wondered if Will really was going to ask her out. It had almost seemed like he was going to before he had been interrupted this morning, but then he had left without a care in the world. She sat back and finished her tomatoes as she thought about Will. If they did start going out, Daphne and everyone else like her would just assume she was doing it for the money. She prayed Will wouldn't think so.

Just the idea of being with Will brought a bright, happy grin to her face. She had dreamed of Will Carson for as long as she'd known him. Tall, strong, hardworking, gorgeous Will Carson. What she wouldn't give to have just one more hug from him.

She threw her plate away, still smiling, and went back to work as two more cars drove up. She spent the first day getting used to everything and everyone. It was a change being around someone as blunt as Betsy, but in some ways it was a relief too. Betsy always let people know what she was thinking. There was no filter between her brain and her mouth. Allison kind of liked it.

At two o'clock one of Will's cousins, a skinny dark-haired boy named Mike, took over for Allison, so she grabbed her keys and purse and waved good-bye to Betsy. She couldn't wait to tell Talon and Aspen about her first day at work.

Betsy waved at her from the small desk in back. "Now you'd better be here tomorrow morning or I'm coming to find you!" she called with a smile.

Allison laughed, knowing Betsy wasn't kidding. "You couldn't keep me away," she promised.

As she hopped in her truck, she noticed something on the seat beside her that hadn't been there that morning—a long, beautiful red velvet jeweler's box with a bright yellow ribbon wrapped around it. Allison's breath hitched in her chest as she wondered what it could be and from whom, although she suspected Will immediately.

She opened it up, not to diamonds, but to colorful macaroni noodles, dyed in food coloring and strung with faded yarn. Allison smiled sadly, picked up the necklace, and lovingly put it over her head, moving her hair out of the way. She patted it in place and closed her eyes as she thought about Bella and all the times she had come up to Allison in school and thrown her arms around her neck. She'd always say, "I love you, Allie. You're my best friend." Allison had treasured those moments because besides Aspen and occasionally Talon, those were the only times anyone ever told her they loved her or showed her any affection.

Allison wiped one more tear away and wished with all her heart that she could have one more hug from Bella. She touched the necklace gently with her fingers and then started the truck. She drove out onto

Main Street and didn't even notice Will Carson standing in the shadows, watching her with a determined yet gentle look on his face. Will had just made up his mind.

SEVENTEEN

The next day Allison came home from work to see a strange car parked in front of the house. She immediately panicked and ran up the front steps, wrenching the front door open. Last time she'd heard, their father wasn't supposed to be let out of prison yet. But people were always getting out earlier than they should be. Thank goodness Talon and Aspen weren't home yet—their bus didn't come for fifteen more minutes.

Allison ran down the hall toward the kitchen but slowed down when she noticed the smell of rosemary and basil. *What?* She hurried into the kitchen and stopped in shock. Bonnie Tierney was standing at her stove, stirring a pot and looking right at home.

Allison stood there for a moment, wondering if there was any way she could just sneak back out, before she remembered she wasn't scared of Bonnie. She cleared her throat, and Bonnie turned around.

"I guess you're wondering what I'm doing in your house? I was thinking I had a fifty-fifty chance that you'd call the police on me. I'm hoping you won't, especially since I'm in the process of making you and the kids dinner. I found this great gluten-free recipe for lasagna on the Internet, and I know how kids like Italian." Bonnie was talking fast, as if she were out of breath.

Allison leaned up against the door frame as her heartbeat slowed down. "Well, Maggie would kill me if I called the cops on her grandma, so you're safe. But just for future reference, it really isn't normal to go into someone's house while they're gone and cook them dinner," she said almost sternly, reminding herself to be sure and lock the door

116

every time she left the house from now on.

Bonnie nodded but then shrugged. "I did the same thing to Maggie the day she moved to Alpine. When I want to do something nice for someone and I get an idea in my head, I just want to get it done right away. I hate waiting. And I didn't want to wait. Allison, I'm sorry. I'm *so* sorry. Maggie and Luke set me straight after you left, and I'm sorry that I was unkind and cruel. That's really not me at all. I like to think I'm a good person and that I'm nice and nonjudgmental. But I wasn't nice on Sunday, and I was being very judgmental. And I'm just sorrier than I can say," she said, twisting a dish towel in her hand and looking at her as if she were a tortured animal.

Allison looked down and huffed out a breath. *When is life going to stop being so dramatic?* She looked back up to see a tear streak down Bonnie's cheek and sighed.

"*Okay,* you're forgiven. Maggie is one very loved woman to have so many people worrying about me being a bad influence on her," Allison said as she walked into the kitchen and put her purse on the counter. She sat down and looked at Bonnie expectantly.

Bonnie sniffed and put the dishrag down. She turned and stirred the pot of sauce quickly a few times and then took it off the heat.

"Well, that's good then. You're a good person if you can forgive that easily. That's something I need to work on—obviously," Bonnie said as she took the drained noodles out of the colander and started placing them in a greased casserole dish.

Allison smiled wryly and rested her chin on her hands as she watched Bonnie begin to layer the lasagna. "Well, that's not altogether true. There are many people who would disagree with you. They think because I've banished my father from our lives, I must be a very unforgiving person," she said quietly.

Bonnie looked up and stared at her in confusion. "Why in the world would protecting yourself and your brother and sister mean you're unforgiving?" she asked as her eyebrows snapped together in a V.

Allison sighed and grabbed a stray piece of cheese off the counter to nibble on. "Thanks for that. So this lasagna is your peace offering then?" Allison asked with a smile.

Bonnie tilted her head and smiled as she turned to take the sauce off the stove and bring it to the counter. "Well, that and I promised you and the kids all the leftovers and you never got them. Just one more thing for me to feel lousy about. Frank had the rest of the fried chicken eaten by ten o'clock that night. I thought about making cookies, but cookies just didn't sum up how sorry I feel. So *yes*. This is my big gesture."

Allison closed her eyes and breathed in the fragrant smells of Italian herbs and sausage. *Heaven.* "Well, it's the best-smelling peace offering I've ever had," she said with a smile.

Bonnie finished putting the lasagna together and slipped it into the oven. Then she turned around with a satisfied smile on her face. "Well, that's just fine then. Now I'm going to put a salad together for you and boil you up some fresh corn on the cob from my garden. Then I'll get out of your hair," she promised as she grabbed the tomatoes and cucumbers from the sink.

Allison grinned as she thought of how good Talon and Aspen would be eating tonight.

"Now, if you like these gluten-free lasagna noodles, you just let me know and I'll order you an extra box next time I put in an order," Bonnie said as she began slicing the tomatoes on a cutting board she had brought with her.

Allison nodded. She studied Bonnie as she worked quickly and efficiently. *What would it be like to have a grandma like her? Someone willing to fight for you and protect you.* She'd never had anyone to fight for her or protect her. Maggie was one of the luckiest people she'd ever met.

"So, Bonnie, since you're here, why don't you fill me in on all things Alpine," she said, just to make conversation.

Bonnie looked up and smiled widely. "And by Alpine, would you happen to mean Will Carson?"

Allison laughed and blushed at the same time. "What has Maggie been telling you?" she demanded.

Bonnie shook her head. "My Maggie's not a gossiper, but last night she did tell me in the strictest of confidences that you had hopes of getting together with Will. She only told me, of course, because, like an idiot, I thought you were . . . well, let's just forget what I thought. Now I don't gossip either, but I do listen more than I should. I was standing in line just this afternoon at Kohler's, and guess who was right in front of me? Lexie Martin. You know, Daphne's mother? Well, she was busy talking her head off to someone on her cell phone and didn't even care how loud she was talking. She was just laughing and smiling and just delirious with happiness. She was going on and on about how depressed Daphne has been since you've moved back because everyone knows how much Will liked you in high school. Well, just this afternoon, it turns out that Will Carson offered Daphne the job of being his secretary at his new little office there on Main Street. Well, Lexie kept saying over and over how this was a sign that Will couldn't care less about you and that he's moved on to more sophisticated women like *her* daughter. Someone who can stand by him proudly and help him make a good impression with his investors," Bonnie said with a disgusted shake of her head.

Allison swallowed a painful lump in her throat and got up to get a glass of water. "Wow. He just offered her the job *this* afternoon. Lexie could be right. I mean, why would Will offer Daphne a job working for him every day if he wasn't interested in her? He's a smart guy. He knows how she feels about him," Allison said, feeling incredibly depressed all of a sudden.

Bonnie sniffed. "Well, it's a good thing you've got me looking out for you now, because as soon as I got out of the store, I called Martha, Will's aunt. I would have called Betsy, but she refuses to talk about Will's personal life. It's *so* annoying. So I got Martha on the line, and I told her what I'd overheard and demanded to know what was going on. Well, Martha's take on the situation is that Will is not interested in Daphne in *that* way. How could he be when she treated him like dirt when they were younger? She's not sure why he hired her, but she's sure there's a reason. And as soon as she figures it out, she's going to let me know. She promised. In the meantime, she thinks you're just darling and that Will and you will make the perfect couple," Bonnie said with a hopeful smile.

Allison tried to smile back as she took her seat at the counter again. "Well, thanks, Bonnie. I appreciate the info."

Bonnie waved her hand in the air. "Get used to it. You haven't had anyone to look out for you. Well, now you do. Consider me your new grandma. I always said I wanted lots of grandkids. Well, now I have me a few more," she said with a kind smile.

Allison grinned and shook her head as Bonnie grabbed the sack of corn on the cob, quickly and expertly husking the corn.

"I'll let you know something about me," Bonnie continued. "I hate being a failure. And when I was your mom's visiting teacher, I always felt like a failure. I wanted to serve your mom and could never figure

Shannon Guymon

out how. And then I was so irritated and annoyed by her, I didn't want to serve her. But that's all in the past. Now I finally know how to do my visiting teaching. It's about five or six years too late, but better late than never. The best thing I can do for your mom is look out for you. You're mine now, honey, whether you want to be or not. You need help? You call me. You need advice? You call me. Someone being mean to you? *You'd better call me.* You need a shoulder to cry on? You're crying on *my* shoulder. Anything at all, you call me. Got it?" she said with a twinkle in her eye.

Allison sat back, stunned. And to think she had just been wishing Bonnie was her grandma. She glanced up at the ceiling, wondering if angels were up there, listening in on her thoughts. She met Bonnie's kind eyes and nodded slowly. "I would actually really love that, Bonnie. Thank you," she said, not knowing what else to say.

Allison continued to watch Bonnie putter around the kitchen and felt her heart warm. But there was something she was still curious about.

"Bonnie? I've tried my whole life to understand my mom. Do you think if she had been married to someone else, things would have been different? That *she* would have been different? Because sometimes I would see glimpses of this woman, and she was amazing. I don't have any illusions about her, but regardless of everything she did and was, I loved her."

Bonnie wiped her hands on the kitchen towel and frowned as she thought about the question. "Well, I do know the people who surround us have an effect on us, whether we want them to or not. That's why teenagers are always told to be careful of the friends they choose. So it's a very interesting question. Heaven knows Max couldn't have been a good influence. Today I've tried to look at your mom with a little more compassion. It's very possible Max manipulated your mom's worst characteristics to suit his lifestyle, but then again, I don't know. Your dad was your dad, but your mom had her agency too. She knew your dad was stealing all that money, and she went right along with it. I wish she were here so we could ask her. Maybe someday you'll get that chance. But in the meantime, you've got me."

Allison grinned and relaxed even more. "That sounds good to me."

Bonnie smiled back as she wiped the counter. "By the way, Thanksgiving is at my house this year, so when Betsy invites you, you just tell

120

her I got to you first," she said with a sneaky laugh.

Allison laughed along with her and then turned around as she heard the front door open and the sound of Talon's and Aspen's shoes on the old wood floor.

"Hey! Allie? Where are you? You weren't waiting for us." Talon said as he came into the kitchen, looking worried.

Allison smiled, realizing this was the first day she hadn't been on the front porch. "Hey, Tal. Hi, Aspen. I came home to find Bonnie cooking lasagna for us. Isn't that nice?" she asked, her eyes going big as she silently begged them not to be mean.

Talon made room for Aspen as they stepped further into the kitchen, looking warily at Bonnie. Bonnie studied them with a sad smile. She took her apron off and folded it slowly. After placing it on the counter, she walked over to Talon and reached up to cup his face in her soft hands.

"Sweetie, will you ever forgive an old stupid woman for being unkind to your beautiful sister?"

Talon looked surprised and uncomfortable. He wasn't used to people touching him, not even kind grandmothers. He blushed slightly but didn't pull away. "We talked about it last night, and if Allie's okay with you, then I'm okay."

Bonnie smiled and patted his cheek. "Then we're right as rain, Talon. And what about you, Aspen? Can you forgive me for being unkind and judgmental? I want you to know that I realize how wrong I was and that now that I know more about your sister, I'm just grateful that Maggie has such a good person for a friend," she said as she took Aspen's hands in hers.

Aspen tilted her head and studied Bonnie. "You know, yesterday at dinner, I wished the whole time that you were my grandma. And then when I found out the things you said to Allie, I was just so sad and disappointed. I'm not mad at you, because I know you were just looking out for Maggie. And besides, Luke said a lot worse. But I just want you to know that from now on, you should really wait and get to know a person before you say mean things like that," Aspen said seriously.

Bonnie looked stricken for a moment but then smiled bravely. "You know, you're never too old to learn, are you? You are a very wise and good girl, Aspen. And just so you know, I've made my peace with Allison, and I've told her in no uncertain terms that I am now her grandma.

She's accepted me as such, which means I'm *your* new grandma now too. If you'll have me," she said hopefully.

Aspen looked to Talon and then to Allison, who nodded her head slightly in the affirmative. Aspen breathed in deeply and smiled.

"I always wanted a grandma who would come over and make yummy dinners for us," she said, smiling generously at Bonnie.

Bonnie laughed happily and pulled Aspen into a tight hug. "Well, you just got yourself a granny who loves to make yummy dinners. And that means there's always an open invitation to dinner at my house. Anytime Allison needs a night off cooking, you know where to go, and I'll be happy to stuff you silly. Now, Frank's part of this too. He wanted me to tell you that if you ever need a grandpa to fix anything that's broken or you need someone to go fishing with or to play chess with, he's your man," she said, turning to look triumphantly at Allison.

Allison grinned. Now she had two good friends, a strangely irritating older foster brother, and foster grandparents. Her family was getting surprisingly big.

"We accept on all counts. Thanks, Bonnie. Do you want to stay and have dinner with us?" Allison asked, standing up as Bonnie began to gather all of her washed cooking implements in a big bag she'd brought with her.

"Frank would be lost without me. I'd better get home and see what that man's up to. I'll be in touch," she said and walked out quickly with a wave of her fingers.

Allison, Talon, and Aspen stared at each other in awe. Alpine was turning out to be an interesting town to live in.

"*Wow.* That was kind of weird," Talon said, walking over to peek in the oven. What he saw put a big smile on his face.

Aspen went and peeked too. "A grandma who cooks—for us. I like it."

Allison laughed and agreed. "What's not to like? As soon as it starts bubbling, we can take it out and eat it. So in the meantime, why don't you guys get your homework done?" she asked.

Talon rolled his eyes and sat at the counter instead. Aspen took the other seat on Allie's right side.

"Nah, we'd rather hear about your first day of work. And when did you start wearing macaroni? Is this a new fashion statement, or is this all we can afford on our budget?" Aspen asked, smiling at the pretty macaroni beads.

Allison smiled sadly as she touched her precious necklace and told her brother and sister of a special little girl who had been her friend. She started to tell them about Betsy too when they heard a knock on the front door.

Talon ran to answer it as Allison began to describe the fruit stand. Then Talon came in, followed by Luke.

"Hey, guys, I was just wondering if you two felt like dusting and trimming today. *Holy cow*, what is that smell?" he asked, going right to the oven and peeking in.

Allison rolled her eyes as Luke made himself right at home. Talon and Aspen filled him in on Bonnie's visit and her offer of grandmotherhood. Luke grinned with satisfaction.

"Good. Now I can rest easy and Maggie can be happy. I think she's getting tired of being embarrassed by her relatives. Me being at the top of that list. So, is there enough for two more?" he asked, opening the oven door again.

Allison frowned in irritation. "If you keep opening the door like that, it's never going to cook. And yes, if you want to call Maggie to come over, we are more than happy to share." Luke grabbed his cell phone out of his pocket as Aspen took out her pre-calc test to show Luke her grade and Talon ran to get a new CD he wanted Luke to hear.

Allison sighed and gave up. Talon and Aspen loved Luke. She really needed to find a way to not be so irritated by him all the time.

Maggie came over ten minutes later, and while Aspen set the table, Allison pulled the corn out of the pot and Talon poured water into the glasses. They all sat down to dinner, and Maggie offered to give the prayer. Before she ended the prayer, she asked that Heavenly Father be sure and keep the Vaughns safe and happy. Allison smiled. She had a feeling that Heavenly Father listened carefully to Maggie's prayers.

Allison served everyone and sat down to one of the most pleasant dinners she'd ever had. It felt like a real family dinner. Aspen and Talon were on their best behavior and didn't say or do anything embarrassing. Luke entertained them with funny stories from the bank, and Maggie pulled out her latest ultrasound picture of the baby.

"So what are you going to name him?" Talon asked as he grabbed his third corn on the cob.

Maggie looked thoughtful for a moment. "I can't seem to make up my mind. I kind of want to name him Robert Luke Peterson, but then again, I kind of want to name him Talon Robert Peterson."

Talon looked stunned and held his corn in his hand stupidly. "You're thinking of naming your son after *me*? Why? I mean, you just barely met me," he said, finally putting his corn down and looking confused.

Maggie grinned as Luke took her hand and smiled at her. "Talon, I have just been so impressed by you ever since I met you. You've had it rough, but yet you are still such an awesome person. So smart, so loyal, and so kind, even though you try and hide it. I just love you, Talon, and if my son can grow up to be like you, then I'll be the happiest mom in the world," she said simply.

Talon cleared his throat and then looked down at his plate, speechless. Aspen patted Talon's knee and broke the silence.

"So if it were a little girl, would you have named her after me?" she asked, trying to look angelic.

Maggie laughed. "Now that's a hard one. I have a few amazing women in my life, and you're definitely one of them. Luke tells me I'm not done having kids, so there's always hope. If I ever do have a girl, for sure I'll name her Lisa Bonnie. But if I have twin girls, maybe the second one could be named Allison Aspen? Or a combination of the two. *Hmmm.* Aspison? Or Alli*sen*?" she said with a grin.

Allison grinned. "I bet you a million dollars you end up naming your son David and your future daughter Madison or something like that."

Maggie shrugged and smiled as she began to eat again. "Think what you want to, Allie, but I believe in naming children after strong, amazing people. Nobody's stronger than you Vaughns," she said as she shoved a huge mouthful of lasagna in her mouth.

Luke nodded his head in agreement. Allison, Talon, and Aspen shared shocked looks but let it go. After dinner, Talon and Aspen disappeared with Luke while Maggie helped her clean up the kitchen.

Allison told her what Bonnie had said about Will and Daphne to get Maggie's take on the situation. Maggie looked horrified.

"What is Will thinking? I never thought he'd fall under her spell. Most men do, granted, but I could've sworn Will saw through her. And with you back now? I've been planning your bridal shower in my head for days. I just can't believe this," she said, disgusted.

Allison laughed in horrified surprised. "You have to be kidding me. You were already planning my bridal shower? We haven't even been on a date yet!"

Maggie shrugged it off. "I guess I could be wrong, but I really never am. Honestly. I just don't get things like that wrong. Well, there's only one thing to be done. We'll have to throw a wrench into that situation," she said, sounding surprisingly serious.

Allison wrinkled her nose nervously. "Maggie, listen. You only have a couple months left till you have your baby. You need to relax and not worry about my pathetic love life," she said soothingly.

Maggie laughed. "Since I've changed my diet, I feel incredible. I have twice as much energy, and I can now rule the world again. And no way is Daphne going to steal your man," she said lethally.

Allison grimaced and thought of a country western song that went along those lines. "Well, this isn't exactly Daphne's fault. I mean, Will is the one who offered her the job. He wouldn't have her there if he didn't want her there. So if he's interested in her, there's really nothing anyone can say or do. Love is love. There's really no logic to it," she said, trying to sound mature.

Maggie rolled her eyes and took out her cell phone. In less than thirty seconds she had Sophie on the line.

"Sophie?" Maggie said. "Sophie, you won't believe what I just found out. . . . I know! Can you believe it? . . . Me either. What should we do? . . . Okay, but what will Sam say? . . . Uh uh . . . . Well, I don't want you to get caught. You know what happened last time. . . . Okay, I'll see you tomorrow. . . . Yes, we definitely have our work cut out for us. . . . Okay, bye!" Maggie hung up, looking determined.

Allison felt faint. "What just happened?"

Maggie took Allison by the arm and steered her to the couch in the family room.

"Now don't panic. Sophie is just going to do a little reconnaissance work for us. She's going into the office tomorrow to check out the chemistry and see what Daphne thinks of her new job. If this is marriage prep, then we bring out the big guns. If this is on the up and up and Will just hired her because he was desperate for a secretary and he didn't care who he hired, then no big deal."

Allison bit her lip and shook her head. "I don't know. I don't think we should intrude at his workplace. That's kind of . . . I don't know . . . pushy?"

Maggie looked at her like she was crazy. "Honey, like a wise woman once told me, you have to mark your territory and mark it big. Just leave it up to us."

Allison winced but nodded. She was very curious as to why Will would hire Daphne practically right after he'd been on the phone with his mom trying to get Allison to be his secretary. Maybe he was just playing games. She frowned at this thought but immediately pushed it away. Will would never do that.

Allison said good-bye to Maggie ten minutes later and then finished wiping down the table. Feeling bored, she ran up to Talon's room and grabbed his laptop. The three of them shared the computer since money was tight. She decided to Google Will and see what came up. She wanted to know what he'd been up to during the last five years.

She opened the laptop and was surprised to see that Talon hadn't logged off of facebook. She frowned. Who would Talon even want to keep in touch with? All of their friends from Dallas had dropped them like hot coals after their father had been convicted and their house and all their possessions were confiscated by the FBI She scanned down Talon's page and noticed a lot of entries by some guy named Bill Kidd. She glanced at his picture, but he'd chosen to use a scene from some island resort instead of his actual face. Allison frowned and clicked into Talon's private inbox.

> Bill: Hey, Tal! Hope to see you soon. It's been too long. Let me know when you can break away from your warden and we'll take off to the beach of your choice. Don't tell Aspen if you think she'll rat you out.
>
> Talon: I don't know, Dad. Allison would freak. We're doing really good here. I don't want to mess it up.
>
> Bill: Son, you've just been brain washed. You can't listen to Allison about anything. She hates me and she wants everyone to hate me. I think she has a mental illness or something. All I've ever done is try and provide a good life for her, and this is the thanks I get! She tries to keep me away from my

own children. Now come on, Talon. You and me hanging out at the beach. Snorkeling, scuba diving, and more chicks in bikinis than you can imagine.

Talon: I'll think about it.

Bill: While you're thinking about it, can you give me your social security number so I can get you a new passport? I'll hold off on the plane tickets, but just in case you change your mind, we'll need that. And if you decide not to, then that's okay too. I love you, son.

Talon: Okay.

Allison looked up, feeling sick and weak. Talon had just given their father his social security number. She looked at the date on Talon's last message and learned that it was just one week ago. She noticed that immediately after he'd given their dad his number, he hadn't heard from him again. She clicked on Bill's page and scanned the information. No friends except Talon. And once he'd gotten what he wanted, he was gone. It was official. Her dad was out of jail and on the hunt.

Allison leaned her head on her hands, knowing what their father was capable of. She glanced out the window and saw Luke washing his car while Talon edged the lawn. She set the laptop down on Talon's bed and ran downstairs. She needed to talk to Luke.

She waved at Talon and walked quickly to Luke's side. He turned the hose off and looked at her strangely.

"Oh my heck, what now? Who else in our family has insulted you?" he demanded.

Allison waved that off impatiently. "Can you come back over to my house for a minute, please? I need to show you something. *Quickly*," she said impatiently, looking over her shoulder at Talon. Talon had his ear buds in and was paying absolutely no attention to them.

Luke nodded and followed her back to her house. She ran up the stairs and brought the laptop down, showing the page of messages to Luke.

"Bill is my dad. *Get it?* Billy the Kid? He's got Talon's social security number, Luke. What am I going to do?" she asked, feeling almost hysterical.

Luke held up his hand as he read the messages, frowning and looking very grim as he came to the end. He finally looked up at her and shook his head.

"You were right to try to protect them, Allison. I'll bet you anything Max has just taken out a few credit cards in Talon's name. And since this was last week, I bet he's already run up thousands of dollars on them. Let me get on this and see what I can do to put a stop to it. All it will take is one call to his parole officer, *unless* he's already left the country. I'll get to the bottom of this. I've seen it before. Kids just like your brother are stuck with ruined credit before they've even started to live. It's tragic. Don't worry, though. There are ways to fight this. I promise."

Allison nodded and wiped a tear off her cheek. "He was so sure his dad would never hurt him. He's resented me this whole time for bringing him to Alpine. But he still got to us. We're not safe anywhere, are we?"

Luke's eyes were the color of a cold green lake. "You moved in right next to me, Allison. I'm an expert on identity theft. Most bankers are. This could have happened anywhere, but here, you've got me on your side. And trust me, Max Vaughn does not want me on his tail."

Allison tried to smile as Luke put the laptop down. He surprised her by giving her a quick hug. "Try not to worry too much about this. Don't tell Talon anything until I do a credit check tomorrow. Let's find out what we're up against before we tell him what Max did."

Allison nodded and watched as Luke walked out of the room. She sat on the couch, feeling exhausted. It seemed like life was one trial after another. And she had been so sure they were due for a break. She logged out of facebook and shut the laptop before leaving the room. *Maybe Luke could tell Talon for me? Maybe it would be easier to take from a banker? Yeah right.* There was no easy way to tell someone that his father used him and stole his identity and his future from him.

eighteen

Allison tried to smile as she went in to work the next day. She didn't want Betsy to take one look at her and pull the whole sordid mess out of her.

"Hey, gorgeous!" Betsy called. "Come over here and help me with this crate of peaches. You're going to be busy today. I just have to put a sign by the road that says 'peaches,' and we're busy from sunup till sundown. It's my favorite time of year," she said with a grin.

Allison helped Betsy lift a crate from the floor to the old wooden table.

"Hey, what's wrong with you?" Betsy demanded as she took a closer look at Allison.

Allison tried to smile bigger, but Betsy shook her head. "Uh-uh, something's wrong," Betsy said, but then grinned as she slapped her thigh. "Oh, you don't have to explain. I know why you're moping around this morning. You must have heard about Will giving Daphne the secretary job," she said with a laugh.

Allison actually smiled for real at that. If only Daphne were her only problem.

"Well, actually, no. That's not it at all," she began but stopped when Betsy held her hand up.

"Please, don't embarrass yourself, sweetie. Don't you worry about it for a second. No way is Daphne going to be my daughter-in-law. No way, sister. Will's a smart man—you'll see," Betsy said with a sneaky grin.

Allison groaned and followed Betsy out to the roadside stand. "Please don't get involved with this, Betsy. Like I told Maggie last night, no one forced him to hire Daphne. He hired her because *he wanted to*. And to be honest, I don't even care. I have too much going on to even think about dating anyone right now," she said, pushing a stray lock of wavy blonde hair over her ear.

Betsy turned back and glared at her. "Are you crazy? Of course I'm involved in my son's life. I have just as much say in who he marries as he does. That's the way the good Lord intended it," she said with a loud sniff.

Allison grinned and felt sorry for Will. "Just keep me out of it then."

Betsy's bright pink lips turned up into a wide Cheshire cat smile. "Like that's going to happen."

Allison sighed and prepared a lecture on agency, but a car drove up, quickly silencing her.

"Oh good, a customer," Betsy said, glancing at her watch. But her smile quickly turned cool when Gage Dulaney pulled himself out of his bright red car. Allison's smile faded too.

"Well, hi, Gage. What brings you to our humble fruit stand this morning?" Betsy asked in a perfectly polite voice.

Gage barely glanced at Betsy. "Oh, it's not the fruit I'm interested in, Mrs. Carson. I heard yesterday from Daphne that Allison is working here now. I couldn't believe my ears. I had to come and see for myself."

Allison glanced at Betsy nervously, hoping the woman wouldn't say anything outrageous. Betsy's face turned a scary shade of red, but her mouth remained pursed tightly shut.

Allison cleared her throat and grabbed the apron off the back of her chair, tying it around her waist. "Well, as you can see, Gage, I *am* working here. And I'm very grateful to the Carsons for offering me this job. It's perfect for my schedule, and I couldn't be happier," she said honestly and with a bright smile.

Betsy's face relaxed a little, but her arms were crossed over her chest and she still looked like she wanted to throttle Gage. Gage was oblivious to Betsy's reaction to him. He continued to stand there, staring at her almost rudely. Betsy let out a huff of irritation and then took out her cell phone and walked quickly back into the shed, leaving

Allison alone with Gage. Allison felt like calling Betsy back. For some reason, she didn't feel comfortable being alone with him.

"Allison, what if I offered you a job at my dad's real estate office? We could start you out answering phones while you take your real estate classes. In six months or so you could be an agent working with me. Dad says he would love to have you on board with us. We're the best realtors in Alpine. You'd love it. And I promise you, you'd like it more than sitting in the sun every day, selling fruit like some nobody," he said with a snide laugh.

Allison frowned and felt her stomach cramp up. She didn't want to work with Gage. If the offer had come from anyone else, she might have jumped on it. But just the idea of those cold, hypnotic, almost reptilian eyes staring at her every day made her want to run.

She was spared having to answer as another car pulled up. It was Will Carson in a sleek silver Maserati. His long legs unfolded from the car, and he appeared a second later, walking toward them with an unfriendly smile on his face.

"Well, Gage, what a surprise. I didn't know you ate fruit. I thought you just sucked the blood out of people," he said in a surprisingly cold voice.

Gage grinned at Will, enjoying himself. "Nah, I don't eat Carson fruit. You know I have high standards. I was just here offering your new employee the job of a lifetime. My dad's willing to pay for her to go to real-estate school if she dumps this job and comes to work for us," he said triumphantly, as if Allison had already agreed to take the job.

Will's face turned to concrete as he looked at Allison. She swallowed helplessly, not knowing what to say. Betsy rejoined the group and put her arm around Allison's shoulder.

"Allison probably needs a few days to think about it. Right, Allison?" Betsy suggested.

Allison jumped on the life line. "Yes! Yes, I do. Thank you so much for the offer, Gage, and please tell your dad how grateful I am. I need to talk it over with Talon and Aspen first. I only have so many hours I can spare, which is why this job here at the fruit stand is so perfect for me right now," she said, twisting her hands in front of her.

Gage frowned and put his hands in his front pockets. "What do you mean you only have so many hours? The real estate game is a serious business, Allison. You and I will need to be able to see clients at night, on the weekends, and whenever we get the calls. I'm going to love having you at my beck and call. It'll make up for all those times you kept me at arm's length in high school," he said with a satisfied grin.

Allison winced and glanced at Will's face. He did not look happy. "Gage, if that's the case, then I think I'll stay here with Betsy. I can't work weekends or nights. I have two teenagers to care for," she said, feeling relieved but trying to look sad for Gage's benefit.

Gage rolled his eyes and shook his head. "Teenagers are practically adults. They can take care of themselves. Just think about it, Allison. Think of what you could do for your brother and sister with the money you'll be making. We'll be paying you two or three times what Will could. And when you start making commissions, you'll be able to move out of that crummy rental you're in. You'll be back living the lifestyle you're used to. Trust me, teenagers these days will trade anything and anyone for some extra cash to play with," he said with a compelling smile.

Will looked down at his feet for a second before looking back at Gage. "She doesn't want your job, Gage. She values Talon and Aspen more than her old lifestyle."

Allison appreciated Will's input and hoped Gage would just take his defeat and leave. Gage laughed.

"I don't think so, Will. Besides, you have nothing better to offer her. Daphne told me she's working for you now. And when it starts snowing, what's she going to do then? Shovel your walks for you? Clean your office and your toilets for you? Don't you know who this is? This is Allison Vaughn. Come on, Allison. Quit right now and come with me. We'll go out to lunch and negotiate your salary," he said, reaching a hand out to her.

Will raised his eyebrows and looked at her. Allison glanced at Betsy, and Betsy gave her an encouraging nod. Allison licked her lips and straightened her shoulders. "I'm fine cleaning toilets or shoveling snow, Gage. Talon and Aspen really are the most important thing in my life right now. Thank you so much for your kind offer, but I'm afraid the answer is no," she said firmly.

Gage swallowed and looked away as he let his hand fall to his side. "Well, if that's the way you want it. I'm a nice guy, though. When you decide you can't take it anymore, you come to me. The job offer stays on the table for however long it takes you to come to your senses," he said and then leaned over and kissed Allison on the cheek.

Allison smiled but felt like wiping her cheek for some reason. They all watched as Gage stepped into his car and roared off down the street.

Betsy looked after the car in disgust. "Good riddance," she said and walked quickly back to the shed, leaving Allison alone with Will. Allison straightened her apron unnecessarily as Will continued to study her.

"Why didn't you take the job? You're crazy not to," he said honestly.

Allison smiled and shrugged. "I might be crazy, but I'm not stupid. If I took that job, it would mean I owed Gage and his dad big time. And I don't think I want to be in that position," she said, feeling shaky now that Gage was gone.

Will clenched his jaw but didn't respond. Allison sighed and wondered what he was thinking. "So what brings you to our humble fruit stand this morning?" she asked, trying to lighten the mood and change the subject.

Will grinned. "You mean, what brings me to *my* humble fruit stand this morning? You, of course. I wanted to see if you showed up to work today."

Allison laughed and straightened the fruit on the stand. "Of course I'm here. Betsy would fire me if I didn't show up."

Will smiled. "That she would. Well, it looks like you have everything under control here. I'll leave you to it," he said and turned to walk away.

Allison turned to watch him and couldn't help calling out. "So Daphne's your new secretary."

Will immediately turned around and studied her face carefully. "That's right. Your old best friend from high school."

Allison polished a peach on her apron and set it back down. "Well, I hope she works out for you. She was always good at talking on the phone."

Will smiled and walked slowly back toward her. "I wouldn't know.

She never called me back then. Of course, neither did you."

Allison looked away and shrugged. "You're right. But then, I never called *any* boys back then."

Will leaned up against the cart and frowned. "But if you *had* been in the habit of calling boys, who would you have called? Just out of curiosity."

Allison kicked a pebble with her old sneaker and smiled wryly. "You mean if I knew my father wouldn't turn my relationship into some kind of business leverage?"

Will nodded.

"Well then, I would have called you," she said honestly.

Will grinned. "Really?"

Allison laughed and pushed her hair out of her face. "Don't be an idiot. You knew I had a crush on you in high school."

Will snorted and shook his head. "No, I did *not*. All I knew was that you went out of your way to talk to me and that you smiled at me a lot. But every time I acted like I was going to ask you out, you started talking about your boyfriend at Harvard," he said, his eyes narrowing at the memory.

Allison grinned and went back to polishing fruit. "Will, just be grateful. Me and my imaginary boyfriend from Harvard spared you from my father. He would have eaten you alive. My father always wanted me to go out with the sons of his investors. I refused. I didn't want to be used in that way. I already had my friends chosen for me. I didn't want my love life controlled too. And if I had brought you home to my father, well, let's just say I liked you too much to see you go through that," she said honestly and with a dry smile.

Will stared at her with an impatient look on his face. "Allison, where is your imagination? We could have snuck around. Remember Romeo and Juliet? We could have hung out at my house. You wouldn't take a chance on being with me because you wanted to spare me? Crap, Allison. You should have told me. I could have planned it all out," he said in irritation.

Allison shook her head and straightened some boxes. "Will, you were working yourself to death just to keep your family afloat. You didn't have the time to sneak around kissing me. Plus, you deserved more. You deserved to be treated with respect. Any girl should have been proud to have been your girlfriend. You didn't deserve to be hidden like something to be ashamed of. I either wanted you out in the open or not at all."

Will looked poleaxed. He opened his mouth to say something and then closed it again. His phone rang in his pocket and he answered it quickly. "This is Will. . . . Oh. . . . Yes, Daphne, I'll be back soon. Thanks, just tell him to take a seat." He slipped his cell phone in his pocket and then stared at Allison again.

"What about now? Do you think you can handle a relationship out in the open now?"

Allison smiled as she felt her stomach do a happy flip. "With *you?*"

Will glared at her. "Of course with me. Who did you think I was talking about? Gage?" he demanded.

Allison shrugged. "Well, things are different now, aren't they? You're the ultra rich one and I'm the poor fruit stand worker. You might want to think about that. What will your business investors think if you start dating Max Vaughn's daughter? I'm pretty much a social liability right now, Will," she said sadly, knowing it was true.

Will put his hands on his hips and laughed. "You're kidding me, right?"

Allison huffed out a breath. "Actually, no. I'm not kidding you. What will you do when people start whispering that I'm only dating you for your money? You might be able to ignore it for a little while, but after a few months, you'll start having your doubts. Sorry, Will, but you'd better stick to your side of Main Street, and I'll stick to mine." Even though she spoke firmly, she hoped he would disagree with her.

Will shook his head at her as his phone rang again. He answered it and said, "Yeah. . . . Okay, I'm coming." After hanging up, he looked coldly at her. "Well, when you're ready to stop caring so much about what other people think, let me know," he said stiffly and then walked away.

Allison felt empty as she watched Will drive quickly away. She was such an idiot.

"Now that's what I'm talking about!" Betsy said, running up to her and giving her a huge hug. "Honey, you are a pro. Will needs a little challenge. This is perfect. I've gotta call Martha," Betsy sang out as she skipped back up to the shed.

Shannon Guymon •∗ ✳

Allison slumped down in her chair and sighed unhappily as two cars drove up. She'd just said no to an incredible job opportunity, and she'd just turned Will Carson down, not for a date, but for a whole relationship. She was just too dumb to live.

Nineteen

Allison was exhausted after work. Everybody in Alpine had wanted their share of the peach crop today. Betsy told her it was going to be like this for two straight weeks. She walked in the house and collapsed on the couch, kicking up her tired feet. A glance at the clock told her she had fifteen minutes before Talon and Aspen got off the bus. She dragged herself to the fridge and grabbed an apple, deciding she'd go sit on the front porch and recharge.

She sank down on the top step, but before she'd taken one bite from her apple, Maggie headed her way, waddling for all she was worth. Allison grinned at the picture she made. Maggie looked beautiful now that her face wasn't so puffy and bloated. And she looked like she'd lost some weight. Allison was starting to see who the real Maggie was, and she could understand why Luke had fallen in love with her. Maggie had an awesome vitality that made everyone else in the world look pale in comparison.

"Hey, Maggie, how are you feeling?" Allison asked as she scooted over on the step.

Maggie grinned and sat down heavily with a bag of Spicy Hot Doritos. She offered the bag to Allison, who dove in gratefully. They couldn't afford fun junk food like chips.

"I'm great," Maggie replied. "Talon's been kicking up a storm today. It's like the kid already knows jujitsu or something," she said proudly.

Allison looked confused for a minute and then laughed. "Are you serious? You're really going to name your firstborn child after my little brother?" she asked in disbelief.

Maggie looked taken aback. "I told you I was. And I like calling the baby by his name. It helps me feel more connected to him," she said with a soft smile.

Allison grinned and took another chip. "Well, that's pretty neat then."

Maggie nodded as she finished chewing a mouthful. "Did you tell him about 'Bill'?" she asked in a more serious tone.

Allison glanced at her and shook her head. Of course Luke would have told his wife. "No. I'm waiting to see what Luke finds out today. He said he'd come over after work and let me know. I'm pretty sure it will be bad news, though," she said, feeling a heavy blanket of sadness enfold her.

Maggie sighed. "I can't even fathom it, to be honest. A father doing this to his own child," she said with a shake of her head. "It's almost unreal. How do you go on after something like this? How have you done it, Allison? I mean, you've been dealing with this fallout for years now. How do you stay so strong? Here you are, taking on the responsibility of two kids. You take them to church every Sunday. You're a good person. How do you do it when you have no foundation and no support from parents?" she asked almost angrily.

Allison sighed loudly and looked up at the sky as she thought about it. "Well, how did your mom survive when she was betrayed by her stepfather? People in general are pretty resilient."

Maggie shook her head. "No, it's more than that."

Allison nodded in agreement. "You're right. It's more than that. When I was about fourteen, I was at girls camp. I'd been there a few days and we had just been to this incredible testimony meeting out in the middle of this clearing surrounded by trees. The Spirit was so strong, I just couldn't stop crying. It was the first time I'd felt the Spirit. It was the first time I knew for a fact that Heavenly Father really was up there and that He loved me. Well, we got back to our cabin, and one of my leaders asked me to give the prayer. I was so choked up, I only got a few words out. But ever since that day, He's been with me. Some days more than others, depending on how faithful I am with my prayers and scripture reading, of course, but He's never left me. Through it all, I knew I was never alone. So yeah, life can be hard and rip your heart out, but when you really know that there's a plan for you and that life has meaning and purpose, then it's not so bad." Allison looked away, embarrassed at sharing such personal feelings.

Maggie smiled at her and put her arm around her shoulder. "Allie, you are too cool. But what about Talon? What's his testimony like? Do you think he's anchored enough to handle this new situation?"

Allison bit her lip as the bus drove down the street. "I honestly don't know. All I can do now is hope he is."

Maggie stood up with Allison and waved to Talon and Aspen as they hopped off the bus. They both waved back happily.

"Well, I'll leave you to your family. Call me if you need me, though," Maggie said, squeezing Allison's arm.

Allison smiled and nodded as Aspen ran up, waving her hand in the air. "Look!"

Allison grinned and grabbed Aspen's hand, looking at the huge school ring hanging off Aspen skinny finger.

"Did you find it in the lost and found?" she asked with a laugh.

Talon walked up and rolled his eyes. "Spare me," he said and walked up the stairs.

"Rowan gave it to me today," Aspen said happily, giggling as she held her hand up to the sun. "It's official. He wants me to be his girl-friend, and he wants the whole world to know it."

Maggie grinned and gave Aspen a quick hug. "I'm happy for you, Aspen, but please tell me you're not going to wait two years for him when he goes on his mission."

Aspen paused and frowned. "Wow, I haven't thought that far ahead. Two years is a long time to wait."

Allison shook her head. "Well, we don't need to decide right now. Come on in and get a snack. All that happiness is going to wear you out if you don't get some calories."

Aspen waved at Maggie and ran in the house. Allison turned to follow but saw Luke drive up, so she walked quickly over to his car instead of joining Talon and Aspen in the house.

Maggie got to Luke at the same time Allison did. She put her arms around his waist and looked up expectantly. "Well?"

Luke frowned and shut the car door, looking at Allison sadly. "It's not good news. He took out five credit cards under Talon's name. Three of them have been maxed out already with cash advances. The other two are almost at their limits. We're looking at over forty thousand dollars right now. I talked to your dad's parole officer this afternoon, and he can't find Max anywhere. He's disappeared. I put a hold on Talon's credit so Max can't take out any more while we try to fix this mess."

Allison's shoulders slumped as her suspicions were confirmed. "Now what? What can we do?"

Luke rubbed Maggie's arm soothingly as he looked toward the mountains for a minute before looking back at Allison.

"The first thing we have to do to clear Talon's name and credit is to file charges against Max. And Talon's the one who has to do it. The credit companies demand it these days. And you might want to think about getting Talon a new social security number. We'll work hard to get this all cleared up, but in three years, Max can just do it again if Talon has the same social security number."

Allison shoved her hands in her front pockets and felt like crying. She held it in, though. She'd done enough crying over her father. "Will you help me tell him?" she asked Luke.

Luke nodded. "Of course. I was planning on it. Do you want Maggie to be there too?"

Allison nodded. "I think if Talon can see all the support he has, it'll be a little easier to take."

Maggie nodded her head in agreement, and the three of them walked slowly back to her house. They walked in to find Talon and Aspen reheating leftover lasagna in the microwave and laughing. Allison felt horrible at having to ruin their happy moods. Talon was just now relaxing and acting like his normal, happy self. Would he revert to being depressed and angry? Luke looked at her and smiled encouragingly.

"It'll be okay," he said softly.

Talon and Aspen finally noticed them and grinned. "Hey, let us grab a snack first before you put us to work," Talon said jokingly.

Luke smiled back and walked over to the pan. "Hey, I could use a snack too."

Aspen smiled and grabbed an extra plate for him. "So what do you have for us today? Bathrooms, kitchen, or yard work?" she asked.

Maggie looked at the two teenagers and burst into tears. "I'm sorry. It must be my hormones," she said apologetically.

Talon and Aspen looked at her in surprise and then noticed Luke's and Allison's grim expressions.

"What's wrong? Is the baby okay?" Talon asked worriedly and put his fork down.

Maggie shook her head. "No, honey, we're good. It's you I'm worried about," she said, turning to cry on Luke's shoulder.

Aspen frowned and walked to Allison. "What's going on, Allie? Are we in trouble again?" she asked, her voice high and nervous.

Allison knew she had to be the one to tell them. It was only right.

"Yes, Aspen, we're in trouble again. Yesterday I went upstairs to use the computer, and Talon had forgotten to log off facebook." She turned to him. "I checked out your profile and saw Dad had left you a few messages. That's when I found out you had given Dad your social security number. I asked Luke to do a credit check on you today, and it turns out Dad has taken out five credit cards under your name and has maxed them out with cash advances."

Talon's face turned white as he stared at his sister. "*No.* No he couldn't have. He wouldn't do that to me," he whispered.

Luke stepped forward to stand by Allison. "It's the truth. Almost forty thousand dollars. I have the printouts right here," he said, pulling a few folded papers out of his jacket pocket and handing them to Talon.

Talon's hands shook as he took the papers and slowly opened them. He studied the numbers for a moment before he carefully put the papers down on the counter. "Why would he do that to me? I'm his son. He's supposed to love me and take care of me and protect me. But he didn't. He used me."

Allison went to Talon and tried to put her arms around him, but he shrugged them off. "We won't let him ruin your life, Tal. Luke is an expert on identity theft. He'll help us fix this."

Talon blinked, still in shock. "How will I go to college now? How will I ever get a car or a house?"

Maggie sniffed and quickly squeezed Talon's hand in hers. "Honey, Luke will take care of it. But you have to be strong now. You have to be strong like Allison has been. The first thing you have to do is file charges against your dad. After that, it's just paperwork."

Luke leaned over to look Talon in the eye. "Talon, I know this is a hard thing that has happened to you. But you're tough. You have your sisters, and you have us to support you through this. You can't let it sidetrack you from your goals. Don't get derailed because of your father's poor choices. Life is too good to let your dad ruin it."

Talon swallowed and looked to Aspen. Aspen was in tears but ran to Talon and threw her arms around his neck. "I'm so sorry, Talon," she said over and over again.

Allison wiped her cheeks and looked away. It was hard to be in pain, but it was so much harder for her to see the ones she loved hurting.

Aspen finally let go of Talon and stood back. Talon sighed and wiped some tears from under his eyes with the back of his hand.

"He started talking to me on facebook, and I was so happy. I thought he had changed, you know? I thought he had learned his lesson and he wanted to be a good dad now. He was going to take me on vacation with him. He said he needed my social security number for a passport or something, and I was so stupid I believed him. What an idiot."

Aspen shook her head. "Dad's been talking to me on facebook too."

Allison, Maggie, and Luke whipped their heads around to stare at her.

"Did you give him your social security number, Aspen?" Luke demanded.

Aspen shook her head. "No. I told him not to contact me anymore. I told him to leave us alone. Then I blocked him," she said tiredly.

Allison sighed in relief, but a second later a new horrifying thought occurred to her. What if her dad had *her* number? "Luke? Did you do a check on me and Aspen?"

Luke nodded. "You're both clean, but I froze your credit anyway, just in case."

Allison nodded and turned to walk to the couch in the family room. She had to sit down or she would fall down.

"Talon, when you're ready, will you go down to the police station with me?" Luke asked kindly.

Talon nodded slowly. "Yeah, okay. Just give me some time."

"You got it, buddy. We're going to take off now. Call me if you have any questions," Luke said. Maggie gave Talon and Aspen big teary hugs and then they went home.

Allison, Aspen, and Talon sat in the family room and looked at each other silently. Life had decided to throw them one more storm.

tWeNty

Allison went in to work the next morning feeling like a dried-up leaf, shoved in an old shoe that had been left in a dumpster. She had stayed up late the night before talking to Aspen and Talon about their choices and their father's choices and where they would go from there. Aspen was sad, but she was okay. Talon had just nodded his head like a zombie and stared off into space. Allison was worried about him. He was still in shock, and there was nothing she could do about it.

Allison walked into the fruit shed and remembered to smile before she saw Betsy.

"Hey, Betsy. How's my favorite boss?" she said, trying to sound chipper and carefree.

Betsy turned around and faced her, looking just as bad as Allison felt. Allison ran to her side and grabbed her arm.

"What's wrong? Are you okay?" she asked, seeing tear tracks down Betsy's face.

Betsy waved her hand in the air and shrugged. "Oh, don't mind me, Allison. I'm just a watering pot today. That happens when your only child acts like an idiot."

Allison stepped back and didn't say anything. She had enough problems of her own. She did not need to get involved in the Will and Daphne drama that was swirling around Alpine. She grabbed an apron off the back of a chair and flipped it over her head.

"Wow, I'd better get out there. With all these beautiful peaches, it's going to be another busy day," she said cheerfully and headed toward the road, humming "I Am a Child of God" as loudly as she could.

"Stop right there, young lady. You're the key to fixing this mess."

Allison stopped humming and turned around slowly to see Betsy looking militant. And that was not good, considering how Betsy was already a force of nature.

"Did you need me to do something in here?" Allison asked, trying to play dumb.

"Do you know what Candy just told me? Daphne went in to get her nails done last night after work. She sat there for half an hour telling Candy how Will took her out to lunch yesterday and how Will treated her like a queen and how Will was going to be the *perfect husband*. I tell you, I won't have it, Allison. You either fix this, or there will be no bonuses for you," she said, nodding her head furiously.

Allison's mouth fell open. "Are you kidding me? It is not my job to fix Will's life. I have enough lives to fix as it is. Talk to Will if you're upset about his love life. I have *nothing* to do with it," she said, starting to get mad.

Betsy saw the fire in Allison's eyes and held up her hands. "Okay, forget I brought up bonuses. That was dumb. But realistically you're the only one who *can* fix this. I thought playing it cool with Will would do the trick, but we're changing gears now. You're jumping to the head of the line. I want you to take a couple of boxes of peaches over to Will's office and tell him to give them to his clients. He loves doing stuff like that. And when you're there, smile a little, flirt a little. Put a little damper on Little Miss Perfect's shine."

Allison sighed and looked up at the ceiling of the shed. After the night she'd had, she did *not* want to traipse over to Will's office and flirt with him just to make her boss happy.

"If you'll do it, I'll give you a bonus this week in your paycheck and all the free fruit you want," she offered with a sly smile.

Allison sighed. She thought of all the things she needed to buy for the kids and caved. Flirting for money. Definitely a new low for her. "Fine. How many boxes?"

Betsy helped her load three boxes of fruit in her truck and sent her off with a smile and a wave. Allison could see Betsy already on her cell phone before she had even pulled out onto the street. Great. She was so glad she could give Alpine something new to talk about.

The brand new office buildings Will worked in had been made to look like they had been built in the 1950s. After parking her car next to Will's, Allison hefted one of the boxes in her arms and headed for the door that said Carson Development. She had to balance the box on her hip as she struggled to get the door open but finally pushed through and walked into a large, sumptuous office that looked more like an upper-class living room than an office. And there was Daphne sitting at an elegant little desk with a cell phone to her ear. Daphne turned in her chair to see who had come in and frowned when she saw who it was.

"Gotta go, Mom. Allison *Vaughn* just showed up. . . . Yeah, *I know* . . . kind of pathetic, huh? Bye."

Allison rolled her eyes and took her time looking around the office, just to bug Daphne.

"Wow, Daphne, what a nice place you work in. I bet you love it here," she said, just to make polite conversation.

Daphne sneered. "Jealous much?"

Allison shifted the box on her hip and looked back to see Daphne giving her the familiar once over.

"Just let Will know I'm here," she said, too tired to play games.

Daphne smirked and got up from her desk, wearing a tight black suit with a hot pink low-cut shirt underneath. Her heels had to be four inches easy, and her bright blonde hair was up in an elegant twist. Daphne was playing the part of the sexy sophisticated secretary to a T. She knocked lightly on a closed door and poked her head in. "You've got a visitor, Will," she said in a low, smoky voice.

Allison yawned loudly as Daphne turned around and glared at her. Then Allison blinked and stood up straighter as Will came through the door, smiling warmly at her.

"Hey, Allison! I was just thinking about you. What do you have there?" he asked, walking quickly to her side and taking the heavy box out of her arms.

Allison smiled in relief. "Thanks, that was an armful. Your mom sent me over. I've got two more boxes in my truck. She wants you to give them to your clients."

Will grinned. "Perfect. Fresh ripe peaches make everyone happy. And a happy client is the best kind. I'll help you bring them in."

They walked outside silently, and Will waited for her to lower the tail gate. "So what's the real reason Mom sent you over here?" he asked with a raised eyebrow.

Allison yawned again before answering. "Oh, you know the story already. Your mom thinks you're going to ask Daphne to marry you any second, and she thinks the only way to save you is to throw me at you every chance she gets," she said tiredly as she pulled the boxes toward her.

Will grabbed her arm to stop her. She looked up questioningly. Will looked aggravated, but she wasn't sure exactly who he was aggravated with.

"Say, I *was* going to ask Daphne to marry me. Would that bother you?" he asked, stepping closer to her.

Allison pursed her lips as she pushed a stray piece of hair back behind her ears. "Will, I just got back in town. Yeah, I used to have a huge thing for you, but honestly? Five years is a long time. If you want to spend eight hours a day, five days a week with Daphne, then that's your business. Would I be sad if you married her? I guess I would be in the sense that I never got the chance to really know you. But if she makes you happy, then marry her. You deserve your little bit of happiness," she said honestly.

Will winced as if she had just punched him. "Ouch."

Allison shook her head. "I don't know what games are going on here, but I just have too much going on to be involved right now. Please tell your mom not to send me over here to deliver fruit anymore. These boxes weigh a ton, and we both know when it comes to comparisons these days, she looks like a runway model and I look like a dumpster diver," she said with yet another yawn.

Will looked like he wanted to argue with her but changed tactics. "So why are you yawning so much? Hot date with Gage last night?" he asked, leaning up against her truck.

Allison laughed and shook her head. "That would have been better. Trust me," she said, pulling at the boxes again.

Will pushed her arms away again, wanting her whole attention. "So what was it? You look exhausted and kind of sad," he said, sounding worried. "Is it your brother and sister? I know raising teenagers has to be rough."

Allison gave up and leaned against the truck too, resting her head in her hands for just a second before looking back up. "It was just a really hard night. It's almost impossible to convince people who have been betrayed so thoroughly to still have hope. To have faith. I feel like

I'm blowing on a match that has gone out, trying to relight it," she said, her voice cracking dangerously.

She looked away and concentrated on breathing deeply. She did not want to lose it in the parking lot of Will's office, especially with Daphne peeking out the window at them every few seconds.

"You know what? I want to take you out to lunch today. Just the two us. Old friends and good conversation. Tell Mom I'm picking you up at 11:30. Tell her you beguiled me into asking you out and that you'll spend the entire time flirting with me or something," he said with a compelling smile.

Allison sighed, ready to say no, but then Daphne's face popped up again in the window, and she had to smile. It would kill Daphne. "I beguiled you? Your mom might actually believe that. What kind of food are we talking?" she asked out of curiosity.

Will grinned and shrugged. "You'll have to come and find out for yourself."

Allison groaned and shook her head. "It's not like I'm dressed to go anywhere nice," she said, looking down at her jeans, already smeared with dirt and her scruffy tennis shoes.

Will laughed. "Trust me, no one will even notice your clothes. You in?"

Allison gave in and nodded. She hadn't been out to lunch in what seemed like years. *Why not have some fun?* "Fine. 11:30, but you'd better feed me. And be sure to tell Daphne you're going out to lunch with me. That will make your mom's day."

Will rolled his eyes and then hefted both boxes in his arms and walked back to his office, opening the door easily with one hand while holding the two boxes in his other. Allison blinked in surprise. *Wow.*

Will smiled and shot his finger at her. "See ya soon."

Allison drove back to work feeling a little better. And when she gave Betsy the news of her lunch date, she had to laugh. Betsy couldn't be younger than her late forties and yet she managed to jump in the air just as high as any cheerleader, shouting and celebrating in front of all the passing cars. To her delight, she even got two honks for her victory dance.

"Sweetie, not only are you getting a bonus in your paycheck, but you are getting paid for taking your lunch break. And it better be a *long* lunch break," she said threateningly.

Allison shook her head but had to laugh. *Only in Alpine.* She almost forgot about her lunch date as car after car after car pulled up. At 11:20 she turned to Betsy, who had come to help her with the rush and shook her head. "There's no way I can leave you. It's way too busy."

Betsy snorted. "Girl, I've been selling peaches for most my life. I think I can handle a rush. Besides, Martha's coming over to keep me company. Now go put on some lipstick and comb your hair. You look like a street urchin. That or you look like you sell fruit by the side of the road."

Allison frowned but went to the small mirror inside the shed and checked her face. She hadn't brought lipstick with her, but she did wipe the smear of dirt off her cheek. *There. Definitely C-minus.*

Will was right on time. Without taking the time to chat with his mom, he walked around to the other side of his car and held the door open for Allison. Betsy waved vigorously as they drove away.

Allison laughed as she buckled her seat belt. "You know, she's so open about her feelings, it's hard to get mad at her. I've never seen a mom love her kid like Betsy loves you."

Will nodded his head with a grim smile. "Yes, she does—maybe too much—but I'll keep her."

Allison leaned her head sadly against the window as she thought of how unloved she and her brother and sister were. "I'll trade you," she said so softly she didn't think Will could hear her.

"Trade me?" he asked.

Allison blushed and shook her head. "Nothing. So where are we going? There aren't any restaurants back this far in Alpine," she said, sitting up and wondering where Will was taking her.

"That's because I'm taking you to my house. I'm going to make you lunch. That way we can have a private conversation."

Allison relaxed and stopped worrying about her clothes. Will drove for five more minutes down a long, winding road before finally pulling into the driveway of a house that looked like it had been taken straight out of *Architectural Digest.*

"Um, Will? You live in Alpine. This house was meant to be on the Washington coast," she said with a smile.

Will shrugged and looked up at his house with love in his eyes. "I saw the plans and fell in love. Come on in," he said as he walked to the front door, opening it with a keypad instead of a doorknob. Allison couldn't help but be impressed.

She walked into the foyer and fell in love too. The colors were exactly the colors she would have picked—warm, inviting, and interesting. The artwork was dramatic and colorful, and the windows drew her toward what made Alpine the special place it was. Outright pristine beauty.

"I guess you hear this all the time, but I love your house. It's intensely stunning," she said, turning in circles.

Will grinned and walked toward the back of the house where Allison could see a glimpse of the kitchen. "I like it. *Intensely stunning.* I'll take that compliment. So what do you feel like? I could grill us a couple steaks, or I could grill us some chicken, or I'll go wild and crazy and grill you salmon."

Allison grinned and slid onto the metal stool at the bar. She couldn't resist running her hands over the tan granite. "I take it you're an expert griller."

Will nodded proudly. "*Grilling* is the operative word. If it can be grilled, then I'll cook. If not? I can do without. And that goes for you too."

Allison thought about it and then went for the salmon. She couldn't afford seafood on her budget. She watched for a while as Will prepared the meat in the kitchen but then got curious and wandered into the family room, which was masculine yet tasteful. She smiled at the gigantic TV and then sat down on the ultra-soft milk chocolate couch and groaned in happiness. She cuddled down into the corner and immediately fell asleep. Twenty minutes later, Will shook her shoulder gently.

"Hey, sleeping beauty. Are you hungry, or would you rather keep napping?" he asked, as if that were really an option.

She sat up in embarrassment and rubbed her eyes. "I'm *so* sorry. I can't believe I did that. Don't tell Betsy or she'll fire me. I have strict orders to make you fall in love with me. And it's hard to do that while I'm asleep," she said with a soft laugh.

Will stood and studied her with his head tilted to the side. "Oh, I don't know. If there's anyone who could do it, it'd be you," Will said as he helped her up and led her to the small dining nook where he had the plates already filled with salmon and salad.

"Bon appetite," he said with a proud flourish of his napkin.

Allison sat down gratefully and waited as Will said a quick prayer. Then she took a bite and closed her eyes in enjoyment. "Wow, Will. You're like the perfect man. Gorgeous, smart, nice, *and* a good cook. I really should give Daphne a run for her money," she teased.

Will looked up from his salmon and watched her. "I wouldn't mind if you did."

Allison decided not to answer that and took another bite instead.

"So tell me about your hard night," Will said. "I'm your friend, Allison. If there's something I can help you with, please let me help you," he said earnestly.

Allison sighed and set her fork down to take a sip of water. She hated people knowing how messed up her family was. But Will said he was her friend. She knew instinctively she could trust him. The only problem was that at the end of their lunch, she would send Will back to Daphne. What sane man would want a relationship with a woman whose family was just plain broken?

Allison studied Will for a moment and then smiled. At least she'd find out soon if he was the sticking kind. She spent the next half hour pouring her heart out to Will. She told him about Talon's facebook page and Luke doing the credit checks and what Max had done. When she told him about Talon's reaction, her hands started to shake, and she had to stop for a moment.

"I just don't know what to do, Will. Our dad crushed his heart. If you can't believe in your own father, who can you believe in? I'm so worried. What if Talon goes off the deep end? What if he leaves the Church over this? Or starts taking drugs? What if he commits suicide?"

Will looked appalled and sat back in his chair as he thought about it. "Well, now I know why you're so uninterested in playing my mom's little games. You've got enough to deal with. If it were me? I don't know how I'd react. I think going off the deep end is actually the normal reaction to something like this. Talon just needs something to believe in and hope in. Luke's working on his financial health. Why don't you let me work on his emotional health?"

Allison ate her last bite of salmon and frowned. "Okay, explain."

Will pushed his plate away and clasped his hands on the table. "It's simple. His emotions are in chaos right now. He doesn't know if he should be mad or sad or what. He needs an outlet for all the chaos.

If he doesn't get it out, then it's just going to eat him up. I'd like to be Talon's mentor. I know he works for Luke after school quite a bit, but how about I steal him from you a couple nights a week? Give me a month, and I promise you you'll have your brother back again."

Allison licked her lips and looked out the window at the green mountains. "What about his homework?" she had to ask.

Will shook his head. "Talon isn't going to care about school or anything else until he works through this mess he has inside of him. If you want your brother to focus on grades, then give him to me for a month," he said.

Allison nodded. He was right. "So what are you going to do with him? This isn't going to be some weird male thing where you sit in a teepee and cut your hair and get in touch with animal spirits, is it?"

Will laughed at her. "You read too much. Just trust me, Allie."

Allison was at the end of her rope. She didn't know what else to do. "What do I tell Talon?"

Will looked away for a second and then back at her. "Just tell him that you're dating me and that you need him to check me out and make sure I'm a good person. Tell him that you won't keep dating me unless I get the okay from him."

Allison laughed but then stopped smiling when Will looked at her, unsmiling and unblinking.

"Are you serious? You really want me to say that? I don't want to lie to him," Allison said, putting her napkin on her plate and looking away.

"I'm very serious, and you won't be lying. You *are* going to date me. One way or another, you and I are going to have our chance."

Allison cleared her throat and looked down at her lap. "Won't that upset your new secretary?"

Will shrugged. "She's my secretary, not my wife. She's not paid to care about my personal life."

Allison looked up in surprise. "Then why did you hire her?" she asked bluntly.

Will grinned. "A few reasons. One, to bug my mother. Two, she's very qualified, and I needed a secretary. Three, I don't date my employees. It's in the handbook."

Allison laughed, smiling into Will's eyes. "Has Daphne read the handbook?"

Will looked naughty. "It was the first assignment I gave her. Whether she read it or not is debatable. Now, shall I get you back to work?" he asked, standing up and stretching.

Allison stood up too, looking longingly at the soft chocolate couch and wishing for just a little nap.

"Yes, we'd better. Your mom's imagination must be going into overdrive right about now. I bet she's hoping we're doing something besides talking," she said with a laugh.

Will walked around the table. "Well, I've got an extra half hour if you do," he said leaning down toward her.

Allison scooted back nervously. "*Hey*. Just because you can grill salmon and you want to help my brother does not mean that you get to kiss me on our first lunch date," she said sternly.

Will looked completely let down. "It doesn't?"

"No," Allison said, walking toward the front door. "But you never know. Our second date could be a lot more exciting," she said, smiling over her shoulder at Will.

Will grinned and followed her to the front door. "Well, then I'll start planning our next date. What time do you get off work?" he asked as he reset the alarm on his house.

Allison sighed happily, rejuvenated from the nap, the food, and the conversation. "I thought you just said something about me getting Talon's approval before I officially start dating you."

Will's jaw set in a hard line, and he walked toward her purposefully. "There's official, and then there's unofficial. Don't play games with me, Allison. If you only knew how long I've waited to be with you," he said frowning down at her.

Allison pursed her lips and thought about it. He was right. They were both too old to play games. "Okay. Unofficially, you're mine then. But I'm warning you—if I find lipstick on your collar, you will seriously regret it," she said, shaking a finger in his face.

Will's face relaxed into a grin as he grabbed her around the waist, lifting her up in his strong arms and pulling her into a hug. "I'm yours. *Finally*," he said letting her go gradually.

Allison couldn't stop smiling. He was so cute. He looked like he was going to lean down again for a kiss, but she stepped back and pointed to the car. "Be good now."

Will gave up gracefully and ran to open the car door for her. "Hey,

I've spent my whole life being good. I've got a lot of vacation time saved up."

Allison and Will both smiled and laughed during the short drive back to the fruit stand. She frowned, though, when Will insisted on walking her over to Betsy.

"Hey, Mom. Sorry if I kept her a little too long," Will said in a sweetly apologetic voice.

Betsy's eyes glittered happily, and she patted his arm. "No worries. We had a lull in traffic. So did you two have a nice lunch?" she prodded, looking back and forth between Will and Allison.

Allison grabbed her apron and pulled it over her head. Will was looking at her expectantly as if she had a big announcement to make. *Oh. Riiight. I do.* She felt shy all of a sudden but then decided to take the bull by the horns. Besides, it would make Betsy's day.

"Well, I guess we did take too long. Probably because I was so busy throwing myself at Will, I lost track of time," she said with a guilty frown.

Betsy's mouth fell open, and she whipped her head around to stare at Will. Will just grinned, still saying nothing, so she turned back to Allison.

"Wow, you really do follow orders," Betsy said in happy wonder.

Will laughed and leaned against the cart. "She has to be the best employee we've ever had," he said dreamily.

Allison laughed and tied her apron in the front. "Rest easy, Betsy. I have beguiled Will to such a degree that he now thinks he's my boyfriend. I have saved him from the perils of Daphne, and his heart is now safe in my keeping," she said, giving up and giggling helplessly at Betsy's expression.

Will laughed too and gave his mom a hug. "Mom, will you relax now about Daphne being my secretary? No more making Allison haul heavy boxes to my office."

Betsy hugged Will back but looked up at him with sharp eyes. "You aren't joking, are you? This is for real, right? You wouldn't tease me like that." She looked worried.

Allison waved as someone drove by and honked. "Betsy, I have no idea why Will would rather date me than his beautiful secretary, but yes, we have decided to try it out. After tasting Will's salmon, I knew it was pointless to fight it any longer."

Will raised his eyebrows at her. "That's all it took? Dang, if I'd known that, I would have brought you fish every day in high school."

Allison began to say something but had the breath knocked out of her when Betsy threw her arms around her.

"You won't regret this, Allison. Will is such a good man. Thank you, thank you," she said, squeezing the life out of her.

Will gently pried his mother's arms from around Allison. "Well, can I get a good-bye hug from my new girlfriend before I head back to work?"

Betsy let go immediately and grinned with happiness. "I think I hear the phone," she said and ran up to the storage shed.

Allison smiled up into Will's eyes. He stared down into her face with a look of such delight, she felt her breath catch. "Well, she took it better than I thought she would."

Will slid his arms around her waist and nodded, still smiling. "We Carsons have no problems expressing our feelings. See, I'm going to do it right now," he said and bent over to kiss her good-bye on the cheek.

Allison felt his soft kiss and wished they were anywhere but on the side of a road. She pushed him away when they heard a car honking. "I don't want to get arrested here. You'd better go."

Will grinned and walked back to his car. "See you after dinner. Remember to tell Talon he has plans tonight."

Allison waved and watched him drive away. *Wow*. Now what had just happened? Betsy flew down the small hill toward her, coming smile first. Allison held up her hand in defense. Her ribs were still aching from Betsy's last hug.

"Sweetie, you moving back to Alpine was the best thing that could have happened. Did you see my boy's smile? He's in heaven."

Allison shrugged, still feeling shy about it. "Well, for the record, I'm pretty happy too. I think I fell for Will the first day of high school. I still remember the first time I ever saw him. He was standing at the drinking fountain after school, and he looked up at me. When our eyes met, I remember thinking he was the most handsome guy I'd ever seen," she said with a sigh.

Betsy's eyes glowed happily. "Perfect. I've been so worried seeing all these girls go for Will because he's rich now. It does my heart good to know he'll be loved for himself and not his bank account. I could die happy," she said with satisfaction as she picked up a peach and took a big bite.

Allison smiled wryly and straightened the fruit. "Betsy, I hate to break it to you, but everyone's going to say *I* went after Will just for his money. I'm not exactly rich anymore."

Betsy swished her hands in the air. "Well, that just goes to show you there are a lot of stupid people in the world. I remember when you used to come buy fruit back when you were in high school. You didn't even know what you were buying half the time. You just stared at Will from the minute you stepped out of your car until the moment you drove away. He didn't have anything in his bank account back then. You don't care about his money. You never have. Nah, I don't care what people say. You're exactly what Will needs in his life. He hasn't had anyone to love. It's just *work, work, work* all the time. Now he can really live. This is going to be a good year. I have a feeling," Betsy said happily. She walked away, humming and reaching for her cell phone at the same time.

Allison tried to smile at how happy Betsy was. But just knowing she was going to be talked about over and over again made her want to hide her head. And to think she used to think Alpine was so quiet and boring.

tWENty-ONE

Later that afternoon as Allison chopped the vegetables Betsy had given her to take home for a chicken stew, she decided to blow off the gossip and just be happy about her new relationship with Will. She had no idea if it would last, but how many people got the chance to go back and date their high school crush?

Wiping her hands on a dish towel, she noticed the time and headed out to the front porch. The bus pulled up right on time, and she smiled as she leaned her hip against the porch post and waited for Talon and Aspen to get off the bus. She frowned as the bus finally shut its doors and pulled away from the curb. She walked down the steps uncertainly looking after the bus. *Where were they?*

She stood there for a moment when Maggie's front door opened and Maggie stepped out. "Where're Talon and Aspen?" she asked worriedly.

Allison had to smile. She wasn't the only one who watched for the bus. "I don't know. They didn't get off. I guess I'll give them ten more minutes to find their way home. Then I'll head down to the high school. Or call the police," she said, looking down the street one more time.

Maggie sighed and sat on her front step, patting the space beside her with her hand. "Well, I'll sit and wait with you. Besides, I have some news. Sophie and I finally have a plan to pry Daphne's claws out of Will. You'll *love* this," Maggie said with a grin.

Allison opened her mouth to tell Maggie there was no need, but

Maggie shushed her. "No! You have to listen before you shoot this down. It's brilliant. Sophie and I are going to go into the office tomorrow morning and demand a meeting with Will. Daphne will try to kick us out, I'm sure. But then, Sophie's going to tell Will that Sam is interested in being the contractor for the park Will's building and donating to the city. Okay, here's where it gets good. Sophie is going to insist that he fire Daphne if they get the job. *See?* Kind of mean, I know, but in our defense, Will has no idea what he's up against with her. And then I'll be there and mention how I could paint some murals for the skate park he's putting in. But the catch will be that he has to go on at least three dates with you. Isn't it perfect?" she asked, pleased with herself.

Allison's mouth fell open in awe. Sophie and Maggie would do all that for her? "Unreal," she whispered, shaking her head at her friend.

Maggie laughed happily. "Sophie is so excited. Her first idea was to sneak in the office and hide under a desk to listen in on Daphne's and Will's conversations, but Sam talked her out of it. Something about him not wanting to take their children to prison to visit their mom. Like Will would press charges. So this is much better. Jacie wanted in on the fun, but she's been so sick with her pregnancy she's either in bed or throwing up."

Allison winced for Jacie. "Maggie, listen, thank you so much for planning to bribe Will. That's just about the sweetest thing anyone's ever done for me. Honestly. I'm going to write it down in my journal. I'm just in awe that you and Sophie would go completely insane for me. But I'm going to have to say no. You can't do it," she said, feeling kind of bad about disappointing them.

Maggie glared at her for a second. "You can't tell us no. We're set! We've both picked out our outfits, and Sophie's going to do my hair so I look really impressive tomorrow. This is the most interesting thing I've done in *months*," she sputtered, looking very put out.

Allison rested her head on her knees as her shoulders shook with laughter. "Maggie, you goofball, you don't have to bribe Will because he took me to lunch today, and we decided to start seeing each other." Allison lifted her head and wiped the tears of laughter from her eyes.

Maggie sat back in surprise, her eyes wide and blinking as she took in Allison's news. "You're serious?"

Allison nodded firmly. "And just so you know, we've already told his mom, and I have her blessing. He's really sweet, Maggie. He grilled me salmon for lunch and let me take a nap on his couch and then listened to me pour my heart out about my life. He didn't run screaming out the door, and when he was getting ready to go back to work, he kissed me on the cheek."

Maggie laughed happily and clapped her hands. "The bridal shower is back on. Yes!" she shouted, standing up and pulling Allison in for a big hug.

Allison hugged her back gently, trying to be careful of the baby. Then she pulled away as she noticed an old red Subaru drive down the street toward them. Allison nodded toward the car. "I believe my lost siblings have arrived," she said, all happiness put on hold as she waited to see her brother and sister.

The car came to a stop in front of them, and Aspen and Talon jumped out, followed by Rowan and a girl Allison didn't recognize. The four teenagers walked up to them, smiling innocently. Allison wished for only the millionth time she could afford cell phones so she could track her brother and sister better.

"So you didn't feel like riding the bus today, huh?" she asked with a friendly smile.

Rowan stepped forward. "Sorry, Allison, but I didn't have to work at the rec center today, so I offered to drive everyone home. We might have stopped at the gas station for a drink too. Um, this is my cousin Sarah. She goes to Lone Peak with us," he said, motioning toward the tall, thin girl with long, brown hair streaked with blonde.

She was cute. Allison looked at Talon. The smile on his face was proof that he had noticed already.

"Hi, Sarah. You guys want to come over to our house? I'm making some chicken stew for dinner. It won't be ready for an hour, but it'll be good when it's done," she promised.

Talon and Aspen smiled gratefully at her and then they turned to Rowan. "Can you stay, Rowan?" Aspen asked hopefully, clasping her hands in front of her.

Rowan grinned and nodded. "I just have to call my mom and tell her where I am. Can I use your phone?"

Allison watched as Aspen led the way to their house. Then Allison stepped down and grabbed Talon's arm before he could follow the group.

"Tal. You hangin' in there?" she asked.

Talon breathed in deeply and let out a slow breath. "Not really. But hanging out with the hottest girl at Lone Peak makes life a little better," he said with a smile that didn't quite reach his eyes. He started to walk away, but she held him in place.

"Hey, just so you know, after dinner sometime Will Carson is coming by. We kind of liked each other when I was in high school, and he took me out to lunch today, and um . . . we'll probably be seeing each other from now on. So, um, he knows about what Dad did, and he wants to hang out with you and um, help you work out your issues," she said lamely, glancing back at Maggie self-consciously as Maggie listened avidly to every single word.

Talon immediately turned irritable. "I'm not going anywhere with some strange guy. He's probably a freak or something."

Allison sighed tiredly as Maggie burst out into laughter. "Will Carson? The man *almost* compares to Luke in amazingness. Not close, but closer than anyone else in Alpine."

Allison rolled her eyes at Maggie's blindness. "Whatever. And *no*. Will is *not* a freak. I really like him, Tal. I want you to go, and while you guys are doing whatever it is he has planned, check him out for me. See if you think he's a guy I can trust," she said, wincing at Talon's stubborn expression.

"I don't need to go hang out with some guy I don't even know. I have Luke. Luke and I can hang out. I don't need any more male bonding. Besides, Frank's my volunteer grandpa. I don't need to be anyone else's charity case," he said angrily.

Allison sighed and bit her lip.

Maggie stepped toward Talon and clasped his arm. "Luke loves you; you know that, Talon. But I know Will Carson, and he's a fantastic guy. He's interested in your sister, and he wants to help you out. You never know. This guy could be your future brother-in-law. He's probably going to take you bowling or to the movies. If you hate it, don't go again. If he's cool, then he's just one more friend you can hang out with."

Talon glared at Allison and shook his head. "Fine. This *once* I'll go, but you owe me. No chores for two days," he said, raising his eyebrows and crossing his arms.

Allison raised hers back at him. Fine. It was negotiation time.

"Okay, Talon. How about this? If you hang out with Will tonight, I won't make you do chores for three days, *if* you promise not to scare him off and you're nice and polite," she said triumphantly.

Talon narrowed his eyes. "How did you know what I was going to do?"

Allison smiled. "I know you, Tal. You were going to give in and and then be so obnoxious Will would come screaming back just to dump you off. I think I'm a little smarter than that."

Talon grinned and shrugged. "Fine, fine. I'll go *and* be nice. But no chores for *four* days."

Allison frowned and shook her head. "That's crazy. No way. Three or nothing."

Maggie smiled as she looked between the two. "How about this, Tal? You take the three days, and I'll throw in a pizza party at my house tomorrow night. All the gluten-free pizza you could ever want and the DVD of your choice."

Talon grinned at that and nodded. "Deal," he said. Then he ran to the house.

Allison laughed weakly and sat back down. "Maggie, you sure come in handy."

Maggie smiled proudly. "Thanks. And by the way, that means you have tomorrow night free, in case Will wants to take you out."

Allison grinned and hugged her friend. Maggie looked surprised and pleased. "Hey, you just hugged me!"

Allison smiled and stood up. "Give me another year, and we'll be braiding each other's hair and having slumber parties."

Maggie laughed. "I'll plan on it."

Allison walked back to the house and found the music turned up too loud and four teenagers in her kitchen, going through the fridge.

"Hey, guys! Dinner will be ready in an hour. Can't you wait?"

Aspen and Sarah shrugged and headed to the couch while Talon and Rowan grabbed some peaches Betsy had given her to take home.

Allison finished chopping vegetables and chicken and added the spices and seasonings as the conversation in the family room jumped from topic to topic so fast she couldn't keep up. She put the lid on the pot and went out to sit on her front porch again. It was too loud inside the house, and it was weird seeing her younger brother and sister flirt. She didn't know if she should send them to their rooms or take pointers.

Three peaceful minutes later, Bonnie and Frank drove up. They emerged from their car, looking grim and holding covered plates. *Hmm. Maggie must have said something.*

"Hey, you two," Allison called out as she stood to greet her visitors.

Bonnie walked quickly up the steps and pulled Allison into a one-armed hug. "Allison, we're here to help. Maggie told us what Max did to Talon. Well, she *had* to. You guys are ours now, and we need to know these things. We're just sick about it. Frank couldn't even sleep last night, he was so mad. We've brought you some rolls and pineapple upside-down cake. I tasted it, and you can hardly tell it's not made with real flour."

Allison smiled at their kindness. It really was nice to have people worry about her. She'd never known how good something as simple as that could feel.

"Why don't you two come in? We're having chicken stew for dinner, and these rolls will go perfectly. Plus, I really do need your help. I have two other teenagers over, and I'm not sure what to do. It's weird," she said helplessly.

Frank laughed and patted her shoulder. "Honey, you just leave teenagers to me. They're my specialty," he said, smiling at the challenge, and walked into the house.

Bonnie laughed. "It's true. They're putty in his hands. I bet he has that music turned down in less than a minute."

Allison and Bonnie waited, smiling at each other, and sure enough, the music was almost immediately turned down.

"Well, I'm glad I have you to myself for a second," Bonnie said. "I know what to do about Daphne. It's the perfect solution," she said, grabbing Allison's hand as the two women sat down on the front steps side by side.

Allison opened her mouth to stick up for Daphne, who had no idea she had so many people plotting against her, but Bonnie shushed her.

"Honey, I told you I'm looking out for you now. Just let me do this. Daphne should be with Gage Dulaney. *Not* Will Carson. Will should be yours. Now this is how we'll do it. Frank will go by and pick up a real estate magazine just to browse and shoot the breeze. And then he'll just *happen* to mention how Will is the greatest guy in the world and how unfair it is that Will got the prettiest girl in town. *See?* Frank will turn it into a competition. Whoever gets Daphne is the best man. Then Gage won't rest until he's stolen Daphne away from Will. Gage has been so competitive with Will ever since he became successful. This will work. I promise," she said, her eyes gleaming just as brightly as Maggie's had earlier.

Allison tapped her chin with her finger. It was actually a brilliant plan. "I like your idea of putting Daphne with Gage. They're perfect for each other. I wonder why they don't see it. But honestly, there's really no need for anyone to go to any more trouble about this situation. I've dealt with it all on my own," she said proudly.

Bonnie looked skeptical. "Honey, I'm an expert at this sort of thing. You should really leave it in my hands."

Allison shook her head. "It's already done. I told Will just this afternoon that he was mine and no ones else's. Then I said that if I ever caught him with lipstick on his collar, he would regret it," she stated matter-of-factly.

Bonnie's eyes opened so wide, Allison laughed. Then she leaned back on her hands and smiled up at the mountains.

"Uh-uh. I don't believe it," Bonnie said.

Allison just closed her eyes and tilted her chin up to catch a small breeze on her face.

"Okay, I believe it. What did Will say?" Bonnie asked, grabbing her hand.

Allison opened her eyes. "Just that he'd been waiting to be with me since high school and a bunch of other mushy stuff you don't want to hear. But it's all true. We are officially seeing each other as of this afternoon. So it doesn't matter if Daphne is his secretary. She's his employee. *I'm* his girlfriend. Now, no more plotting against Daphne."

Bonnie smiled but sniffed in disappointment too. "Well, it was out of the goodness of my heart. I have certain talents, but I only use them when it's an emergency. *Darn.*"

Allison smiled and stood up. "Well, if it makes you feel any better, I think your idea of setting up Daphne and Gage is brilliant. I say you go for it as long as you're only doing it because you want to see two people happy together."

Bonnie looked thoughtful as they walked into the house but stopped when she saw Frank and all the kids playing a hand of cards at the dining room table.

"Want to join us for a game of Rummy?" Frank asked.

Bonnie joined in the game as Allison finished making dinner and sliced the rolls. After Frank and Aspen both won a hand, Allison called an end to the game and set the bowls out. Her table was just barely big enough to fit everyone. Allison grinned at the picture and admitted she never thought she'd see her house so full of people. It warmed her heart.

Bonnie said the prayer, and everyone devoured the soup to the last spoonful. After dinner, Rowan had to take Sarah home, and Aspen walked over to see if Maggie needed any help. Frank took Talon in the backyard to talk and throw a baseball while Allison and Bonnie cleaned up.

"I think if your dad ever showed up in town, Frank would take the man out back and teach him what's what," Bonnie said with a firm shake of her head.

Allison sighed tiredly. "Where was Frank ten years ago? My dad's been scamming people for so long he doesn't know what else to do, I guess. But if someone like Frank had been there the first time, I think life would be very different."

Bonnie frowned and nodded. "You're right. We'd probably have to go back to his childhood to fix what's wrong with him. Makes you wonder how a man raised in the Church and married in the temple can go through life without a conscience."

Allison sighed sadly and wiped down the table before putting the leftover rolls in a large baggie. The knock on the front door made her stomach flip over in anticipation. *Will.*

She quickly walked to the front door and opened it wide with a smile. But it wasn't Will. It was Daphne. Allison frowned and stepped forward.

"Daphne? What a surprise," she said, noting the redness in Daphne's cheeks and her clenched fists.

"Please tell me this is a bad dream," Daphne said, flipping her blonde hair over her shoulder. "Please tell me that you are *not* dating Will Carson. Betsy just came by the office to congratulate Will *very loudly* on his new girlfriend."

Allison bit her lip. "Well, yeah. We are dating. We talked about it today over lunch, and we decided to start seeing each other. I'm sorry if you're upset by that."

Daphne stepped closer, breathing faster. "*Upset?* Are you serious? Do you know how long I've been trying to get together with Will? *Hmm?*"

Allison didn't say it, but it was probably right after Daphne found out he was rich.

"No, Daphne."

Daphne closed her eyes. "For one whole year, Allison. A year of my life. And you come in and ruin everything with just one stupid lunch date? How did you do it? I really want to know," she said, tapping her foot. "Because look at you. You dress like our cleaning lady. You live in an old shack. Your nails look like garbage, and you have nothing. *Nothing.* And Will picks you over *me*. I don't get it, Allison. I'm not leaving here until you can explain it to me."

Allison sighed, seeing real hurt in Daphne's eyes. She stepped out onto the front porch and shut the door to Bonnie's curious ears.

"Look, Daphne, I can't speak for Will. I don't know what happened between the two of you before I got here. Has he asked you out before?"

Daphne looked away and frowned. "Not exactly. But I knew he was working up to it. And yesterday at work, he took *me* to lunch. And he really talked to me, you know. He wanted to know my opinion. He treats me like I'm smart and I'm competent, and I love that."

Allison winced. "I've always liked that about Will too. He treats people like he wants to be treated. Probably because he was treated so badly when he was younger."

Daphne shook her head. "I know I didn't treat him well in high school, but you can't judge somebody based on high school. Everyone's an idiot back then. I thought . . . I thought he'd gotten over all that stuff," she said, sounding unsure.

Allison hugged herself and leaned on the door frame. "Daphne, maybe this is something you should talk to Will about. I'm sorry you're mad and upset. But to be honest, I've liked Will ever since my first day at Lone Peak. I've always liked him. And I think he's always liked me."

Daphne's eyes blazed with anger as she stared at Allison. "I don't believe it. You're doing this just to hurt me. You never were my friend in high school. I overheard you complaining to your dad about me one time. I know he forced you to hang out with me. And I don't even care.

Guess what, I didn't like you either. It was all for show back then. So if you think I'm going to sit back and watch you ruin my life for old time's sake, think again. I was meant to be with Will. *You?* You were meant to sell fruit on the side of the road."

Allison felt a little nauseated as she watched Daphne walk briskly away with her head held high. Bonnie opened the door behind her. "Allison? You okay?" she asked softly.

Allison nodded as Daphne's car sped off down the road. "There goes one angry woman."

Bonnie nodded. "I'll get to work on Gage."

Allison sighed. "The sooner the better."

The two women walked into the backyard and watched Talon and Frank throw the ball for a few minutes before Bonnie mentioned that Frank's favorite CSI show was coming on soon. Talon and Allison smiled as Frank practically ran from the yard.

tWENty-tWO

As Frank and Bonnie drove away, Talon looked thoughtful. "He says I should try out for the baseball team. That would be kind of interesting. I mean, if I made it. I didn't exactly grow up playing Little League."

Allison grinned. "Hey, don't count yourself out. I can just see me now. Sitting in the stands, eating hot dogs and getting a tan. Yeah, I say we go for it."

Talon shook his head. "Nah. You got the picture all wrong. You'll be too busy watching me hit home runs and catching fly balls. You won't be holding any old hotdog. You'll be holding up a huge sign with my name on it," he said, smiling faintly at the picture in his head.

Allison liked his picture better and wished with all her heart it would happen. The doorbell, rang and Allison's stomach once again flipped over a few times. *Please be Will.* If she saw Daphne on her door-step again, she was going to hide in her closet. She opened the door and smiled at the dozens of red roses in Will's hands.

"I hear girlfriends like getting roses," he said, handing her the flowers.

Allison's heart melted as she smelled the flowers. She had no idea if she even had a vase big enough for them. "Well, *your* girlfriend defi-nitely does. These are beautiful, Will. Thank you," she said and kissed him on the cheek.

Will's cheeks reddened as he followed her into the house. Allison led him back to the kitchen, where Talon was leaning against the counter, looking sullen. Allison glared at him warningly, so he stood up and looked sullen.

"Hey there. You must be Talon," Will said, holding out his hand for a shake.

Talon looked surprised but shook Will's hand. The front door flew open and Aspen ran down the hall, breathing fast and looking excited. "Oh my heck! Maggie just told me. Allison, why didn't you tell me your *boyfriend* was coming over tonight?" she said in breathless glee, staring at Will.

Will cleared his throat nervously and looked at Allison, who just laughed. "Will, this is my little sister, Aspen. Aspen, this is Will."

Will walked over and shook Aspen's hand too. "It's nice to meet you, Aspen."

Aspen stared at him for a moment and then looked at her sister. "He really does look like Hugh Jackman."

Will blushed and looked at Talon, who was laughing at him. "So I guess we're going to head out," he said, leading the way down the hallway with Talon right behind him.

Allison and Aspen followed them toward the front door and watched as they got in Will's car. Allison waved as the car drove away.

"He is so hot," Aspen whispered in awe.

Allison laughed and hugged her sister. "Yeah, well thanks for embarrassing my new boyfriend. Watch him dump me now."

Aspen rolled her eyes. "Who would dump you? You're the best. Okay, I gotta head back to Maggie's and finish sweeping. But you and I have *so* much to talk about," she said as she walked across the lawn.

Allison sighed. Now that the drama was over, she was all alone. The kitchen was clean, and she had two choices. She could go for a walk or she could relax. Allison turned around and decided on the relaxation. She headed automatically for the couch but then changed course and walked upstairs. She went to Talon's room and opened up the laptop. The facebook home page was still up, but Talon had logged out this time. She hadn't asked him for his password and didn't want to.

She logged on to her old facebook account and winced at the number of friends she had. At one time she'd had over three hundred. Now she had eighty-nine. And most of them were people she barely knew from college. She checked Talon's page and read the most recent posts on his wall. They were mostly from kids at school. She smiled, happy that

Talon had made a few friends at least. There was nothing new from Bill Kidd, though. Of course, if she'd had Talon's password she could check his personal messages, but she had a feeling that now that her dad had gotten what he wanted, he wasn't going to stick around. She scrolled down Talon's list of friends until she got to her dad's picture of the ocean. She felt anger pump through her body as she pictured her father lying on the beach, enjoying all of the money he'd stolen.

Then she bit her lip and sent her dad a message:

> Stay away from my family. They're not yours anymore. They're mine, and you don't get to hurt them or steal from them or break their hearts anymore. Just go away and never ever come back.

Allison sighed, knowing she probably wouldn't get a response. Her father didn't care about them anyway.

She wandered back downstairs and watched television until Aspen came home. Then Allison spent the next hour regaling her sister with every detail she could remember about her lunch with Will. Aspen was so happy for her, she wouldn't stop bouncing on the couch.

"I still can't believe those flowers. I know if Rowan could afford them he'd bring me some," she said with yearning in her voice.

"Of course he would. Who wouldn't want to bring you flowers?" Allison smiled.

Aspen grinned back at her and then stood up. "Speaking of which, I'd better get to bed. I want to look amazing tomorrow."

Allison yawned and looked at the clock. It was almost ten. Maybe she should have reminded Will it was a school night. She decided to watch the news and dozed off. At ten thirty, Will and Talon walked in the door. Allison jumped up and ran to see them. They looked okay. They were smiling. And miraculously, Talon didn't look sullen anymore.

"So what did you guys do?" she asked as Will and Talon sat their drinks on the counter.

Talon shook his head. "This guy is crazy, Al. He took me to this gym and they taught me how to box. No kidding. Will and I got in the ring at the end, and—tell her, Will. Tell her how hard I punched you," Talon said proudly.

Will held up his hands when he saw Allison's face. "Hey, now. Don't get upset. Lots of padding was involved. No injuries were acquired. Just two guys getting a little aggression out. And yes, Talon has a great right hook," he said, punching Talon on the shoulder hard enough to make Allison wince.

Talon grinned and punched Will back. "So, next Tuesday? Same thing?"

Will smiled and nodded. "You and me in the ring."

Talon shocked Allison by giving her a quick kiss on the cheek before he headed upstairs for a shower.

Allison looked at Will with raised eyebrows. "Boxing?"

Will grabbed her hand and pulled her toward the couch. "Yes. Boxing. I knew if I told you, you'd say no. But Talon loved it, Allison. And like I was telling you at lunch, he needs a healthy way to release all that anger and aggression. This is it."

Allison frowned and grabbed a pillow as Will scooted closer to her and clasped her hand.

"If you can promise me he won't get hurt, I'll try to be okay about this," she said, narrowing her eyes at him.

Will frowned and shook his head. "Nah, that's not how it works. I can't promise he won't get hurt. It won't just be boxing, though. I'll take him rock climbing too. Maybe cliff jumping. I don't know. The point is, I'll do my very best to keep him safe, but every now and then, yeah, he'll get hurt. But he's *already* hurt, Allison. This is cathartic."

Allison sighed and leaned back. "Okay. I guess. But what makes you such an expert on aggression therapy? How do you know exactly what to do with an angry teenage boy?" she asked curiously.

Will smiled and put his arm around her shoulders. "I'm an expert because I used to be an angry teenage boy. My dad died when I was just a kid. We were dirt poor, and my mom had to work hard just to keep food on the table. My sister always needed so much help or she was sick. And then being treated like crap at school wasn't very much fun. I had a lot of anger. My uncle knew what I was going through, and he had some boxing gloves. Me and my cousin Chris would pound each other into the ground sometimes."

Allison winced again and shook her head. "Um, maybe you guys could move on to rock climbing sooner than later."

Will grinned and intertwined his fingers with hers. "Just so you know, rock climbing is even more dangerous."

Allison groaned. She closed her eyes and found her head lying on Will's shoulder. "Well, he did look happy," she conceded.

Will nodded and played with her hair. "We talked a lot in the car too. We talked about your dad and school and girls. He's a pretty amazing kid."

Allison smiled and snuggled closer to Will. "Yeah, he is. I love him. So does he approve of you?"

Will laughed and kissed her forehead. "Well, he didn't come out and say he gave me his approval, but when we were in the car coming home, he said I was a lot better than your ex-*fiancé*. Care to fill me in?"

Allison opened her eyes and wrinkled her nose. "There's not much to tell. Aspen and Talon hated him. We dated for about six months before he asked me to marry him. I don't know why I said yes, but I did. He dumped me two months later when my dad's face was splattered all over the newspapers. I was a huge embarrassment to him."

Will looked happier than he should have. "What an idiot."

Allison sniffed. "Yeah, he really was."

Will put his hand on her knee as he looked in her eyes with a very serious expression. "I just want you to know that I could never be ashamed of you. I don't care what your dad did or how much money you have in the bank. None of that matters to me."

Allison smiled and reached up to run her fingers through his hair. "I believe you."

Will leaned down like he was going to kiss her when Aspen cleared her throat very loudly from the kitchen.

"Anything good on TV?" she asked innocently.

Will sat back and looked like he'd just been caught with his hand in the cookie jar. "Well, it's getting late. I'd better get going," he said, standing up.

Allison glared at Aspen behind his back and walked him to the door. Since Aspen had followed them to the front door, Will settled with a quick hug and then left.

Allison shut the door and locked it before turning around to kill her sister.

"Hey, don't get mad at me. You told me that was one of the rules. No kissing on the couch. You can't break your own rules."

Allison rolled her eyes. "Those are rotten teenager rules, not awesome adult rules."

Aspen shook her head. "My seminary teacher says rules are for everyone, regardless of age. Sorry, Allie, but you have to set a good example. I've already told Rowan the rules, but if you want to change a couple, we could," she said with a wicked smile.

Allison groaned. "You're grounded. Go to bed."

Aspen ran upstairs laughing as Allison went around the house, turning all the lights off. Rules were rules. Tomorrow she'd have to tell Will about all the complex and somewhat restrictive dating rules she'd come up with for Talon and Aspen. And she really might have to rethink some of them.

tWeNty - thRee

The next day was Friday, and the most exciting thing to happen to her at work was having Sophie stop by to buy a box of peaches and chat. Sophie did mention three times how disappointed she was that she couldn't have helped Allison with Will in a more hands-on way.

Allison took Sophie's cash and smiled. "You're kind of an excitement junkie, huh? You know you would have gotten caught."

Sophie grinned and didn't deny it. "We all have our faults."

Allison had a great idea as she handed Sophie back her change. "Actually, you might be able to help. It's Bonnie's idea, really. She was thinking that in order to stabilize Daphne, we should push her and Gage Dulaney into a more romantic relationship."

Sophie made humming sounds as she thought about it. "Well, it's kind of weird, isn't it? They've been friends forever. They hang out all the time. I always see them going places together. I wonder why they haven't gotten together on their own."

Allison sat down in her chair to get out of the sun. "Maybe they just need a push in the right direction."

Sophie sighed. "I make it a rule not to get too involved with what's going on in Daphne's life. Of course, I make exceptions when she's messing things up for my friends, but to actually go out of my way to help her? I don't know. That would mean I'd have to be charitable, forgiving, and Christlike," she said, wincing.

Allison raised her eyebrow. "Hey, you're not exactly evil. If you can forgive me, then you can forgive her, right?"

Sophie tilted her head and studied Allison. "You do make a good point. To be honest, I kind of hated you more. With Daphne, I knew it was in her nature to be cruel, but it wasn't like that with you. So you're right. I guess I am incredibly Christlike. I had no idea."

Allison smiled sadly and sniffed. "If I haven't said thank you before, I'd like to say it now. Thanks for listening to me and believing me. I'm really glad you forgave me, Sophie. Maybe someday Daphne will be grateful too."

Sophie rolled her eyes and grabbed her box of peaches. "I'll think about it. But that's as far as I'll go. Oh, before I forget, Maggie's really wanting to throw you a welcome home party. She was planning on having it at her house, like a surprise party, but I talked her out of it. She's too close to delivery, and I don't think the stress would be good for her or the baby. So guess what? It's going to be at my house," Sophie said with a grin.

Allison's mouth fell open. "Why would you do that for me? I mean, I'm glad you've forgiven me and we're working at having a friendship, but that's a lot to ask of you. Let's cancel it. I'll talk to Maggie. Please, please don't go to the trouble. I'd feel so bad."

Sophie held up her hand and waved it in the air. "I love throwing parties. I love nothing better than being with people I love, eating good food, and having great conversation. Besides, this will give us a chance to get to know each other better and start our friendship off on the right foot this time. Seriously, we're doing it. You can't say no to pregnant women. Trust me, I've been one."

Allison jumped off her chair and hugged Sophie. "Thank you so much. You are the best person in the world."

Sophie nodded in agreement. "One of them, anyway. I'll call you later with the details."

Allison walked Sophie to her car and opened her trunk for her. Sophie shoved the box of peaches in and slammed the back of her Escalade shut.

"I hear Will's taking you out tonight," she said as she pulled out her keys and got in her car.

Allison smiled. "I hadn't heard. Where am I going?"

Sophie shut the door and rolled down the window. "Dress cute but casual. And that's all you're getting out of me."

Allison waved as Sophie drove off. She wondered when Will was going to get around to actually asking her himself. She was surprised when Will didn't stop by that day to see her, and she asked Betsy about it.

"Oh, didn't you know? I thought Will would have told you. When Will got home last night, Daphne was on his doorstep, crying her eyes out. She quit on him. He's at the office, answering the phones and doing everything himself. He's swamped. A temp agency is sending him someone tomorrow, but right now he's pulling his hair out."

Allison frowned and went back to work. *Interesting.*

Later that day when she got home from work, she found Gage Dulaney waiting for her on her front porch. She almost didn't get out of her truck. By the frown on his face, she could tell this wasn't going to be fun.

"Hey, Gage. What brings you to this part of town?" she asked, leaning up against the stair railing. She didn't want to invite him inside, so they'd have to talk out on the porch, whether he liked it or not.

"Daphne told me that you and Will have started seeing each other. Is it true?" he asked, looking at her coldly.

Allison nodded her head. "Yes, it's true. I know Daphne's pretty upset about it."

Gage tilted his head and studied her. "Didn't you know I would have given you anything? I would have given you the best job. I would have bought you new clothes. Heck, I would have even bought you a new car. Why wouldn't you give me a chance, Allison? You've always known how I've felt about you. And you've never given me anything but friendship," he said bitterly.

Allison swallowed and glanced over her shoulder at Maggie's house. She might need backup.

"Well, you're right, Gage. I've only offered you my friendship because friendship is all I've ever felt for you. I'm sorry if that hurts your feelings, I really am, but I've always had feelings for Will, and when he asked me out, I said yes. I hope that means you and I can still be friends, though," she said, wincing at his stormy expression.

"*You* and *me*? Friends? That's just perfect. Will Carson, rags to riches. Everything he touches turns to gold. And now he gets you too. That's just great. Sure, Allison, let's be friends. And as your friend, I'm going to let you in on a little secret. You're dating someone just like your dad. Will is so traumatized by growing up poor that he'll do *anything* to be rich now. He has so many deals going now your dad would be impressed. Most of those deals are legal, granted. But some of them? I don't think so, and my dad doesn't either. Haven't you had enough of living on the edge? Will only cares about money now, Allison. I thought you were smart enough to know that. This is pathetic. I'm out of here," he said, his voice rising and his pale face turning an unattractive mottled shade of red.

Allison clenched her hands by her side as she silently watched Gage drive away. Then she sat down on her steps and rubbed her arms. He had been so furious. Almost enraged. And all of those things he'd said about Will—they couldn't be true. Not Will.

She leaned her head on her hands for a moment and breathed in deeply as she tried to calm her heart. Gage had to be insane to think Will was like her father, but she couldn't help remembering her conversation with Bonnie when they'd talked about what had turned her father into the man he was today. Maybe a long time ago, her father *had* been like Will. Just a young man trying a little too hard to be successful.

Allison stood up and paused when she saw Maggie. She waved and ran over to Maggie's yard so Maggie wouldn't have to walk so far. "Hey, Maggie," she said breathlessly.

Maggie looked her over. "I saw Gage storm off. You okay?"

Allison sighed and shoved her hands in her back pockets. "Yeah, I guess. He just called me stupid for dating a man just like my dad. He said Will's involved in some illegal deals," she said, feeling sick just repeating what Gage had said.

Maggie looked horrified at first but then smiled wryly. "Gage is so slick, Allison. He's trying to drive a wedge between you and Will. And he'd love to be your rebound guy, I'm sure. Just ignore everything he said, Allison. Seriously, I know people, and Will would never stoop that low."

Allison bit her lip and felt miserable. Gage had done a pretty good job of putting doubts in her head. No way did she want to be with anyone even remotely like her father. Maybe she had rushed into this relationship a little too fast.

"Do you want me to ask Luke? He would know about something like that. And he's also in a position to hear the gossip if Will was involved in anything dirty."

Allison nodded silently, feeling horrible. But she couldn't just go on Maggie's gut feelings on this. Her relationship with Will didn't just affect her. It would have an impact on Talon and Aspen too. She couldn't be too careful.

Maggie looked a little disappointed in her but agreed to do it. "I'll call you and let you know, okay? And tell Aspen I want to see her new outfit before Rowan picks her up tonight."

Allison nodded and turned to walk away. But Maggie called her back.

"Allison? I know it's almost impossible for you to trust people after what your father put you through, but just remember that some people are worthy of trust. And they deserve to be given it."

Allison winced and turned around without saying anything in response. She walked back to her house just as the bus drove up. She smiled as Talon and Aspen got off the bus and relaxed when she realized they were both so excited about their plans for that night that they wouldn't even notice she might have just made a huge mistake with her life.

tWeNty-foUR

Just as Sophie said he would, Will called a half hour later to ask Allison out to dinner. She had to remind herself that people were innocent until proven guilty, so she said yes. Then she forgot about herself for an hour and helped Aspen get ready for her date. It was Aspen's first official date, and she was bursting with excitement.

"What was your first date like?" Aspen asked as she went through Allison's box of earrings.

Allison lay across Aspen's bed and smiled. "Well, I was actually at college before I went on an official date. In high school we just kind of all hung out together. So I was pretty excited for my first date. His name was Peter, and he was this super-tall blond guy with bright blue eyes. One of the nicest guys I've ever known. He took me to a great Italian restaurant, and then we went to a concert where his roommate played in the orchestra. It was a really nice first date."

Aspen frowned. "I don't remember you ever mentioning anyone named Peter. What happened?"

Allison sighed and picked at the yarn on Aspen's quilt. "Oh, the usual. We didn't have the right chemistry," she said, thinking of Will and their crazy chemistry.

Aspen smiled and picked the earrings with rhinestone jewels hanging from a spray of metal shards. Allison smiled her approval. "Perfect for your new jeans and shirt."

Aspen agreed and then walked to the bathroom. "Can you help me with my makeup? I never wear any, but I want to look glamorous tonight."

Allison followed her willingly and smiled when Talon joined them. He must have been feeling lonely.

"So what's the deal? All this effort for going to the movies? You've got to be kidding me," he said, sounding irritated.

Aspen rolled her eyes. "Tal, if you'd just ask out Sarah, then you could have someone going to a lot of trouble for *you*."

Allison raised her eyebrows at Talon but kept silent. Talon looked at his feet for a moment but then smiled. "Do you think I should? I've got all that money I've been saving, and I could borrow the truck."

Allison groaned inwardly at the thought of her brother driving their only transportation to take Sarah on a date. She trusted her brother. *Sort of.* But then again, she remembered what kind of driver she had been at sixteen. "Why don't you guys double date with Rowan and Aspen?" Allison asked quickly.

Aspen smiled and nodded. "Well, not tonight, of course. There's no time to ask her, but why don't you ask her out for next weekend and we can plan something fun?"

Talon smiled and leaned up against the door as Allison applied a smoky shade of eyeliner on Aspen's eyelids.

"Okay. Maybe I will," he said and walked out again.

Allison smiled at Aspen in the mirror. "You're a good sister."

Aspen nodded serenely. "I know."

Allison finished Aspen's hair and makeup and wasn't the least surprised to see how gorgeous she was. "We're going to have to hide you from the model scouts from now on. I can't have you going off to New York without me."

Aspen laughed and turned in a graceful circle. "I wish Mom could see me now," she said wistfully.

Allison winced and hugged Aspen. "Are you missing her?"

Aspen shook her head. "Nah, she just always acted like I didn't matter as much as you or Talon because I was never really pretty. Maybe if she could see me right now, she'd finally think I mattered."

Allison's heart hurt as she rubbed Aspen's back. "You've always mattered, Aspen. Just because you're gorgeous now doesn't make you matter more."

Aspen smiled and hugged her sister back. "I know. Don't be sad, Allie. It's okay. What matters now is that I get to go on a date. He should be here in ten minutes."

The two sisters ran downstairs and peeked out the window when Allison remembered Maggie wanted to see Aspen before her date. All three Vaughns walked over to Maggie's house and knocked on the door. Luke was the one who answered, and his expression was the best compliment Aspen could have gotten. She giggled delightedly at his shocked expression.

"*Aspen?* I don't believe it. Maggie! We have a poor lost model on our front porch!" he called over his shoulder.

Maggie hurried to his side with her camera. Allison smiled in gratitude. She should have thought to take a picture.

"Aspen, you're just like Cinderella. You've transformed into the princess. Look at her eyes, Allison! I hope you'll let me paint your portrait after the baby gets here. You are just too beautiful for words," she said, going on and on. Aspen started turning red at all the compliments, so Talon jumped in.

"What? I'm not model material? You've never said you wanted to paint me," he said, sounding huffy.

Maggie turned and looked at him thoughtfully. She grabbed his chin and turned him this way and that way in the sunlight. "Actually, you would make a good model. And everyone knows Allison is gorgeous. Maybe I'll do all three of you," she said, sounding thoughtful.

Aspen whipped her head around as she heard Rowan's car drive up. She ran down the porch stairs and over to the curb as Rowan stepped out and slammed the door shut. He walked around the car and stopped when he got a good look at Aspen, who was standing still, smiling at him shyly. His eyes got round, and his mouth went slack as he walked slowly forward. Maggie hurried toward the couple, taking picture after picture.

"*Aspen?*" Rowan asked.

Aspen nodded her head, blushing. Rowan cleared his throat and tried again. "Aspen, these are for you," he said, handing her a small bouquet of daisies, carnations, and baby's breath.

Aspen looked as if she'd just received three dozen roses.

"They're beautiful," she said, reaching for them. Maggie took the money shot and looked back at Allison victoriously. "I got it!" she whispered.

Allison laughed but then choked up and had to wipe a tear from her cheek. Her baby sister had just gotten flowers. Talon sighed deeply and looked at Luke for a manly sneer, but Luke looked charmed by the scene as well.

"Let me give these to my sister so she can put them in water," Aspen said, turning back to Allison. Luke took that opportunity to walk quickly to Rowan, shake his hand, and talk quietly into his ear for a moment. Allison looked at Luke suspiciously when Rowan turned pale and looked nervous.

Allison took the flowers from Aspen and gave her a quick hug and kiss. "Have the best time of your life, sweetie. But be home by eleven."

Aspen laughed and nodded. "I'll be home on time. Bye, everyone!" she called out. Then she skipped to Rowan's side. He quickly opened the car door, aware of their audience, and blushed accordingly.

They all watched happily as Aspen drove away.

"So what did you whisper in Rowan's ear?" Allison asked Luke as the car turned the corner.

Luke shrugged but then he saw Maggie's expression and laughed. "*Fine.* I'll tell you. Aspen doesn't have a dad here to look out for her. And Talon would be too embarrassed to do it, so I put the scare on him. It's no big deal. I just said he'd better be the perfect gentleman with Aspen or I'd find him and put him in the hospital." He laughed at Allison's and Maggie's horrified expressions.

Talon laughed and gave Luke a high-five. "No wonder he looked scared to death."

Maggie and Allison watched as Luke and Talon walked into the house, already discussing their movie choices for the night.

"Can you believe him?" Maggie asked with a shake of her head.

Allison smiled. "I think it's kind of sweet. I'm actually glad he did it. I could have said the same thing, but its scarier coming from Luke."

Maggie raised an eyebrow and sat down on the porch swing. "You'd better watch it, Allie, or you might actually start liking Luke."

Allison laughed and sat down next to her. "I'll admit it; he's starting to grow on me."

Maggie sighed happily and glanced at her camera. "I know what I'm giving Aspen for her birthday now. A scrapbook for all these pictures. She's going to love it."

Allison smiled warmly. "Threats *and* pictures. You guys are the nicest people in the world. Thank you."

Maggie grinned and pointed to a new car pulling up. "Allie, I think this date is yours."

Allison jumped up and ran down the sidewalk. She had completely forgotten about the time in her excitement for her sister. Will got out of the car and glanced at her dirty jeans with a frown.

"Did you change your mind?" he asked.

Allison grabbed his hand and pulled him toward her house. "Bye, Maggie! Um, *no*. I didn't. I just need to change into something nicer. I'll be ready in five minutes," she promised.

Will looked doubtful but followed her into the house. She ran up the stairs and threw open her closet. She had no time to consider and just grabbed the first thing, which happened to be an outfit she hadn't worn in years because she'd gained a little weight. She studied the white jeans and the burgundy silk scooped neck shirt and decided to go for it. If it was still too tight, then oh well. Will wouldn't care anyway. He liked her in old jeans and an apron. She slipped out of her clothes quickly and right into the outfit. As she buttoned the jeans she closed her eyes tight and winced. Then she looked down in surprise. She must have lost a little weight. A grin spread across her face as she thanked all the fruit she had been hauling around lately.

She ran to the bathroom, quickly brushed her teeth, ran her hands through her hair, and reapplied her lipstick. Then she grabbed her sandals in one hand and ran down the stairs.

tWeNty-five

Okay! I'm ready," she said, out of breath, as she bent down to slip her shoes on.

Will looked shocked and delighted at the same time. "Whoa. That was incredible."

Allison grinned and grabbed her keys, motioning for him to go out the door so she could lock up.

"I am a woman of many talents," she promised as she followed him to his car.

Will grinned and opened the door for her. "I have never once doubted that," he said. As he walked around the car, he frowned at the Petersons' house. "Why did I just see Maggie Peterson taking a picture of me?" he asked suspiciously before turning the key in the ignition.

Allison laughed and told him all about Aspen's first date and her future scrapbook. Will smiled good-naturedly. "Well, I guess she's planning yours too. I can see it now. A picture of me helping you into the car with the caption, 'Will falling in love with Allison for the second time.'"

Allison felt her heart skip a beat and wasn't sure how to react to that. "Actually I can see her doing that," she said, blatantly ignoring the fact that he had practically just told her he was in love with her.

As they drove down Main Street, Will asked her all sorts of questions—her favorite music group, color, movie, book, everything. Allison concentrated so much on answering that she looked up in surprise when Will pulled into the parking lot of Lone Peak High School.

"The high school? Are you taking me to a play tonight?" she asked, looking at all the cars in the parking lot.

Will shook his head and hopped out. Allison opened her door and stood up before he could reach her.

"There is a play rehearsal going on tonight, but that's not why we're here. I have permission from the principal to show you something. Come on," he said, grabbing her hand and pulling her toward the front entrance.

Allison grinned as all the memories swamped her. She'd had so many good times walking these halls. Will sped up as soon as they were inside and Allison almost tripped as she tried to keep up with his long legs.

He finally came to a stop at the drinking fountain by the gym.

He motioned toward the fountain as if it were something special. She walked closer, peeking into the basin in case he'd hidden something inside. She hated scavenger hunts.

"Don't look irritated, Allison. Do you remember this spot?"

Allison looked again at the white drinking fountain and raised one eyebrow. "This is our first date, so I'm going to go along with this. Yes, Will. I do remember this water fountain. There were many times I even stopped here to get a drink on occasion."

Will shook his head in pity. "No, Allie. This is the place where I first saw you. You were coming out of the gym right after cheerleading practice, and I had just finished making up a test for English. We reached the water fountain right at the same time, and I motioned for you to go ahead and you just stood there and looked up into my face and kind of grinned at me, like you were happy to see me or something. After you took your drink, I took mine. When I stood up, you were still there leaning up against the wall and you said, 'Hi, I'm Allison.'"

Allison leaned up against the wall in the same spot she had so many years before and grinned up at Will in just the same way.

"I remember. And then you said, 'I'm Will Carson,' and you sort of blushed a little. I wanted to find out more about you, but some of the girls came out right then and interrupted us."

Will studied her face across the drinking fountain. "That moment when you smiled at me and told me your name was one of the best moments of my life. I remember thinking, 'If only I could have a girlfriend like her.'"

Allison laughed and stood up. She walked over to Will and put her arms around his neck. "Guess what I was thinking? I was thinking, 'Oh my heck, he's the most gorgeous guy in the world. What I wouldn't give to have a boyfriend like him.'"

Will grinned down into her eyes and wrapped his arms around her, pulling her in closer. "You wouldn't believe the daydreams I used to have of kissing you right here at school."

Allison's expression turned serious. "What's stopping you now?"

Will leaned down and took her mouth with his as if he had been waiting his whole life for just that moment. He brushed her lips gently with his before kissing her more fully.

Suddenly two boys with paint on their hands tore down the hall, heading toward the bathroom. Allison pulled away regretfully, blushing at the snickers and knowing grins the boys gave each other.

Will cleared his throat in embarrassment. "Sorry about that. I guess when you've waited as long as I have for one little kiss, it's easy to get carried away."

Allison reached up and gave him a quick peck. "I'm glad you did."

Will's smile bloomed in his eyes first and then spread to his whole face as he grabbed her hand and led her back outside to the car.

"Now for our second destination."

Allison frowned, wondering where they were headed next and if there would be food there. Will drove back toward Alpine and stopped at the city park. After parking the car, he led her toward the gazebo. He waited while she sat down before he said anything.

"You have to know why I brought you here," he said almost hopefully.

Allison looked around. Will was taking a trip down memory lane, which was sweet, but also kind of tricky when she couldn't remember the things he hoped she would.

"Um, you saw me here at the park?"

Will looked disappointed. "Well, yeah. Do you remember that time Bella decided she wanted to go to the park by herself? She had asked my mom to take her but she had to work. She asked me, and I said no; I had too much homework to do. So she got mad and walked down to the park all by herself. Well, by the time we realized she had taken off, she had been gone for probably an hour. We were driving all over town, looking for her. We'd called the police, and as I was driving down this road, I saw you pushing Bella in the swing."

Allison nodded. "She told me she just wanted to feel the wind in her hair. I had been on my way home from the store and saw her all by herself, so I decided to stop and see if she was okay. And she was."

Will sat down beside her and took her hand. "When I saw you pushing my sister on the swing, that was the exact moment I fell in love with you. Couldn't you tell?" he asked softly, kissing each finger of her hand.

Allison sighed in pure happiness. "Really? Well, I thought you were looking at me kind of funny. At first I thought you might be mad because you weren't smiling, but then you just walked up to me and you said—"

Will interrupted her. "I said, 'You're the most amazing girl in the world.'"

Allison grinned and leaned into Will's chest, resting her head on his shoulder. "I couldn't stop smiling for a week."

Will kissed the top of her head and then stood up, pulling her up with him. "I wanted to take you in my arms and kiss you that night, but I was too scared. I knew who you were then. How could Will Carson kiss the richest, most popular girl in Alpine?"

Allison put her arms around his waist and lifted her head. "Tell you what. I'll let you kiss the poorest, most unpopular girl in Alpine. It might not be as wonderful, but it's all I have to offer you."

Will shook his head. "You're magnificent. You always have been, and you always will be." He dipped her low over his arm and kissed her.

When he finally let her up, she felt dizzy and had to sit down for a moment.

Will leaned on the railing and just looked at her with a half-smile. Allison blushed as she felt her heart pounding. She'd never felt like this before when other dates had kissed her. She finally knew what it was like to go weak in the knees.

"You know, I never even kissed a boy until I went to college," she said lightly as her heart continued to pound.

Will frowned and crossed his arms over his chest. "Hmm. I think I specifically told you not to kiss anyone until you moved back to Alpine and became my girlfriend."

Allison laughed and stood up. They walked back to the car holding hands.

"So who was your first kiss?" she asked curiously as they buckled up.

Will looked surprised by the question and then a little embarrassed. "There was a really pretty girl in one of my classes that I used to study with. Her name was Deidre, and it only lasted for about three weeks. Her missionary came home, and that was the end of our study group."

Allison smiled at Will as he drove toward Kohler's. "Deidre, huh? Two-timing me with Deidre. I can't believe it."

Will grinned at her before pulling into the parking lot of the grocery store. "Hey, I've never been engaged. That would be you."

Allison got out of the car and winced. "That would be me. I'm so grateful he dumped me. If he hadn't, I would have never known what it was like to be kissed by you," she said, still thinking about the last kiss.

Will pulled her in close to his side as they walked down one of the aisles.

"So is this where you feed me dinner?" she asked doubtfully.

Will laughed and stopped right in front of the almond M&M's. "I promise you'll go home full. Be patient for just a little longer. I had to show you this spot because it's very important to me. After you moved away, I kind of felt like part of me died. All of that love I had for you was so big, and I had nowhere to put it. I had no one to give it to. I went on a mission, I went to school and to work, and I dated a lot of girls. But part of me always felt empty. And then one day I look up, and there you are. You're standing right there in front of me, trying to steal my candy. And all that love for you that I had shoved away in a corner somewhere in my heart was right there again. This spot is where life began again for me," he said as he took both her hands.

Allison swallowed and blinked back a few tears. "How can you be so sweet to me? I don't deserve this," she whispered, turning her head away from curious shoppers.

Will leaned closer, kissing her cheek gently. "I took you to all these places tonight because I wanted you to know this is very serious for me. I've never given my heart to anyone but you. You've always had it. I love you, Allison."

Allison threw her arms around his neck, holding him tight. "Will, I love you too. I always have," she whispered.

Will pulled back, not caring that an elderly couple was glaring at them, and kissed Allison with a joy that was apparently shocking.

"Excuse me! Oh my word. Will Carson, what are you doing making out in the candy aisle?" demanded a very irate voice.

Will let go of Allison and stepped back. "Oh, hi, Bishop Henderson. I'd like you to meet my girlfriend, Allison Vaughn."

Allison's mouth fell open, and she said the first thing that came to her mind as she stared at the older man who was looking questioningly at her. "It's not what it looks like."

The man raised his eyebrows as his mouth split into a grudging smile. "Well, it kind of looks like Will here was showing a little too much affection for public viewing."

Allison blushed and stammered for a few more minutes as Will grinned and stayed silent. Finally Bishop Henderson held up his hands.

"We'll talk on Sunday," he promised Will, pointing at him. Then he strolled away with his cart.

Will and Allison looked at each other and burst out laughing. They ran from the store and drove quickly back to his house, where he had a catered dinner waiting for them. They ate chicken cordon bleu with wild rice, asparagus, and salad. For dessert they had dark chocolate torte with vanilla bean ice cream.

Allison sat on Will's couch and watched nervously as he walked toward her. She remembered every rule she'd ever lectured her brother and sister on dating and worried that Will would want to start kissing her again.

He saw her expression and grinned self-consciously. "You don't have to look at me like that. You can trust me. Besides, there's a good reason I spent all that time kissing you in public instead of here. I didn't want you to have to face Aspen tonight when she asked you if you followed all the rules."

Allison smiled in relief and immediately relaxed. Will sat down and slipped an arm around her shoulders. They spent the next two hours talking about their past, their dreams, their disappointments, and what they wanted for the future.

When Will took her home that night, she knew she'd never have a date as amazing as the one she'd just had.

tWeNty - six

That night was the beginning of a month of fun, exciting, and adventurous dates. Sometimes Will would take her to dinner and a movie, but other nights, he would take her fishing or hiking. Once he even took her spelunking. Her favorite date of all was when he surprised her with tickets to a Rascal Flatts concert. She had never liked country music, but she found herself on her feet dancing the entire time and never enjoyed herself more. She was now Rascal Flatts' biggest fan. Will even bought her a concert T-shirt that she was scared to wear because she loved it so much. It was the best month of Allison's life. And every day, she could feel herself falling more and more in love with him.

But it was his effect on Talon that was almost magical. Talon didn't seem so lost or angry or even worse, zombielike. Will's aggression therapy was working wonders.

But that didn't stop the doubts. Gage's words would flash through her mind at the oddest times, during conversations with Will or even right before she went to sleep. She had to remind herself over and over again that Will was innocent until proven guilty. She knew she loved him. Why couldn't she just relax and trust him?

A week after the Rascal Flatts concert, Betsy walked down to the fruit stand where Allison was just taking cash from Luke for a box of mixed fruit.

Betsy gave Luke a quick hug and sent him on his way before turning to her.

"I hate doing this to you, especially since it's Gage Dulaney, but could you drop some fruit off at his office on your way home tonight? He said he'd pay double, and I never say no to money. I'll split the difference with you," she said with a wheedling smile.

Allison sighed and rolled her eyes. "I've never told anyone this before, but I just feel so uncomfortable around Gage. Is there anyone else who can do it?" she asked, knowing she sounded whiny.

Betsy frowned and shoved her hands in her pockets. "Well, it's no secret he wanted you for himself. I think if you show up there and you show him how happy you are with Will, it'll just put his hopes for you to rest. Everyone knows you and Will are crazy in love. Sorry, Allison. I think you should go for his own good. Then maybe he can move on to someone else," she said and pointed out the three boxes of fruit for Gage.

Allison felt like stomping her feet but kept her mouth shut, thinking of the extra money that could go toward the dental checkups she needed to take Aspen and Talon to.

She shoved the fruit in the back of her truck and drove out of the parking lot with a half-hearted wave to Betsy. She headed down the road to the Dulaneys' real estate office and parked in back. She knew how careful the Dulaneys were of their image. She didn't want to scare off good-paying clients with her rusted out truck.

She carried the first box into the office and immediately smiled as she took in her surroundings. The office smelled amazing—clean and as if someone had just baked fresh rolls. On every wall was a picture of an old-fashioned home from the early days of Alpine. The photos were framed and matted beautifully. The furniture was expensive but comfortable, and the colors were muted and relaxing. It had professional decorator written all over it.

"Well, there you are, beautiful. I was just wondering when you were going to stop by," Gage said from behind her.

Allison quickly turned around and placed the fruit in Gage's arms.

"Um, yeah. I've got two more boxes for you out in my truck. I'll just go grab them," she said, wanting to leave as he stood and stared at her.

Gage smiled and put the box of fruit on the ground, pushing it toward the wall negligently.

"Oh, you can keep the fruit. I just asked for a delivery because I wanted to talk to you. You know, friend to friend."

Allison frowned and shook her head. "You could have just called me. It would have been a lot cheaper."

Gage shook his head and motioned her toward a couch. She followed him and sat down hesitantly.

"You're worth every penny. Now, why do you look so alarmed?"

Allison blushed and looked down at her jeans and her clenched hands. She relaxed her hands and looked up to meet Gage's gaze.

"Well, it's hard to forget our last conversation, Gage. You were pretty upset with me, and you said some very derogatory things about Will."

Gage nodded and rubbed his chin. "Yeah, I'm sorry about that, Allison. But you have to realize that when I first saw you back in town, I immediately thought—*hoped*—you and I would end up together. I have to admit that I was *very* disappointed things didn't work out the way I wanted them to. But I'm taking this friendship thing seriously, and that's why I invited you here today. As your friend, I want to look out for you. I want to tell you something before anyone else has the chance to rub it in your face."

Allison's heartbeat sped up, and she felt her hands go cold and clammy. "What, Gage? What is it you want to tell me?"

Gage turned to the coffee table and picked up a financial magazine. "There's an article in this magazine that mentions your dad and what he was pulling down in Texas."

Allison refused to take the magazine.

"Well, that's very thoughtful of you, Gage. I still wish you'd just called me and told me," she said, standing up.

Gage's eyes went steely and cold. "Sit down, Allison."

Allison bit her lip and knew she could leave if she wanted to. But Gage was acting funny, like he knew something she didn't. She did what he said and sat down.

"What is it, Gage? Stop playing games and just lay it on the line," she said, returning her hands to her knees.

Gage leaned back on the couch and smiled in satisfaction. "The writer of the article called your dad the most soulless predator to have a business license. Did you know that he actually advertised his special investment opportunities in magazines for the elderly? He would do seminars at all the retirement communities. Just think about it,

Allison. Your dad actually went after the weak and infirm to make a buck. The writer said your dad was moving on to the mentally disabled when he got caught. Scary, isn't it, what some people are capable of?"

Allison felt her hands begin to shake, so she clasped them together until the bones of her knuckles turned white. "Why are you doing this to me? Why are you torturing me?" For some reason she wasn't able to look way from her hands.

Gage smiled with a shrug. "I'm not torturing you, Allison. Like I said, I'm just being your *friend*. I want you to know what people are reading about your father and the fallout that might come your way. It's better to be prepared. Trust me." He paused and then said, "I just think it's so interesting."

Allison took a deep breath and looked up to see Gage looking at her with pity. "What, Gage? *What* is so interesting?" She was trying hard not to cry.

Gage studied his fingernails for a moment before answering. "Well, that you would pick someone just like your dad. That's all."

Allison stood up and started walking toward the door. She refused to waste another minute looking at Gage's triumphant smirk.

"Will's not building that park, Allison. He's turning all that beautiful land into crappy, cheap condos for old people. Do you want to know why, Allison? Because nothing matters more to him than making a quick buck. *Just. Like. Your. Dad.* He doesn't care if he's breaking promises left and right. He doesn't care. Think about it, Allison. They have *so much* in common. Neither one of them can keep their word. It's called integrity, Allison. And the man you think you love so much doesn't have any."

Allison flung the door open but looked back one last time. "You and I are *not* friends. Stay away from me," she said before fleeing to her truck.

Allison raced home and ran up to her room where she could punch her pillow and cry as loud as she wanted to. She hated Gage. She hated him for making her feel like dirt. She hated him for throwing her father in her face like acid. But mostly she hated him for making her doubt the man she loved. She sobbed into her pillow as she realized that he had accomplished what he had set out to do. He had poisoned her feelings for Will as surely as if he'd injected her heart with arsenic. She sniffed and wiped her eyes. She had a choice now. She could let the poison and the doubts sit there and fester, or she could get rid of them once and for all. She couldn't be in a relationship without trust. If she was going to love Will, she had to trust him. She would talk to him about it tonight.

He had asked her out to dinner days ago and had mentioned dressing up. Tonight was supposed to be special. She hated to bring negativity to the evening when Will had planned something so romantic, but she couldn't stand these thoughts for another day. If Will denied Gage's snide accusations, then she could finally rest easy. If he confirmed them . . . Allison burst into more tears. She didn't even want to think about what she'd have to do if he confirmed them.

tWeNty-SeveN

Three hours later, she got in Will's car and wondered why Will couldn't tell something was wrong. When he showed up on her front porch, he'd kissed her and given her red roses like he always did. True, he spent at least a half an hour talking to Aspen and Talon about their plans for the night. There'd been so much laughter and giggling that no one had noticed she hadn't said a word. And he'd been so excited to surprise Talon with a new pair of boxing gloves that he must not have noticed the strain in her eyes as he helped her into the car.

"So where are we going?" she asked, trying to act normal.

Will smiled. "Oh, it's this little restaurant up in Salt Lake I've been to before. Its French, so I hope you've taken a few language classes."

Allison smiled. "Sounds good to me. I can't wait." The last time she had eaten French food had been the night Jason had called off their engagement, so it wasn't the best memory.

She and Will talked about the fruit stand and people they knew from high school on their drive to Salt Lake. Instead of going downtown, Will drove down a canyon road and pulled into a long winding lane that lead to what looked like a French château. *La Caille*, she read on a small unobtrusive sign. She remembered hearing her parents talk about it when they'd lived there five years ago. The view from the road to the front of the restaurant was gorgeous, with manicured gardens and beautiful water fountains. Her dad always took his most important clients to this restaurant. It was extremely elegant and very expensive. She glanced down at the simple black dress an old roommate had given her and hoped it was up to the job tonight.

A valet was waiting for them when Will pulled up to the front of the restaurant. Her door was opened immediately, and a hand helped her out. Will handed the keys to the valet and then took her hand automatically as they walked in together. She was silent as she took in the opulence and the incredible beauty that surrounded her. She had almost forgotten the impact this kind of lifestyle could have on the senses. The flowers alone were staggering.

Will held her chair out as they sat down at a table in the far corner of the room, overlooking the gardens. Allison sighed happily. There were some things about being rich she missed. This was one of them.

"This is wonderful, Will. Thank you for bringing me here," she said, smiling across the table.

Will sat back in his chair and studied her with a half-smile. "I always dreamed of taking you somewhere like this. I was so in love with you I couldn't see straight. And for some reason, I thought if I just had enough money, I could buy the cool car, pick you up in style, and show you the time of your life. Then you'd fall in love with me and you'd never smile at another football player ever again. But then I'd wake up," he said with a soft laugh.

Allison frowned and looked down at her lap before she spoke. "If only we had been mind readers. Of course I knew you sort of had a crush on me, but I never dreamed you felt that strongly."

Will shrugged and took a sip of water. "Would it have made a difference?" he asked seriously.

Allison looked away from his searching eyes and stared unseeingly at the peacocks walk around the lawns. "Maybe it would have. If I knew you felt the same, I'd like to think I would have done whatever it took to be with you. But I didn't know for sure. I knew my father and how he would have treated you. I guess we should both just be glad we're out of high school and we're adults now," she said with a wry smile.

Will smiled back and reached across the table for her hand. He leaned over and kissed the palm of her hand as he stared at her. "You're right. The past is the past. I am who I am today because of everything I went through, just like you are who you are. I don't think I'd be half as successful today if I hadn't wanted to prove to you and to everyone else in Alpine that I was worthy of you."

Allison pulled her hand away and sat up straighter. "You never had to prove anything to me, Will. You were always good enough. I'm *not* like my father. And who cares what everyone in Alpine thinks? If I had come back to Alpine and you were still selling apples on the side of the road, what do you think would have happened between us?" she asked, curious and upset at the same time.

Will sat back and looked at her in disbelief. "You're saying that if you had bumped into me at Kohler's and I'd been in dirty jeans with dirt under my fingernails and I was still working the fruit stand that you'd be with me tonight?"

Allison smiled at the picture and nodded her head immediately. "I've had all this Will," she said, motioning with her hands around the large restaurant. "And now I have nothing. I promise you, I'm happier without the money than I ever was with it. If I had bumped into you at Kohler's and you had been just as poor as you were in high school, I would have been just as thrilled to see you. I was actually confused that you weren't in dirty jeans, to be honest," she said, looking him straight in the eye.

Will looked away. "You would be my girlfriend even if all I could do is take you to Wendy's for the dollar menu?" he asked quietly.

Allison laughed but nodded. "Yep, I was pretty much yours for the taking regardless. I actually thought about not going out with you when I found out how rich you are, just because I didn't want people to think I was only dating you for your money. You would have had an easier time if you were still poor." She smiled as the waiter walked up to their table.

They both ordered, with Will choosing the crab cocktail and pan roasted duck and Allison picking the paté with onions on toasted baguettes and the grilled tenderloin with béarnaise sauce. Allison couldn't help but notice that Will seemed moody all of a sudden.

"Are you okay? Are you mad that I'm not here for the money and that I'm only dating you because you're eye candy?" she asked, trying to get a smile out of him.

Will gave in and smiled but set his fork down. "I guess it's just hard to realize that everything I've worked so hard for these last five years doesn't mean anything to you."

Allison frowned and looked out the window for a moment. "If it was all gone tomorrow, Will, and you and I were all that was left, that would be enough."

Will looked into her eyes and smiled. "I'm being stupid, aren't I? For the last three years, I've had women chasing me from Alpine to Salt Lake just for my money, and now I'm ticked because you couldn't care less. Go figure," he said, relaxing into a laugh.

Allison shook her head and grinned at him. But just at that moment, everything Gage had told her that afternoon overwhelmed her. She needed answers.

"Now that that's settled, tell me about this amazing park you're building for Alpine. Your mom even mentioned it the other day. She said you were planning on calling it Bella's Park. I love that. Maggie said she might paint the murals. And Talon said all the kids are excited because you might put in a small skate park," she said, moving her water glass as the waiter arrived with their food.

Will waited until the waiter walked away to answer. "That's not a for sure thing, actually. I was in talks with Alpine to donate the park *last* year, but since then I've had an offer from a builder who wants to build high-end twin homes like the ones in Draper for wealthy older couples. I could make a fortune off this deal. If this deal goes through, I can start planning my retirement," he said, grinning at the thought.

Allison felt her blood turn cold as she stared at the man sitting across from her. Will had that spark of conquest in his eyes. The same spark she had seen in her dad's eyes all her life. Gage had been right.

"So, you're *not* going to build the park," she said in a quiet voice.

Will shrugged and took a bite of duck. He smiled and closed his eyes in pleasure. "*Mmmm*, this is good. The park? It's all still up in the air. I told the city I wanted control over the design, and it's been nothing but headaches ever since. They're not willing to work with me, so it only makes sense to move on," he said, taking a roll from the bread basket.

Allison swished a morsel of tenderloin in the sauce and popped it into her mouth, not tasting anything. "Will, do you mind if I ask you a question?"

Will looked up in surprise. "Of course not. Ask away."

Allison sighed and leaned closer to the table. "What's the most important thing in your life?"

Will ate the bite that was halfway to his mouth but then set his fork down and wiped his mouth with his napkin. "The most important thing to me right now? *You.*"

Allison stared into his eyes and wished she could believe him. "Are you sure it's not money?"

Will's eyes turned icy as he leaned back in his chair and crossed his arms over his chest. "What's on your mind, Allison? If you want to say something, just say it."

Allison took a deep breath and clasped her hands in her lap. "I'm just worried. You've done nothing but work and earn money these last few years. You're more interested in building duplexes than parks. And you think that if you have a big enough bank account, then that means you're just as good as everyone else."

Will's eyes burned angrily. "It's not a crime to work hard, Allison. And I know I'm just as good as everyone else. The difference now is that everyone else knows it too."

Allison shook her head as tears formed in her eyes. "I don't know if I can do this, Will. I loved you in high school. Believe me, I did. I still do. But I refuse to be with someone who's like my dad—someone who values things and dollar amounts more than people. When Gage told me about the park, I just couldn't believe it. He said you broke your promise to the city of Alpine just so you could make money off the elderly. Please, please tell me that money isn't the most important thing to you," she pleaded.

Will threw his napkin on his half-eaten food and stood up. He tossed some large bills on the table and pushed his chair in as the waiter practically ran to their table, asking if anything was wrong with the food.

"I just lost my appetite," Will said. Then he walked off toward the front of the restaurant, not bothering to wait for her. Allison slipped out of her chair and ran after him. She caught up to him at the door and grabbed his arm.

"Please! Will, *just wait!*" she whispered urgently as he opened the door and signaled the valet for his car.

"Are you okay getting a ride home with me or do you want me to call you a cab?" Will asked coldly, refusing to look at her.

Allison stepped back as if she'd been slapped. "*What?* Will, don't act like this. I didn't mean to upset you, but can't you see why I'm worried?"

Will ignored her as the valet drove up with his car. She slipped into her seat as Will walked around the car, feeling the tears she'd been holding back slip down her cheeks. She turned in her seat and stared at Will as they drove down the road and out onto the main street.

"So when were you and Gage talking about me and my business dealings?" Will asked angrily.

Allison swallowed and smoothed her dress over her knees. "He came over to my house a month ago when Daphne told him we were together. He was pretty upset. He told me that I was dating someone just like my dad and that you had so many deals going you could make my dad jealous. Then he said that some of those deals were illegal," she said quietly, staring at his face. His jaw was so tense it looked like it was going to crack. "I didn't believe him, Will. But then today he arranged it so I had to deliver fruit to his office. He told me how my dad had been going around defrauding the elderly and disabled. And then he told me about you. I didn't want to believe it," she continued when he didn't say anything. "But when you started talking about money and the duplexes, I had to know. I'd rather call a halt to our relationship right now before, . . . *before* . . . ," she said, faltering.

Will turned and looked at her. "You mean, before you break my heart again?"

Allison shook her head. "No. Before you break mine," she said as more tears slipped down her cheeks.

Will saw the tears and sighed. He reached over like he would touch her, but then pulled back. "Gage is a liar. He and his dad do mostly real estate, but they develop subdivisions as well. I beat them out on some property last year, and they've held a grudge ever since. They accused me of bribing the land owner, but I didn't. It was all straightforward and legal. I had the higher bid. I got the deal. They lost. I'm not going to apologize for making a living, Allison."

Allison sighed and looked out the window. "Money is like a drug, and my dad is a junkie. I don't want to see the same thing happen to you, Will."

Will glared at her and drove faster. "I am not your dad, Allison," he bit out. "Not every rich person you meet is going to be a soulless sociopath. Alpine is full of the nicest, most generous, giving, *wealthy* people in Utah. And not one of them is like your dad."

Allison bit her lip, feeling miserable. "All I'm saying is that maybe we should slow things down. We kind of jumped into this relationship pretty fast. Maybe we should both step back until we're sure."

Will looked like he wanted to explode. "You mean *you* want to step back."

Allison nodded her head slowly. "Yes. I think that would be best."

Will didn't say another word as he drove home. Allison felt sick to her stomach as the minutes crept by. When they finally drove into Alpine, she had a migraine and felt horrible, guilty, and uncertain.

Will pulled up in front of her house and finally looked at her. "You're everything I've ever wanted. But I refuse to be with someone who won't trust me or believe in me."

Allison didn't even bother wiping her tears away now. There were just too many. "When you can't trust your own father, it's really hard to trust anyone. I'm sorry, Will. Maybe I'm wrong. I hope I am. But as much as I want to be with you, I can't be with someone whose whole purpose in life is to make more and more money."

Will's eyes glittered as she stared at his hard, cold face. "I can't make you believe anything, Allison. That's what faith is. You have to believe in me. But I'm not going to sit here and beg you to stay with me. Either you will or you won't."

Allison leaned over and kissed him on the cheek even though she felt like she was bleeding inside. "I don't know where we go from here, but even though we're not seeing each other exclusively, I'd like to think we can still be friends. I care about you," she said, trying to smile.

Will looked as if she'd slapped him. "Allison, when you love someone so much it hurts, it's not possible to be friends. All I've ever hoped for is to have you love me. No, we can't be friends. Just seeing you is going to kill me," he said, closing his eyes and leaning back in his seat.

Allison watched him for a moment before slipping out of the car. She didn't know what else to do. She watched silently as Will drove away, leaving her alone and heartbroken.

twenty-eight

Allison changed into jeans and waited up until eleven when Aspen came floating into the house. Aspen described everything about her date with Rowan and the Mexican restaurant and the food in such detail that Allison felt like she had been on the date with them.

"So did he kiss you good night?" Allison teased.

Aspen blushed and took her earrings off. "*Yeeessss.* Just a little one, though. He doesn't want to get caught up in anything physical right before his mission. Rowan's completely the most honorable, trustworthy, incredible guy in the world. But it was a great kiss."

Allison laughed softly and fell back on Aspen's bed. Why couldn't her love life be as simple and sweet as her sister's romance?

"So what about *your* date? I've talked you to death and you haven't said one word about Will. Where did he take you tonight? Was it dinner or did you go horseback riding or something?" Aspen asked as she began to wash the makeup from her face.

Allison sat up and tried to smile as she described the outrageously expensive restaurant. Aspen turned around and looked at her carefully.

"Are you okay? Did you and Will get into a fight or something? You look kind of sad," Aspen said, putting the wash cloth down and walking over to the bed.

Allison shrugged as her face collapsed. "I am sad. I broke things off with Will tonight."

Aspen's mouth fell open. "But you're so in love with him! I mean, when he kisses you, it's like the movies. All that passion and romance. What did he do?" she demanded.

Allison brushed new tears off her cheek and sighed. "I told him I was worried that he cared too much about money and making *more* money, and he got pretty mad. And then I told him that I wanted to slow things down and just be friends with him. And that's when he said no. He doesn't want to be friends with me. He doesn't even want to be around me anymore." Allison buried her head in her hands as her misery overwhelmed her.

Aspen patted her back comfortingly. "What a dumb thing to say," she said simply.

Allison raised her head and stared at her sister. "Me or him?"

Aspen wrinkled her nose. "*You*. Everyone knows you don't tell a man you're in love with that you just want to be friends. That's the worse thing you could ever say. What were you thinking?"

Allison sniffed and stared at her sister in surprise. "I can't be with someone like Dad, Aspen. You of all people should understand that."

Aspen got up and continued getting ready for bed as Allison sat still, stunned by her sister's reaction.

Aspen shook her head in the mirror. "Will isn't *anything* like Dad. Will loves people. I think he even loves Talon, and that's not the easiest thing to do. Dad couldn't even love his own children. So what if Will makes good money. That doesn't mean he *steals* it."

Allison looked down at her feet and felt like pulling her hair out. "Are you saying you think I just made a mistake?"

Aspen pulled out her pajamas from her drawer and didn't even look at her sister when she answered. "Yep."

Allison stood up and walked out of Aspen's room. She went downstairs and got a drink of water. Had she made a mistake? All she'd said was that she wanted to slow things down. That didn't necessarily mean that they couldn't resume their relationship at some future date.

Allison winced as she went over their conversation again in her head. She'd panicked. Pure and simple panic. If Aspen was right, and Allison's heart was telling her that she was, Allison had just hurt the really amazing man she was in love with and possibly pushed him away forever. Or maybe she was right to protect herself and her family. Allison put the glass down and stood up when she heard the front door open.

Talon walked into the kitchen, smiling. Their dad had done everything to crush him, but here he was laughing and telling her about the movie he and some friends had just seen and the girls from school they had run into. She sat at the bar stool and listened happily to every word, even laughing when Talon showed her the phone number that Hannah Price had written down for him.

She hugged him good night a half hour later and went and sat in the family room. She couldn't sleep. There was no point going to bed. If she did, she'd just wake up and start the day knowing that Will was no longer her boyfriend. At least she had two days before she had to face Betsy.

Saturday and Sunday passed by so slowly, she was almost glad when Monday morning did arrive. She had never noticed it before, but when she was with Will, she was so happy, time flew. But now that they were apart, she was so miserable, every minute felt like an hour.

Allison arrived at work right on time, even though she had dark circles under eyes and it looked like she hadn't slept in two days. Mostly because she hadn't. Betsy stood in front of the fruit stand with her fists on her hips and blood in her eyes. Allison sighed from the bottom of her soul and opened her truck door. She pushed a stray strand of hair out of her eyes and walked slowly toward her boss. She shoved her hands into her front pockets and came to a stop a few feet away from Betsy in case Betsy decided to jump her. Betsy was tough, but Allison could outrun her if it came to it.

"You think you can dump my boy? Break his heart just like that? Because he's *rich* now?" Betsy demanded, punctuating every word with a wave of her hand.

Allison didn't say anything because she had a feeling Betsy wasn't finished.

"He came over broken-hearted on Friday night. Do you know how long he's protected his heart? Too long! And then you come back and the first thing you do is smash it to bits. Who do you think you are? Well, I'll tell you what, you have another thing coming if you think you can treat Will like that. Will can have any woman he wants. *Anyone.* He's handsome, smart, and rich. Those are good things, missy."

Allison nodded silently and continued to watch Betsy carefully, keeping a safe distance between them at all times. Betsy went on for another fifteen minutes, waving her arms and getting redder and redder in the face.

"Aren't you going to say anything? Are you just going to stand there looking like the world just ended?" Betsy demanded, coming to a stop in front of her.

Allison bit her bottom lip and shook her head. "I don't know what to say, Betsy. I love your son. But I can't be with him," she said simply. Then she walked around Betsy to grab her apron. She had a feeling she was fired, but she needed something to do while she had her rear end chewed to bits.

Betsy followed her out to the fruit stand. "You love him but you can't *be* with him? That's about the most ridiculous thing I've ever heard."

Allison grabbed a box of apples and hefted it onto the top shelf. "Betsy, I know you're mad at me. Will's mad at me. My little sister is mad at me. Any second now, everyone in Alpine is going to be mad at me. But I can't be with someone like my dad. Friday night, just hearing Will talk about money and how he would rather build duplexes than a park because of all the money he could make made me realize that we're very different. I don't want to live that life again. I *can't* live that life again," she said almost desperately.

Betsy stared at her silently for a moment and then grabbed another box of apples to set next to the other one. "Okay. I can understand that. But did you ever stop and think that maybe all Will needs is a good woman to show him the right way? Maybe you're right. Maybe these last years Will's priorities have been mixed up. Well, don't you think that will change when he gets married and becomes a husband and a father?" Betsy asked, wiping dust off the chair.

Allison smoothed the wrinkles on her apron and looked at her feet. "My father had a wife and children. It didn't make any difference."

Betsy snorted. "Get your head on straight, girl. Look at what you have in front of you before you lose it all. Will is the best thing that ever happened to you. He's a *good* man. You could make him better. *Or* you could watch him walk away and know that you'll never be loved like Will would have loved you," she said before turning to walk away.

Allison felt her heart bleed as Betsy's words hit her like knives. But first she had to know something.

"Aren't you going to fire me?" Allison called out before Betsy was out of ear shot.

Betsy turned around and smiled evilly at her. "Do you really think I'd make it that easy on you?"

Allison watched Betsy disappear into the fruit shed and then slumped in her chair. She was starting to get the feeling that she might have seriously messed up. The rest of the morning was busy with car after car pulling up. At one in the afternoon, she had a break and sat down to eat a peach. She had been hoping Will would stop by to talk to her. If he tried to get her to change her mind, she would probably jump in his arms and beg him to take her back.

She'd thought all day about what Aspen and Betsy had said, and she was starting to realize that maybe they were right. She was just being paranoid. There had to be a way to make things right. Maybe if she called Will up after work they could get together and talk it out. She felt a little better at the thought and smiled as she saw Sophie get out of her car, followed by Jacie. Sophie looked fantastic in jeans and a T-shirt, but Jacie looked just horrible—pale, greenish, and limp.

"Hey, guys," Allison called out with a wave and a smile.

The two women walked toward her purposefully, not smiling.

"Are you kidding me?" Jacie said with a sneer, but then she looked at the fruit and had to close her eyes and breathe through her mouth slowly.

Allison blinked in surprise and looked to Sophie to explain. Sophie rolled her eyes and shook her head.

"We had plans, Allison. What do you think you're doing messing everything up? I just got a call from Daphne. She's back at work, *with Will.* She's ecstatic and wanted to share her joy with me. You just made Daphne the happiest woman in the world, Allison. What were you thinking?"

Allison groaned and kicked a rock out of her way. Jacie went to sit in her empty chair and tilted her head back in exhaustion.

"Is she going to be okay?" Allison asked with a tilt of her head toward Jacie.

Sophie winced. "She's usually like this for the first four or five months. Just ignore her and focus. This is your life. *Why?* Just tell us why you did it," Sophie said, looking genuinely confused.

Allison felt defensive and very young. "I can't be with someone like my dad. Will just seemed so into money and power. I can't be with someone like that."

Sophie rolled her eyes again. "Give the guy a break. He grew up dirt poor. He bought his clothes at the DI, and everyone knew he got free lunch at school. So he's enjoying having money in the bank. Who wouldn't? Don't you remember the way everyone would tease him and make fun of him? Okay, he's gone a little overboard on the get-rich plan, but can't you have a little sympathy for him? He just needs to loosen up and have a little fun. That's where *you* come in. You're not supposed to break his heart and send him running into Daphne's arms," Sophie said as she took out a pack of soda crackers from her purse and handed them to Jacie.

Allison leaned her head back, closed her eyes, and yelled as loud and as long as she could. When she was hoarse and tired, she stopped yelling, opened her eyes, and saw Sophie, Jacie, and now Betsy staring at her with wide eyes and shocked expressions.

"I can't take this anymore!" she yelled, just because she felt like it. "Okay, I messed up! I panicked and did something really stupid. Now what am I supposed to do?"

Betsy grinned at her and Sophie giggled. Jacie took a break from morning sickness to let out a little laugh.

Then Sophie walked over and hugged her. "Okay. Now you know what a bad thing you did. Now we can fix it. Jacie? We need a five-step plan. Fast."

Jacie groaned and tried to sit up. "Grovel. That's step one, two, three, four, and five," she said, looking even more green.

Betsy smiled and walked over to Allison, squeezing her arm affectionately. "There's my girl. I knew you couldn't be that stupid. Jacie's right. You have a lot of apologizing to do. Better get to it," she said. Then she walked off, whistling happily.

Sophie sighed and took Allison's hand in hers. "Remember your welcome home party? Well, it's this Friday at my house. I want to see you *and* Will at your party *together*. You have five days to fix this. And Jacie's right. Groveling is probably where you need to start. Come by the salon after work, and I'll fix your hair and makeup before you go see Will."

tWENty-NiNe

Betsy grinned and waved as Allison left work and headed straight for the salon. She hoped Sophie wasn't planning anything crazy because she only had about twenty minutes before Talon and Aspen came home. She walked into the salon and saw Sophie immediately. She was standing by her mother, and they were both looking through a hair magazine. Candy's hand was on her daughter's shoulder. It was such a simple thing, but that gesture alone told Allison that these two had a close and loving relationship. Allison's mouth turned up at the picture they made. She'd never had that kind of relationship with her mom, but maybe someday she'd have it with her own daughter.

"Hey, guys," she called out, interrupting them.

Sophie and Candy both looked up and smiled at her.

Then Candy beckoned her over, gave her a hug, and patted her back. "Don't worry, Allison. I'll tell you a little secret about men. If Will is as in love with you as he's said he is, he won't give up on you this easily. I bet a little apology and a kiss will make everything as good as new."

Allison tried to smile. "Thanks, Candy. I hope you're right."

Sophie pushed her into a chair and twirled her around. "Okay, you little stinker. What am I going to do with you? We need some hair magic to help this relationship."

Allison laughed and shook her head. "Does good hair fix every problem?"

Sophie looked surprised by the question. "Just about."

As Candy stood on her other side, Sophie pulled the rubber band out of Allison's hair. Then they both picked up handfuls of her hair and stared at it for a while. Sophie fluffed it out around her face, pulling it this way and that.

"You've got to be kidding me," Candy said in awe.

Sophie sighed. "I tried to tell you. If everyone looked like Allison, we'd be out of business."

Candy stepped closer. "Well, I do like the highlights you added."

Sophie nodded and picked up a brush, smoothing the hair. "That's all I could do, really."

Candy grinned at Allison's reflection. "We can't do anything for you, sweetie. Heavenly Father got there before us. You have beautiful hair. What about makeup, Sophie?"

Sophie studied Allison's face closely, making her blush. "Maybe a little eyeliner? Darken the brows and some lip gloss. That's all she needs. Can you believe it?"

Allison laughed uncomfortably. "Sorry there isn't more for you to do."

Sophie waved her hand. "It's okay. I'll get over it. You'll be out of here in three minutes."

Candy darkened Allison's eyebrows, and Sophie did the eyeliner. Two minutes later, Allison looked perfect.

Sophie shrugged good-naturedly. "Well, looking good's easy for you, but now's the hard part—groveling. Do you know what you're going to say?"

Allison looked at the clock. She still had fifteen minutes to spare. And if it did take longer than that, she was sure Talon and Aspen would survive. Okay. What to say?

"No. I have no idea. What do you think I should say?" she asked, biting her lip and feeling like an idiot.

Candy leaned up against the chair next to Sophie's station and tapped her chin. "I think you should just walk into his office, go right up to him, put your arms around his neck, and kiss him like he's never been kissed before. Then say, 'Will, I'm so sorry. Please forgive me for being so stupid.'"

Allison groaned and stood up, grabbing her keys. "I've never in my life been called stupid, but I think everyone I know has called me that in the past couple days. I'd better fix this fast or I'll get a complex."

Sophie grinned at her. "Stupid would be letting Will get away. Smart is realizing that what you did was wrong and making things right. If you fix this, we'll take the sign down we put on your house."

Allison laughed. "Let me guess. The sign says, 'Here lives the dumbest woman in Alpine.'"

Candy patted her back and led her to the front door. "Don't worry about it, Allison. We're women. We're allowed to change our minds. Now hurry before everyone in Highland and Cedar Hills finds out too."

Allison waved good-bye and then drove to Will's office. His car was there, she noticed with relief. She hopped out of her truck and walked into the office, wanting to get this part over as fast as she could. Daphne wasn't at the front desk. Maybe he hadn't rehired Daphne. Maybe he was still using the temp service.

No one was in the front office, so she walked over to Will's office, where she heard voices. She didn't want to interrupt a meeting, but maybe he was just talking on the phone. Allison walked over to the partially opened door and peeked in. Daphne was standing right in front of Will with her arms around his neck. Will was laughing down into her eyes as he lifted his hands to her arms. Daphne quickly leaned up and kissed him on the mouth. Allison gasped and covered her mouth quickly as she stepped back, stumbling in her haste to get to the door. Will erupted from his office so fast he must have heard her. His hand slammed the front door shut before she could pull it open.

"Allison. What are you doing here?" Will asked in a perfectly calm, normal voice.

Allison's hands were shaking as she lifted her shocked green eyes to Will's. Daphne's lipstick was still on his mouth. Allison looked quickly away, feeling sick to her stomach.

"I came over to apologize for the things I said to you the other day. I realized how wrong I was, and I wanted to see if we could start over."

Will took his hand off the door but leaned against it with his hip so she was still stuck. Allison stared expressionlessly at Daphne as she walked back to her desk with a bright, sunny smile on her face.

"Oh hi, Allison. We were just talking about you. Wow, don't you look pretty today," she said sweetly as she sat down and picked up some papers.

Allison ignored her and put her hand on the doorknob. "Please move, Will."

Will shook his head. "So you thought you could just walk in my office and apologize to me and everything would go back to the way it was? You can break my heart one day and fix it the next? That easy, huh?"

Allison felt her cheeks heat up as Daphne listened in to their conversation and grinned. But she remembered Jacie's advice. Groveling left no room for pride. And she had been wrong. But then again, he'd been kissing Daphne just seconds before. Maybe she didn't want him back. She looked up at Will and saw real pain in his eyes. She'd grovel.

"Will, I panicked. I'm so incredibly sorry I hurt you. I never want to hurt you again. If you give me another chance, I promise I'll trust in you and have faith in you. *Please*, Will."

Will's face softened, and he reached up to push a strand of blonde hair behind her ears. Daphne shot up from her desk and walked toward them on her five-inch heels.

"Life just doesn't work that way, Allison. Will is an *amazing* man, and he deserves to be treated like a king. If Will took *me* to La Caille, I would have been in heaven. I for sure wouldn't have treated him like dirt. Will, you're better off without her."

Allison glanced up at Will's face and saw he had closed off from her. Daphne's words had closed the door she had cracked open. Well, she just had more groveling to do then. But not here in front of Daphne.

"You're right. I treated him like dirt. He didn't deserve it. But then again, he didn't deserve to be treated like dirt in high school when you enjoyed making fun of him so much, did he? I'll let you two get back to work, or whatever it was you were doing," she said. Will had moved back from the door, so Allison opened it and walked out.

Allison knew Will wouldn't follow her, so she got in her truck and didn't look back. She thought over the kiss she had seen between Daphne and Will and knew Daphne had been the one to initiate it. But for some reason, that fact didn't make her feel any better. Will was the one who had let her get close enough to do it. But then again, Will was a single man, and he had one beautiful secretary. Why shouldn't he kiss her?

Allison slammed out of her truck as the bus pulled up. She pushed her problems to the side as Talon and Aspen jumped off the bus and ran toward her.

"Allie!" Aspen said, breathlessly. "Allie, I just saw Dad."

Allison gasped. Talon nodded his head. "I could swear it was him. We were sitting in the back of the bus, and we saw this cool old-fashioned Mustang drive by. You remember how Dad loved old cars? Well, we looked, and it was Dad. He was wearing a baseball hat and he has a beard now, but I'm telling you it was Dad. He's here for us."

Allison felt as if the wind had been knocked out of her. Maggie walked out onto the front porch, shielding her eyes from the sun. "Hey, guys. Everything okay?"

Talon and Aspen ran to her side and told her what they'd seen. Maggie's face turned ashen. "We can deal with this. Luke was saying just this morning that he was going to talk to you again about going down to the police station to file charges against Max. Today sounds like the perfect day. Let me call him and see if he can hurry home," she said, disappearing into the house.

Aspen and Talon returned to Allison's side, standing close to her and looking nervous.

"What do we do if he comes to the door? What if he tries to take us, Allie?" Talon asked, trying not to sound scared.

Allison rubbed her face with her hands. "He can't take you. I have legal custody of you. After we file charges, we'll get a restraining order. It'll be okay. I can't believe he's here. This is the one place he shouldn't be if he wants to stay out of jail," she said, shaking her head.

Maggie joined them, and they all walked into the house. Talon and Aspen threw their backpacks down in the hallway and headed for the kitchen. Maggie followed them and picked up the phone.

"Hi, Grandma? We're in trouble. Can you come over? Yeah, Talon and Aspen think they just saw Max driving down the road. Bring Grandpa too."

Maggie held a hand under her stomach as she leaned against the counter, looking worriedly at Talon and Aspen. "We're not going to let anything happen to you two. I promise."

Allison smiled. "Maggie, you are one amazing neighbor, you know. I can just see it now. A pregnant woman holding off Max Vaughn with a broom."

Talon and Aspen smiled at the image, and Maggie grinned. "I may look non-threatening right now, but when I'm in my prime, I can take on anyone. But no, you're right. I won't fight your father off with a broom. I'll fight him off with Luke. When Luke gets mad, he's scary. No one can stand up to Luke," she said proudly.

Allison rolled her eyes. "Will totally could," she said and then frowned, looking away.

Maggie walked over and sat next to her. "Allie, I just heard this morning that you dumped Will. You should have called me. Are you okay?"

Allison shook her head as Talon and Aspen listened carefully for her answer. "Oh yeah. I'm great. I went over to Will's office to apologize and found him kissing Daphne. Yeah, life is wonderful. And now to find out my dad is here in town. It just can't get any better, can it?"

Maggie winced at the sarcasm and looked at Talon and Aspen. Aspen took a sip of chocolate milk before she spoke. "Allie, don't worry about Daphne. Will's just mad and hurt. Of course he's going to let Daphne kiss him. How else can he make you hurt as much as you hurt him?"

Allison closed her eyes and leaned her head back on the couch. "How do you know so much about men?"

Maggie looked curiously at Aspen, waiting for her reply. "Yeah, Aspen. That's kind of perceptive for a sixteen-year-old."

Talon sighed loudly. "You grow up quick when you're a Vaughn."

Aspen shrugged. "Everyone has their talents. Mine is being able to see relationships as they really are."

Maggie looked intrigued. "Me too. I can tell who's real and who isn't. What do you see when you look at me and Luke?" she asked.

Aspen joined them on the couch, soon followed by Talon. "Hmm. Well, that's easy. I see two people who love each other so much that it's almost scary," she said, looking serious.

Maggie frowned. "What do you mean by scary?"

Aspen looked uncomfortable for a moment. "Well, it's a great thing. Don't get me wrong. I'm glad I can see you and Luke every day and see that kind of love. I never saw it growing up, so I wasn't even sure it existed. But the scary part is, what if something happened to you or Luke? What would happen to the other one? It's like Romeo and Juliet. If one goes, so does the other. Life would be over."

Maggie frowned and looked out the window as she thought about it. "I don't know if I agree with the life being over part, but you're right.

It would be hard. I think for someone who doesn't have the gospel, that might be the case. But when you love someone as much as I love Luke and you have eternity, you can handle anything. It comes down to covenants."

Aspen's eyes went wide, and she nodded her head. "Wow. That's good."

Talon looked at Allison. "Is that what Allison had? Because I swear she's looked half dead ever since she broke up with Will."

Maggie and Aspen smiled and looked at her. Allison tried to smile, but that just made everyone wince.

"You don't have to pretend, Allie," Maggie reassured her. "You *are* half dead. When things are right with Will again, you'll be back to normal."

Allison leaned her head against the couch and felt like crying. "And what if that never happens? Am I doomed to walk the earth alone, like some ghost, just breathing and eating and getting through the day so I can get up and do the same thing the next day? No joy, no happiness, no life, no love."

Maggie didn't say anything, and Aspen looked down at her fingernails. Talon looked disturbed and jumped up when he heard a knock on the door. Allison jumped up a second later and raced after him, followed by Aspen and Maggie. She got to the door just as Talon opened it. It was Luke. Allison sighed in relief, and Talon pulled the door wider for Luke to enter.

"Come in, Luke. Please," Allison said.

Luke slapped Talon on the back and squeezed Allison's arm comfortingly. He leaned over and kissed Maggie on the lips and then smiled at Aspen. "Okay. Let's go sit down and go over everything," he said, taking charge.

Allison followed everyone back to the kitchen table. Bonnie and Frank arrived moments later, and they all listened as Talon and Aspen recounted what they'd seen. Luke thought it would be wise to go to the police station immediately. Allison naturally insisted on being there with Talon when they filed charges against Max.

Half an hour later they were finally sitting in front of Officer Townsend, who didn't look surprised to see them.

Allison had to ask. "You act like this is normal. We're not the only ones?"

Officer Townsend looked up and grimaced. "Identity theft is one of the fastest growing crimes we have. We see it every day. And it's usually a family member doing it. Wait right here. I'll be right back with copies of the paperwork."

After Officer Townsend left, Luke walked over to Talon and sat down next to him. "You're amazing, Talon. You're handling this very well."

Talon looked sick. "I wish Will would take me boxing again. I think if I could just pound the bag for an hour, I would feel better."

Allison felt even more guilty and sick at heart. Luke glanced at Allison before taking out his phone and quickly dialing a number. "Hey, Will. How's it going, man? You been golfing lately? . . . Well, I'm calling because me and Talon here are thinking about doing a little boxing. You want to come along and show me the ropes? Talon thinks he can take me. I need someone there to make sure I make it home in one piece. . . . Perfect. Okay, I'll see you at seven."

Luke looked at Allison apologetically but grinned when he saw Talon's face. Talon jumped up, pumping his fist in the air. "Yes! I can't wait. Rock climbing was cool, but boxing is the best. I hope he doesn't back out just because Allison dumped him."

Luke winced and stood up gratefully when Officer Townsend walked back in the room. They finished the paperwork and left the police station quickly. As Talon jumped in Luke's car, Luke grabbed Allison's arm before she could follow.

"How about you? Are you okay?" he asked.

Allison frowned and shrugged. "I'm *always* okay. I've survived this long. I'll survive a little longer," she said pensively.

Luke shook his head. "I mean about Will. Maggie told me you broke things off with him. You just seem kind of . . . miserable."

Allison hugged herself as a breeze ruffled through her hair. "Miserable. That pretty much sums it up. I messed everything up. Right now, he's probably making out with Daphne. But that's life, right? You mess up. You deal with the consequences."

Luke nodded his head. "Well, for what it's worth, I'm sorry things didn't work out. I really like Will. I thought you guys would be perfect together. And just so you know, everything Gage said was total crap. Will is one of the most honest businessmen I know. But there are a lot of single guys around. Just because it didn't work out with Will doesn't mean you can't still go out and have fun and date. I've got a buddy I know from my mission I could set you up with if you want. You say the word, and you can be back in the dating scene."

Allison looked surprised by the offer and smiled. "Luke, you just keep surprising me. I honestly can't believe you've turned out to be such a nice guy. I'm so glad I don't hate you anymore," she said with a laugh and got in the car.

Luke grinned and got in too. "What are brothers for? Right Talon?"

Talon grinned and slapped Luke on the shoulder. "If I had to have a brother, I'd totally pick you," he said honestly.

Luke smiled and nodded. "Now let's get back home and see if Bonnie and Frank have barricaded the house. I bet you a million dollars Bonnie's making cookies and Frank is checking all the locks."

When they got home, they discovered Luke was almost right. Bonnie was making a pumpkin loaf, and Frank had finished checking the locks and moved on to fixing the leaky faucet. They all sat down to a broccoli and chicken casserole as Luke told everyone how the visit to the police station had gone.

After everyone cleaned up the kitchen, Allison couldn't help noticing it was almost seven o'clock. She looked nervously around for Luke and Talon. But they had gone over to Luke's house so Luke could grab his gym bag. Frank was helping Aspen with her homework, and Bonnie and Maggie were sitting on the couch laughing and watching TV. That left her to answer the doorbell when Will arrived.

Maggie and Bonnie acted like they hadn't even heard it. Allison sighed and straightened her shoulders. She could do this. She could face down an ex-boyfriend on her front porch. One she had apologized to. One she wanted back. *One who didn't want her back.* She could do this. She opened the door slowly and pasted a serene, polite smile on her face.

Will stood on her front porch, dressed in black sweat pants and a black T-shirt. He looked mean, he looked strong, and he looked like he was very ready to go boxing. Maybe Talon wasn't the only one who needed to get rid of extra aggression.

"Allison," he said when she didn't say anything.

"Talon and Luke are over next door. Luke just needed to change clothes."

Will nodded and turned to glance at Luke's house. "So how are you doing?" he asked politely.

Allison pursed her lips as she pretended to consider the question. "I'm doing great, Will. Really, *really* great. And how about you? Are you having a nice day?" she asked in an overly sweet voice.

Will's eyes became intense as he stared at her. "Daphne's the one who kissed *me*. Just in case you were wondering or cared."

Allison sighed and leaned in the doorway. "Yeah, you were really fighting her off. By the way you were smiling, it almost looked like you were enjoying it. You two make a really cute couple. All glossy and gorgeous and perfect for each other."

Will smiled tightly. "Yeah, we do, don't we?"

Allison suddenly felt like doing a little boxing herself. "So, have fun tonight. And thanks for taking Talon boxing. He's had a rough day. He could really use this."

Will shrugged. "I was going to come by for Talon anyway. Luke didn't have to call me."

Allison looked at him suspiciously. "Seriously? We broke up and you were *still* planning on helping out Talon?"

Will raised his eyebrows slightly at her. "*We* didn't break up. You dumped me. And yes. When I give someone my word, I stand by it."

Allison stared up into Will's eyes and felt her heart lighten. He was telling the truth.

She smiled up at Will and stepped closer. "Will? I just want to say again how sorry I am. If I could take every thing I said back, I would. I—"

"Will!" Talon yelled from across the yard, running toward them and interrupting whatever it was Allison was about to say.

Will looked impatiently at Allison after he waved at Talon. "What were you just about to say, Allison?"

Allison blushed and shrugged as Talon ran up the stairs and punched Will in the arm. "Hey, man, let's go. I can't wait. Luke's going down."

Will grinned at Talon and put him in a headlock. "Dude, you're the one going down. By the way, you're driving tonight," he said, letting Talon up and digging the keys out of his pocket.

Talon stood up, his hair messed up from the wrestling, with such a look of utter joy on his face that Allison had to laugh.

"No. Way," he stuttered as he grabbed the keys out of Will's hand and ran to show Luke.

Will turned back to Allison. "Now, where were we?" he asked, looking intently at her.

Allison took a deep breath and stepped closer to Will. She leaned up on her toes and kissed him very softly on the lips. "I was just going to say that I love you, and I would really love it if you would just forgive me."

Will's eyes softened and his hands came up to grasp her waist. "Allison—"

"Will! Come *on!*" Luke and Talon shouted at him.

Will's face closed up and he stepped back. "I'm sorry, Allison. I need time to think about it." He frowned at her and then turned and walked down the steps to join Luke and Talon.

Allison watched as they drove away, and Maggie and Bonnie joined her on the porch.

"You have your work cut out for you, honey," Bonnie said.

Maggie nodded. "If I'd kissed Luke like that and begged for his forgiveness, he would have been putty in my hands. Will is either really upset, or Daphne has finally got her claws into him."

Allison shoved her hands in her pockets and sighed. "Well, Jacie said the first step was groveling. Step two, three, four, and five are the same. Maybe when I get to step five he'll forgive me."

Maggie smiled uncertainly. "Yeah, maybe. Hey, why don't I call my mom and we can go get some ice cream or something?"

Bonnie jumped on the idea and ran to get the phone. Aspen was thrilled at having something fun to do, so Allison was forced into going, although the only thing she wanted to do was hide in her room and stare at the ceiling in misery.

Lisa showed up fifteen minutes later. Everyone piled into Bonnie's Jeep, and they drove to Iceberg. They sat in a corner booth, consuming way too much ice cream and taking turns trying to cheer Allison up.

Lisa sat opposite Allison, Aspen, and Maggie. She leaned over the table and smiled at Allison.

"It hurts, huh?" she said.

Allison nodded. "*Oh yeah.* It hurts."

Lisa swirled her spoon in her towering ice cream creation and sighed. "If it makes you feel any better, it wouldn't hurt so much if you didn't care so much. It sounds kind of like you love him," she said bluntly.

Allison glanced at everyone at the table and looked down at her melting ice cream. "Yes. I've always loved Will. And I have a feeling that I always will."

Lisa tilted her head and studied Allison. "So what are you going to do to win him back?"

Maggie stuck up for her friend. "She's done everything, Mom. She's apologized twice and she even kissed him. He didn't even budge. He told her he'd have to think about it. What else can she do?" Maggie asked, sounding irritated.

Bonnie laughed and shook her head. "Honey, just because Luke would have been over it yesterday doesn't mean every man is like that. I know Betsy and the Carsons. They're proud people. Allison insulted his honor. She'll have to do something more than apologize." Bonnie looked at Allison with a wince. "Sorry."

Allison shrugged. "Don't worry about it. At least you didn't call me stupid, like everyone else has. So what can I do? What kind of gesture can I make? I have no money. I have nothing."

Lisa took a big bite of ice cream and looked thoughtful. Bonnie tapped her fingers on the table as she racked her brain for any ideas. Maggie rubbed her stomach and leaned back in the booth, thinking hard. Allison turned to Aspen, who had been quiet the whole time.

Aspen studied her sister and squinched her face up. "I think you're going to have to challenge Daphne for the right to his heart. Like some kind of duel. Or maybe a contest."

Maggie snorted but then sat up. "Hey! That might actually work. What do you think, Mom?" she asked, turning to look at Lisa.

Lisa bit her lip as she considered the idea. "I don't think so. Will would see through that. I honestly think it'll just take some time. Let him cool off, and then we'll see what happens."

Maggie and Aspen hated that idea and went back to devising strange and somewhat embarrassing contests between Allison and Daphne. Allison laughed as the women considered every ridiculous way there was to win back a man's heart. They finally left Iceberg full and a little lighter of mood.

Allison waited up for Talon again, but Will didn't come in. He drove off before Talon even reached the door. As Talon turned to go upstairs, Allison held up her hand. "Wait, Talon. Did Will say anything about me?" she asked timidly.

Talon frowned and thought about it. "Hmm. He did say something when Luke punched him really hard in the stomach. He said, 'Man, that feels just like when Allison dumped me.'"

Allison's face crumbled as Talon apologized and quietly left the room. She followed her brother up the stairs and went to bed. It had been a long, depressing, horrible day. Tomorrow had to be better.

thiRty

After Talon and Aspen left for the bus stop the next morning, Allison ran up the stairs and opened the laptop. *Perfect.* Talon hadn't logged off of facebook. She scanned down her brother's page and looked for any more comments from Bill Kidd. Nothing. She checked his personal messages and quickly skipped over three from Sarah. There was nothing from their father. She frowned and wondered what Max could be doing in Alpine. Maybe his being there had nothing to do with them and everything to do with a business deal. She could only hope. She logged off and then logged back in as herself. Her eyes widened in surprise. She had a message. She scrolled down to it and felt adrenaline pump through her veins when she saw it was from her father.

> Allison, you were always so melodramatic. What's mine is mine. Stay out of it or you'll be the one who gets hurt.

Allison felt her stomach dip and her hands fist into tight balls. *Stay out of it?* She was just supposed to stand back and let her father steal everyone blind? She was supposed to support him? He was absolutely crazy. She was all Talon and Aspen had. She had to protect them. She printed off the message quickly and shoved it in her jeans pocket before leaving for work.

Betsy looked grim when Allison arrived at work. Allison held her hands up defensively. "Please don't hurt me. I did everything but get down on my knees and beg."

Betsy blew out a puff of air and nodded. "I know you did. He told

219

me all about it. Good try, by the way. I guess this is something he just can't get over. Or *won't*. I can't help thinking, though, that if he does end up with Daphne, her influence on him won't be positive. He'll just focus more and more on everything that doesn't matter. I thought that if he married you, everything would be all right. That he'd finally be able to slow down and take a break. That maybe, just maybe, he could stop trying to prove to everyone that the Carson name is one to be proud of," she said with a sad shake of her head.

Allison tied on her apron and sighed as Betsy wandered away, looking deflated. She fixed her ponytail and straightened the tables of fruit before she headed down to the roadside. She sat in her chair for a few moments before the cars started pulling in. She was grateful it was apple season now. The busier she was, the less time she had to think about Will. But later as she sat and munched on some sliced tomatoes Betsy had brought out to her, she thought long and hard about Jacie's five-step plan to get Will back. Groveling hadn't done anything. If Will was going to forgive her, then he'd just have to decide to do it. There was no grand gesture she could make. And Maggie was right. If he wasn't going to let it go after her apologies, there was nothing she could do except move on. Will was working hard on moving on. Maybe she should too.

The next few days passed slowly and painfully. Each day she didn't see Will was excruciating. There was no getting around it; he was making his position very clear. The least she could do was respect his wishes. Sophie and Jacie stopped by to offer more advice on getting him back. But all of it was bad. Even Bonnie came by the house one night with a magazine article from Oprah's *O* magazine on how to apologize correctly. Allison smiled and thanked her and then threw it in the garbage without reading it. Will didn't want an apology. He wanted to forget about her. She'd try to make it easy on him. She had started asking people who stopped to buy fruit if they knew of any job openings, and the only one that would possibly work for her would be working at Sophie's salon as a shampoo girl and shop assistant. That meant when she wasn't shampooing, she'd be sweeping, ringing people up, cleaning the bathrooms, and running errands. With winter coming and no more fruit to sell, she decided to hand in her resignation to Betsy.

Friday afternoon she folded her apron and handed it to Betsy, trying to smile when Betsy pulled her into a big, crushing hug.

"You gotta do what you gotta do, honey," Betsy assured her.

Allison nodded and smiled again. "I do. But I'll miss you, Betsy. You're the best boss I've ever had," she said honestly.

Betsy grinned and shook her head. "I'm probably the only boss you've ever had. But I'll take it. If you ever need anything or you want to come back, you just say the word. I know it's been hard this past week, what with Will and Daphne parading around town, but you've kept your chin up. You've got grit, girl. I'm just so sad you won't be my daughter-in-law. You know I had my hopes set on you. But you'll be okay. You'll probably meet someone just like Will and fall in love before you know it," she said with a sad smile.

Allison looked away and tried not to cry. Even Betsy wanted her to date other guys. Maybe it was time she listened.

"Well, thanks again, Betsy. If you ever need extra help, you call me."

Feeling drained and empty and very much like a failure, she drove home and sat on the porch. The wind gently caressed her face, and she closed her eyes and lifted her face up to the fall sky. She sat like that, trying desperately to feel some kind of peace, until Talon and Aspen got home. When she heard them coming she smiled, stood up, and asked about everything that had happened that day at Lone Peak. She was getting really good at acting like nothing was wrong when everything felt nothing but wrong.

Aspen heated up leftovers in the microwave and smiled hopefully at Allison. "Please, *please* can Rowan and I come to your party?"

Talon turned down the volume on the TV to hear her answer. He had been begging to go too.

Allison smiled and shook her head. "Adults only. That's what Sophie said. You two are so gorgeous, I don't want Aspen getting hit on by some thirty-year-old or Talon hanging out with some gorgeous twenty-five-year-old. Nope, you two will stay safely at home tonight."

Aspen's eyes brightened at the thought. "Rowan would be so jealous," she said giggling delightedly.

Talon shrugged. "Well, Sarah already has a date tonight. It would serve her right if I started dating some hot older lady."

Allison grimaced. "Actually, it would be illegal and gross. So forget about it. Luke said you guys could raid his DVD collection if you wanted to."

Aspen and Talon started talking about what they wanted to watch that night, so Allison went upstairs to shower and get ready for the party. But all she really wanted to do was curl up on the couch with a bag of popcorn and hang out with Talon and Aspen. She didn't want to go smile for three hours and look happy and carefree. It was going to be torture.

Aspen came in to watch her get ready and sighed unhappily at her closet. "I still don't get why the FBI had to confiscate the entire contents of our house. You used to have the most beautiful clothes in the world. And now you dress like a bag lady."

Allison sniffed in offense. "I do not look like a bag lady. I look shabby. Big difference. But you're right. If they would have just let us have our clothes, life would be a little better. Remember that long tan suede skirt I used to have? Oh I loved that skirt," she said longingly.

Aspen nodded. "I was always hoping I could borrow it someday. And now I'll never get to. At least you got to keep the clothes that all your roommates borrowed."

Allison rolled her eyes. Her roommates had borrowed half her closet of clothes. When she had called to get what she could back, she'd only gotten a fraction. And what she did have was a little too tight now.

"What about this? I mean, it's a little fancy for a casual party, but it's this or jeans," Aspen said, pulling out a light blue dress styled after the fifties. It was cute and vintage and perfect. The simple feminine lines were very accepting of curves, and the belt around her waist would make her look just like a 1950s pinup. Allison smiled.

"It's perfect, Aspen. I'm so lucky to have you around."

Aspen grinned and watched as Allison transformed herself into a glamorous woman right before her eyes. She straightened her wavy hair with a round brush and her blow dryer but did an exaggerated Veronica Lake wave through her bangs. She picked a bright red lipstick to finish the effect.

"What do you think?" she asked, twirling in her dress and feeling a little better.

Aspen's eyes were wide open as she shook her head. "I feel so bad for Will. When he sees you tonight, he's going to regret being so stubborn."

Allison's smile dimmed when she heard Will's name. But she

pushed the pain away. Tonight was a night for fun, not misery. "Will won't even be there. Why would he? He and Daphne are probably going to be out shopping for engagement rings. And besides, even if Will did want to come, Daphne wouldn't let him anywhere near me," she said certainly.

Aspen nodded sadly. "Well, anyway, the point is, you've never looked more beautiful than you do right now."

Allison smiled gratefully. There was nothing like a sister to boost her self-esteem when she needed it. A few minutes later, she blew kisses at her brother and sister and reminded them to lock the door and not to answer it no matter what. Luke and Maggie were giving her a ride, so she walked over to the Petersons'. She noted sadly that the leaves were already turning color and wished that life didn't have to change so quickly.

She knocked on the door and waited. Luke answered it and stood in shock as he stared at her. Maggie joined him and she looked surprised too.

"Holy crap, Allison. You're absolutely stunning," Maggie said, pushing Luke aside. "Please promise me you'll let me paint you. I pay very well, by the way. Talk about the perfect part-time job," she said, moving Allison by her shoulders so the light hit her face at a different angle.

Allison blushed and felt embarrassed by the attention. "It's just an old dress and some red lipstick."

Luke shook his head and shut his mouth. "Wow. I can't wait to see Will's expression tonight."

Maggie nodded in agreement. "There are many ways to win a man back. This might just be the perfect way. Forget groveling. Just be irresistible."

Luke ushered the ladies to the car and drove quickly up the mountain. Conversation mostly centered on the lack of any more sightings of Max Vaughn. Luke seemed to think that maybe Talon and Aspen might have made a mistake. Allison hoped he was right but told Luke and Maggie about the message she had gotten on facebook from her dad. Luke brushed Max's threats off and made her feel better. When they arrived at Sophie's house, they walked up to the door and waited as Luke rang the doorbell.

Sam, Sophie's husband, did a double take when he met Allison for the first time. "Whoa. You must be Allison," he said, smiling warmly at her and shaking her hand.

Allison liked him immediately and walked in. They were a half hour early so they could help Sophie set everything up. Sophie grinned when she saw Allison and shook her head. "Tonight is going to be a night to remember."

Allison just hoped it was a night she could get through. Soon enough the doorbell started ringing, and she was the one in charge of answering it. Sophie thought it would be a good way to start the party since Allison was the guest of honor. Allison was delighted to meet all of her old acquaintances from high school and couldn't believe how many people showed up. An hour into the party, she was surprised to hear the doorbell again but got up when Sophie pointed to her. She walked quickly down the hallway and opened the door with a bright, welcoming smile.

It was Will and Daphne this time.

She said the first thing that came to her mind. "What are *you* doing here?" she asked. Then she blushed and wished once again, she could take back her words.

Daphne answered since Will was busy looking at Allison as if he were drinking her in with his eyes. "We were invited, of course. Will and I wouldn't miss your welcome home party for anything, would we, baby?" Daphne said, slipping her arm though his possessively.

Will nodded but kept staring at Allison. Allison cleared her throat and smiled as she opened the door wide. "Well, in that case, thank you for coming. Please come in," she said politely and moved to allow them to walk in.

Daphne pulled off her bright pink jean jacket covered in gaudy sequins and handed it to Allison as if she were the coat girl and not the guest of honor. "Make sure it doesn't get squished," she said as she wandered down the hallway.

Will turned and waited for Allison as she shut the door. "You look beautiful tonight, Allison."

Allison moved her hair out of her eyes and smiled up at Will, trying to look as if seeing him with another woman wasn't killing her. "You're so sweet," she said. Then she turned to walk away.

Will's hand flashed out and grabbed her arm gently. "I'd like to take you up on your offer, Allison," he said with a half smile.

224

Allison's heartbeat sped up as his words sank in. *They could start over again?* Her face lighted up with hope. "I'm so glad, Will," she said, moving a step closer to him.

Will looked down at his feet. "Yeah, I realized that I do want to be friends with you after all."

Allison's heart burst into tiny pieces, but the smile stayed fixed on her face. Will turned with a brittle smile of his own and walked away, following Daphne. Allison leaned up against the wall as she tried to catch her breath. Will wanted to be friends with her. That was it. All hope that she had for winning Will back died immediately. She counted to ten and tried to compose herself before she rejoined the party. But how could she? How could she stand there and laugh and smile while Will was with Daphne? She didn't know if she could.

The sound of the doorbell broke through her distress. She stood up shakily and opened the door. The man standing on the front porch looked a lot like Sam. He was taller, though, and slightly more handsome. His eyes lit up with good humor and appreciation as he looked at her.

"I can't believe my luck. I've just met the most gorgeous woman ever born," he said charmingly as he stepped forward with his hand outstretched.

Allison smiled and shook the man's hand. "Hi, I'm Allison Vaughn. I don't think I remember you, though."

The man grinned down at her and refused to let go of her hand. "I'm Sam's younger brother, Trey. I'm sorry I'm late. If I had only known you'd be answering the door, I would have been the first one here," he said with a playful smile.

Allison had to laugh, even after her encounter with Will. They walked together into the house and back into the party. She threw Daphne's coat on the floor in the office and then walked with Trey over to Sophie and Sam.

Trey hugged Sam and kissed Sophie on the cheek. "Please tell me this gorgeous woman is single," he begged, loud enough for everyone to hear.

Daphne, who had been standing just a few feet away, answered quickly for them. "She is!"

Trey looked like it was Christmas morning. "Well then, today really is my lucky day. Sophie, how fast can you plan a wedding?"

Sophie grinned at her brother-in-law and shook her head. "Trey, you are the biggest flirt in Utah. You'd better watch it or you'll frighten her off."

Sam slapped his brother on the back. "Good luck, Trey."

Sophie stood up and whistled for everyone's attention. "Okay, everybody. I think since we're all here now, we should sit down. This party is to officially welcome Allison back home. We're all so glad she finally came back to us," Sophie said with a warm smile.

Allison smiled self-consciously as everyone looked at her. Trey squeezed her arm and winked at her. Daphne sighed rudely.

Sophie glared at Daphne and went on. "So what I'd like to do is go around the room and have everyone tell their favorite memory of Allison, okay? Oh, and those who didn't know her, we can just skip you," she said, noticing her husband's pained expression.

Allison listened as women who used to be on the cheerleading squad with her talked first, and then girls from her Young Women group went next. Allison laughed at some of the memories and winced at others. But it was heartwarming to realize that there were people in this world who wouldn't judge her by her parents and who surprisingly still wanted to know her and be friends with her.

When it was Jacie's turn, Sophie couldn't help feeling nervous. There was just no telling what she would say. Jacie stood and held her hands up for everyone's attention.

"Okay, everyone. My best memory of Allison goes way back. We were in the ninth grade and *someone*," she said throwing a glance at Daphne, "someone had sat behind me in class and written all kinds of insulting things with a *permanent* marker on the brand new hoodie I had just gotten for my birthday. When Allison saw what had happened, she immediately took her jacket off and traded with me. She wore my hoodie the whole day just to make a point," Jacie said and smiled gratefully at Allison.

Allison sighed in relief. Jacie could have mentioned the Blake experience but she must have taken pity on her. Allison saluted Jacie with her cup of punch. Trey leaned over and whispered in her ear. "This is great. It's like I'm getting to know your whole history in just one night."

Allison smiled up at him but then frowned when she saw Daphne stand up next. She groaned quietly.

226

"Well, I have more memories of Allison than anyone here. Let me see. My favorite memory. Hmm," Daphne said, drawing out the drama and enjoying having everyone's attention.

Sophie rolled her eyes. "Daphne, why don't we move on to someone else while you think about it?" she said, motioning for Will to go next.

Daphne held up a hand as if she were royalty. "Back off, Sophie. Okay, I've got it. There was this one time Allison's dad, you know, *Max Vaughn*, flew us to New York for spring break. It was fashion week, and we walked around New York, pretending to be models. We had a group of college guys following us around all day. Allison refused to meet up with them to go dancing, so she totally ruined it for me, but it was still one of the best days ever," she said wistfully.

Allison's eyebrows hit the roof. Daphne could have taken the chance to really embarrass her but instead had chosen a good memory. What was that about? She shared a confused look with Maggie and Sophie but then frowned when Will got up. She knew he was going to say that his most memorable experience with her was when she had dumped him. She sighed heavily and glanced at the clock, wondering if it would be rude to slip out of her own party early. It shouldn't take her too long to walk down the mountain. In heels.

Will stood up and looked at Allison for a moment and then surprised her by smiling tenderly at her.

"I have a lot of great memories of Allison. Some of the best ones were when she would take the time to talk to my little sister, Bella, or even sit down and eat lunch with her. Bella loved that. But for me personally, I'll always remember the time I was working after school, selling apples at our fruit stand and a truck full of kids from school slowed down and stopped. Allison jumped out and walked up to me and asked if I wanted to join them after I got off work. They were all going up to Sliding Rock for a party.

"Man, I wanted nothing more than to spend the afternoon with her, having fun and relaxing. But I couldn't. My sister was sick that day, and my mom was at home with her. I had to stay until all the apples were sold or until seven o'clock, whichever came first. I told her I couldn't come, but she wouldn't listen. She took out her checkbook and bought every single apple we had there just so I could go with them. She always went out of her way to try and include me, regardless of what some of her friends thought or said. Some of the kids put up a fight and didn't want me around because I didn't live in a house like theirs or wear clothes like theirs or drive cars like theirs. But she didn't care about that. Knowing Allison was the best part of high school for me," Will said, smiling sadly before sitting down.

Allison looked away from Will and blinked quickly. She'd almost forgotten about that day up at the little waterfall. How in the world was she going to get over Will?

Sophie cleared her throat. "Wow, Will. That was intense. Um, I guess I'm the last one to go then. Okay. My best memory of Allison was when I was a junior in high school. I had gone to the mall the day before and bought the coolest shirt ever, or so I thought. Well, when I got to school the next day, I was wearing my new shirt and I felt amazing and so stylish, until this one person started making fun of me. I'm not talking laughing and pointing. I'm talking, this person got a crowd around me and then tore me apart from my clothes to my hair. I was just crushed. Allison walked up and saw what was going on, and she stuck up for me. She told me that she thought I was one of the cutest girls at school and that anyone who could make fun of me was either blind or just stupid. And then the very next day, Allison wore the *exact* same shirt I had been wearing to school. She must have gone to the mall right after school to get one. She did that, just for me," Sophie said with a grin.

Allison smiled, remembered it had been Daphne who made fun of Sophie. She and Daphne had been on the outs for a week over that incident until her dad had ordered her to back down and make nice. Allison glanced at Daphne. Daphne was studying her nails and looking bored.

Allison stood up. "Thanks, everyone. It's nice to know you guys have good memories of me. It's been a hard year, but reconnecting with all of you has been wonderful. Thank you so much," she said gratefully.

Trey stood up, smiling down at her. "Wait a second. I haven't shared my favorite memory."

Allison laughed nervously. "Um, I've only known you for about half an hour."

Trey sighed theatrically. "If you had known me in high school, we'd have two kids by now. So my best memory is of meeting you tonight.

Love at first sight is a great memory to have," he said as everyone laughed and hooted. Everyone except Daphne and Will. Will looked supremely irritated by Trey's outrageousness.

Sophie stood up and kissed Trey on the cheek. "Thanks for sharing, Trey. Okay everyone, let's mingle, eat, and have a great time."

Trey grabbed Allison's hand and his plate of food and dragged her to a deserted corner. They sat down and nibbled on the finger foods while they got to know each other. She'd never had a man react to her like this. Trey was over the top. But he was so funny, good-looking, and kind that it felt good. After her week of rejection from Will, being in Trey's company was like swimming in the sun. She felt warm and beautiful and smart and funny. She couldn't help but like him.

Sophie had Sam and Luke move all the furniture out of the way, and she put on some music from their high school days. Everyone started dancing and having a good time while she and Trey talked. Trey finally stood up and pulled Allison up with him.

"We better join this party. I feel bad keeping you all to myself, but who can blame me," he said as they joined the dancers. The music immediately turned to a slow song, and Trey pulled her into his arms. She was surprised at how perfectly they fit together. She frowned as she realized the last time she had gone dancing had been with Will.

"Hey, why the sad face?" Trey asked.

Allison looked up and caught sight of Will dancing with Daphne. It looked like Will and Daphne fit together perfectly too. She ordered herself to forget Will and focus on the present.

"I'm fine, Trey. I'm just glad you came to my party tonight. I have a feeling that I wouldn't be having such a good time if you weren't here," she said honestly.

Trey smiled happily. "So was Daphne telling the truth when she said you were single?" he asked rather loudly so he could be heard over the music.

Will and Daphne had ended up right next to them at this point, and Allison tried hard to pretend they weren't there, listening to the conversation. She took a deep breath and tried to smile.

"You can't get any more unattached than I am. Why do you ask?"

Trey laughed. "Are you kidding me? I show up to this party thinking I'll just stay for fifteen minutes, and the first thing I see when the door opens is the most beautiful woman I've ever met. For the record,

I'm single, and you are welcome to change my status any time," he said teasingly.

Allison laughed and was glad Trey was so comfortable with himself. She liked that there wasn't a shy bone in his body. After the dance was over, she excused herself to get a drink while Trey went to talk to a friend he knew from BYU. She wondered why there was nothing to drink but punch or Fresca. Sophie and Maggie immediately joined her as she popped the top on the soda.

"Ooh, this is working perfectly. I don't know why I didn't even think of it," Sophie said delightedly as she munched on a lettuce wrap.

Maggie clapped her hands together happily. "Did you see his face, Sophie?"

Allison looked at the two women curiously. She had no idea what they were talking about.

"He looked like he wanted to strangle Trey! And I love Trey, so we can't allow that, but can you imagine?" Sophie said.

Maggie nodded quickly. "Where's Jacie? Her plan needed step number six: make Will so jealous he can't see straight."

Allison frowned and felt depressed all over again. "Would you two stop it? Will and I are over. He told me when he got here that he just wanted to be friends with me. *There is no more plan.* It's over. Now, the good news is that I just met Trey, and he's a lot of fun. I'm actually having a good time tonight, even with Daphne here. So please just let everything else go," she pleaded.

Maggie and Sophie looked at each other and grinned as both of them shook their heads. "Not on your life, Allie," Sophie said with a toss of her red curls. "Will is still in love with you. While you were dancing with Trey, he looked like he was going to burst into green flames."

Maggie grabbed Sophie's arm. "No! He looked like he wanted to grab Allison, throw her over his shoulder, and run off with her."

Allison laughed and rolled her eyes. "Girls, the fairy tale is over. Time for reality. Will has what he wants. He has Daphne."

Maggie looked at her like she was demented. "Fine, if you don't believe me, then why is Will standing over there staring at you like he's starving to death and you're chocolate cake?"

Allison looked over Sophie's shoulder and caught Will staring at her as he stood by a window all by himself. She swallowed nervously and tried to look away, but his eyes held her. He didn't smile, he didn't blink. He just looked at her. It was like a magnet was pulling her. She left Maggie and Sophie without saying another word and walked over to Will's side.

"Are you okay? You look like you're mad at me," she said quietly.

Will grabbed her hand and pulled her closer. "What are you trying to do to me?" he asked in a low, hard voice.

Allison shook her head. "I'm not trying to do anything, Will. Like you said, you want to be friends. I tried everything I could to make things right with you. You've moved on, Will. It's time I did too," she said, pulling her hand away so she could walk back toward her friends.

But Will grabbed her elbow and made her turn back. "I don't want you dating Trey Kellen," he said darkly.

Allison raised her eyebrows at that and yanked on her arm. Will kept tight possession of it though. "I'll date who I want to, Will. Trey is a really nice guy. I think you'd like him."

Will's smile was almost ferocious. "I don't care if he's the nicest guy in the world. I'm going to pound his face into the dirt if you dance with him one more time," he promised.

Allison's mouth fell open in shock. "Don't you dare threaten him. You can kiss and date whoever you want to, but I'm not allowed to *dance* with anyone? Will, you're always telling me not to play games with you. But you're the one who doesn't know what he wants," she said, yanking her arm away from Will furiously.

Will sighed and rubbed his face with his hands. When he looked back at her, his eyes were just as intense. "I know exactly what I want, Allison. That's the problem."

Daphne walked up to them right at that second and diffused the tense atmosphere. "Of course you know what you want, Will. And I'm right here."

Allison kept her eyes on Will's, ignoring Daphne. "Exactly my point," she said. Then she walked over to Trey, who was looking for her.

She spent the rest of the night ignoring Will and Daphne's presence with a vengeance. She might have laughed harder at Trey's jokes than she usually would have. She might have smiled more brightly up into Trey's eyes than she should have. And she might have let Trey put his arm around her waist when she shouldn't have. But she had a point to make. When Will and Daphne got ready to leave, they found her sitting on the arm of the chair Trey was sitting in.

"Great party, Allison," Will said, looking livid.

Trey's eyebrows went straight up as he looked between Will and Allison. Allison smiled coolly. "Thank you so much for coming, Will. It was nice to see old friends from high school again."

Daphne laughed a high, artificial laugh as she wrapped her arms around Will's middle. "We had to come. Sophie would have killed me if we didn't show up. Oh, and Trey, be careful with this one. She's hard on men."

Allison glared as she watched Daphne and Will walk away. She wanted nothing more than to throw her drink in Daphne's face.

"Let me guess. She was the head cheerleader who tortured you all through high school?" Trey asked, pulling her attention back to him.

Allison licked her lips and shook her head. "Wrong. I was the head cheerleader, and Daphne wouldn't have dared. But she's sure making up for lost time now," she said tiredly.

Trey stood up and stretched. "Let me drive you home. You look like you're ready to go."

Allison stood up too and stuck out her hand. "Oh, I already have a ride home, but thanks. It was so good to meet you tonight," she said wholeheartedly.

Trey took her outstretched hand with a wry smile on his face. "Get rid of your ride and let me take you. I don't want to let you go just yet."

Allison glanced across the room to where Maggie and Luke were cuddled up on the couch. Maggie, who had been watching them the whole time, gave her the thumbs up.

Allison smiled and waved. "Okay then. I guess I'll ride home with you. Let's tell Sophie and Sam good night first. I need to thank her for throwing this party for me."

Trey held her hand as they went to look for Sophie and Sam. They found the couple in the kitchen with their arms around each other.

Trey cleared his throat loudly and theatrically. "You two act like you're still newlyweds. Every time I go into a room, this is what I find."

Sam laughed and let go of his wife.

232

"Trey, are you giving Allison a ride home?" Sophie asked, her eyes lighting up.

Trey looked proud as a peacock. "Of course I am. She's mine now whether she knows it or not," he said, aiming a wicked wink at her.

Allison shook her head at him, knowing he was just teasing her. She kissed Sophie on the cheek and thanked her and Sam for the welcome-home party.

Sophie walked them to the door with a hand on both of their shoulders. "You drive safely down the hill. And watch out for deer!" she called as they walked toward Trey's large black Dodge truck.

Trey helped her into the truck since it seemed like it was a mile off the ground. She couldn't help comparing it to her rusty truck. Inside it was almost as nice as Will's car.

Trey kept her entertained on the way home and even managed to catch her hand in his.

Allison felt kind of guilty for giving him the wrong impression. As much as she enjoyed Trey's company at the party, she knew she wasn't ready to jump into a relationship with another man. She needed time to get over Will. Trey didn't deserve to be a rebound guy.

Trey pulled up in front of her house and turned the truck off. "So Will, that guy who looked at me like he wanted to kill me all night long, is your ex, huh?"

Allison looked at him surprise. "We dated for a short time. How did you know?"

Trey shrugged and turned in his seat to look at her. "I asked Sam what was going on with Will, and he told me. So if you're not ready for this, I can understand, but when you are ready, I'll be waiting for you," he said, serious for the first time that night.

Allison smiled at him and relaxed. Maybe she was ready after all. Trey was amazing.

"You're definitely the first in line," she said finally.

Trey grinned and opened his truck door. He came around to her side and helped her out.

"This incredible evening just got even better," he said, looking grateful and happy in the moonlight.

He walked her up her porch steps and held her hand before she could unlock the front door.

"Here's my card. You call me when you want to see me. The

answer is *always* going to be yes, just so you know."

Allison shook her head in wonder. "You're the perfect man, Trey. Where did you come from?"

Trey grinned, back to his cocky self. "I'm one of a kind. Good night, beautiful," he said and leaned over to kiss her on the cheek. Allison smiled at him and waved as he walked back to his truck.

thiRty-ONe

Allison walked into the house and immediately frowned. All the lights were off. She walked into the dark kitchen and turned on the lights. It was eleven thirty. Where were Talon and Aspen? Then she noticed a piece of white notebook paper on the counter and grabbed it.

Hey Sis,

Hope you had a good time at the party. We heard some strange noises and called Frank and Bonnie. We tried calling the number you left, but no one answered. So come and get us when you're done. Here's Bonnie's number. She said if we want we can spend the night. But call us. We're kind of freaked out.

Talon

Allison looked around the house nervously and wondered what kind of noises would send her brother and sister running. She walked through the first floor of the house and checked the doors and windows before going upstairs. She walked through all the rooms, turning on the lights, checking the closets, and even getting on her knees to check under the beds. Her heart was beating fast as she walked back downstairs to call Bonnie. The house was just as it should be. Clear of all boogey men, ghosts, and monsters. She smiled to herself, thinking how she would tease Talon and Aspen for being such scaredy cats.

"Hi, Allison."

She whirled around and screamed as the outline of a man appeared behind her. She had turned the light on in the living room, but now it was off again.

"Who are you?" she asked as she stumbled backward toward the kitchen and the old phone hanging from the wall.

The man followed her nonchalantly, coming into the light. "Just your dear old dad," Max said with a little laugh.

Allison tried to breathe normally. She should have known immediately.

"How did you get in?" she demanded, walking as quickly as she could to the phone and picking it up. She held it to her ear and dialed 911 but frowned when she didn't hear the dial tone. She held up the phone and noticed that the cord had been cut.

"I didn't want to take any chances. I was sure that my own daughter wouldn't call the cops on me, but I had to cover all my bases. Good thing I did," Max said, leaning comfortably against the counter and staring at her as if he were amused by her.

Allison let out a shaky breath and hung up the phone. For the ten millionth time, she wished she could afford a cell phone.

"What do you want? Why are you here?" She spoke calmly, but the whole time her mind was calculating if she would be able to get out the back door before he caught up to her.

Max slicked back his dark blond hair, so much like hers, and smiled. "I'm just here to check on the kids—tell you all how much I've missed you. See if you need anything," he said with a sarcastic grin.

Allison felt her stomach cramp at the outright lies and edged backward toward the door. "Yeah right. What a joke. Just between you and me, did you *ever* love us?" she asked curiously.

Max chuckled as if her question was funny but then looked thoughtful. "I thought I would, but I never got around to it. Maybe if I'd had better kids. Maybe if you hadn't been so cold. Who knows, who cares," Max said with a shrug as he opened the fridge. "What crap. Jeez can't you even afford to eat real food? You look like you've gained at least fifty pounds. You must be hiding the good stuff somewhere," he said with a sneer.

Allison ignored the insult and took the chance to walk to the edge of the counter closest to the door before he looked up.

"Where are Aspen and Talon? This family reunion calls for a party," he said, shutting the fridge door and walking slowly toward her.

She held her hand up and he stopped immediately. "They're not here."

Max nodded. "Yeah, I saw the note. Who are Frank and Bonnie?" he asked curiously. "Friends from school?"

Allison nodded quickly. "Yep. They're just kids from school. They live somewhere in Highland, I think," she lied, twisting her dress in her hands nervously.

Max laughed. "You're the worst liar I've ever known. That's okay. I don't need them. All I need is you," he said happily.

Allison swallowed nervously and knew she would have to run for it. She didn't know what her dad's plan was, but she didn't want any part of it. She would not be an accessory to anything he wanted to do.

"I'm afraid I don't feel like helping you after you stole Talon's social security number and took out all those credit cards," she said, her voice sounding stronger and surer.

Max smiled apologetically and opened his hands palm out. "Yeah, I was sorry I had to do that. But a man's gotta live. And who else should help out their old dad when he's down on his luck than his own children? That's what family is for. Isn't that right, Allison?" he said in an overly sweet voice that turned her stomach.

"Yeah right. You just use us. That's not what a family is for. You don't steal from your own family. That's just sick," she said with disgust.

Max's eyes lowered dangerously. She'd hit her mark. "Don't you judge me. You don't know what it's like to try and support a family. You have no clue. I did what I had to do. You just remember that," he said angrily.

Allison shook her head. "I'm supporting my family just fine, and I haven't had to steal from anyone."

Max threw back his head and laughed. "Yeah, I heard about that. Selling fruit like some loser on the side of the road. That's how you're living now? *Pathetic*," he snarled.

Allison straightened her shoulders and stood up tall. "There's no shame in doing honest work if it puts food on the table. I hope Talon and Aspen have learned that."

Max slammed his hand on the counter with a crack. "Shut up. Enough of this crap. I don't need to stand here and be judged by some stupid girl. What a waste you've turned out to be. Give me your social security number and Aspen's too, and I'll be on my way," he said, reaching in his back pocket for a small pad of paper and a pen.

Allison felt a moment of relief, thanking her lucky stars for Luke Peterson. "I could, but it wouldn't do you any good. Luke Peterson is helping us now. He's an expert on identity theft, and he's had our credit frozen. We're untouchable now."

Max looked thunderous at this knowledge, but then his countenance cleared. "That's okay, I know plenty of people who will pay for your information, and they won't know about the freeze."

Allison thought about just making up a number but knew she could be giving her father a valid number. Then it would be her fault if her dad stole from whoever the number belonged to.

She shook her head. "No. I won't and you can't make me."

Max lunged for her and Allison screamed. She ran for the back door, but Max grabbed the back of her dress. She heard the fabric begin to tear as she stretched for the doorknob, still screaming when he ripped her head back by her hair. The sound of splintering wood didn't even make Max pause.

Allison continued to pull away from her father, screaming and reaching for the door, ignoring the pain. Ignoring everything but the urge to get as far away from her father as she could.

"*Get your hands off her!*" someone roared as he ran into the room.

Max pulled her around to face the newcomer. Allison stopped screaming and opened her eyes to see Will Carson standing in her kitchen, breathing fast and looking deadly.

"I'll give you one more second to get your hands off her before I tear you apart," Will warned, walking toward them with blood in his eyes.

Max dragged her to the opposite side of the counter and put his arm around her throat.

"This is just a little family business. It's none of your concern. I'm her *father*," Max said, trying to sound casual and normal, while holding his arm on her throat, making it hard for her to breathe.

Will's eyes sharpened, and he leaned over the counter. "If you don't move your arm off her throat, I'm going to break your wrist," he promised, looking like he wanted any excuse to attack.

Max lowered his arm and she gasped for air.

"So is this your boyfriend, Allison? You sure work fast. You found someone to pay the bills for you, huh?" he asked with a sneer.

Will stood taller, flexing his arms as his jaw tightened. "That's right. I'm looking out for Allison now."

Allison tried to talk. "Will, please be careful," she whispered.

Will ignored her. But her dad looked intrigued. *"Will?* Oh, you've got be kidding me. You're Will Carson. The *fruit stand* Carsons," he said, laughing delightedly.

Max shook his daughter's shoulders roughly, making her head bounce around. "You hooked up with a Carson? Oh, this is perfect. You can't get lower than a Carson. I knew you had a thing for him back in high school. All those stupid boxes of fruit stinking up the house. I still remember all the fruit flies. I warned you to stay away from him. Remember, Allison? I said, 'Stay away from losers or you'll become one. It's contagious.' And look at you, Allison. You're just as bad as a Carson now. Nothing but a loser. Dirt poor nobodies. That's all Carsons are. You should be ashamed," he said scathingly.

Will's face turned to stone, but his eyes looked murderous. Allison was filled with fury at her father's words. She stomped on Max's foot as hard as she could and elbowed him in the stomach. Max groaned and immediately let her go. She ran for Will, who took her in his arms and hugged her tightly, asking her if she was okay. She nodded and turned quickly to see that her dad was already recovering and standing up. He glared at her with hatred in his eyes.

Allison felt for Will's hand and held on tightly. "You have no right to put down Will's family. They're hard-working, honorable, kind, *good* people. They're the best Alpine has to offer. I'd rather be a Carson any day than a Vaughn," she said, feeling the strong security of Will's arms around her.

Max spit on her kitchen floor and ignored her. "If that's the case, then let's make a deal. Give me ten grand and I'll disappear. You won't see me again," he said, looking at Will appraisingly. "How much is your girlfriend's peace of mind worth?" he asked as he continued to massage his stomach where she had elbowed him.

Allison gasped in outrage. "Will, don't even think about it."

Will pushed her gently away and reached in his back pocket for his wallet. He took out his checkbook and immediately wrote out a check for ten thousand dollars. Allison's mouth fell open at the same time Max began to grin.

"Now look there, Allison. You might be right. Maybe Carsons are good for more than selling crap at the side of the road," he said with a laugh.

Will gently pushed Allison toward the fridge and then held the check out to her father.

Max grinned and walked over to take it. As he reached over the counter to take the check, Will launched himself across the counter and tackled Max.

Allison screamed and ran for the back door. She didn't know what was going to happen, but she needed to call the police, and the nearest working phone was at Luke and Maggie's.

She flew across the cool grass to get to the Petersons' house. When she got there, she ran up the steps and pounded on the door with both fists. Luke opened the door immediately, still wearing the clothes he'd worn to the party. She tried to tell him, but she couldn't catch her breath. She gestured toward her house, and he took off immediately, leaping down the stairs and running toward her house faster than she could have imagined. Maggie appeared seconds later in a large bath-robe and immediately wrapped Allison in her arms, pulling her into the safety of the house.

Allison finally got her breath. "It's my dad. He pulled on my dress and ripped my hair out. He wanted our information. Will came to help me, and that's how I got away. They're fighting. Will needs help," she said, feeling sick with worry.

Maggie hugged her quickly and then ran to the kitchen. She called 911 and spoke urgently into the phone. Allison pulled the curtains up and stared at her house, trying to see any movement. She gasped when the figure of a man erupted out of the back of her house and ran down the street, followed moments later by someone else.

"*Maggie!* I think Luke is chasing my dad down the street!" she screamed as Maggie ran to the window.

Maggie continued to talk into the phone, but Allison had to know if Will was hurt. She ran out of the house as Maggie called to her to come back. She jumped up the stairs of her own house and through the now-open door to see someone lying on the ground, gasping and coughing. She couldn't tell who it was until she rounded the counter.

She knelt down by his side and grabbed his hand, leaning over him.

"Will! Are you okay?" she asked urgently.

He opened one eye and groaned. "He had a taser," he said, turning on his side and rising up to his knees.

Allison had her arm around his shoulders as she helped him stand up. He leaned over the counter, trying to breathe. "Just give me a minute," he said, sounding shaken.

Allison heard sirens a moment later as Maggie walked in through the back door. She hurried to Will's side and took his face in her hands.

"He got you good, huh?" Maggie said with a commiserating wince.

Will nodded in embarrassment. "Talon will never let me live this down," he said with a half-smile.

Allison steered him toward the couch and then sat by his side as the two policemen came in and began questioning them. One officer immediately went after Luke and Max, while the other stayed back to call the paramedics to check out Will.

Luke walked in the house a minute later, looking disappointed. "He got away," he said in a surprised voice.

Maggie looked stunned. "What? How could he get away from *you*?"

Luke looked even more embarrassed at his wife's surprise. "He had a car waiting for him. He jumped in and was gone before I even knew what had happened. That man is as slippery as a snake. When I got here, he had already used the taser on Will, and he almost got me too. Man, what a night."

It was a long time before Allison called Talon and Aspen and told them what had happened. Bonnie got on the phone and insisted on keeping the two teenagers for the night.

When the last police officer left, Allison was left standing in her house with Will and Maggie and Luke. "Well, your door is shattered thanks to Will," Luke said, looking at the completely demolished shards of wood.

Will looked apologetic. "Sorry about that. But when I heard you scream, I just went crazy. It was the fastest way in."

Allison smiled. "It's okay. I have renter's insurance. I'll call tomorrow and see if I can get someone to fix it."

Will frowned. "You do have someone to fix it. *Me.*"

Allison raised an eyebrow at that but stayed silent.

Maggie spoke up quickly. "Well, you can't sleep here tonight, Allison. It isn't safe, considering Max is still out there and you don't even have a door now. Why don't you come sleep on our couch tonight? It's pretty comfortable," she offered.

Allison was just about to accept when Will shook his head. "Nah, she'll stay at my mom's house. My mom has an extra bedroom with its own private bath. She'll be more comfortable there."

Maggie looked like she wanted to argue, but Luke cleared his throat just in time.

"Well, now that that's settled, I think I'm going to take my exhausted wife home. She could have the baby any day now, so she needs all the rest she can get." He pulled Maggie toward the door.

Maggie yawned. "He's right. I've gotta go. I'm not used to late parties and break-ins. Good night, Will, Allison." The two of them disappeared in seconds.

Allison was left alone with Will and felt shy and uncertain all of a sudden. Will leaned up against the wall and looked at her silently.

"Why were you on my front porch tonight, Will?" she asked, leaning up against the opposite wall.

Will looked away for a second and then turned back to face her. "I wanted to talk to you. I knew Trey was taking you home tonight, and I couldn't stand it. I came by to set things straight between you and me," he said, standing up and taking a step closer to her.

Allison stayed where she was and frowned. "Will, we've already gone over this. We both decided that we should just be friends. Right?"

Will's eyes gleamed almost dangerously at the hated word. "No."

Allison looked up into his eyes since he was standing right in front of her and swallowed nervously. "But that's what you said at the party," she pointed out as Will's hand closed lightly around her arms, just above her elbows.

Will shook his head. "That was my pride talking. Now listen to my heart. I want you to call Trey and tell him you never *ever* want to see him again," he said, leaning down to kiss her lightly on her upper cheek.

Allison pushed Will back, but he didn't move. "Trey is a very nice man, Will. He's funny and he'll treat me like I should be treated," she assured him, knowing she was pushing him over the edge.

Will tilted her chin up so she had to look him in the eye. "Trey doesn't exist to you anymore."

Allison couldn't help smiling as she shook her head. "Give me one good reason I should forget about Trey. You and Daphne are practically engaged. You won't accept my apologies. I've begged you to take me back, but you won't. If you won't have me, then Trey will be very happy to," she said, pointing out the facts.

Will leaned down and kissed the side of her mouth as he thought it over.

"I don't love Daphne and she doesn't love me, although she's spent a lot of time trying to convince herself that she does. I was working up to accepting your apology, but I was going to make you suffer for another week. You hurt me Allison. I love you, but it killed me that you didn't trust me and that you thought I was like your dad," he said, leaning down to nuzzle her neck.

Allison gave up and put her arms around Will's waist. Then she leaned her head against his chest. She sighed deeply as she felt his strong, even heartbeat against her cheek.

"I'm so sorry, Will. I never want to hurt you ever again," she whispered.

Will held her tightly, leaning his chin against the top of her head. "Apology accepted," he said with a smile. "So are you going to see Trey again?" he asked.

Allison laughed into Will's shirt. "Are you ever going to let Daphne within ten feet of you again?" she responded.

Will sighed long and loud. "She's the best secretary I've ever had."

Allison pulled away and glared at him.

"Okay, *okay*. She just got a great job offer from Gage Dulaney anyway. She told him she was going to think about it. I'll tell her on Monday that she should take it."

Allison smiled and relaxed into Will's arms again. "This feels good, doesn't it?" she murmured tiredly.

Will rubbed her back and nodded. "Nothing has ever felt so good."

A few minutes later he pulled away to call his mom on his cell phone. He drove her over to his mom's new house and waited as Betsy fussed over Allison. Will kissed Allison good-bye and promised to be back for breakfast. Allison fell asleep immediately in the strange bed and didn't wake until Will kissed her cheek the next morning at ten.

"Wake up, sleepyhead," he said, laying a red rose by her pillow.

Allison grinned and sat up and stretched. They ate breakfast with Betsy and gave her all the details she hadn't gotten the night before.

Betsy looked worried. "I can't believe it," she kept saying over and over again.

Allison nodded sadly. "I know. He's my father and yet he would do this. It makes me really wonder about my DNA."

Betsy shook her head. "Now don't go there, Allison. You might have your parents' DNA and that's why you look the way you do, but your spirit is all your own. You just remember that."

Allison smiled gratefully. She had said the same thing to Talon and Aspen herself, but hearing it from Betsy made it sink deeper into her own heart.

"You should have seen her though, Mom. He started putting us Carsons down for being poor nobodies, and that's when Allison stomped on his foot and elbowed him in the stomach. I've never seen her so mad," Will said with a proud grin.

Betsy's eyes went huge. "Are you kidding me?" she asked in shock.

Allison blushed and shook her head. "It was just horrible the things he was saying. As if being poor was a crime or something to be embarrassed about. He acted like he was better than you, and I just snapped. Will is the most incredible man I know. I couldn't stand there and let my dad tear him down," she said, feeling angry all over again.

Will grinned happily at her as he stuffed French toast in his mouth. "It was worth breaking down that door just to hear it, Mom."

Betsy smiled at Will but turned back to Allison. "So when you had both men standing there in the same room, did you see much of a similarity?" she asked gently.

Allison blushed and looked at Will, who was waiting for her answer. "None whatsoever," she said quietly but firmly.

Will nodded his head and smiled at her. "Now that that's settled, Mom, you won't believe who Allison was dancing with last night at her party," he said, enjoying the shock on his mother's face.

Allison laughed as she and Will both gave their versions of the story to Betsy, who immensely enjoyed being referee. At the end of breakfast, Betsy had smiled so much, her face was sore. Allison stood up, thanked Betsy for her hospitality, and asked Will to take her to pick up her brother and sister at Bonnie and Frank's.

Betsy stood on the front porch and waved good-bye to them but then surprised them by running down the front porch and over to the car. Allison rolled her window down so Betsy could stick her head in.

"Allison, I want you and your brother and sister to have Thanksgiving at my house this year. It'll be wonderful," Betsy assured her.

Will looked thrilled at the suggestion, but Allison grimaced. "Sorry, but Bonnie and Frank have already asked us," she said, wincing at Betsy's stormy expression.

Betsy shook her head. "Oh, is that right? Well, Bonnie and I will just have to have a little chat is all," she said. Then she stood back as Will reversed out of her driveway.

Will chuckled as he waved at his mom. "Poor Bonnie has no idea what she's in for now."

Allison smiled. "No, she does. When she asked me, she already knew your mom wouldn't be happy about it. She's ready for a fight. She might even be looking forward to it."

Will shook his head. "It's going to be World War III over who gets to be with you. Good thing you're mine either way."

Allison tilted her head as she studied the man sitting beside her. "What exactly does that mean? *Yours*?"

Will turned his head to look at her. "Just what it sounds like. You're mine. No one gets to hurt you, or scare you, or treat you badly. No one gets to *dance* with you or date you or fall in love with you. They'll have to go through me first," he said cockily.

Allison shook her head and laughed as she looked back out the window. "When you said I was yours, I thought that you meant we have some kind of commitment or something."

Will blinked and made a humming noise in his throat. "Hmm. Commitment? That sounds kind of serious."

Allison sniffed and decided to ignore him.

Will reached over and grabbed her hand. "Are you saying you want to officially be my girlfriend, Allison?"

Allison pulled her hand away. "I'm thinking about it," she said casually.

Will scowled. "There's no thinking about it. You are, and that's the end of the story," he said firmly.

Allison grinned and shut her eyes as she leaned back in her seat. "Okay. I accept."

Will relaxed and laughed. "I never knew having a girlfriend was going to be so complicated."

Allison opened her eyes and sat up in her seat, turning so she could take Will's large strong hand in hers. "Will, I haven't said it yet, but thank you. Thank you for coming to my rescue last night. If you hadn't been there, I don't even know what would've happened. I know I wouldn't be sitting here, happy and safe, that's for sure."

Will looked over at her and trailed his hand down her cheek. "I love you, Allison. I'll never let him hurt you again."

Allison smiled and leaned over to kiss Will on the cheek. Will grabbed her hand again, and they spent the rest of the ride over to the Tierney's in comfortable silence.

After picking up the kids, Allison let Will give them all the details of what happened. He told the story with so much exuberance, Talon and Aspen sat in their kitchen with their mouths hanging open. When Will got to the part where Max tasered him and took off, Talon looked relieved, shocked, and disappointed all at the same time.

"Wow. I've seen you fight. My dad's like ancient, and he got you? That's embarrassing," he said with a snotty smile.

Will grinned and shrugged. "Let's focus on the results. He's gone, and you're all safe. Besides, I can't beat up my future father-in-law, no matter how corrupt he is," he said, looking at Allison's dazed expression with a grin.

Talon whooped and gave Will a high-five. "Was that a proposal?"

Allison glared at Will. "No, that was *not* a proposal. A proposal is romantic and wonderful and *planned out.*"

Will shrugged. "Just get used to seeing me around," he said.

Aspen clasped her hands happily. "Allison Carson. I love it! But what will happen to me and Talon?" she asked, looking at Talon nervously. "Where will *we* live? With you guys?"

Will looked at Talon and Aspen and then at Allison's worried face. "When I marry your sister, you'll be coming with us. We'll be a family. Where else would you go?"

Allison sighed and put her arms around Will's waist as she looked up to receive his kiss. "My very own family. I can't wait."

Will grinned down at her. "Me either."

Talon groaned in disgust and stood up. "Luke told me he has some yard work for me. I'm taking off. This is way too mushy for me."

He stood up and disappeared out the door.

Aspen stood up too. "Rowan's picking me up in an hour to take me fishing. I'm going to go take a shower."

Allison was left by herself with Will in the kitchen. "And I have a door to fix," Will said, rubbing Allison's arms.

Allison smiled gratefully. "It seems like all I'm ever saying to you is thank you."

Will pushed her hair over her ears. "And I don't mind that one bit," he said, leaning down to kiss her.

The pounding on what was left of her front door interrupted Will. Allison walked cautiously toward the front door. Trey Kellen stood on the other side of the door, looking worried and upset.

"Allison! I just heard from Sophie what happened," he said, pushing through the door. Then he noticed Will standing behind her.

Trey ignored Will and grabbed Allison's hands, looking down into her face. "Are you okay, sweetheart? I can't believe this all happened right after I left. I'm so glad Luke was just next door to chase your dad off," he said, pulling her into a tight warm hug.

Allison hugged him back quickly before pushing away. Will stood right next to her and put a hand on Trey's chest, physically moving him away from Allison.

"Whoa, watch the hands." Trey warned in a low, mean voice that made Allison raise her eyebrows.

Will didn't care. "Luke wasn't the one who came to her rescue. *I was.* I'm looking out for Allison now."

Trey stared Will in the eyes and crossed his arms over his chest. "The only thing you were looking out for last night was Daphne. You always want what you can't have, don't you Will?" Trey said in a hard voice.

Allison held up her hands to stop the argument, but Will grabbed her hand out of the way.

"Daphne is just a friend. Allison is the woman I love. We've had our problems, but they're fixed now."

Trey glared at Will and then looked at Allison. "You told me last night you were single and that Will was your ex. You spent the entire evening with *me.* You can't be with him just hours later," he said with a scowl.

Allison blushed and felt helpless. "Will did come to my rescue last night. He and I both realized afterward that maybe we should give it another chance. I love him, Trey," she said, sorry at the disappointment and anger she saw in his eyes.

Trey closed his eyes for a second, and when he opened them, they were clear. He looked at Will and shrugged. "If she leaves you again, even for a second, I'll be there. And trust me, she won't go back to you again," he promised before turning and walking out of the shattered door.

Will stood and looked out the door as Trey drove away in his truck. "I believe him."

Allison felt horrible about leading Trey on the night before. She'd had no right to do that. "Maybe I should call him and apologize," she said as she bit her lip.

Will spun around and grabbed her shoulders. "Over my dead body," he warned.

Allison smiled and nodded. "Okay, relax, big guy. You're not going to turn into one of those weird super jealous boyfriends, are you?"

Will frowned. "Wow, I hope not, but seeing you dance with him last night was one of the worst experiences of my life. You could probably have danced with any other guy there, and I wouldn't have cared, but I saw the look in Trey's eyes. He was completely enthralled by you. And you were enjoying yourself way too much for someone with a broken heart. Yeah, you're not going anywhere near him," he ordered. Then kissed her before taking off.

Rowan drove up right after Will left, so Allison chatted with him about the previous night's events while they waited for Aspen to come downstairs. After Rowan and Aspen left fifteen minutes later, Allison was by herself. She tried cleaning up the door as best she could and put all the pieces she could find in the trash. She laughed when she got a call from Bonnie, who had just gotten off the phone with Betsy. Bonnie was determined to keep them and Allison laughed harder when Bonnie told her Betsy had bribed her with boxes of free fruit. Allison hung up the phone smiling and wondered where they would end up for Thanksgiving. Then she made herself a sandwich and wondered if her father was still in town. She wished with all her heart he was in a different state.

thiRty-two

Allison straightened up the house and then helped Will hang their new front door. She couldn't help being impressed with the way he put the door on quickly and expertly.

"Wow, there aren't even any instructions. You just did it," she said as she helped Will pick up the tools.

Will grinned sideways at her. "Well, I worked construction so I could earn more money for my mission the summer before I went. It comes in handy."

Allison smiled and gave him a quick hug. "*You* come in handy for sure. Thanks again."

Will beamed and went to put his tools in the back of the truck. Allison frowned as she saw Gage's red sports car drive up behind Will. She didn't feel like another confrontation right now. She sighed and walked slowly toward the sidewalk. Gage got out of his car and, completely ignoring Will, walked right up to Allison and took her hands in his.

"Allison, I need to talk to you. *In private*," he said urgently.

Will walked up behind Gage, overhearing everything he said.

"Allison and I don't keep any secrets from each other, Gage. I'm staying right here," Will said coldly.

Allison sighed and nodded her head. "It's okay, Gage. Whatever you need to tell me, just tell me, okay?"

Gage let her hands drop as he considered changing his mind. Allison frowned. Gage looked completely rattled. Whatever this was, it was serious.

"What is it?" she prodded.

Gage ran his hand over his chin and shook his head. "I saw something last night. I saw something I wasn't supposed to see. I've been up all night and driving around all morning, because I don't know what to do."

Allison frowned and glanced at Will. Will shrugged but looked intrigued.

"Gage, come in the house. We'll sit down and talk it out, okay?" she said, reaching out for his arm. Gage sighed and nodded. She guided him into the house in case he decided to bolt. She was very curious now.

They sat down in the family room, she and Will on the couch and Gage in the opposite chair. Gage looked down at his feet for a few moments as he struggled with what to say. Allison started to feel the strain and cleared her throat.

"Is this about Daphne?" she asked.

Gage laughed humorlessly and shook his head. "No, of course not. Allison, I saw your dad last night."

Allison gasped and covered her mouth with her hands. Will reached over and laid a comforting hand on her knee.

"Where?" she asked in a choked voice.

Gage gritted his teeth almost painfully and clenched his hands. "I saw him in my dad's office. Talking to my dad. Laughing and joking," he said bleakly.

Allison looked at Will in confusion. Will had both eyes on Gage.

"Were you able to hear what they were talking about?" Will asked in a calm voice.

Gage groaned and cradled his head in his hands. "Yes."

Allison felt lost. What was going on here? "Gage, what did they say?" she prodded.

Gage looked up at Allison and stared at her with bitter eyes. "They talked about how five years ago when your family had to leave the state, your dad stashed most of the money he had stolen with my father. My father hid it for him. And now that your dad's back, they're going to split it. Your dad's going to take off out of the country. He said something about an island somewhere, and my dad said he'd been waiting for this day for over five years. Allison, when your dad got caught scamming everyone over those real estate deals, my dad was involved.

250

The police couldn't find any proof to tie him to anything, but from the way they were talking last night, they were in it together, right from the beginning."

Allison felt horrible for Gage. But she'd been dealing with her father's illegal activities for so long, she wasn't even surprised.

"I'm so sorry, Gage. It's a shock, isn't it?"

Gage sighed raggedly and nodded. Will sat forward, looking tense. "Gage, where is Max *now*? Is he still with your dad at your house?"

Gage looked at Will and grimaced. "Yeah, I think so. They're going to hit the bank on Monday. My dad has all the money stashed in some safe deposit box at a bank in Salt Lake. I'm not sure which one, though. After that, Max is taking off."

Will stood up and started walking out of the room. "Where are you going, Will?" Allison asked, standing up and grabbing his hand as he started to walk past her.

Will stopped and leaned over to kiss her cheek quickly. "We're going to the police, Allie. We've got to stop your dad or he'll just be back to hurt you again. Come on, Gage," he said, assuming Gage would go with him.

Gage stood up and shook his head. "No way, man. I can't turn my own father into the police. What kind of son would do that?" he asked, turning red in the face and looking increasingly upset. "I came over here to tell Allison because I thought she deserved to know, but I can't bring my own father down. Max probably forced him to do it," he said desperately.

Will looked at Gage with pity. "If you don't help us get Max, then he'll just start up somewhere else and steal from more people. He'll ruin more lives. Maybe if your dad gives the police all the information they need, he can get a plea bargain. He might not have to go to jail, Gage. But if you don't help us right now, then *you're* an accessory. And you have too much integrity for that."

Gage's head went up as if he'd been hit. His eyes were wide and panicked. He turned to look at Allison for help, but she shook her head. "It's up to us to stop this, Gage. You don't want to be like your dad."

Gage looked tortured by her words. "That's the only thing I've ever wanted to do. Be like my dad."

Allison couldn't help herself. She walked over to Gage and gave him a hug. "Trust me, I know what you're feeling. My little brother,

Talon, has been struggling with those same feelings. It's so hard to realize that your parents aren't perfect, and even worse, that they're not good people. But you can survive, this Gage. You're a good man. Don't let your dad make you into a bad one," she said softly.

Gage stepped back from her and breathed in deeply as he made up his mind. "Okay. Let's get this over with. But my mom and my older brother will probably never speak to me again."

Will grabbed his truck keys and motioned for everyone to walk ahead of him. He took out his cell phone and called Luke. "Hey, Luke, we're heading down to the police station. Gage knows where Max is. Want to come along? . . . Okay, we'll meet you there."

Allison and Will followed Gage down to the police station. She sighed in relief when Gage didn't change his mind and speed off. Will leaned over and kissed her gently on the cheek. "This is almost over, Allie. It's going to be okay."

Allison leaned into Will's arm for a moment as she closed her eyes. "I hope so."

They joined Gage and walked into the police department together. Officer Townsend was there, so it didn't take long before three police cars were on their way to the Dulaney residence. Luke walked in twenty minutes later with Talon right behind him.

"Sorry I'm late, guys. Maggie wasn't feeling well, so I wanted to wait until her mom could come by and sit with her. What's going on?" he asked.

Will filled Luke and Talon in, while Gage sat in a corner, staring off into space.

Talon looked almost cynical as he shook his head in disgust. "And this man is my father. I just don't get it. He was raised in the Church! He's held high positions. He went on a mission. He *knows* right from wrong. Why is he like this?" he asked Allison as Luke and Will listened in.

Allison didn't know how to answer that, so she just put her arms around him and hugged him. Will sighed and pulled out a chair to sit in. "There are quite a few members of the mob who go to Catholic mass every week. There are members of the KKK who consider themselves good Christians. There are many evil people out in the world today who do horrible things and yet they go to church every Sunday. It's not about religion, Talon. It's about conversion."

Talon looked away and sighed, his shoulders slumping. "I guess you're right. But I just feel so angry at him. Honestly, I don't think I'll ever be able to forgive him for everything he's done."

Luke sighed and patted Talon's shoulder. "I'll tell you what I know about forgiveness. Maggie and her mom taught me this. It's just something you gotta do. It doesn't have to happen today. But you do have to work at it. Do a little bit here and there, but forgiveness is a work in progress. Some people have small things to forgive, and then there are people like you who have a lot to forgive. Compare it to eating. You have a twenty-foot submarine sandwich to eat. You can't eat it all at once, so for right now, just focus on taking one bite at a time. Someday, with a lot of prayer, you'll get to the end of it. I promise."

Will smiled at Luke and gave him a thumbs-up behind Talon's back. Luke sighed and wearily leaned back in his chair.

Talon nodded his head in understanding. "That kind of makes sense. But do you think my dad will ever repent and try to be a good person? Do you think we'll ever be able to have a relationship again?"

Allison frowned, wanting to know the answer to that question too.

Will leaned his elbows on his knees. "That's completely up to your dad. It's all about the Atonement. Your dad has a lot of work ahead of him. But that doesn't mean it's impossible. The first thing he'll have to do is realize that what he's done is wrong. He'll have to take responsibility for his actions before he can make any progress. For people like your dad, that's the hardest part of the process."

Allison sighed, wishing for Talon's sake that Max would make that long, hard journey, but realized that the likelihood of it happening was pretty small. Talon wasn't finished, though.

"Sometimes, just living here in Alpine kills me, you know. At school, all I see are hundreds of kids who have moms and dads who love them unselfishly. Moms and dads who would take a bullet for them. It's so unfair. I used to like going to seminary, but almost every day they sing 'I Am a Child of God.' I totally and completely hate that song," Talon said fiercely.

Allison held up her hand before Will or Luke could say anything. "I've got this one. I had the same problem, Tal. When we first moved here, I met with the bishop and told him what we were going through. And then I told him how much I hated hearing that song and how I hadn't gotten parents *kind* or *dear*. He told me a new way to sing it so it makes sense for me."

Allison started to sing the song, changing the words, to "kind of weird" and watched as Talon smiled sadly.

"See? The bishop told me to sing that song to myself every day for a week with those words, and you know what? It helped a lot. We don't have the perfect, typical Mormon family. But we do have each other. And if it makes you feel any better, I'd take a bullet for you," she said sincerely.

Talon lowered his head and nodded before surprising everyone by getting up and throwing his arms around his sister. "I'd take a bullet for you too, Allie," he whispered in her ear.

Allison hugged her brother back tightly, not wanting to let go. He pulled away in embarrassment a moment later and decided he needed to use the restroom. Will leaned over and kissed Allison's cheek after Talon had left the room.

"You are amazing," Will said with a shake of his head.

Allison swiped the tears off her cheeks and gave him a lopsided grin. "No, I'm not. I just love them. Besides, I have my own issues. I still don't know if I'll ever be able to honor my father. How can you honor a criminal?"

Will looked perplexed by that one, but Luke smiled gently at her. "Allison, you're already doing it. You honor Max by leading an honorable life. I think out of all the people I know, you're one of the most honorable. I don't think you have to worry about breaking any commandments."

Allison stared at Luke for a moment and then stood up, walking the two steps over to Luke and then leaned over and hugged him. "Thank you for that, Luke. You really are a great brother."

Luke looked stunned but then grinned, his eyes turning bright blue. "See, I knew you'd come around."

Allison laughed and sat back down by Will. Luke left to get drinks out of the machine for everyone, including Gage. When he got back, he took it upon himself to sit down by Gage and try to talk to him.

Will turned to Allison and took her hand as he stared into her eyes. "How about you? How are you handling the anger? How big is your forgiveness sandwich?"

Allison looked down at her hands for a moment as she thought about it. "I've been working on it for a while with my bishop. He's really helped me deal with a lot of the anger. I'm not angry at my dad. I don't hate him. And believe it or not, I forgive him. I just don't ever want to see him again."

Will winced and shook his head. "You know, when my dad died, I think I would have given *anything* to see him just one more time. I can't even imagine not wanting to have my father in my life. But then again, he would have cut off his right arm before he hurt us."

Allison looked up at the fluorescent lights above her and wished life had turned out differently. "You're lucky. You will get to see your dad again someday. A dad who loves you and wants to be with you. Your chain is unbroken. Mine? Shattered. Busted. Gone," she said as she massaged her forehead.

Will rubbed her back. "Your dad broke the links in your family chain. Now you get to forge your own, Allison."

Allison looked up and smiled as Will looked into her eyes. She'd have to be a dummy to not get his implication. He leaned over and kissed her gently on the lips to make his point crystal clear.

Luke finally gave up trying to talk to Gage and came back to sit by them. Talon walked back into the room five minutes later. Allison huddled in the corner with Will's arm around her shoulders and Talon on her other side. The room was eerily quiet as they were all lost in their own thoughts. Allison kept going over in her mind everything that had happened.

Finally breaking the silence, she wondered aloud, "If he had all that money stashed with Gage's dad, why did he break into our house and try to steal our information? It doesn't make sense," she said with a shake of her head.

Will sighed. "It does if you're a businessman. It's called covering all your bases. You have to have insurance. You have to have a plan B *and* a plan C. You were plan B. If he wasn't able to get the money from Jared Dulaney, then at least he would have some backup money."

Allison felt sick to her stomach and buried her face in Will's shoulder. They sat like that for another twenty minutes before a police officer came through the door.

"Well, thanks to Gage, Max Vaughn is now in custody. Your family can sleep easily now," he said with a kind smile.

Gage stood up and walked quickly to the officer, grabbing his arm. "What about *my* dad, Jared Dulaney?"

The officer frowned and nodded. "We have your father as well. We're holding him for questioning, but he's requested a lawyer. They both have. You can't speak to him right now, so I suggest you go home. There's nothing more you can do at the moment."

Will, Allison, and Talon hugged each other while Luke talked to the officer for a few more minutes.

When Allison looked around again, Gage was gone. She frowned sadly but knew this was something he'd have to work out for himself. Luke went home to check on Maggie while everyone else went home and waited for Aspen so they could fill her in.

Allison felt exhausted by all of the drama of the last twenty-four hours. All she wanted to do was take a nap. Talon and Will were sprawled on the couch watching a baseball game, so she went upstairs and flopped onto her bed.

An hour later, she woke up to Will gently nudging her shoulder. "Allie, wake up. Maggie just left for the hospital. She's in labor," he said, looking worried.

Allison jumped off the bed and hurried downstairs. Talon was on the phone, and Aspen was hurrying around the house grabbing jackets and her purse.

"Allie, we've got to hurry," Aspen said, shoving a jacket in her hands. "Maggie's water broke. She could have the baby any second."

Allison smiled but put her jacket on to make her sister happy. "Aspen, I don't know a whole lot about child birth, but I hear it takes hours."

Talon hung up the phone and turned to face them. "Luke's almost to the hospital. He says her contractions haven't started yet, but that she feels horrible. He forgot to lock up the house and turn off the oven. So I'll run over and do that while you guys get in the car." He quickly walked out of the kitchen.

Allison grinned at Talon's cool competence. "Okay then. Let's go see this new Peterson. I hope for little Talon's sake, he takes after Maggie."

Aspen shook her head at her sister. "Hey now, Luke adopted you. If Talon looks like Luke, you still have to love him. Now come on, let's go," she said, taking Allison's arm and dragging her toward the door.

Will followed after them, locking up. "Why don't we take my car? It's faster."

Aspen changed directions immediately, and they all got into Will's sports car. Seconds later, Talon joined them and they were on their way to the American Fork Hospital where they weren't surprised to find Bonnie, Frank, Lisa, and Terry already there.

They spent the next three hours keeping Maggie company and playing cards until the nurse kicked them out. Maggie's contractions kicked in with a vengeance, and even though she had an epidural, she was still under a lot of strain. In the end she only wanted Luke in the delivery room with her when Talon Luke Peterson was born, weighing seven pounds, ten ounces.

Allison and Aspen both got teary-eyed as they watched from the window in the nursery while Luke gave little Talon his first bath. He was so red and tiny, he didn't look like Luke or Maggie. Bonnie stood a foot away just shaking as Frank held her shoulders comfortingly.

Lisa walked over and put her arms around her. "He's beautiful, isn't he?"

Bonnie wiped her eyes and looked up at Lisa as Allison and Aspen stepped closer. "He looks just like Robbie's baby pictures, Lisa. They could be twins."

Allison and Aspen looked at each in confusion. How could anyone tell?

Lisa smiled and hugged Bonnie even tighter. "I hope you're right, Bonnie. Robbie would have loved that, wouldn't he?"

Luke came out twenty minutes later, beaming and grinning. "Did you see him?" he kept asking everyone over and over again.

Lisa hugged him and gave him a big kiss on his cheek. "Of course I saw my new grandson. He's the best-looking baby there."

Allison grinned as she noticed Luke's eyes were the most brilliant green she'd ever seen. Today was a very happy day.

thiRty-thRee

❤

SIX MONTHS LATER

Allison pushed her cart down the grocery store aisle as she headed straight for the almond M&M's. She smiled as she thought of the first time she had come to Kohler's looking for candy. Meeting Will again over a bag of M&M's had been just the beginning. She glanced down at her empty ring finger and sighed. Will was sure taking his time proposing. They'd been together every day for the last six months, and the way Betsy kept hinting around, she knew Will was going to propose soon. She just hoped it was more romantic than the first time he'd tried when he'd been standing in her kitchen.

Allison stopped her cart and reached down to grab two bags of candy.

"Well, well. If it isn't Allison *Vaughn.*"

Allison's head popped up and she turned in surprise to see Daphne standing beside her.

"Hi, Daphne, how's it going?" she asked with a polite smile. She hadn't seen Daphne much since she went to work for Gage Dulaney. From what Sophie told her, though, she was actually very good at selling real estate. She couldn't help noticing the large opulent ring on Daphne's left hand.

"So I guess everyone had fun at Maggie's birthday party last night. Smart to have the party and reopen her art gallery all at once. She probably sold a few paintings," Daphne said with a small frown.

Allison winced. Daphne hadn't been invited. "It was mostly just family." And about twenty other close friends. But Daphne was right about Maggie selling a few paintings. Will had bought her two—one Maggie had painted of Talon and Aspen and one of Alpine that she had fallen in love with.

Daphne sniffed and glanced over the candy, finally deciding on a bag of Almond Joy. Allison couldn't help but notice that Daphne had gained at least ten pounds and looked fabulous and healthy.

"I haven't seen her lately, but I heard she lost all her baby weight. What a shocker. I thought she'd have to go on *The Biggest Loser*."

Allison smiled and leaned against her cart. "Well, she hasn't lost all of it. I heard before she got pregnant she was a size zero. Probably because she had celiac disease and didn't know it. But yeah, she looks amazing. She's training for a marathon too, so I'm sure that's helped."

Daphne sighed and looked down at her feet. "Some people just have the perfect life. Everything is so easy for them. Friends, love, . . . *money*," she said forlornly.

Allison frowned. She knew Maggie's life hadn't been a walk in the park. It was far from it. But she could see how Daphne would think so. "Is everything okay, Daphne? You seem kind of down," Allison prodded, wondering what she could have to be sad about.

Daphne shrugged and looked away. "Yeah, everything's great. Gage proposed last month, and we're planning on getting married in June. It's going to be huge. My mom's planning the reception down at Thanksgiving Point. You'll be invited, of course."

Allison tilted her head and studied the unhappy woman in front of her. Something was on her mind. "What's going on, Daphne? You can tell me."

Daphne looked up with tears in her eyes. "Life just doesn't work out the way you want it to sometimes, that's all. I mean, after Gage's dad went to jail, Gage has been scrambling to keep the company going. I'm doing everything I can to help, of course, but it'll take years to restore the Dulaney image. You're lucky. You get to change your name someday. Me? I love Gage and everything, but now I'm going to be Daphne *Dulaney*. It's just awful. His father ruined everything. And when I told Gage I wanted to keep my own last name, he just flipped out. We almost called off our engagement," she said as two more tears slipped down her cheeks.

Allison nodded her head in understanding. "It's hard, especially for Gage, I'm sure. You're right, it's going to be a battle to make the Dulaney name honorable again, but Gage can do it. You just have to have faith in him and keep doing what you're doing. Talon and Aspen have struggled with that too. Especially Talon."

Daphne sighed with a roll of her eyes. "I hear he's the most popular kid at Lone Peak now. I don't think he has anything to worry about."

Allison grinned and nodded. Talon was doing amazing at school. He was happy, he was getting good grades, and he was dating one of the prettiest girls in Alpine. "You're right, things are going really well for him, but in the beginning he had a lot of doubts about himself. It doesn't matter what your last name is, though. It's up to you. It's the life *you* lead that counts."

Daphne twisted the ring on her finger. "I guess it's easier for you. They shipped your dad back to Texas to finish out his prison sentence since he skipped out on parole. But Gage's dad is still in the news *every* week. I can't stand turning on the TV anymore. I mean, I'm glad the police were able to return most of the money to all those people they stole it from. And it's kind of nice to see Ben Dalton driving a decent car and his wife smiling again. But do they have to write about *all* their victims and how happy they are now that their money has been returned?" Daphne asked with a pout.

Allison smiled happily as she thought of Rowan and his family. They hadn't gotten all the money back that Max had taken from them, but even getting half of it back had helped their family tremendously. Rowan had already put in his mission papers, and as soon as school was out, he'd be at the MTC. Being able to support their son financially on his mission was one of the biggest reasons Rowan's family was smiling these days.

"It makes people feel good to see justice done, Daphne. It'll die down pretty soon, though. Some new drama will grab people's attention any minute now."

Daphne shrugged. "Maybe the park will take away some of the attention."

Allison glowed happily. Will had gone ahead and given twenty acres of land to the city of Alpine for a park. Tonight was the ribbon cutting ceremony. Tomorrow construction would begin. She couldn't be more thrilled.

"I hope so. The kids will love it. Part of it will be a skate park, part of it will be traditional, and then there will be water fountains and murals. It's going to be the most beautiful park in the world," Allison said proudly.

Daphne narrowed her eyes at Allison. "Yeah, that Will is really something, isn't he?"

Allison blushed and quickly changed the subject. "So are you coming to the ceremony tonight?"

Daphne shook her head and took a step away with her cart, signaling the conversation was over. "Better things to do. I'm sure your face will be all over the news, though. Enjoy," she said with a jealous frown and walked quickly away.

Allison sighed and shook her head. She felt bad that Daphne was having a hard time. Not as bad as Daphne was feeling for herself, but then again, who could?

Allison finished her shopping and then hurried home. Talon and Aspen would be home from school any minute. She put the groceries away and walked out to the front porch where she lifted her face to the cool spring breeze and enjoyed the sight of Maggie's tulips and daffodils. This was one of her favorite parts of the day—the return of her family.

She stood up as the old red Ford truck rumbled down the road. She'd let Talon and Aspen have the truck when Will insisted on loaning her his old Honda Civic. She waited for them to hop out before she walked down the steps.

"Hey, guys! How was school?" she asked, noting their happy faces as they walked toward her.

Talon grinned and motioned toward Aspen. "They just did the voting for the yearbooks. Guess who got most beautiful."

Aspen's cheeks turned a rosy pink as she giggled. "Me! Everyone voted for me. Can you believe it?" she asked, still looking shocked.

Allison screamed and grabbed her sister in a tight hug. "Of course I believe it! You're the most beautiful girl in the world," she said proudly, hugging her once more for good measure.

Aspen beamed happily but then pulled away. "Well, that's not all. Guess who was voted most likely to succeed?"

Allison's mouth fell open as she turned to Talon. "You?" she whispered, putting a hand over her heart. "They voted for you, didn't they?"

Talon looked happy but confused. "Isn't that crazy?" he said with a shake of his head.

Allison immediately shook her head. "No. It's not crazy at all. You are who you want to be. You're going to do amazing things in this world, Talon. And everybody knows it," she said, sniffing back a tear.

Talon and Aspen rolled their eyes and laughed at their sister before running into the house to get a snack. Allison took a moment to control her emotions as she stood by the railing.

"What kind of tears are those?"

Allison laughed and turned to see Maggie walking toward her, pushing baby Talon in his stroller.

Allison walked down to meet them on the sidewalk. "These tears are some of the happiest tears you'll ever see. Aspen was voted most beautiful at Lone Peak, and Talon was voted most likely to succeed," she said, her voice still shaking with joyful awe.

Maggie grinned happily. "Luke will be so proud. He was voted most likely to succeed too. This calls for a celebration."

Allison held her hands up. "We're still recuperating from your party last night. Besides, we've got the ribbon-cutting ceremony tonight. You promised to be there to unveil your ideas for the murals."

Maggie leaned over and picked up her son. She fixed his blanket and then put him on her shoulder. "Are you kidding? I can't wait. You couldn't keep me away."

Allison's heart melted as she stared at Maggie's baby. Her heart hitched every time she thought of herself being a mother and holding her own child.

"Oh, he's so beautiful," she whispered as she touched his little ear.

Maggie smiled contentedly. "I know. I can't stop painting him. Is it completely cliche to think that your baby is the most beautiful baby ever born?"

Allison laughed softly. "Not at all. Besides, you happen to be right."

The women talked for a few more minutes and then Allison went in to remind Talon and Aspen not to eat everything in sight since Will was taking all of them out to dinner after the ribbon-cutting ceremony.

Two hours later they stood in front of a large crowd as the mayor handed Will a pair of very large scissors.

Will took the scissors in his hand and stared at the bright red ribbon. "You know, this day almost didn't happen. I had made up my mind to develop this land into luxury twin homes. But a very special woman changed my mind. She reminded me that there was something more important than money. She reminded me that people were what mattered most. My little sister, Bella, would have loved this park. The pictures of the murals that Maggie Peterson will paint feature my sister in every scene. I know her spirit will be here with the children as they play and have fun. Today is one of the greatest days of my life. But what would make it perfect would be if Allison Vaughn would agree to spend the rest of her life reminding me of the important things in life. Allison, will you marry me?"

Allison gasped as everyone stared at her in delighted anticipation. Will handed the scissors back to the mayor and then walked toward her. He knelt down in the dirt and held a beautiful but simple ring up toward her.

"Please," he said.

Allison swallowed and took one step toward Will. Her hand was steady as she reached for the ring and held it up for everyone to see. And with a huge grin, she slipped it onto her left hand.

"Will, I would love to spend the rest of my life nagging you," she said as everyone erupted into laughter and cheers. Will jumped up and threw his arms around her, squeezing her tightly before giving her a kiss that probably lasted a little too long. Then together, with both of their hands on the scissors, they cut the ribbon for Bella's Park.

Afterward, Will took them all out to dinner to celebrate. As everyone pigged out on Mexican food, Allison looked across the large table at all of her dear ones. Maggie, Luke, the older brother and sister she'd always wanted and needed, were there with their baby. Bonnie and Frank, the grandparents she'd always ached for, were there too. Sophie and Sam and Lisa and Terry were also there—good steadfast friends she could trust to be there for her, even through the hard times. And then there was Talon and Aspen, happy and laughing and enjoying themselves—finally. And of course, there was Betsy. Allison finally had her mom.

She couldn't help comparing this night to that night so long ago when she'd felt so alone and so defeated as Talon's and Aspen's misery had almost overwhelmed her. Heavenly Father had stepped in and helped her. He'd helped save her family and bring peace back to their lives. She had so much to be grateful for. She turned and looked at Will. And now she had love. She leaned over and kissed Will's cheek. Even though her life hadn't been easy, it had brought her the most amazing gift of all.

About the Author

Shannon Guymon lives in Utah with her husband and six children. She enjoys spending time in the mountains, gardening, traveling, being with her family, and, of course, writing. She is the author of *Never Letting Go of Hope, A Trusting Heart, Justifiable Means, Forever Friends, Soul Searching, Makeover, Taking Chances,* and *Child of Many Colors: LDS Stories of Transracial Adoption.*